LOTTO LUCY

A James Bay Novel

KATHLEEN IRENE PATERKA

DEDICATION

For M. L.

1958 ~ 1995

.

ACKNOWLEDGMENTS

A novel is not born of solitary musings, but rather is the culmination of many individuals whose valuable contributions assist authors in bringing the story to fruition. I owe a huge debt of thanks to many people who generously shared their time and expertise in helping me research and develop Lucy's story. Special thanks to the following:

Jenna Mindel. My luck changed the day I met Jenna. She's been with me since the beginning; the best of friends, the best of mentors, not to mention the best brainstormer in the business. How appropriate that it was Jenna sitting beside me when the inspiration for Lucy was born.

Christine Elizabeth Johnson. A wonderful friend and an extraordinary author who sees things in my writing that I am clueless about. Thank you, dear Christine, for constantly urging me to step it up to the next level.

Catherine Chant and Edie Ramer, for their continuing encouragement, support and advice.

William Kanine, C.P.A., for his patience and assistance in helping a mathematical dummy (me) understand the financial ramifications involved in winning the lottery.

Anne Victory, for her rich detail when it comes to editing; Karen Duvall, for her priceless cover artwork; Amy Eye, the Queen of Formatting.

And, as always, my husband Steve... my biggest critic and my biggest fan. None of this would be possible without his patience, tolerance, encouragement and support. With Steve beside me, I've won the lottery in things that matter most: life and love.

CHAPTER ONE

I'm a cash-only girl and I've never been a gambler—with my money or my life. So when Kris Henderson and I stroll into Pete's Place, our small town's gas station and convenience store to pay for my gas, Pete Kelly's suggestion I buy a lottery ticket has me chuckling and shaking my head before the words are even out of his mouth.

"Aw, come on, Lucy. Whatdya got to lose?" His craggy eyebrows lift high. "It's only a buck."

"Sorry, Pete, but you're talking to the wrong girl. I don't gamble." When you live in place like James Bay, ticking off the wrong people can come back to bite you. But Pete—a fixture in our town for the past seventy years—and I have always gotten along. I like Pete just fine. Thing is, I like my money more.

"What's the big deal?" he says. "Do yourself a favor and buy a ticket. Besides, you're in the Lottery Zone."

"And what's that supposed to mean?" I ask.

"The Lottery Zone." He straightens behind the counter and points upward. "See that? The salesman from the State Lottery Commission stuck it up there a couple days ago."

Kris and I glance up to see a neon-glo sign swaying above our heads. LOTTERY ZONE glitters in bold swirls against stripes of yellow and black.

"It's some damn promotion they've got going," he says. "If I don't ask for the sale, you don't pay for the ticket."

"Sorry, I don't gamble. Why don't you ask Kris?" I nod at my colleague. "Spending money is her hobby."

"Hey, speak for yourself," she splutters in protest. "Besides, I'm broke."

Pete eyes me over the cash register. "You never know, Lucy. Buy a ticket and you could end up the lucky winner. You could even get your name in the headlines on the front page of that paper of yours."

Kris and I trade glances, then laughter. As reporters for the *James Bay Journal*, it's our job to write the news, not make it.

Pete rolls his eyes. "Maybe you girls think it's funny, but I don't. My sales are down, and I've got a quota to meet. You want the state to yank my machine?"

Now it's my turn to roll my eyes. Pete's Place has the busiest gas pumps in town, not to mention the best prices on beer and wine. Hard to believe his store doesn't do a thriving business selling lottery tickets.

"Sorry, Pete, but I'm only buying gas today." I scrounge through my latest purse, digging for my wallet. The oversized leather pouch resembles a duffel bag and things inside have an odd way of disappearing. Today it's my wallet that's a no-show.

"You could save yourself some time and hassle if you paid at the pump," he says.

2

Kris snorts. "And use her credit card? Lucy would rather die than break out the plastic."

"It's only for emergencies," I say, trying not to sound too prissy.

She eyes me suspiciously. "Define *emergency*."

Too bad someone hasn't defined the word for Kris. Maybe then she wouldn't have a problem keeping her own credit cards tucked safely away where they belong. But my colleague isn't going to suck me into playing semantics today. We spent too much time gabbing over lunch and I'm running late. The Hospital Foundation's latest ribbon-cutting ceremony starts soon and I'm scheduled to cover the story.

"I prefer to operate on a cash-only basis," I say. "If I can't afford it, I don't buy it."

She huffs a long sigh. "There's your problem, Lucy. Why are you so scared of spending money?"

"The better question might be why don't more people feel that way? Too much easy credit gets people into trouble. Thanks, but no thanks." I come up with my wallet and slide my last two twenties across the counter. With payday still another week away and the price of gas soaring higher than the scorching summer temperatures, I can't afford to bask in thinking I've got money to burn. I've never lived on easy street. In fact, there's a flashy *For Sale* sign decorating the front lawn of the modest house where Grandma raised me. Plus, a mortgage still due and no takers in sight. The way I'm going, I'd need a million lottery wins to get me out of my money mess.

Pete counts out my change, then dangles the bills just out of reach. "Whatdya say, Lucy? You've got seven dollars

3

here. That equals seven chances to win. All it takes is one ticket."

"Sorry, but you're wasting your breath. Like Grandma always said, *the best way to double your money is to fold it in half and stick it in your wallet.*"

"That grandma of yours didn't know everything," he mutters.

I have to give him credit. When it comes to being successful in business, my old friend Pete learned the secret a long time ago. Never give up. But two can play at that game.

"Pete, how long have you known me?"

He scratches his bald head. "Pretty much all your life, I guess."

"Exactly," I say. "Now think back a few years. Remember when I won the Miss James Bay Contest my senior year of high school?"

He frowns. "Can't say that I do."

I cluck my tongue, holding back the smile. "How about last year when I landed the biggest trout in the annual fishing tournament and won the thousand-dollar prize?"

The furrow in his brow deepens. "I thought Bob Campbell took first place last year." He hesitates. "Or maybe it was the year before?"

Poor guy, he still doesn't get it. "It was last year," I say gently. "Bob won the contest, not me."

"But you just said—"

"I was only kidding," I say, suddenly ashamed of myself for egging him on.

He peers over the cash register. "What about that Miss James Bay thing?"

"Honestly, can you see me entering a beauty contest? I'm the unluckiest person you'll ever meet. So me buying a lottery ticket would be like throwing good money away. Guaranteed I wouldn't win. I never win anything."

"Seems like I remember you winning some scholarship or something to the university," he muses.

"Partial scholarship," I correct him. Though a lot of good it did me. The money barely made a dent in my student loans. Four years later, I'm still paying the bills, the most recent of which arrived two days ago. It's still unopened on my kitchen counter where I tossed it. I haven't worked up the nerve to rip it open and see how much interest has accumulated.

Kris plucks a candy bar from a display and shoves it on the counter. "What's the big deal? Buy the ticket, it's only a dollar."

"And so is this chocolate," I reply. "Buy your own candy."

"Come on, Lucy, please? I'm a little short on cash. I'll pay you back."

"Where have I heard that line before?" I push the candy bar back at her.

Kris eyes the chocolate with a woeful face. "Just so you know, I'm holding you personally responsible if my blood sugar plummets and I keel over. My family is hundreds of miles away. Who'll take care of me?"

"I'll drive you to the E.R. myself," I promise, trying not to smile. My colleague Kris Henderson is irreverent, witty, and everything I wish I could be myself (spiky blond hair excluded). But Kris hasn't lived here very long. And though I've spent twenty of my twenty-five years in this little town, that doesn't mean I'm naive enough to believe I've earned local status. That right is reserved solely for people like my father and Pete, both born and raised in James Bay. You could live in this town for fifty years and still be merely a *local wannabe*.

I turn to Pete with an open palm. "Could I please have my change?"

"You want your money, here's your money." He slaps the bills into my hand. "Glad to oblige. After all, it's not like you owe me. At least, not much."

"Owe you for what?" I ask warily. That sly smile on Pete's face has stripped away some of his seventy-plus years and I suddenly have a funny feeling I'm being set up.

"No big deal, it was just an interview," he reminds me. "Remember? You came waltzing in here a couple days later, thanking me for all the great quotes I gave you and telling me how people were writing letters to the editor... plus how that Kendall guy that runs your paper actually gave you a compliment. But don't let that get you feeling guilty. You keep your money. Like I said, you don't owe me. It was just an interview."

Maybe if he hadn't fetched up that hilarious hound-dog expression, my mouth and wallet would have stayed shut. But Pete and I have been friends since I got my driver's license and started pumping my own gas. And all kidding aside, Pete makes a good point. I *do* owe him. That interview he gave me last month about the escalating price of gasoline had some colorful quotes about the little man getting screwed. My story made the front page above the fold and generated a slew of heated letters to the editor.

Letters to the editor sell papers. People buy extra copies, happy to see their name in print.

"When's the last time someone told you what a great salesman you are?" I say, laughing. "All right, I'll buy a ticket. But only *one*," I warn him.

"Thatta girl." He waltzes behind the lotto machine. "You want to choose the numbers or you want an easy pick?"

"Oooh, let me pick the numbers." Kris snatches a coupon and grabs a pencil stub. "We can use our birthdays. Pete, what month and day were you born?"

I squint at the plastic beer clock 3-D display over his shoulder. I'm due at the hospital in ten minutes, plus I still need to drop Kris off at the *Journal* office. "Just give me what you've got."

"One easy pick, coming right up." The machine spits out a ticket, which Pete presents me with a flourish. "Big jackpot drawing Saturday night. Sixty-five million dollars."

"Thanks, but I won't hold my breath." I trade him a smile for my ticket and change and throw them in my bag where they settle in the mess pooled at the bottom.

"Don't forget to check your numbers," Pete calls as we head out the door. "Who knows? You might get lucky."

Me, lucky? I'm still laughing as I drop Kris off downtown, then head for the hospital. People like me have two chances of winning the lottery. Slim and none. Like Grandma always said, *the only sure bet is the one you make on yourself.*

I'd like to bet that I'll make it out of this town someday, but so far the only thing I've ever won is that partial scholarship. One journalism degree later, my hometown connections landed me a job on the *Journal* staff. Being back in James Bay, working for the local daily, isn't the career fast track I intended, but it keeps me near Grandma and plus, it's a job. Lots of people my age with college degrees flip burgers for a living. And while being a journalist might sound important, I doubt it pays much better than a stint behind a hamburger counter.

Winning the lottery? Maybe other people have time to sit around and dream about hitting the jackpot, but I need to hustle faster than someone slinging hamburgers if I want to keep my job. With the internet and cable news available twenty-four seven, newspapers are becoming paper dinosaurs, headed for extinction. But until that happens, I've got things to do.

Like make today's interview on time.

Like finish my latest article on the rezoning of Loon Lake.

Like visit Grandma at the nursing home.

Talk about a reality check. Each time I visit, it gets harder to force myself to walk through the door. Grandma took up permanent residence at Whispering Pines six months ago and she won't be going home. I dread the day when the *For Sale* sign comes down. Blessing or curse, it will mean her house is sold and mark the end of everything important in my life. But I've run out of options. The monthly bill from Whispering Pines averages seven thousand dollars, and Grandma's savings account is almost tapped out. The balance dwindles with every statement and it's nearly disappeared.

Just like Grandma's mind.

"You girls want another beer? More iced tea?"

Kris hoists her empty beer mug and salutes our waitress. "No thanks, Nettie. I've got a date with a camera and eighty high school seniors, and my eyeballs already feel a little loose." She slides me a sideways grin. "That would make quite the story in Monday's *Journal*. **BOOZED-UP REPORTER BASHES BACCALAUREATE**. Detailed coverage, see page three."

I stir up a smile with my straw, then drain my iced tea as I conjure up a mental picture of the *Journal*'s managing editor, scowl firmly in place. "Who knows? If it helps circulation, Charles might give you a raise."

"Like that's going to happen." She shoves her mug aside. "Two beers are my limit, but somebody ought to buy Charles Kendall a six-pack. That man needs to lighten up."

I lose my battle fighting off the giggles. My own life lightened up earlier this year when Kris joined the *Journal* staff. She covers the crime beat, court docket, and schools, while I focus on municipal and nonprofit groups.

"Whoa, check out the guy at nine o'clock." Her eyes disappear in a deep squint. "He looks familiar. Do we know him?"

Chuck's Tavern and Grill is standing-room only for a Saturday night. I scan the crowd. "Where?"

"Halfway down the takeout line." She nods toward the cash register. "Definitely your type. Baby-faced, casually dressed, up-north appeal."

"I'm not interested in dating tourists," I say with a sniff. Summertime in northern Michigan means warm sunny days and crisp cool nights. Those of us who live here year-round have some names reserved for these eight to ten weeks of summer. *Pure heaven. Tourist hell.*

"No, I'm sure I've seen him before. I think he lives around

here. See the guy I'm talking about? Blue jeans, brown hair, white polo shirt."

I crane my neck and swivel in my chair, but the only thing in my line of vision is a crowd of hungry strangers jostling for takeout.

"Wait, I've got it," Kris crows in triumph. "Remember the interview I did last month about that kid's camp on Loon Lake?"

Her words alone are enough to raise goose bumps on my arms.

"Please do not mention that place in my presence." The last thing I need on my night off is to hear about Loon Lake. Bad enough Charles forced me to cover the rezoning issue for the *Journal* during working hours.

"That guy is their new camp director. His name is Max Graham. And Lucy, he is perfect."

"Perfect for what?" I ask, though I already suspect I won't like what I hear.

"For you, naturally. You're two of a kind. Just look at the poor guy, all alone, ordering takeout on a Saturday night." Kris leans closer. "We should ask him to join us."

"No, I don't think—"

"Come on, Lucy, loosen up. You'll never know unless you ask. I bet he says yes." She aims a high-beam smile directly at the takeout counter. "Will Lucy Carter find love and happiness in the arms of a stranger ordered up from the takeout line? Talk about a terrific feature story."

"Don't you dare!" I grab her arm midair. Kris is always sniffing around for the next splashy feature that will get her name above the fold, but I'm not putting my reputation on the line as a romance guinea pig to further her career. "I am not interested," I hiss.

"You're never interested." She slumps back, throws her hands in the air. "You drive me crazy, Lucy, you know that? I swear, if you weren't my best friend..." She shakes her head. "Girl, you need to get a life."

"I have a life, thank you very much." My voice sounds as stiff as my spine.

"Could have fooled me. When's the last time you went out on a date?"

"I don't remember. Besides, when do I have time? I've got a job—one that keeps me busy most nights."

"My point exactly," she says. "You're way too busy taking notes in the back row at those boring commission meetings. You're missing out."

"That's not true."

"No? Turn around and take a long, hard look at Max Graham. The man is living proof. Go on, I dare you."

I sit and stare at her in stony silence.

Kris's eyes hold a challenge. "Or maybe you're scared to face the truth?"

"My life is perfect the way it is, thank you very much. I don't need any distractions. Especially the male variety."

She lets out a long sigh. "I'm only trying to help."

"What makes you think I need help?" I ask, chin tilting higher. Sometimes my stubbornness amazes even me.

"You're twenty-five years old and having dinner with a girlfriend on a Saturday night." She rolls her eyes. "How pathetic is that?"

"Speak for yourself." I fling my straw across the table, missing her nose by a good inch.

"I'm happily involved, remember? And if I wasn't, you'd do the same for me. Isn't that what friends are for?"

Kris is right, of course. But then, she doesn't need my help finding dates. She's been involved in a long-term, same-sex relationship since college. I've never met her friend Toni, but I've heard all about her.

"Don't you dare write a story about this," I mutter as Kris waves Max over. There's no escaping the inevitable. I've been taken prisoner in a crowded bar and grill.

Or maybe not. I straighten as he nears the table. Tall, lean build, warm brown eyes, engaging smile. Definitely a seven-point-five. Maybe even an eight. I note the slight limp slowing him down.

"Kris Henderson, right?"

"Nice to see you again, Max." Her voice oozes charm. "This is Lucy."

He turns a 120-watt smile on me and sticks out his hand. "Max Graham."

Warm handshake, firm grip. My fingers tingle at his touch. "Hi. I'm Lucy Carter."

His eyes widen slightly. "Lucy Carter from the *Journal*? The same Lucy Carter covering the Loon Lake issue?"

I squirm under his heated gaze. Being a reporter in a place like James Bay makes you small-town famous. Which can be a good thing or a bad thing, depending on the reader's politics and-or point of view. "That's me," I admit.

His smile broadens. "Nice to finally meet you. I've been reading your byline all winter. I'm one of your fans."

I'm guessing my face is as red as the grease pencils we use to mark up the *Journal*. When I envision my reading public, it's not people like Max who jump to mind. More like Pete Kelly and the gas-station crowd.

"You're doing a great job on the rezoning story," he says. "Let's hope the county planning commission notices."

"Thanks." I swallow down the compliment. Max hasn't quit staring since Kris introduced us and it's a little unsettling. I feel lost without my notepad. Call me a control freak, but things are much more comfortable when I'm the one conducting the interview.

"There's something different about you, Max." Kris eyes him thoughtfully, then brightens. "You shaved your beard."

"It itched." He scratches his chin and grins. "Plus, camp starts in a week. I don't want to scare the kids."

I blink. Nothing about Max Graham could be conceived as scary. Beard or no beard, he would attract kids.

And women. *Definitely* women.

He turns to Kris. "I've been watching for your article about camp, but I haven't spotted it in the *Journal* yet."

"It's scheduled to run on the feature page soon."

"I appreciate that. We could use the publicity." He brushes a hand through the thick brown hair grazing his collar. "We don't have a full roster yet. Hopefully if enough people read the article, we'll fill up for the rest of the summer."

"I'll talk to our editor and see what I can do," she promises. "Look for it next week. I'll get you some extra copies." Kris flashes me a pointed smile. "I'm sure Lucy would be glad to deliver them personally."

My mouth drops open. There's a fine line between helping things along and blatantly promoting, and my ex-friend Kris just crossed it. I stare at my empty glass, kicking myself for not taking Nettie up on her offer of more iced tea. I could use some cooling off.

"Lucy's great, very accommodating," Kris continues. "She's always willing to help out. Isn't that right, Lucy?"

Subtlety isn't one of my colleague's most endearing qualities, and being put on the spot isn't one of my strong points. But with Max watching, there's not much I can do but acknowledge him with a gracious smile.

And glower at Kris when he's not looking.

"Sure, I'll be glad to play delivery boy," I mumble.

"Thanks. I suspect I won't get into town much once camp is in full swing." He steps aside as Nettie pushes past him and gathers our empty plates. "I'd better get going."

Kris grabs his arm. "Why don't you sit down and eat here? We'll keep you company. Right, Lucy?"

That's a maybe, depending on if she plans to stay. Kris grew up with three brothers and she's a natural when it comes to chatting with the opposite sex. Unfortunately, I am not Kris. And since I'm an only child, I have no brothers. Plus, no dad. When it comes to men, I operate best armed with a notepad, pen, and long list of questions.

Nettie levels Max with a dark scowl. "I've got people lined up waiting for tables. If you're eating, find yourself a chair and make it quick."

"You can have my seat. I have to get going." Kris grabs her purse. "Lucy will keep you company. Oh, and could you give her a ride home? I've got eighty high school seniors in caps and gowns waiting for me to immortalize them for the *Journal* archives. God knows how long that will take." She throws some bills down, tosses us a brisk wave, and scoots out the door.

"Is she always like that?" Max asks as he settles in her chair and scans the menu.

"You mean bossy?" I say, watching with an evil eye as my ex-friend departs.

One corner of his mouth turns up. "I was trying to be polite. But seeing how you mentioned it, bossy works."

"It goes with the job. You get used to not taking *no* for an answer." I fiddle with the paper wrapper off my straw and keep my eyes low. It's safer that way. As I told Kris earlier, I don't need distractions. And Max's warm, steady gaze providing heat across the table is a distraction. A very tempting distraction.

"Know what you want?" Nettie is back, armed with check pad and pen and a pointed glare for Max.

"I'll have the fish and chips." He hands over his menu and flashes me a smile. "How about you?"

"I already ate, thanks."

He eyes my empty glass. "Buy you a drink?"

"Nope, I'm good." I squirm in my seat, simultaneously cursing and missing Kris. If he plans on ordering a big meal, this could prove a long night.

"At least let me buy you a glass of wine. I don't like to drink alone."

"I already said no." The words come out flat and firm, faster than I expected, and immediately I regret them. There's no need for me to play defense. Max seems like a nice enough guy. "I don't drink," I add softly.

"Okay. Sure, sorry." He sits back slightly, uncertainty registering in his eyes. "Would it bother you if I do?"

Now I'm the one surprised, not to mention impressed. Nobody's ever asked my permission before. Usually they press me for the reason I don't drink, why I've never touched alcohol, why I never will.

I have no desire to end up like my mother.

But from the look on Max's face, I've definitely inherited her sharp tongue.

"Sorry, I didn't mean to be rude. Go ahead and have your drink."

"You sure?" He eyes me hesitantly.

"Absolutely." I shake my head so hard, I feel my ponytail swing.

"Make it a beer." He smiles up at Nettie. "Whatever you've got on draft."

She doesn't budge. "Let's see some I.D."

"No problem." He pulls out a leather wallet and flashes his driver's license. "I'm legal."

"Barely," Nettie says with a sniff and turns away.

Barely? What exactly is that supposed to mean? He has a day's worth of stubble grazing his chin, but so do teenage boys. "How old are you?"

"Why?" Max asks. "You worried?"

The sparkle in his eyes catches me off guard, as does the zing shooting straight down my spine and into my toes as I realize he's flirting with me. The thought is intriguing, exhilarating, and utterly ridiculous. Doesn't he know I'm romantically challenged?

"You've got the rules mixed up," I loftily inform him. "It's supposed to be the other way around."

His eyebrows lift.

"It's a woman's prerogative to keep her age a secret," I explain, "not the man's."

His eyebrows rise even higher, but one corner of his mouth turns up. "That's rather sexist, don't you think?"

"What I *think* is that you're trying to evade the issue." I tap his wallet with one finger. "Exactly how old are you, anyway?"

"Old enough to know better and young enough not to care." He slides his wallet into his pocket. "How's that for an answer?"

"Not nearly good enough."

He props an elbow on the table, leans forward, chin in hand, and squints a smile. "You're a very nosy woman, Lucy Carter. Anybody ever tell you that?"

"All the time, but I never let it stop me. I'm a reporter, remember? Being nosy and persistent is part of the job." Keeping up a sober expression is proving hard work. Who knew I'd enjoy hassling him like this? "Not to mention I have access to records," I add. "I can always check you out with the DMV."

"Touché." Max fingers his forehead in mock salute. "Okay. I'll tell you mine if you tell me yours," he says as Nettie plunks a plate and beer in front of him. He waits as she disappears, then turns to me with a cocky grin. "You first."

"Twenty-five," I challenge.

"Twenty-two," he says, devouring a French fry.

Three years younger than me? I stink when it comes to math, but even I can figure this one out. Max is barely out of college. *If* he went to college. Do people need degrees to work at summer camp?

He eyes me casually as he spears a piece of fish from his plate. "You have a problem with younger guys?"

A problem with him being younger? For having no degree? For making my toes curl and suddenly wishing I'd paid attention while the other seventh-grade girls primped in front of the bathroom mirror? *Yes, I have a problem.* With a ponytail scrunched high atop my head and glasses perched on my nose, I'm not exactly the kind of girl men are interested in. My closet is crammed with banker boxes full of books instead of fashionable clothes. Keeping up with the latest styles requires time and money, and I have neither to spare. I'm plain old Lucy Carter. No man would look twice.

Who cares?

Sitting across from Max, I suddenly realize someone cares.

Me. I care very much. Until now, my femininity or lack thereof never seemed particularly relevant. But sitting here any longer will only prolong the inevitable. Why make him suffer?

"Sorry, but I've got to go. It was nice meeting you." I bounce up, chair screeching against the scarred wooden floor. "Enjoy your dinner."

"Wait, you're leaving?" His eyebrows arch as he leaps to his feet. "What's wrong? What did I say?"

"Nothing," I stammer. "Believe me, it's nothing."

I'm the one who's nothing. And if I stay any longer, he'll figure that out.

"Look, Lucy, I'm not sure what's going on, but I didn't mean to say something to make you mad. I get joking around sometimes, but I don't mean anything by it. I guess it comes from being around kids. Don't hold that against me."

"Never mind, it's okay." I grab my purse.

He sighs. "If you're that intent on getting home, give me a minute. I'll get this in a to-go box and meet you at the door. My car isn't far." He flags Nettie over.

I swallow hard, not an easy task when the inside of your mouth feels as parched as the Sahara desert. "That's not necessary. I don't live far."

"No problem. I'm parked right around the corner."

And my apartment is just down the street. Damn Kris Henderson. Now I have to 'fess up and admit the truth. Why did she ask him to drive me home? Kris has a big heart and an even bigger mouth. First thing Monday morning, she and I are going to have a little chat and establish some ground rules.

Rule No. 1. No messing with Lucy's love life.

"I don't need a ride." I ball up my fists, jam them in my pockets. "I live right here downtown, one block away."

His face scrunches up like he's trying to figure out why he got an incomplete on a final exam after pulling an all-nighter. "But I thought Kris said..."

It's worse than I thought. Max still doesn't get it. No wonder he didn't go to college.

"She lied," I blurt out. "She told you that I needed a ride because... well, because she thinks I need some excitement in my life. And I guess she thought that you... that you and I might..."

We stare at each other for what seems like forever as he ponders my explanation and I ponder diving under the table. But the thought of crawling around on top of those crunchy little peanut shells littering the floor isn't one I relish.

Then suddenly he gets it, and the sympathetic look that washes across his face is more than I can handle. A man feeling sorry for me is the last thing I want. *Lucy's Pity Party* is an exclusive club with sole membership limited to myself and the occasional guest, like Kris.

"Look, Lucy, it's okay—"

I hold up a hand, blink back hot tears threatening to spill over. I am not going to cry. I refuse to be reduced to tears, especially in front of a man.

"Honest, Max, you seem like a nice guy, but I can fend for myself. I've been doing it for years." I fling my purse over my shoulder and head for the door...

He grabs my arm before I make it two feet.

"Did I mention how much I hate eating alone? It's a hang-up I've had since I was a kid." His voice softens and his hand on my arm loosens a bit. "Come on, stay and keep me company. You'd be doing me a favor."

And then he smiles. Actually, merely one corner of his mouth lifts, but it's good enough to qualify as a smile. Maybe Kris is right. If I leave now, I'll never know what's got me scared, why I'm constantly running away from life instead of embracing it. And if nothing changes, nothing changes. If not now, when will I learn?

Maybe my first lesson is standing right in front of me.

"I'll even share my French fries," he offers.

My eyes narrow. "Are you trying to bribe me with food?"

"Only if you think it will work." He grins and I feel the Lucy-deep-freeze beginning to defrost.

"I wasn't kidding about hating to eat alone," he adds. "Plus, I'd appreciate a chance to pick your brain and find out what you think about the rezoning on Loon Lake."

"I'm not allowed to have an opinion," I say. "I'm covering the story for the *Journal*. I'm supposed to be neutral."

A flat-out lie. When it comes to Loon Lake, they can turn the place into a swamp, a desert, or a firing range, for all I care. I fought from the get-go not to be assigned to cover the story. A conflict of interest, I argued with Charles Kendall, citing my family history. But, as usual, the *Journal*'s managing editor blew off my concerns.

"At least tell me the latest," he says.

I drop my purse on the table and plop down across from Max. "What do you want to know?"

"The planning commission recently passed the application on to the township engineer for review and approval. Think they're close to a resolution?"

"Maybe." For once I'm not in the loop with the township officials. I thought it odd they're being so closed-mouthed, but seeing how it's Loon Lake, I haven't pushed the issue. "Why do you ask?"

Max leans forward. "You might say I've got a vested interest in the matter. Our camp is surrounded by the property they're debating."

"I think I'm beginning to understand." The Loon Lake rezoning has been controversial from the beginning, and it's not going away any time soon.

"It's a disaster waiting to happen." He shakes his head in disgust. "Our camp has been around for fifty years. If the rezoning passes, we might as well board up the cabins and call this our final season."

I get what he's saying. If money makes the world go around, Northern Michigan has been spinning out of control for the past ten years. It wasn't like this when I was growing up. It used to be that a family cottage on the lake meant an idyllic summer retreat. But times have changed, and inheriting property uncaps the land value. In this economy, especially with lakefront property taxes soaring, heirs are desperate to sell. That's when developers with cash in hand swoop in like ugly black crows and buy up the property. With more than enough acreage for a Planned Unit Development, the PUD application was filed one month ago.

"They're trying to force us to shut down," he says. "Once they do that, they'll grab our property, too. They know there's no way we can run a boy's camp smack in the middle of mega-mansions and an eighteen-hole golf course."

Like it or not, I get the point. Loon Lake is an inland lake, and one of the last pristine bodies of water in our region. Jet skis, powerboats, thirty-five-foot cruisers will destroy it.

Not that I care. I've hated that lake since I was five years old.

"Hey, I've got an idea." Max straightens, brightens. "Why don't you come out and see the place for yourself? I can give you a guided tour. We'll hike the property."

I swing my head so hard, my ponytail whips in my eyes. "Sorry, but you're talking to the wrong girl." Loon Lake is the last place on earth I want to visit. "I hate bugs and dirt. I hate anything to do with the great outdoors."

He chuckles. "Obviously your parents didn't send you to camp when you were a kid."

"No, they didn't," I say flatly. Summer camp is for kids with loving parents who can afford it. I had neither.

"Come on, Lucy, at least give it a try. What have you got to lose?"

The thought of a path overgrown with slimy moss, of dark hiking trails winding through the forest brings a shudder down my spine. Who knows what dangers might lurk beyond the tree line?

"Did I mention snakes?" I add. "I hate snakes."

Max grins. "I've seen some garter snakes around camp, but they won't hurt you."

"You're right," I agree with a fierce nod. "Because I won't be around to give them a chance."

"It's not the jungle, Lucy. It's only a summer camp."

His eyes gleam and I know he's teasing, but somehow it's okay. He's having fun *with* me, not making fun *of* me. There's a huge difference between the two and Max seems to understand the difference.

"The famous Lucy Carter, afraid of snakes. Who would believe it?" He grins, shakes his head. "You come across so brave and fearless in those articles you write."

"It's called literary license. I use it to full advantage."

"Okay, forget about hiking the property. Come out and see what we've got to offer. I'll even throw in dinner." His eyes crinkle in a smile. "Roasting hot dogs over an open camp fire. No one in their right mind could call that dangerous."

"Depends on how sharp the stick is that you're cooking them with," I say with a quick smile. I can almost hear Kris cheering me on from the sidelines. Max is trying so hard to be nice. The least I can do is meet him halfway. Plus, there's a free meal involved. "Okay," I relent.

"Great. I'll call you at the *Journal* and set something up."

"Give me a few days." Reporter or not, I'm still a girl. And before I go anywhere near that camp, I intend to pay a visit to our local hardware store and buy myself a pair of thick rubber boots. A pair of boots a snake can't bite through. I'm not sacrificing my toes to some slimy reptile.

"I can't wait to show you around. You'll love the place."

"Don't be too sure about that," I warn him. Poor Max. He has no clue what he's gotten himself into. Unfortunately, I do. And while I knew this day would eventually come, I didn't expect it to arrive so soon. I was counting on having another twenty or thirty years—or better yet, never—before facing the truth.

But being a reporter means following leads, taking risks, and facing facts. I guess it's time I did just that.

I'll start with Camp Call of the Loon.

Maybe then I'll find the courage to finally face Loon Lake.

CHAPTER TWO

"Hello, Lucy. And how are you on this beautiful Monday morning?"

Given my profession, staying connected is important. But some connections I can do without. Like Didi Taylor, the local realtor I signed with to sell Grandma's house. She's living up to her reputation as the *Rottweiler of Real Estate*. The woman hunts me down at the most inconvenient times.

"Lucy, are you there? Damn this phone, did I lose the connection?"

"Yes, Didi, I'm here."

Kris, not-so-politely eavesdropping from her desk adjacent to mine, sticks out her tongue and rolls her eyes at the mention of Didi's name. That's one thing I like about Kris. Even on a Monday morning, she manages to pull off subtlety.

"I'm disappointed in you, Lucy. I thought you were going to call."

"Sorry." Didi sounds upset and the last thing I want is her mad at me. Rottweilers snarl and bite if they're not properly handled. "Was I supposed to?"

"I haven't heard from you since we talked last week. Have you made a decision about dropping the price?"

No. A bargain-basement sale isn't an idea I'm eager to buy into. Grandma worked hard all her life to keep the two of us together in the house where my dad grew up. It doesn't seem right to let it go just to make a fast buck. Didi wants a quick sale, a quick commission. But what I want, I can't have. Grandma won't be coming home.

"Lucy? Am I losing you again?"

"No, I'm still here," I say, holding back a sigh.

"What about the price?"

"I'll think about it."

"Don't think too long," she warns.

I screw up my courage. "It's only been on the market two months."

"Two months is too long when it comes to moving real estate... especially in today's market."

I bite my lip and try to ignore Kris, who's given up any pretense her attention is occupied elsewhere. She's settled back in her chair, enjoying her coffee and my dilemma at being caught up in this lopsided conversation.

"A man called yesterday about the property," Didi says. "I'm showing it this morning. I'd like to tell him you're considering all offers."

"Offers? What offers?" I frown. "You never mentioned we've gotten other offers—"

"Precisely. Because we haven't. You have the price listed too high." Didi's voice no longer flits across the line like a butterfly intent on catching a morning breeze. "Lucy, listen to me. If you're serious about selling, I suggest you do the smart thing and drop the price. It's an old house and it needs work. Someone is going to have to sink some money into it to make the place livable."

"It's not that bad."

"Seriously?" The Rottweiler bares her teeth. "It's not worth much. Damn little, if you want the truth."

I'm too old to pout, though I feel like doing exactly that. Grandma lived in that house nearly all her life. I lived there myself until a few months ago.

"Do you want to scare off potential buyers?"

"No." I hate that my voice sounds tiny over the phone. I hate myself for not speaking louder. I hate that I'm not standing up to Didi.

Grandma never would have allowed the Rottweiler to stop her.

"I'll call you after I show the place. But if the buyer walks, don't say I didn't warn you. Meanwhile, I suggest you give some thought to what I've said." Her voice softens. "For your own sake."

Kris sniffs as I end the call. "Whatever possessed you to sign with Didi Taylor?"

"Name recognition is everything in this business." I defend my decision with a direct quote from Didi and hope to hell she's right. *The devil is in the details*, my journalism professor always said, though I probably should have done my research into Didi's sales record when she contacted me a few months ago about listing Grandma's house. I was surprised to take her call, especially since we'd never met.

But with Didi's face on more than half the *For Sale* signs in town, I felt like I knew her.

"Her name and listings are all over the *Journal*'s realtor page," I add.

"Just because she drops money on advertising doesn't mean she's selling houses," Kris retorts. "Frankly, Lucy, the woman scares me."

"She's not bad, once you get to know her," I say. Though truth be told, Didi scares the hell out of me, too.

Kris flashes me a look blacker than the coffee in her mug. "The less I see of her, the better."

"I doubt that will be a problem." James Bay has its distinct social divisions, and Kris and I run in a different circle than Didi. We're the downtown type who enjoy free concerts in the park (major emphasis on the word *free*), while Didi keeps company with the James Bay Yacht Club crowd. A petite dynamo in stylish suits and killer heels, she's armed with a realtor's license and confident attitude that convinced me to sign her listing agreement on the dotted line without reading the fine print. Now I'm stuck with this dynamo for the next six months.

Hopefully she'll convince some buyer to go brain dead and sign on the dotted line. I'll breathe easier with the sale complete and Didi out of my life. That woman sucks every bit of air out of the room when she's around. She's the closest thing to a human vacuum I've encountered.

"I've had enough of Didi Taylor for one day, and it's not even nine o'clock," Kris said. "Finish what you were telling me about Max before we were so rudely interrupted."

"There isn't much else." I taste my cold coffee, grimace, and swig it down anyway. When it comes to caffeine, a reporter learns fast to drop the java attitude and take what she can get, when she can get it. "He invited me out to visit him at camp."

"Way to go, girl," Kris says with a triumphant smile. "You work faster than I thought."

"Don't go thinking crazy. I'm not interested in Max Graham and he's not interested in me. He's interested in the story I'm covering on the Loon Lake rezoning."

"Give yourself some credit. You're cute, you're smart, you're funny, you're available—"

"And I'm also three years older than he is. Thanks, but no thanks." I jostle my mouse and the screen jumps to life.

"Three years is nothing," she blithely pooh-poohs. "So, when is he giving you the grand tour?"

I hold back a sigh. Kris is notorious for running away with conclusions. The last thing I need is my personal life ending up the caboose on her freight train. "He said he would call."

Will he? More important, do I want him to? I've been second-guessing myself since yesterday afternoon when I bought those rubber boots, now in a box on the floor beside my bed. I must be crazy. I've made it a point not to go anywhere near Loon Lake unless it's a dire emergency. One emergency in a lifetime is enough for anybody. I maxed out my quota at Loon Lake twenty years ago.

Maybe I can return the boots. Fred, the manager of the hardware store, is a nice guy. Plus, I still have my receipt.

Kris quiets down to work at her computer and I do a quick scan of my email. Nothing much of interest, save for a notice about the special meeting for the proposed parking-meter ordinance. I scribble myself a reminder. Downtown Main Street remains meter-free, but not if our current mayor has his way. His plan isn't popular and the meeting is guaranteed to be well-attended. I'll be in the front row. Parking meters don't exactly make for Pulitzer Prize material, but controversy sells papers.

And as Charles Kendall is fond of reminding us, anytime Kris and I are unhappy with the stories he assigns, we're free to switch departments and write the type of copy that truly counts in the newspaper business. Advertising copy.

"Have you heard from Charles?" I eye the empty chair of the managing editor's desk positioned in the center of our small editorial department. The page-one deadline is due within the hour, and it's my responsibility if Charles doesn't show. "He should be here by now."

Kris shrugs. "The phone's been quiet. So has the scanner."

"Ladies, have I got a story for you," Charles says moments later as he blows into the office and tosses his daily copy of the *New York Times* on his desk. "I was over at the coffee shop and it's all everyone is talking about. We've got bona fide breaking news in James Bay."

"Let me guess. You bought coffee for everybody this morning," Kris says with a poker face and a quick wink for me.

"Lucky for you, Henderson, I'm going to ignore that remark." He rocks back and forth in his wingtip shoes, looking like he's about to bust. "I'm talking big news. Bigger than you ever dreamed. Somebody in our little town won the lottery."

Kris's head snaps up. "The Big Game?"

"Someone from James Bay?" I straighten in my seat. News like this is guaranteed to knock the parking-meter debate off the front page.

"Winner takes all." Charles folds his arms and perches on a corner of his desk. "A seventy-million-

dollar jackpot."

Kris's whistle ricochets around the room. "That's some serious cash."

"I've got the winning numbers. They're posted on the website." He fumbles inside his coat pocket, draws out a folded scrap of paper. "Two, four, six, twelve, thirty, plus the mega ball, thirteen." He jabs a finger in my direction. "You are going to track down the person who won."

My heart pounds in my ears. "You're giving me the story?"

"Against my better judgment," he says with a scowl. "Pete Kelly sold the winning ticket. I swung by his store after I left the coffee shop and tried to interview him, but he refuses to budge. He insists on talking only with you."

God bless Pete Kelly. He's giving me an exclusive. Looks like all those years of pumping gas at his place are finally paying off.

"The guy is going nuts. His place is a mess, with reporters and camera crews everywhere. The Fox News truck showed up just as I was leaving." Charles levels me with a heated stare. "I want you to get out there pronto before Pete changes his mind and talks to somebody else. The last thing I want is some clown from Detroit or Lansing scooping us on a hometown story."

I grab my notebook. "I'm on my way."

"And make sure you get the whole story. Pete's pretty excited. From what they said at the coffee shop, he'll be claiming a nice check for selling the winning ticket."

"Define *nice*." The grin spreads across my face so wide it hurts. Lucky Pete, lucking out like this. It couldn't happen to a nicer guy.

"Four hundred thousand dollars. A little less than one percent of the jackpot."

A second whistle from Kris echoes around the news room. "Pretty nice change just for selling a lottery ticket."

Charles slaps the paper printout on my desk. "We'll hold the front page. You've got three columns to fill. Call Pete and tell him you're on your way. And make sure you find the winner. Your interview with them will run tomorrow."

I grab the receiver, but instead of a dial tone, I hear the static of an open line.

"Lucy?"

"Pete?" I stare at the phone. Funny, expecting to hear his voice when I haven't dialed. Dead silence greets me for a minute.

"It's Max Graham."

"Oh. Hi, Max."

Charles glares, Kris's eyes pop, and my heart skips a beat.

"You sound a little funny," he says. "Everything okay?"

"Things are fine. I'm just… a little busy."

"Working on the rezoning story?"

"Not exactly." I swivel in my chair, turn my back on two pair of eyes blazing at me. This conversation had better be fast or I'll end up with holes in the back of my favorite blouse. "I was just on my way to an interview. What's up?"

"Are you busy tonight? I was thinking I could give you that tour of camp. I'm coming into town later today for some things. I could swing by the *Journal* and pick you up. There aren't many people who've had a ride in my Jeep."

"Is that supposed to be a privilege?" I smile into the phone.

"Depends. You can decide for yourself once you see the Jeep."

I laugh softly. Our conversation last Saturday night was a first in the *Lucy Chronicles*. Totally unplanned, totally unguarded, and totally fun time chatting with a guy. A younger guy. One who poses no threat. Max is funny, cute, plus he's too young for me, which makes him perfect. There's no pressure. It's easy being around him, unlike when I'm with guys my own age or older. The other night with Max, I found myself being just me.

Maybe I can practice on Max until the real thing comes along.

"So, what do you think? Is it a date?"

I twirl in my chair, swiveling to a stop directly in front of Charles. "Get going," he mouths with a furious stare.

"Sorry, Max, but I need to get to my interview."

"What about tonight?"

Charles points at his watch, points at the door.

"Tonight's fine," I say. "See you then."

Kris gives me a thumbs-up. "I told you he would call."

"Unless that was the lottery winner, I don't care who called." Charles scowls. "Get out to Pete's Place. Now."

"I'm going, I'm going." I grab my purse and escape out the back door into brilliant sunshine.

Pete's Place is busy as a casino, with people milling through the aisles and the cash register sounding *ca-ching ca-ching* every thirty seconds. I smile to myself as I shoulder my way through a group of reporters clustered around the coffee machines. Little do they know that the girl passing by the beer and bologna coolers is here for the exclusive from Pete they're seeking. I detour down the cupcake aisle, past a heavyset woman debating breakfast, and end up near the till. A pimply faced boy struggles to keep up with the steady stream of customers. Pete is planted behind him, arms crossed, policing the scene.

"Wow, this is something." I pause for breath, feeling flushed as a Vegas high roller for simply having reached the counter.

"Crazy, isn't it? Go figure. It's been like this all morning." He grabs my arm and hauls me around the counter, through a door, and into a cramped office where he nods me into a seat. He sinks into a cracked leather chair behind a scarred wooden desk. "I've never seen anything like it. If things keep up the way they're going, I'll be out of beer before noon."

"Pete, are you okay? You look a little—"

"Excited?" His eyes burn bright. "Damn right I am."

I'm leaning more toward *agitated,* myself, especially given his flushed face and untucked shirt. But Pete's never been the debonair type. Plus, I'm a firm believer that a little sympathy goes a long way in loosening people's minds and hearts... plus their tongues. And right now, the gift of gab is what I need from Pete. I'm on a deadline for what could be the biggest story of my life.

"Damn, I never expected this," he says. "The place is lousy with reporters. I called my wife and told her to get over here and help. She hates working at the store, but I'm going nuts. Everybody wants to know who bought the winning ticket."

Everybody, including me. Our loyal *Journal* readers are clamoring for the story. I clear my throat, click my pen, take a slow, deep breath. Pete needs to be handled gently. There's a wild look in his eyes that has me feeling a little wild myself.

"Do you blame them?" I say. "It's a big story."

"It's a lot of money. Seventy million before taxes."

"Have you ever sold a winning ticket before?"

"Some guy a few years ago won ten thousand dollars. But nothing like this." Pete snorts, sits back in his chair, shakes his head. "Seventy million dollars. Hell, Lucy, what do people do with that kind of money?"

"I don't know," I say, though I know exactly the first thing I'd do. Pay off my student loans. They were a blessing at the time and helped me make it through college. But I dread the monthly statement arriving in the mail. At the rate I'm going, I'll be retired way before my education debt is.

I scribble a few notes. "Any idea how many of your customers play the lottery? Describe a typical player." My money is on gullible fools with grandiose dreams. But Pete might have other ideas and I'm willing to listen. With Charles barking orders at me to get on the story, I didn't have time to do research. When it comes to gambling, I'm a virgin. Not to mention in certain other aspects of my life.

"Anybody over eighteen with a dollar to blow can play," he says. "We card anybody that doesn't look old enough. The State's pretty strict. I don't want to lose my machine." Pete settles back in his chair, calmer now he's finally talking. "We make a nice profit off our regular players. They come in to buy their tickets, and they usually end up buying cigarettes, a tank of gas, maybe even a six-pack while they're here." His grin widens. "Naturally, we card them, too. Can't take a chance on selling to minors."

"Naturally," I say, smiling. Pete's a stickler for following the rules and woe to the customer who doesn't comply. A sign above his cash register offers a *FREE RIDE IN A POLICE CAR* to anyone caught shoplifting from his store.

"I understand you're getting a nice check for selling the winning ticket."

"Gravy for my retirement." He stretches in his chair with a speculative gleam in his eye. "Think I might finally buy me that motor home I've been wanting and head on down to Florida this winter. Ditch the snow and cold for palm trees and ocean breezes. What do you think? Sound nice?"

Can money buy happiness? Pete's asking the wrong girl. I've got no clue. Money was tight at Grandma's house when I was growing up. All the kids in school knew whose parents had money. It wasn't hard to figure out. Those kids were part of the popular crowd, especially once we hit high school. The girls wore cute clothes, the guys drove cool cars. I wasn't invited to one single party.

"Tell me more about the Big Game." My grip tightens around my pen. "How big is it? How many tickets do they usually sell?"

"We're talking nine states. The more people play, the higher the jackpot. The higher the jackpot, the more people play." Pete chuckles. "If there's no winner, the jackpot turns over. That's when things really get interesting. Eighty percent probably buy an easy pick. Five numbers and the mega ball. It's fast, and your odds are the same. Maybe even better. After all, the winning numbers are just a random series. And I'm selling those damn tickets about as fast as the machine can spit them out," he informs me in a gleeful voice. "It's been churning since six a.m. Guess since somebody hit the jackpot in my store, people figure they might get lucky, too."

Gambling fever. The thought makes me shiver. Thank God I never succumbed. With my luck, I'd be dead broke by now.

"How did you find out you sold the winning ticket?"

"Ha!" Pete scoffs and nods at the door. "A couple of them were waiting when I showed up this morning. The State posts everything on the lottery website." He shakes his head. "If this keeps up, I'll have to hire more help. Know anybody that needs a job?"

"Sorry, Pete." I could use some extra money, but running a cash register isn't exactly what I had in mind. More like writing feature articles. And when it comes to articles, I still have Pete's exclusive to write. Charles is holding three columns on the *Journal*'s front page.

I peer across the desk at Pete. "Any idea who the winner might be?"

"Naw, it could be anybody. All we know is the computer says the winning ticket was sold here last Thursday." He cocks his head with a thoughtful stare. "Say, didn't I sell you a ticket last week?"

A dim recollection of me purchasing a lottery ticket collides with the preposterous notion of hitting it big. I shrug off the idea as fast as it hits. "Forget it, Pete. Things like that don't happen to people like me."

He scoffs. "It happens every day, kiddo. You don't think so? Hey, just look at me. Who would have dreamed my store would hit the jackpot? And until somebody comes forward to claim the big prize, it's anybody's guess who won. But man oh man, would I like to know."

Pete, and everybody else in town—including me. Charles made himself pretty clear. I'd better locate the winner and grab an exclusive… or else.

"Do you think it's somebody from James Bay?" I'm gambling—hoping—praying that's the case. I'll have a much better shot at tracking them down if the winner is someone local. People in this town love to talk. Someone's sure to have the scoop.

"Sorry, Lucy, I don't have a clue. Though I hope it's one of my regulars." A big wolf-grin spreads across his face. "Wouldn't that be something? One of our own, hitting the jackpot. Now, there's a story that would sell some papers."

"What happens if no one comes forward?"

"Hell if I know." He looks surprised. "Why wouldn't they?"

I stumble over the thought. Why would a person want to hide their good fortune? My fingers tighten around my pen as my brain wraps around the notion of anonymity. Pete's Place is crowded with reporters. The parking lot is jammed with news trucks. What if it was me? What if I was the winner? Would I welcome the notoriety? The mere thought sends a shiver snaking down my spine. Life as I know it would never be the same.

Not to mention the balance in my bank account.

"They get one year to claim their prize," he says. "One year from the day the numbers are drawn. Some people take their sweet time, get things set up with lawyers and accountants before they head to Lansing and pick up the money."

"Seventy million dollars," I muse out loud. "You'd need a big purse for that kind of cash."

"Check your numbers," he reminds me. "You never know. You could be the one."

I swallow hard. Leave it to Pete to get my heart racing.

"We done here?" He clears his throat, straightens in his chair. "I need to get back out front and make sure things are running smooth."

"Let me get a few pictures and I'm all set." I fish the digital camera out of my bag and snap a few shots of Pete posed behind his desk.

"Just remember what I told you, Lucy." He bounces to his feet and wags his finger as he ushers me through the door. "Check your numbers."

Two hours later, Pete's picture is splashed across the page-one banner. The *Journal* is an afternoon paper and today's issue is a guaranteed sellout. I'd be a liar if I didn't admit some satisfaction at having scooped the other print journalists, as well as the local television evening news. But today's news is tomorrow's trash. All of us are now hunting for the same story.

Who won?

I spend my afternoon working the phone lines and combing the downtown area. James Bay is buzzing. Everyone is eager to talk, but no one has real news. I chat with shoppers and storekeepers alike, including my landlady, Polly Mitchell, who pounces on me as I stroll into her dress shop. She crows with the news that her nephew holds the winning ticket—one he bought at Pete's Place. My breath catches as Polly dials the number and gets her nephew on the line. Sure enough, he scored at Pete's... and he's already claimed his one-hundred-dollar prize.

I head back to my desk, hot and dusty. Tomorrow's front-page exclusive isn't looking good. I've exhausted my resources and tapped out my contacts. Even Grandma's pie-baking buddies from the Rosary Altar Society don't have a clue. Charles can complain all he wants, but until someone steps forward of their own volition, I'm fresh out of ideas.

I sink into my chair and stare at the computer. The lottery website printout is taped on the screen. The winning combination is two-four-six-twelve-thirty, and the mega ball is thirteen. The name of Pete's store is printed at the bottom as the winning location. A little voice stirs in my head, and I remember Pete's admonition to check my own ticket.

Where is it? I barely remember buying it, let alone what I did with it. I scrounge through my purse, eventually turning it upside down on my desk, where I sort through the mess. No ticket. I tear through desk drawers, paw through aging paperwork. Nada. Desperation drives me to my knees and I dive under my desk, hunting through the cardboard recycling box I keep at my feet. Maybe I accidentally tossed the ticket without realizing it.

"Lucy, you've got a visitor."

"I'm in no mood to talk." I sink back on my heels, swipe the sweat from my face and peer up at Kris from my spot under the counter. "Tell whoever it is that I'm not available."

"If you want me to leave, you should at least have the courtesy to tell me to my face." The words drop to the floor beside me as a pair of rugged hiking boot lines up directly behind Kris's navy blue flats.

My heart clutches as I recognize the voice. And the boots. The heavy-duty kind made for traipsing through the forest. Over hill and dale. Around a summer camp.

"You're early." Reluctantly I accept the hand he offers and rise to meet him.

"I finished up sooner than expected." Max nods at my knees. "Sorry about disturbing your prayer time."

"Ha, ha, very funny." I swipe a hand through my hair and clothes, brushing off a layer of dust. Our nightly cleaning people need to do a better job.

"What exactly were you doing down there? Or maybe I shouldn't ask?"

"I lost something." Just my luck, having Max show up an hour early. There goes my plan for a quick run home. Maybe I stashed the ticket in my basket of unpaid bills. "Would you mind stopping by my apartment? I need to check something. It will only take a minute."

"No problem."

"You're sure? I don't want to interfere with dinner."

He grins. "Hot dogs don't take long to cook. You like baked beans?"

"Love 'em. My grandma used to make a pan every Saturday night." I swallow down a sudden hunger pang. Lunch is a distant memory; a few stale crackers from the hallway vending machine and a spoonful of peanut butter from the emergency jar I keep stashed in my desk.

"Roberta makes the best baked beans you'll ever taste," he says. "Molasses is the secret, so she tells me. That, plus a pinch of mustard."

My mouth waters. Maybe it would be better to just chuck this whole find-the-missing-ticket scavenger hunt and head on out to camp. It wouldn't be polite to keep the cook waiting.

Then again, I still need to stop by my apartment. There's another matter that can't be overlooked. A *size ten* matter neatly tucked in a box on my bedroom floor. Growling stomach or not, I have no intention of going anywhere near that silly camp without my new rubber boots.

"Hey, I almost forgot. This is for you." Max twirls a navy blue baseball cap in his hands. The hat has a black-and-white loon featured on the front with the words *Camp Call of the Loon* embroidered underneath in fancy red print.

"We sell them at the camp store. I thought you might like one."

"Thanks. That was sweet." I twirl the cap in my hand. Do I tell him I never wear hats? That I hate hats? Always have, always will.

"You'll need it, riding in an open Jeep. Plus, I know how girls are about their hair."

Max probably knows more about women and their hair than I do myself. I flip the cap over a few times, praying he won't notice the flush climbing my cheeks or the way my heart is pounding against my chest. Max has it all wrong. Other women worry about their hair, not me. Other women get presents from men, not me. I'm not like other women.

Then again, maybe I'm more like other women than I realize. At least Max seems to think so.

I jam the hat on my head and flash him an uncertain smile. "How do I look?"

"Like you're ready to roll. So, first to your apartment and then out to camp."

My mind is suddenly chasing dust bunnies. Dusting has never been high on my list of priorities, and I wasn't expecting visitors. I never have any, save for Kris, but she doesn't count. What's a little dust between friends?

Hopefully Max is someone I can count as a friend.

I snatch the lottery printout off my computer screen and tuck it in my pocket. With a brief wave for Kris, out the door we go.

Max was right. I definitely need the hat riding in his Jeep. "Sorry, I know it's a mess. I use it to run around camp. I've been meaning to get it cleaned."

He must be kidding. A thousand car washes won't help this Jeep. With no doors, merely a roll bar for a roof, plus numerous dents and dings, it doesn't exactly ooze style. Yellow foam shoves up through cracked vinyl seats.

"It's quite the car." I fasten my seatbelt, then double-check it as Max pulls into traffic. He drives like a fiend. My dust-bunny worries blow away in the wind as we make the quick spin three blocks down Main Street.

"Pull in next to that little VW." I grab the Jesus bar as we skid to a halt at the rear of the two-story building. An upscale dress shop run by my landlady, Polly Mitchell, occupies the ground floor. My apartment is directly above. "Here we are. Home sweet home."

Max follows me up the weathered, outside staircase. He waits as I fish out my keys and struggle with the wooden door.

"Got a problem?" he asks from behind.

"It's the humidity. Sometimes it sticks." I jiggle the knob but the door won't budge. I fight off the urge to give it a swift kick. I pay my rent on time. Why can't Polly make sure my door opens on command?

"Here, let me try. I'm getting good at this kind of stuff." Max nudges me aside. One well-aimed shove of his shoulder, a twist of the knob, and the door swings open.

"Very nice. I'm impressed." I lead him inside.

"You get handy living around a camp. Give me a screwdriver, hammer, and some nails and you'd be surprised what I can fix."

"Do you rent out?" I ask with a quick smile. "My landlady isn't exactly Mrs. I'll-Have-It-Fixed-For-You-Today." While I wouldn't call Polly a slum landlord, lately every other sentence out of her painted-on mouth comes punctuated with a sigh and a mini-lecture on the high cost of maintaining her rental apartments. Mentioning the sticky door will only set her off on another of her tirades.

"I'll bring my tool belt next time," he promises.

I throw my keys on the table and lead him into the living room, trying to ignore his promise of a next time. "This won't take long. Make yourself at home."

He glances around. "Nice place."

"Little place," I correct him. His loop around the tiny living room lasts exactly thirty seconds. Sagging couch, slip-covered armchair, creaky rocker. Vintage Grandma's house. I scan the end table next to the rocker, fish through the magazines stored in the basket beneath, then scowl. Where did I put that stupid ticket?

"Wow, look at that view. James Bay and Lake Michigan, right across the street."

The sight of Max in front of the window, rubbernecking like a tourist, puts the smile back on my face. I picked this apartment solely for the view. Sparkling blue waters, evening sunsets. "You know what they say," I remind him. "*A view of the bay is half the pay.*" And my checking account is living proof.

Max sticks his hands in his pockets and throws me an expectant look. "Want some help trying to find whatever it is you're looking for?"

I glance at my bedroom door, then back at Max. "Let me check one more place."

He picks up a copy of yesterday's *Journal*. "Sure. Take your time."

I slip from the room as he settles in Grandma's rocker. Five minutes, I promise myself, and then I'm giving up. No use wasting my time, or Max's, either. I've got a feeling that ticket is long gone. I tear through my bedroom, jerk open the closet door and search the shelves. Nada. I sink on my knees and peer under the bed. Nothing, save for a thriving population of dust bunnies plus a paperback romance novel that went missing months ago. I fish it out and slap it on the nightstand, then turn to my dresser and paw through the drawers.

"Everything okay in there?" Max's voice is muffled through the bedroom door.

"I'll be right out," I yell, hands on hips. The last thing I need is him in my bedroom, especially in its semi-disheveled mess. I yank open the last drawer and woefully stare at the meager heap of lingerie. If thinking about money can drive a person insane, then I've gone certifiable. Never in a million years would I have tucked that lottery ticket in my bras.

"Need any help?" he calls.

"No!" I slam the drawer shut and take one last glance around the room. Four walls, a double bed, rubber boots in the box. As usual, everything neat and tidy. Unlike my purse...

I spin around so fast, it makes me lightheaded. I blink, breathe, and take in the sight of my duffel-bag purse on the bottom of the closet floor, still in the exact same spot where I dropped it the other day after switching bags. I grab it, flop down on the bed, and upend the purse on top of the pink chenille bedspread, digging through the mess. Comb, notepad, gas station receipt. I draw in a sharp breath. Tucked between a wad of clean loose Kleenex is the missing lottery ticket.

My heartbeat pounds a drum roll in my ears as I pinch the ticket between my thumb and forefinger and hold it up for scrutiny. The numbers two and four swim before my eyes. Were those two numbers on the winning ticket? Easy enough to find out. The lottery printout is in my pocket.

The ticket vibrates slightly between my fingers, and something about it suddenly has me spooked. I hold it at arm's length. What are the odds? How many people match one number, or even two? Millions of people play the Big Game. Millions of people expect to win.

How many of those millions shop at Pete's?

I head into the living room, pinching the ticket gingerly between two fingers. My heart is racing so fast, it feels like it might explode out of my chest and shoot through the window straight into James Bay. I clear my throat and stand before Max. "Do me a favor?"

He throws the *Journal* aside. "Sure."

I tug the printout from my pocket and hand it to him, praying he won't notice my hand is trembling. "Would you read the numbers to me?"

"The lottery?" His eyebrows lift. "Funny, I didn't peg you as the gambling type."

Sweat beads pop on my upper lip. Max can think what he wants. Right now, the only thing I care about is eliminating myself from the pool of potential lottery winners.

"Two, four, six."

My hand shakes. The first three numbers are a match.

He glances up with a quick smile. "Got a winner yet?"

"Just read the numbers." The words come out sharper than I intended, and I bite my lip. "Sorry. I didn't mean…" I sigh, shake my head. "Please, Max? It's important."

"Sure." He frowns slightly, his voice drops. "Twelve, thirty."

There's no need for him to finish. I already know what that last number is. Inside I've gone cold and clammy, like I've climbed outside my own skin and am floating high above the room. Hovering. Hallucinating. No way this can be for real. *No way.*

"The mega ball number is thirteen." My voice sounds tinny and far away to my ears.

"How did you know?" His voice hits the right note of incredulity, perfectly in tune with the queasy feeling in my gut.

It's me. I'm the one. I won the lottery.

Seventy million dollars.

No more wondering who the lucky winner is. No more wondering who I'll interview for the *Journal*'s front page tomorrow.

I can interview me.

"Lucy, you okay? You look a little funny."

The room is hot and dry and suddenly I can't breathe. "I don't know. I feel like… I think I'm going to be sick."

"Sit down," he orders. "Put your head between your knees."

I'm vaguely aware of Max's hand on my elbow, guiding me backward to the couch. I sink into the cushions. A broken spring pops to life and hits me under my hip. My stomach opens in a yawn as I bend forward. The winning ticket flutters out of my fingers and settles on the floor. I blink and stare at the scrap of paper nestled against my shoe.

A wrinkled slip of paper worth seventy million dollars.

Nausea and disbelief collide midpoint between my stomach and brain and rush to my throat.

"Breathe through your mouth." Max crouches beside me and grips my knee. "Drink this. Slowly."

I sip the cool water. Max must be a magician, for he's produced a glass of water out of nowhere. I blink and finally recognize the plastic tumbler is from my kitchen cupboard.

"Lucy? You going to be okay?"

Am I okay? His question would have me doubled over with laughter if I wasn't already sitting with my head between my knees. Poor Max. He has no clue. Nothing in my life will ever be okay again.

"So, I guess you won?" He picks up the ticket and hands it to me without eyeing it. "From the look on your face, it must be a lot of money. How much? Ten thousand?"

I've never been good at math. How many times do you multiply seven times ten in order to come up with seventy million dollars? Seventy? Seven hundred? Seven thousand? "Obviously you haven't read today's *Journal*," I manage to choke out.

"Nope." He rubs the back of his neck and stares. "Why? Something happen I should know about?"

The irony isn't lost on me. I'm with the one person in town who hasn't the slightest clue. I swallow bile rising in the back of my throat. "You'll find today's *Journal* in my bag. Out on the kitchen table."

Max frowns as he comes to his feet. "Which article am I supposed to read?"

"Start with the front page," I croak, rubbing my forehead as I say the words. I wish everything could stay the same. The minute he reads it, he'll understand, and everything will change. Money changes things. It changes people. And I don't want money changing the way he looks at me.

Max is a quick reader. He's back, mouth open, eyes wide with disbelief.

"Any questions?" I ask weakly.

He shakes his head silently, still staring at me.

"Good, because I've got one for you." I stumble to my feet. If I'm going to be sick, better it happens in the bathroom than on the living-room carpet. "What exactly do I do now?"

CHAPTER THREE

Most lottery winners probably celebrate in expensive restaurants over champagne and caviar. Max and I celebrate in my tiny kitchen over bowls of chicken soup. It's the only thing my stomach can handle.

He pushes his bowl away. "Feel better now?"

"Actually, I do." I shove my bowl aside. "You were right. The soup was perfect." I prop my elbows on the kitchen table and offer him a weak mile. Max and Grandma have something in common. Chicken soup as a cure-all reminds me of when I was ten years old, and Grandma ruled her kitchen and my world.

But I'm all grown up now. And thanks to that little slip of paper anchored to the table by the saltshaker, my world has changed overnight.

"I still can't believe it." I grab another Kleenex and blow my nose. "Things like this don't happen to people like me. It feels like I'm stuck in a dream."

He smiles softly. "It's no dream. I'm right here with you."

I stare at him with round eyes. "Yes, but how do I know you're not part of the dream?"

"Trust me, you're wide awake. Want me to pinch you and prove it?"

Max looks dead serious, but I'm discovering he's a big tease. Is it any surprise he works around kids? They probably love him. Lots of guys my own age are full of themselves and their careers, but Max doesn't seem too concerned about himself or the fact that working at a summer camp probably isn't the best of career moves. Maybe he's just a big kid at heart, but I can't fault him for that. He gave me something to cling to tonight as I rode out the financial tornado that tossed and turned and spit me out on my bathroom floor with no yellow brick road in sight.

Wherever I've landed, it sure isn't Kansas.

"Seventy million dollars," he muses. "Wonder how much that equals after taxes?"

I rub my forehead. So much money. So much to think about. "I suppose I'll find out soon enough."

He gives me a curious smile. "It's a lot of money. Be careful you don't blow it all in one place."

"Very funny," I mumble as my stomach gives another wild lurch. My insides spin like I swallowed a yo-yo, my legs ping like loose rubber bands, while the rest of me feels like a bag of cement. I haven't budged from my chair for an hour. I don't dare. The last thing I want is to end up on the bathroom floor again.

"Got any plans on how you'll spend it?"

I shake my head. "I have no clue."

"Everybody dreams about hitting it big."

I swing my head, feel the hair brush soft like silk against my cheek. "Not me."

He eyes me across the table like he doesn't believe me. "Practical and pragmatic?"

"What's wrong with that?" My dreams died twenty years ago, and no amount of money will bring my father back. That's when I quit dreaming. I kept myself busy going to school, trying to keep my scholarship while working two part-time jobs, doing my best to keep it all together, trying to help Grandma. "I've never been a dreamer," I inform him. "I never had the time or money."

"Let me clue you in on something. You've got the money now."

His words slam me back in my chair. I shake my head, trying to shake away the dazed feeling clogging my brain. Max is right. I *do* have the money. No more student loans. No more worrying about how to pay the bill for Grandma's nursing care. There'll be no need to sell her house.

Maybe I can afford to start dreaming after all.

"My car needs new tires. I guess now I can buy them." I've been saving for weeks, despite Kris's urging to use my credit card. But unlike my co-worker, I refuse to let the words *charge it* rule my life.

Max offers a brief smile. "New tires? Why not buy a new car?"

The thought thuds in my brain as I realize he's right. "Maybe I will." I feel a slow grin start across my face. "Wait till I tell Kris. She's never going to believe this."

"Sounds like you two are pretty tight."

I nod fiercely. "She's the best."

"What about your job? Do you plan to keep working?"

My grin widens as I envision waltzing into the *Journal* building and into Charles Kendall's office. Finally I'll be able to tell him exactly what I think of him... just before I pronounce those magic words, *I quit.* "Who knows? Maybe I'll buy the *Journal*."

"From new tires to a newspaper," Max replies with a laugh. "Now you're thinking big."

"Wouldn't that show Charles exactly who's in charge?" I sit back, delighted as possibilities begin to present themselves. I can quit my job. I can buy a new car. I can pay off my student loans, help Grandma out. I can do what I want. Travel, see the world. My brain feels like it's in overload. This having-more-money-than-I-know-with business will take some getting used to. Too much stimulus. Too many dollar signs.

"What about you?" I eye Max across the table. "What would you do with that kind of money? Buy the camp and save it from the developers?"

"I wish it were that simple." His grin slips away, replaced by a sober stare. "The camp owns the property. It has for a number of years. But if the development goes through, it will destroy Loon Lake. We'll have to shut our doors." His eyes narrow, darken. "But I'm not giving up. That place is part of me, and I'm not going down without a fight."

Many people in James Bay aren't happy with the booming development in the North Country, but few try to change things. But I have no doubt that Max means every word. He's not afraid to get down and dirty. Living at that camp, he's used to being around dirt.

Max clears his throat. "It might be a good idea to put that ticket someplace safe."

"What could be safer than right here in front of me?" My hand creeps to the saltshaker and I finger the edge of the ticket.

"Do you have a safe-deposit box?"

"No, I never needed one. Besides, they cost money."

"Well, you need one now. And you can afford it. In fact..." His eyebrows rise. "You can't afford *not* to have one."

Max sounds so serious, he has me spooked. "I'll go to the bank tomorrow—"

"No," he interrupts, fierce determination in his voice and eyes. "Lucy, listen to me. I think this is something you need to do tonight."

I blink. "The bank has been closed for hours. It's nearly nine o'clock."

"They'll open up once you explain."

I bark a short laugh and shake my head. "I doubt it."

"Wanna bet?" His eyes hold a challenge that makes me swallow hard. "That ticket needs to be under lock and key. There must be someone from the bank you can call. Someone with a key who can open up after hours."

I eye the slip of paper holding my financial future. The wooden saltshaker guarding it can't weigh more than two or three ounces. It's safe enough to hold down a grocery bill, a scribbled address or a laundry receipt. But is it safe enough for a scrap of paper worth seventy million dollars?

Max is right. I need to get to the bank. Fast.

"Kent Phillips has a key," I say hesitantly, "though we're not exactly on a first-name basis." The President of our small, hometown bank is a board member of the Hospital Foundation and was at the ribbon-cutting ceremony last week, posing for pictures. Hopefully Mr. Phillips will remember me from the photos instead of the shaky balance in my checking account.

Max flips through the phone book. "Here's his number."

I'm slow to pick up the phone. James Bay is a small town, but people like me don't phone people like Kent Phillips and expect them to jump. Not at nine o'clock at night. Not even at nine o'clock in the morning. He's president of the bank. I'm just Lucy Carter.

"He's probably not home," I say. "He's very community oriented. I'll bet he's at a meeting."

"Or maybe he's home watching TV," Max chides gently. "Come on, you're supposed to be the fearless reporter. Are you afraid to make the call?"

Me, afraid? Not of Kent Phillips.

"Have you ever met his wife?" What if Edie Phillips answers the phone? "She's had it in for me since last year when I accidentally ran her picture on the society page with Luella Peterson's name underneath."

Max merely smiles.

"Do you know Luella Peterson? She must weigh at least three hundred pounds," I add quickly. "Edie took it personally. She still hasn't forgiven me."

Max sighs and rolls his eyes. "Make the call. Trust me, Lucy, you need to get that ticket someplace safe."

"Trust me, Max. Edie Phillips can make my life a living hell."

Our stare down lasts several seconds. Long enough for me to realize he's not giving up. When it comes to being stubborn, maybe I've met my match. I grab the phone, punch in the numbers, and wait.

A woman's throaty voice floats across the line. "Hello?"

Just my rotten luck. My spirits take a nosedive, but I take a deep breath and suck up my courage. "Hi, Mrs. Phillips, it's Lucy Carter."

"Who?"

What an absolute witch. She knows exactly who I am. I bite my tongue, reminding myself why I'm calling, why I need access to a safe-deposit box tonight. "Lucy Carter. From the *Journal*."

"Oh." The chill factor in Edie's voice plunges ten degrees.

"Sorry that I'm calling so late." I eye Max darkly. He's picked up my ticket and is examining it intently. It would serve him right if I handed over the phone and made him finish the call. This was his lamebrain idea, not mine. "Is Mr. Phillips available?"

"Why do you want to speak with Kent? Is there a problem?" Her words stab like icicles.

"It's urgent."

Edie's patronizing *harrumph* speaks volumes. I've always wondered how women with money and social status can say so much merely by clearing their throats. I drum my fingers against the worn kitchen table and try to ignore Edie's thinly veiled hiss *it's-that-awful-Lucy-Carter-reporter* I hear on the other end.

"Hello?" A deep male voice rumbles across the line.

"Hi, Mr. Phillips, this is Lucy Carter. Sorry to bother you at home so late at night." Kent Phillips seems amiable enough in public, but with some people you never knew. Not to mention the teensy-weensy fact that he's married to Edie. "Lucy Carter," I add. "From the *James Bay Journal*."

"I know who you are. What can I do for you?"

I swallow hard and pray he can be trusted to keep a secret. I'm not eager to give up my anonymity, but I doubt he'll agree to unlock the bank without a good reason.

Though I have a sneaking suspicion that seventy million dollars might be just the catalyst to get him behind the wheel of his car headed downtown.

"Mr. Phillips, have you read today's *Journal*?"

Our conversation doesn't last long. Long enough for me to convey the news. Long enough for him to exclaim *wow* several times, and then some. Long enough for him to agree to open the bank.

"We're to meet him in front of the bank in fifteen minutes." I grab the ticket, grab my purse. Max grabs my arm.

"Hold on, Lucy. Before we go, do yourself a favor." He holds out a pen. "Sign the back of the ticket."

"Why should I do that?"

His face is solemn. "You know it's your ticket, and I know it's your ticket, but who's to say it's your ticket once it's out of your hands?"

I scoff at the notion that anyone would think otherwise. "You're talking crazy. Of course it's mine."

"Can you prove it? Possession is nine-tenths of the law."

"But why would—"

"Some people will do anything for that kind of money." He stares me down. "I looked the ticket over while you were on the phone. Once you sign the back, it's legally yours." He hands me the pen. "Your ticket, your money. Don't you want to make sure it stays that way?"

Enough said. My hand shakes as I grip the pen. Max serves as my witness as I sign on the line marked *Claimant*. "Good," he says with a confident smile. "Now it's official."

My fingers tremble as I slip the ticket in my wallet. It's a good thing one of us sounds certain of what's happening, because I'm not sure of anything now. A mere scrap of paper controls my destiny. Anything could happen. What if something does?

Max is right. The faster the ticket is out of my hands and safe in the bank, the better off I'll be.

The night sky envelopes us in darkness as I lock the door. It feels strange to be headed out so late on a weekday night. Normally I'm arriving home from meetings at this hour. I trail Max down the stairs, gripping the wobbly banister tightly. I'm already off balance. This whole thing has a surreal feel to it, like we're about to depart on some secretive spy mission.

But spies don't limp. Max is rubbing his leg as we reach the bottom step.

"Are you okay?" I ask.

"My leg fell asleep." He shrugs off my concern under the glow of the street light. "How did Kent Phillips take the news?"

"He seemed a little shook." Not to mention extremely interested in my future plans for the money. If a banker gets that zealous that quick, how are other people going to react?

"It's a lot of money. It's going to change your life."

I swallow hard as I climb into the Jeep.

Don't remind me.

I breathe easier once the ticket is secure in my new safe-deposit box. I snap the lid, double-check, then triple-check that it's securely locked, then slide the box back into its narrow space and tuck the key deep in my purse.

The ticket is safe, but I'm not so sure about my future.

I slump against the cold metal boxes lining one wall of the vault. Kent Phillips and Max are waiting outside the door, but I need a minute or two to myself. I've stumbled across some odd things reporting the news, but today's events seem too weird and bizarre, even for me. If I were reading this particular story in the *Journal*, my first instinct would be to check the date for April Fools'.

Me, the lottery winner? Talk about a fool. The joke's on me. That's when the tears start and I have a good cry. A few minutes later, my tears are spent and the absurdity of what I'm doing hits me. I'm huddled inside a bank vault crying over the thought that I've just won seventy million dollars. I swipe away the last tears with a shaky laugh. Hopefully there aren't surveillance cameras in the vault or the bank employees will think I'm nuts. I just won the lottery. What do I have to cry about?

With seventy million dollars, I could buy the vault.

I could buy the bank.

But I don't know anything about dealing with money. Another wave of frustration and fear sweeps through me. How am I supposed to find my way through this? I feel like I've ended up somewhere over the rainbow, a place where all my dreams could come true. But unlike Dorothy, there's no Scarecrow, no Tin Man, no Cowardly Lion to save me. Not even a loyal little Toto trotting alongside, wagging his perky tail, assuring me things will be fine. I'm on my own, save for a few friends like Kris and Max. Grandma can't help. And as for Lila…

My heart slams shut. Not Lila. *Never Lila.*

"Lucy? You okay?" The faint sound of Max's voice filters through the heavy steel door.

"I'll be right out." I swallow hard. This is insane. What am I afraid of? Being rich doesn't take any particular courage. Courage is knowing you don't have money, that you'll never have money, but still hauling yourself out of bed every morning to face the world.

Something Grandma did every day of her life.

The vault door closes behind me with a heavy thud.

"Mr. Phillips and I were talking," Max says. "He has some ideas you should think about."

"I can use all the help I can get." I sling my purse over my shoulder. Funny, but it seems lighter now the ticket is gone.

"You know how this town is, Lucy. News travels fast." The bank president's smile is not encouraging. "You'll probably get bombarded with people and phone calls. It might be a good idea to lay low for a few days. At least until you figure out how you want to handle things."

He makes a good point, I think to myself, remembering my research from earlier this afternoon. The internet was jammed with horror stories about lottery winners being easy prey. Big money attracts scam artists, and lots of winners find themselves broke within a few years. I'll have to be very careful. Everyone will have their own agenda. Even close friends and family members...

My stomach lurches in a sickening one-eighty. It's a sure bet my mother will be very interested once she hears the news. Seventy million dollars equals seventy million reasons to keep things quiet. The last thing Lila needs is unlimited access to unlimited funds.

"You need to protect yourself," Mr. Phillips continues. "Don't make hasty decisions you might later regret. I recommend you get yourself a good attorney. Plus, you should hire someone who knows their way around taxes."

I wince at the thought of owing Uncle Sam. Bad enough paying my taxes each April when I file my 1040EZ. Winning the lottery puts things into a whole new perspective. And swings me into a whole new tax bracket.

My fingers tighten around my purse. "Do you have any suggestions?"

He thinks for a moment. "As for attorneys, Rose Gallagher is on the Board of Directors here at the bank. Do you know Rose? She's got a private law practice here in James Bay, and she's married to Mike Gallagher, the fire chief."

"Rose and I went to school together." I leave out the part about Grandma having cleaned house for the Gallagher family for nearly twenty years. I grew up subjected to weekly rundowns of Rose's accomplishments, as well as her hand-me-downs. She was an inch or two shorter than me and her clothes never fit right. Rose was kind and never said a word, but the other girls knew.

"Rose is sharp. She'd give you good advice. Though I'm not sure she's back to work yet. She had a baby about a month ago." Mr. Phillips rubs his forehead. "When it comes to accountants, I'd recommend Sam Curtis. He's a CPA and financial advisor with a solid reputation."

"I can vouch for Sam," Max offers. "He does our books at camp. He's a good guy. I think you'll like him. He's easy to work with."

I like my privacy, but with seventy million dollars at stake, it's definitely time to get some professionals involved. Especially given the fact I can barely balance my checkbook. I file their suggestions away in my head as we start for the door.

"Thanks again. You've been a big help tonight, Mr. Phillips." I wait as he locks up.

"My pleasure." He punches in the security code and double-checks the door. "But please, no more Mr. Phillips. Call me Kent."

The bank president and I are now on a first-name basis? Whoever said money changes things wasn't kidding. I stick out my hand. "Thank you... Kent. I appreciate it."

"And we appreciate your business." He ignores my hand and gives my shoulder an affectionate squeeze, just like a father. "Take care, Lucy. We'll be in touch."

The sidewalk hangs in deep shadows as I trail Max to the Jeep. "Where to now?" he asks.

I climb in next to him and buckle my seatbelt. "Home, I guess."

He glances at me. "You okay?"

"I'm fine," I assure him, though it's a lie. My mini-meltdown in the bank vault has me seriously depressed, and I'm not looking forward to being alone with my thoughts. Max has been a huge help tonight, but how am I going to get through the next few days? I squeeze my eyes shut and gulp the cool night air. I wish my stomach would calm down. I wish life would lose this crazy tilt. I wish... I wish...

Be careful what you wish for, Grandma always said, *because you just might get it.*

Why am I so scared? Why do I feel like running away? Even if I did, where would I go? Everything's flip-flopped and there's nothing left for me in the life I left behind.

Nothing but debts, deadlines, and responsibilities. I've never felt so lonely in my life. Not even the day I put Grandma in the nursing home.

"Max, I wish you—"

"Lucy, I've been thinking—"

Our words collide and we stare at each other in confusion, then share an uneasy laugh.

"Go ahead," he says with a gallant smile.

"No, you first," I insist.

"Okay." He scratches his chin, rakes a hand through his hair. "Remember what Mr. Phillips said, about how you should lay low for a couple of days until you decide what to do?"

I nod slowly. *Protect yourself*, was his suggestion. And I'm trying. I even turned off my cell phone when we left the bank.

"Why not come back to camp with me? You can hang out there."

"At Loon Lake?" Max expects me to escape to the one place I've done my best to avoid for the past twenty years? I can barely wrap my mind around the thought.

"Camp doesn't start until Sunday. That will give you a day or two of privacy while you figure out what to do. We've got plenty of room. You can stay in the nurse's cabin."

"Thanks, I appreciate the offer, but I don't think so." Things aren't that simple. He'd understand if he knew my history.

"I thought it might give you a chance for some peace and quiet before your life gets too crazy." His voice softens. "I was only trying to help."

Which he's been doing all night, looking out for me and my interests. Dear Max. Maybe I'm more like Dorothy than I thought. But Max isn't Toto. And Loon Lake definitely isn't Oz. More like the witch's castle, complete with those creepy winged monkeys.

Max pulls up behind Polly's dress shop and cuts the engine.

Loon Lake. I swallow hard. It wouldn't be forever. Only for a day or two. Time enough for me to make plans. No one would know where I was. Best of all, I wouldn't be alone.

"Can you wait?" I suddenly hear myself asking. "I need to pack a few things."

Under the street light I catch a glimpse of his smile, which erases any further doubt in my mind. I made the right decision.

"Take as long as you need."

"Five minutes." Enough time to grab some clothes and my toothbrush.

And those damned rubber boots.

The light from Max's flashlight bounces along the dirt path as we make the hike from the staff parking lot. I swat at mosquitoes as the woods crowd near us. A scurrying sound from the brushes near my feet has my neck prickling with fear, my hair standing on end, and me grabbing his arm. "What was that?"

"Relax, will you?" He gently pries me loose. "Probably just a porcupine."

"Just a porcupine..." I cringe. Do porcupines bite? Do they attack without warning, shooting their quills at innocent victims? I won't stand a chance.

"Then again, it might have been a skunk," he adds.

"Oh, God," I mutter, inching even closer to Max. I stay that way the last few hundred yards until a floodlight mounted high atop a pole signals our return to semi-civilization.

"Here you go." Max throws open a door. The nurse's cabin doubles as the infirmary. Cement floor, rough-hewn walls painted a pristine white. He assigns me to a narrow single bed covered with a gray blanket. "It's a little Spartan. Hope you don't mind."

"It's fine." I throw my overnight bag on the bed, relieved that there's finally a closed door between me and Mother Nature.

"The bathroom is in there." He thumbs toward a door near the foot of the bed. I peek inside. A single toilet, wash basin, and stand. Definitely not the Ritz, but at least it's clean. Besides, beggars can't be choosers. And that's exactly what I am tonight... a beggar.

"You lucked out. The infirmary is the only cabin with indoor plumbing."

"You're joking, right?" Lack of modern facilities ranks up there with being attacked by a porcupine or stepping on a snake.

"Afraid not," he says, chuckling softly. "They don't call it *camp* for nothing. We've got two separate buildings out back of the cabins. One has showers, the other has sinks and stalls. The kids don't seem to mind, but you know how kids are. They're pretty resilient."

Resiliency was a major word in my vocabulary growing up, but it didn't include a nightly stroll to an outhouse. I shudder at the thought of a young camper armed with only a flashlight when nature calls.

"Let's store your gear and get you something to eat."

My stomach's still jumpy. The night air is chilly and I rub my arms. "Do you have any milk?"

"If there's one thing around here in ample supply, it's milk. This is a kid's camp, remember?" He gives me a quick smile. "Come on, we'll get you some milk, and me something to eat. Maybe you're not hungry, but I am."

My cheeks burn. I know he didn't mean anything by it, but I can't help feeling guilty. Tonight's menu was supposed to be hot dogs on an open campfire. Instead, Max was stuck with me, eating chicken soup.

"If we're lucky, we'll find some of Roberta's baked beans left over."

"Who's Roberta?" I trail him out the cabin and down a dirt path, where I promptly trip over a large tree root.

"Whoa, watch your step." He grabs my arm and steadies me without missing a beat. "She's our camp cook. Her husband, Bob, is the caretaker. They live out here year-round and pretty much run the place."

A massive lodge looms before us. Old-fashioned lanterns illuminate a wide, covered porch which wraps around the front of the lodge, offering a sweeping vista of the moonlit lake. Sturdy wooden rockers in fluorescent hues are lined up in a row, inviting visitors to sit a spell.

"Nice chairs," I comment, though I've no desire to rock away the hours contemplating Loon Lake.

"Roberta's husband makes them. Woodworking is his hobby." Max halts and fumbles with the screen.

An eerie cry from the lake splits the night silence.

I nearly jump out of my boots. "What was that?"

"It's a loon. Watch, it's going to land." He points over the railing to the water, where a long dark shadow circles low across the moonlit lake. It skims the surface, lands, and disappears into some reeds. Seconds later, the same shrill cry rises from shore. The long, plaintive sound is like a lost soul crying from a watery grave.

"It settled on its nest," he tells me. "Loon Lake is their natural habitat."

I shiver in the darkness and hug myself close. "This lake gives me the creeps."

"The loon's call is very distinctive. When I was a kid, I actually thought the lake was haunted."

I swallow hard. If Max wants haunted, I can give him haunted. The silvery water hangs shrouded in silence. Even the loons are quiet. In the inky blackness, I can almost swear I see my father's ghost.

"Hold on a minute and let me hit the lights." Max flips a switch as I follow him inside. Suddenly the rustic room is flooded in a warm honey glow reminiscent of a campfire.

"Wow," I breathe softly. Rows of wooden tables with benches tucked neatly underneath, wagon-wheel chandeliers, floor-to-ceiling windows. If the main lodge wasn't impressive enough, the huge fieldstone fireplace at one end of the cavernous room makes me gasp. It could easily roast a wheelbarrow filled with marshmallows in one magnificent blaze.

"I've got a little apartment upstairs. It's not much, but who needs space when you've got a place like this?" He reaches out and reverently strokes one of the wooden beams. "I love it here. This is home."

A swift, fierce longing surges through me. No wonder Max feels the way he does about Loon Lake. His summers were spent surrounded by all this. Plus friends to laugh with during canoe trips, sing-alongs, and nature hikes. The only summer hikes I took were to the corner store with Grandma's grocery list.

Max props one foot against a wooden bench. "The board hired me last winter to turn things around. The place has great bones, but it needs some work."

"It looks fine to me."

"You'll see what I mean when the sun comes up." His gaze wanders the walls, ceiling, floor. "My goal is to get things back to where they were twenty or thirty years ago. Back then, the camp was filled to capacity all summer long. One hundred boys, every session."

"How many are signed up for this season?"

"We've got seventy-five kids coming in on Sunday." He shoves his hands in his pockets and squares his shoulders with a quick, hesitant smile. "We've got a solid program and well-qualified people. Things will work out." He nods as if he's trying to convince himself. "We'll be fine."

The unspoken words hang between us. Bugs, snakes, primitive plumbing aside, Camp Call of the Loon is part of Max. But if the developers win, a way of life that's existed for decades will be destroyed when they bulldoze the first tree.

He gestures with his flashlight. "Come on, let's get you that milk."

I trail him into the biggest kitchen I've ever encountered: gleaming stainless-steel counters; a deep, triple sink; and a huge cook stove, complete with griddle and ten separate burners. Open-faced shelves above the sinks display rack after rack of utilitarian dishes. I flash on the mental image of table upon table of hungry little boys pounding their silverware and chanting for their dinner. "I hope to God you've got a dishwasher."

Max opens a massive, stainless-steel refrigerator and hands me a carton of milk. "Grab yourself a glass."

I find a plastic tumbler in a cupboard. The milk is ice-cold and soothing on my stomach.

"Ahh, look what I found." He pulls out a bowl sealed with plastic wrap. "Roberta's baked beans. Want some?"

"No, thanks." I watch as he heaps a good-sized portion on his plate. My stomach is still jumping. It doesn't need beans. I watch as Max slathers peanut butter on a thick hunk of fragrant bread; the kind you never see on a grocery shelf. My mouth waters as he adds a heaping spoonful of strawberry jam. "Is that homemade bread?"

"Fresh out of the oven this morning. Roberta bakes six or seven loaves every week for the staff." He waves it close with a tempting smile. "Sure you're not hungry?"

It smells delicious. "Maybe just one piece," I say. Probably I can handle bread and milk. By the time I polish off my second slice, I've forgotten I wasn't hungry.

"That was heavenly." I lick the last of the jam from my fingers. "I'm sorry I missed meeting Roberta at dinner. Her bread tastes nearly as good as what my grandma used to make."

"Why don't you tell her yourself? Let me finish up here and I'll introduce you." He moves around the kitchen like someone who's used to taking care of himself. "She and Bob live in a cabin right across the yard."

"I don't know. Do you think we should?" The fewer people who know I'm here, the better my chances of keeping things quiet. "Maybe they went to bed."

"You'll meet them tomorrow anyway. I can't hide you in a cabin."

"What are you going to tell them?"

"I don't know, I'll think of something." He opens the screen door. "Come on, their lights are on. We'll only stay a minute."

I trail him across the dirt yard. It's cold by the lake when the sun goes down. I rub my arms against the night dampness as Max raps on the door of a nearby cabin. The porch light snaps on. A stocky woman in blue jeans and a sweater-vest peers across the threshold. Her face breaks into a smile as she catches sight of Max. "Hey there, kiddo, we missed you at dinner."

He winks at me as he pulls me into the circle of light. "I want you to meet Lucy. She's a big fan of your homemade bread."

Roberta's laugh rumbles straight from her belly, which looks like she's sampled one too many pieces of her own cooking. She and Grandma come from the same school. One that includes lots of tasting by the cook before they finally yell *Come and Get It!* Roberta waves us into a cozy living room. "You must be the mystery girl Max told us about."

He's been talking about me? I slide him a sideways glance, but Max merely shrugs and smiles.

"Sorry about missing dinner. We got caught up with a couple things downtown." He rakes a hand through his hair. "Lucy's going to be staying with us for a few days."

"You look familiar." Roberta peers at me. "Have we met before?"

"I don't think so." I squirm as her green eyes take me in from head to toe, halting for finally on my thick rubber boots. Maybe coming out to camp was a mistake. Roberta doesn't strike me as a pushover. The last thing I need is her snooping around, asking a bunch of questions.

"Lucy's with me." Max's hand clasps my own and he squeezes tight. I catch my breath at the feel of his fingers laced in mine.

"So it's like that, is it?" Roberta chuckles. "About time."

"Lucy's not much for nature. I'm hoping to get her interested in camping."

Exactly what does he think he's doing? I came out here to hide, not to fall in love with the great outdoors... or Max, either.

"Take my advice, Lucy. If you're interested in Max, you'd better get interested in camping, and fast. I've known him since he was five years old, and it's God's truth he lives and breathes for this place. In fact, you're the first girl he's ever brought out here." Roberta claps him on the shoulder. "I was beginning to think he was only interested in the mating habits of raccoons."

"Thanks a lot," he says with a good-natured grin. "Keep it up and you'll ruin my reputation."

I play my part with a shy smile. Maybe Max isn't as clueless as I thought. His hand tightens around my own, and this time, I squeeze right back.

The sound of hearty laughter and raised voices floats from an adjoining room.

"Come on, Bob's out in the kitchen. I'll introduce you." She grabs my arm. "He'll be glad for the break. We're whipping his butt at euchre."

"A word of warning," Max whispers as we trail her into the kitchen. "Bob and Roberta are fanatics about cards. Don't play unless you know what you're doing. They'll take your last penny."

"Everybody, look who's here. It's Max. And he brought a girl."

A wiry little man half his wife's size springs to his feet and pumps my hand. "Nice to meet you...?"

"Lucy," I supply. "Lucy Carter."

"Carter?" Roberta whistles through her teeth. "No wonder you look familiar."

The other two players at the cramped kitchen table turn sideways in their chairs.

"I'm Sue Gerbeaux." The first woman's face is wreathed in a curious smile. "Nice to meet you. I've been reading your column so long I feel like I already know you."

I can only nod. My mouth has gone dry and the smile is frozen on my face. I stare at the other woman staring back at me.

"Hello, Lucy."

I flush a deep red and flinch as I hear my name cross her lips. There's no escaping the small, crowded kitchen or being polite. I give a brief nod. "Hello."

"I loved your story in the *Journal* today." Sue's eyes gleam. "Imagine, Pete Kelly selling the winning ticket. I can't wait to read tomorrow's paper and your interview with the winner. Do you know who won yet?"

"I really can't say," I mumble as my stomach does a one-eighty.

"I hope it's someone from town. It's all everyone's talking about—"

"I... I'm sorry, I've got to go." I whirl and bolt from the room. My feet barely touch the floor as I fly through the living room and out the door.

"Lucy? Hey, Lucy, stop!"

I sprint for the main lodge, my heart hammering against my chest. Footsteps pound behind me but I don't stop. Why did I think things would be different tonight? Facts are facts, and the fact is that Loon Lake is bad news. It always has been and it always will be. I can't change the past. But I can change the present.

I put on another burst of speed, but Max proves faster. He snags me halfway across the yard. "What the hell?"

"Let me go." I blink back hot tears and struggle to catch my breath. Stupid, stupid, stupid, coming here tonight. Major mistake on my part. I never should have let myself get sucked in by him.

"Take it easy, Lucy. Your secret is safe."

"Let me go." I've pushed away the pain so long, and I don't want to feel it now. Not here, not like this. Especially not in front of Max.

He holds me at arm's length and eyes me in the moonlight. "What's wrong? You look spooked. Like you saw a ghost."

If he only knew.

"I don't get it," he says. "Everything was fine, then you take off like a banshee. What happened?"

I swipe away my tears. Poor Max. He got more than he bargained for when he stopped by the *Journal* office this afternoon. He searches my face, straining to understand as we stand there in the moonlight. I feel like I've let him down. The least he deserves is some kind of explanation. I blow out a small breath. "Do you know those two women in there?"

"Sure, they play cards with Roberta and Bob on Monday nights. Sue works at the post office."

"Not her. The other one."

"She's a cashier at the grocery store. Why? Do you know Lila?"

"You might say that." He's bound to find out sooner or later. Why try and hide the truth? "She's my mother."

CHAPTER FOUR

If that infernal pounding doesn't stop soon, someone's going to be sorry.

I shift under scratchy sheets, open an eye with a bleary look around. A small crack of sunshine peeks through shuttered windows, but the rest of the room is shrouded in darkness. The fragrant smell of pine assails my nose.

I bolt upright in the narrow bed and fling off the sheets. Bad enough my sleep was broken with bad dreams. I'm wide awake and stuck in a nightmare.

Still at camp. Still at Loon Lake.

The hammering increases against the door.

"Hold on a minute." I struggle into my jeans, take a quick whiff of yesterday's shirt, shrug, and pull it over my head.

"Lucy? Open up. I need to talk to you."

I draw in a ragged breath. How did she find me? I comb my fingers through my hair and unlock the door.

"Are you okay?" Kris peers at me as she steps inside. "You had me worried, disappearing like that."

"What time is it?" I rub my forehead with the heel of my hand. Blinding sunshine bounces off the white infirmary walls and hits me square in the eyes. Lack of sleep, lack of caffeine. Give it an hour and I'll have a major headache.

"It's after ten. I've been trying to reach you all morning."

"I didn't get any calls."

"You haven't been answering. Charles and I kept getting your voicemail."

I groan, remembering how I shut off my cell phone when I left the bank last night. I fish it out of my pocket and flip open the screen. Nine voicemails. Three from Kris, four from Charles, plus one from my landlady, Polly, and another from Didi Taylor, my realtor.

"Charles is going crazy. He sent me to find you."

My mouth feels grainy, like I've swallowed lots of sand, courtesy of the beach a hundred yards or so away. I can't believe I spent the night on the shore of Loon Lake. I can't believe I let Max talk me into staying. He promised me a ride back to town this morning in exchange for the explanation I promised to give him over breakfast about my mother.

"How did you know where I was?"

"A lucky guess. Your car is still down at the *Journal* office. Last time I saw you, you were walking out the door with Max. I called him this morning, and he confirmed what I already guessed."

Max told her? Resentment blazes inside me. "Where is he?"

"Up at the lodge."

What a coward. Afraid to face me himself.

"Is it true?" Kris's voice drops. "The rumors are flying all over town."

"Is what true?" I hedge. How much did Max tell her?

She shifts on her feet and stares at me a long moment. It's a rare thing to see Kris at a loss for words.

"They're saying you won the lottery," she finally blurts out.

Am I ready to give up my anonymity? We've known each other less than a year, but working in cramped quarters and allied against Charles, we've grown tight. Kris and I count on each other. We cover for each other.

If I can't trust Kris, the world will be a sad lonely place.

"It's true."

"Ohmigod." She backs up two steps and promptly trips across the door ledge, falling smack on her butt.

"Don't look at me like that," I beg as I help her to her feet. Her eyes are as wide as newly minted quarters and her face is flushed a peculiar shade of green, like the reflection off a crisp new one-dollar bill. "Nothing's changed. I'm still me, the same old Lucy."

"No, you're not," she whispers. "You're rich. You'll never have to work again."

For one horrible second, I think I glimpse a flash of pure, unadulterated envy on her face. A look of jealousy at someone else's good fortune. At my personal good fortune. I blink it away. Not Kris. Never Kris. There are people around town who fault her for who she is and the way she lives her life, but we've been friends since the day we met. She would never envy me. It isn't in her nature. I blink again and chance another look, grateful to see the envy gone. My imagination has quite a sense of humor.

"Rich!" Her screech hits the ceiling and ricochets off the infirmary walls. "You won the lottery! Do you have any idea what this means?"

"It means, for now, we need to keep things quiet." I grab her wrists and try to keep her happy dancing to a minimum. "That's why I'm out here. I need a few days to figure out what to do before the story explodes and the world finds out."

Kris freezes mid-dance, and winces.

I don't like that look on her face. "What's wrong?"

She hesitates. "I think it might be a little too late."

"What do you mean?"

She bites her lip.

"Don't you dare hold back on me," I demand.

"I saw the mock-up for today's *Journal* headline," she finally admits. "You're not going to like it."

I've got a sneaky suspicion she's right. "What does it say?"

"You know how Charles gets, especially when he thinks we have the exclusive. He's determined to break this story."

I don't like the guarded tone in her voice. Or the way she refuses to meet my eyes. I grab her shoulders and shake her slightly, determined to shake the truth loose. "Tell me. I have to know."

She gulps. "**LOTTO LUCY!** ***JOURNAL*** **REPORTER HITS LOTTO JACKPOT!**"

"No. he wouldn't. He couldn't." But he did. The news hits like a sucker punch to my stomach. My legs are suddenly gone, and I sink down on the bed. My anonymity shot to hell by my managing editor, and I can't refute it. There's no getting around the truth. I never asked for any of this. I never even wanted to buy the damned ticket. "I can't believe Charles would print the story without talking to me first."

"He talked to someone," she blurts out. "I told him I didn't want any part of it, but he said—and I quote—"*Too bad, Henderson, I've already got the byline; I wrote the damn article myself.*" She plops down on the bed beside me and squeezes my hand. "I'm sorry, Lucy."

"I still don't understand how he knows I'm the winner. We were so careful."

Her face scrunches in a question mark. "We?"

"Max," I explain. "He was with me when I found out I won. He's the one who suggested I spend a few days here at camp and lay low while I figured out what—"

My heart drops into my stomach. Is he the one who betrayed me? Did Max make the phone call to Charles? It could have been, though I hope it wasn't. Yet, how well do I know him? We've only met twice.

"It wasn't Max," Kris says, like she's reading my mind. "Charles got a phone call early this morning. From a woman."

Telegraph, telephone, tell a woman. The old adage holds true, especially in James Bay. I can think of plenty of women in this town who live just for gossip, who thrive on being the first to know. Women who take perverse pleasure in sharing with their friends over lunch the latest juicy story to hit James Bay. And today, I'm the juicy story.

"Charles was so excited when he got off the phone, I thought he was going to wet himself," she continues. "That's how I know it was a woman. He's quoting her as an anonymous source. He said that she hadn't seen the winning ticket, but that her husband had."

A woman. A woman with a personal ax to grind. A woman who either eavesdropped or was privy to a private conversation between her husband and me.

"It doesn't matter," I say. "It's too late now."

And too late for Kent Philips. He just screwed himself and his bank from getting any of my future business.

"What are you going to do now?" Kris asks slowly.

"Go back into town and face things, I guess," I say. "There's no sense staying out here. Everyone will know I'm the winner as soon as they read today's *Journal.*"

"I don't have to tell him where you are," she says. "I'll say I couldn't find you."

It's a tempting offer, but I can't let Kris take the heat. "You're sweet, but no thanks. He'll find out eventually. I don't want you taking the brunt of his bullying."

"Do you think I care? I don't give a damn about Charles and what he thinks," she scoffs. "You're the one I'm worried about."

I rub my forehead. This is ridiculous. My brain doesn't want to work. I feel like a financial fugitive. I need coffee, food, a shower.

I need my life back.

"Okay, here's what we're going to do." I stand up and haul Kris to her feet. "You go back into town, tell Charles you found me, and that I'll be in later this afternoon."

"That's it?" Her eyebrows scrunch together. "But he'll want to know—"

"Screw Charles and what he wants. For now, don't tell him anything." I open the screen and push her out the door.

"But he's going to run the story. Don't you want to talk to him? Don't you want to make sure he has the facts straight?"

"Nope." I shake my head. "Not my problem."

"But, Lucy—"

"And it's not your problem, either." I give her a gentle shove down the path. "The only thing you need to worry about is figuring out what questions to ask during your interview this afternoon."

She frowns. "What interview?"

"The one I'm giving you," I say with a grim smile. "Charles only has a headline and some anonymous source. You, however, are getting an exclusive. When it's picked up by AP and Reuters, you'll have the byline. Let Charles choke over that for a while."

I envy Kris as she heads down the trail. Facing Charles Kendall will be easy compared to what I have waiting for me. Max expects a story from me. One I promised to deliver. And unless I intend reneging on that promise, I've just exhausted my deadline.

Grabbing my rubber boots, I trudge up the path toward the main lodge.

His gaze lingers on my face. "You look like her."

"No, I don't," I state flatly, though I know he meant it as a compliment. Even pushing fifty, Lila is still a flawless beauty, with soft features, smooth complexion, perfectly styled hair. But *pretty is as pretty does*. Inside, Lila is an ugly mess.

A mess I want no part of.

"You have her eyes."

"Hopefully that's the only thing I inherited," I mumble. Max hasn't the slightest clue about the kind of woman my mother is, but I wouldn't expect him to. He's got that easy sense about him of someone who grew up in a loving home. Save for the slight limp, he could be a poster boy of the All-American Kid, complete with a mother and father who obviously doted on him. They might not have had the financial resources to send him to college, but somehow they managed to scrape enough money together to send him to summer camp.

"I take it you and your mother don't talk?" he asks.

"Talking requires a two-way conversation." I squirm on the wooden bench and grip my coffee cup. "Lila is only interested in one thing. Herself."

"Lila from the grocery store." Max props his elbows on the table, chin in hand, and shakes his head. "I still find it hard to believe. If you hadn't told me, I never would have—"

"Guessed? That's what people always say when they find out she's my mother." Not that I go around broadcasting the truth... or buy my groceries at the downtown store where she works. I do my shopping at Bayside Market. It's a few more miles down the road and a little more expensive, but it's worth every penny if it means avoiding Lila.

"From what Roberta said, I take it your mom hasn't lived in town long."

"Too long, as far as I'm concerned. She showed up in James Bay about six months ago," I say. "Right around the time Grandma got sick and I moved her to Whispering Pines." I feel the frown tug at my forehead. "I don't know why she came back, but I wish she'd leave."

"Maybe she realized there wasn't much time left." His brown eyes soften. "She wanted to make things right before it was too late."

"It is too late," I state flatly. "Twenty years too late." I have no sympathy for her. Lila probably got fired from her latest job. Once she heard Grandma was in the nursing home, she probably headed north, figuring to hit me up for a few bucks. And when Lila hears I won the lottery? My stomach rolls at the thought of the ticket, safely stashed in the bank vault. No doubt she'll try and her best to weasel in and collect a piece of the fortune. Just claiming what's rightfully hers, to her convoluted way of thinking.

"Family stuff is hard," Max says. "Dealing with elderly relatives and all that. I'm sure your mom figured you could use the help."

"Well, I don't," I say stiffly. "I've managed fine all these years without any help from her. Why doesn't she go back where she came from?"

"Maybe she feels guilty about not spending more time with her mother."

I feel the horror slide over my face. Good thing Grandma isn't around to overhear his comment. Guaranteed she'd fall right out of her wheelchair. "My grandmother is not Lila's mother."

"But I thought—"

"You thought wrong." My eyes narrow. "My grandparents raised me since I was five years old. My father was their only child." I finish my lukewarm coffee in silence. Anger and resentment simmer not far from the surface, bitter as the coffee. I push away the feelings. It's safer not to think about things. Not to remember. It keeps away the hurt.

"I'm sorry. Sounds like you had things pretty rough."

"Not as rough as Grandma. She lost everything, including Grandpa Carl." My voice sounds flat and dull to my ears. "He died when I was six years old. Grandma always said it was from a broken heart, but Lila killed him. Sure as she killed my father."

Max's eyes pop. "You mean, she murdered—"

I close my eyes, shutting out the shock on his face. It's not so easy to shut out the grief in my heart. "Grandpa Carl died of a heart attack. My father died the year before. He drowned in Loon Lake."

So hot. So hot. My hat is gone. It's clutched in Daddy's fingers as he slips beneath the waves. The boat drifts in aimless circles. I'm crying. My mother is screaming. She's in the water. Wet. Wet.

"Lucy, snap out of it!"

I gulp for air as the bright flashing lights begin to fade. Steady arms snatch me from disaster. I latch on tight. If I can't save myself, maybe someone else can.

"It's okay." Max's breath is warm and soft against my hair. "I'm right here. It's okay."

The nausea is back. The same nausea that always follows one of my visions. I blink several times, try to slow my ragged breathing and my racing pulse. Try to shake off the fluid memories that for years have brought me screaming awake from a never-ending nightmare.

"Better now?"

I nod silently, unable to trust myself to speak.

His arms tighten around my shoulders. "What the hell just happened?"

I feel cold to the bone, despite the brilliant sunshine flooding the main lodge. Death is closer than it has been in years, and today it came to collect me. Death is right outside, lapping at the shoreline.

"I hate this place. I've always hated this place." And I burst into tears.

Max wraps me close in his arms. His shirt smells like pine trees, fabric softener, and a faint trace of aftershave. For one brief moment, I give in to the luxury of being held by a man, of allowing myself to believe everything will be okay.

"Shhh, don't cry. Nothing's going to hurt you. It's okay."

But it isn't okay. It will never be okay.

"I was only five years old." The memories are waterlogged and bleary from being submerged so long, but they've floated to the surface and there's no holding them down. "We were in a boat, out on Loon Lake. My father, my mother, and me. It was a hot day." I swallow hard, remembering. "Lila was angry. She was shouting at my father. I was crying."

Somewhere from the murky recess of my mind, a new memory floats to the surface. "I lost my hat."

I lost everything that day. My hat. My family. My home.

"Then I was on shore. I don't remember much, except that I was cold and wet and sitting in the sand." A bitter taste fills my mouth and I swallow down the bile. "And I remember sirens and lots of men. My mother kept screaming. She wouldn't stop screaming."

I shudder at the memory, breathe deep, wait. Wishing— and dreading—that the twenty-year-old fog will finally lift. But the memories refuse to surface. Except for one.

The smell of alcohol.

As usual, Lila had been drinking.

"She never should have been in the boat," I say. "She doesn't know how to swim."

"Did she fall overboard?"

"I don't know. Maybe she fell, maybe she jumped. Does it matter?" I pull away. His arms can't hide me from the truth. "My father jumped in to save her, but instead, he was the one who died."

The oomph sucks out of Max in one long whoosh. "No wonder you didn't want to come out here. I knew there had to be some reason you didn't like the place." He sounds winded, defeated. "This camp—this lake—has been a part of my life since I can remember. I thought if you got a chance to see it through my eyes, you'd see things different." He laughs bitterly. "So much for good intentions."

"It's not your fault. You didn't know." My family history is no big secret to the locals of James Bay. There are people in town who remember my parents, who knew my father, who know my mother's past. You simply have to know who to ask. Everyone knows the truth.

Lucy's mother is a drunk.

"Lila had a nervous breakdown after my father died. They sent her to a sanitarium. My grandparents took me in and raised me as their own. After Grandpa Carl died, it was just Grandma and me. Everything I am today, I owe to her."

The Grandma I used to know. The woman who loved me, who worked hard every day to make sure I grew up safe and happy.

"Sounds like she loved you very much."

"She did," I say, nodding as the tears keep falling and the memories keep coming. Grandma cooking, ironing, cleaning toilets. All for me, in order that I could have a good life. "She does."

"She's still alive?"

"Yes," I say softly, "if you can call it that. She's not Grandma anymore. She has Alzheimer's."

There's no way to pretend when you say it out loud. I swallow over the lump in my throat. "Around the time I finished college, it was obvious she was having problems, so I moved back home. Lucky for me, I landed a job at the *Journal* so I could stick close. It didn't take the doctors long to make a diagnosis."

Max's eyes are soft with sympathy.

"Things got bad fast. She was always self-sufficient, but soon it got to the point where I couldn't trust her. One day while I was at work, the neighbors found her wandering in the street. I hired someone to stay with her. Then one night, I woke up at three a.m. The smoke alarm was going off. Grandma had gotten up in the middle of the night and turned on the stove to make some soup. But then she went back to bed. The pot burned up." I shudder, remembering that horrible night. "We both could have burned up. That's when I knew I had to do something... for Grandma's safety as well as my own. Moving her to Whispering Pines was the right thing to do, but it's hard seeing her there. Even when she's having a good day, she barely remembers my name."

My tears are no longer the tears of a five-year-old. They're adult tears, born of love and loss. Of all that is gone, and that I'll never have again. But crying won't change anything. And sitting here won't get anything done. I stand up, look at Max. "Could you please take me back to town?"

"You don't have to go," he says. His eyes and his face hold regret.

"There are things I need to do." Starting with some phone calls. Returning the realtor's call can wait, but I'm concerned about my landlady. Hopefully my bathroom plumbing didn't burst and flood her dress shop like it did last spring. And then there's the lottery ticket to deal with. Do I contact the lottery people, or should I call the accountant first? What was his name? Sam something-I-can't-remember. My brain feels like it's been through four cycles on the washing machine and now it's on spin dry. I think harder. *Sam Curtis*, that was his name. And I probably should call Rose Gallagher, too. Just the thought of Rose makes my stomach churn. Will she remember me? We went to school together, but we weren't exactly chums. I was Winnie Carter's granddaughter. My Grandma worked for Rose's mother. She vacuumed the Gallagher's floors, scrubbed their toilets, did their laundry.

Talk about ironic. Twenty years later, and now I'm hiring Rose to help me figure out the legalities of how to manage my money. Then I'll spend it paying someone to do things for me, just like Grandma did for Rose's family.

I gather up my things and climb in the Jeep beside Max without a backward glance. He can sing the camp's praises all he wants, but if I never see this place again, it will be too soon for me.

We bounce along the dirt two-track and head for the main road. "Would you drop me off at the *Journal* office?" I ask after a moment. "I need to pick up my car."

He flashes me an encouraging smile from behind the wheel. "No problem."

I scrunch low as we zip through downtown. Tourists mill along the sidewalks, cars jam the Main Street corridor, kids play shuffleboard in Marina Park. A typical summer day in James Bay. Nothing's changed, but everything's changed. Especially the future balance of my bank account.

Minutes later, we pull up behind my VW bug. Max turns to face me. "Are you sure about this? I feel bad, leaving you alone."

I force a smile, though smiling is the last thing I feel like doing. "Don't worry about me. I'm going home to shower and change. Then I've got an interview with Kris."

"Call me," he says, more a command than an invitation. "Let me know how you're doing."

"I will." I lean across the console and kiss him on the cheek, taking us both by surprise. "You're very sweet, Max. Thanks for everything."

"You. Take. Care. Understand?" He catches my hand and squeezes my fingers. A warm hum of electricity flows between us and it's hard to let go. Max waits in the parking lot while I climb into my car. I throw him a wave and watch as he disappears down the street and rounds a corner. That's when I back out of my parking spot and swing down the shady street away from downtown. Going home will have to wait. I need something else a whole lot more than a shower and fresh clothes.

I need to talk to Grandma.

CHAPTER FIVE

I find her slouched sideways in her wheelchair, third in the lineup parked down the hallway. Elderly folks, patiently waiting, never questioning why. Better for them they don't remember. Too bad for me that I do.

They're waiting to die.

At least the hallway doesn't smell. As soon as I have that lottery money in hand, I'm signing Grandma up for a private room. One with a view and without a roommate like the one she has now, who wears diapers and cusses like a seasoned sailor. Grandma deserves better.

"Hi, Grandma. It's me. Lucy." I crouch close beside her wheelchair and brush her cheek with a kiss. Sometimes she remembers who I am, sometimes she doesn't. My heart lifts to see recognition instead of cloudy confusion in her faded blue eyes. Today is one of her good days.

"You look pretty today, Grandma." I stroke her thin white hair. It's freshly washed and she's dressed in the blouse I bought her last month. She's even wearing a necklace. The sparkling purple beads are entwined between her fingers. I reach out to touch it.

She pulls away, her eyes suddenly wary. "Mine."

I sit back on my heels, giving her some space. "Where did you get the necklace?"

"Pretty." She fingers the beads, looking as proud as a five-year-old who's raided her mother's jewelry box.

"It is pretty," I agree, trying to steal a closer look. Then I notice it's not a necklace. It's a beautiful crystal rosary made of amethyst beads, her birthstone.

"Grandma, where did you get this rosary? It's not a necklace. You don't wear it, you pray with it."

"No!" She grabs the beads with a fierce look that tells me there'll be no getting it away from her without a fight. I give up and let go. As long as she doesn't strangle herself, what's the harm? Grandma has been a devout Catholic all her life. If God is truly loving, He'll understand.

"Winnie looks good today, doesn't she?" A young aide sporting pink-and-lavender hair and multi nose piercings strolls up the hall. She's pushing a wheelchair holding an elderly gentleman with a stained lunch bib tucked around his neck. "We got her all dolled up for church. You going to pray for me, Winnie?"

I swallow down a flash of annoyance. Another new aide, barely out of her teens, talking down to my grandmother as if she were a two-year-old.

"Mass starts at one o'clock," the aide chirps over her shoulder as she breezes past us. "You can take Winnie in if you like. The activity room is all set up."

"Come on, Grandma, let's get you a good seat." I ease her wheelchair down the hall and park her in front of the makeshift altar hiding the big screen TV. If Grandma still prays and God still listens, the least I can do is make sure they each have front-row seats for their conversation.

"Unh." A familiar grunt catches my ear as a wheelchair rolls up beside me. My spirits lift as I catch sight of the woman with the drooping face and drooling mouth.

"Hello, Mary Margaret." I give Grandma's old roommate a careful hug. Despite the recent stroke that robbed her of speech and the use of one arm, Mary Margaret still has that Irish sparkle in her eyes. "Welcome back. We missed you."

"They transferred her back from the hospital yesterday afternoon."

I glance up at the woman pushing Mary Margaret's wheelchair... straight into Lila's face.

"What a nice surprise to see you here, Lucy. Are you here for Mass?"

The blood rushes to my face. Why am I here? She's got some nerve. What is *she* doing here? "I came to visit Grandma." My voice is stiff as my spine.

Lila nods and smiles. "Winnie looks good today, don't you think? Her color is so much better than last week."

Last week? I'm speechless. Since when did Lila start visiting Grandma? She has no business being anywhere near her. I don't want Grandma upset.

"She seems more alert than usual. Except for the rosary beads."

I draw myself up, towering over Lila a good several inches. "It's not Grandma's fault," I snap. "She doesn't know what she's doing."

"Did you think I was making fun of her?" Lila looks contrite. "I'm sorry, that's not what I mean. I know Winnie can't help herself. And who knows? I'm sure God doesn't mind." Her face softens in a smile. "Perhaps in a little corner of her mind, it's Winnie's way of praying."

My eyes narrow as I watch her take a seat on a folding chair on the other side of Grandma. "You're staying?"

"Why, yes, I'm here every week." Her eyes are suddenly wary. "I thought you knew."

Does she think I'm stupid? If I'd known Lila was a regular visitor, I would have slapped a *No Visitors Allowed* request on Grandma's chart.

"I come with Father Greg every Tuesday afternoon when he's here to say Mass." Lila nods toward the faithful gathered in an untidy semicircle of wheelchairs and walkers around the altar. "I set things up and help him distribute Communion."

Since when has Lila become a devout Catholic? I don't remember my parents taking me to church. I stare in stony silence at the makeshift altar covered with snowy-white linen. Two tapered candles flicker at each end. If Lila thinks lighting a few candles and helping a priest will make up for her past sins, then she's even more a fool that I originally thought.

"I try and spend some time with your grandmother every week after Mass is over. We sit and talk." A tiny smile flits across her face. "Well, to be honest, I'm the one who does most of the talking. But Winnie's a good listener." Lila's voice drops slightly. "I hope it gives her as much comfort as it does me. You and your grandmother are all I have left in the world."

The blood roars through my brain, and my heart pounds so hard, I'm sure the entire room can hear. Lila visits Grandma to find some comfort for herself? Where is the justice in that? Lila's brought nothing but pain and misery to those around her. The last thing she deserves is peace in her life.

"Please rise if you are able to do so." Father Greg Kozminski, parish priest from Our Lady of the Lakes, bows before the altar, then turns to face us. "Let's join together in Hymn Number Thirty-One, 'Now Thank We All Our God.'"

"Sing nice and loud," Lila whispers to me over Grandma. "We need all the help we can get."

I press my lips tight together, blocking my ears and heart as elderly voices warble in a hymn of praise and gratitude. What do I have to be thankful for? My grandmother is confined to a wheelchair, robbed of her memories and mind, and I'm trapped in a room with my mother. Bad enough I have to drive an extra five miles to avoid the grocery store where she works. I never expected having to worry about bumping into her at the nursing home.

"Let us pray."

I bow my head, close my eyes and listen as Father Greg leads us through the ritual prayers I learned at my grandmother's knee. The gospel reading speaks of suffering. His short homily speaks to those in misery and distress.

"God never forsakes His children, even in their darkest hour. His greatness and goodness shines through each of you as you live your purgatory here on earth. God bless you in your daily suffering. For truly you are ministers, allowing us to be Christ's hands and feet and heart for each of you. We ask that you pray for us, for you are indeed close to heaven. God bless you on your way home. God bless you all."

I peek at Grandma during the breaking of the bread. The rosary is still around her neck, but her hands are clasped, her face smooth with peace, and her lips move slightly. I blink back tears that spring from nowhere as I realize she's praying. Somewhere in Grandma's mind, something still registers. Something infinitely good.

If Grandma prays for me, does she also pray for Lila?

"Let us join hands and pray with confidence to the Father in the words our Savior gave us," Father Greg chants. "Our Father, who art in heaven, hallowed be thy name..."

I reach for Grandma's hand and squeeze gently as her feeble voice joins with others in reciting the familiar prayer.

"Forgive us our trespasses as we forgive those who trespass against us." The words catch in my throat. *Forgive.* How can a loving God expect me to forgive? Lila robbed us of everything. She killed my father, destroyed my grandfather's health, ruined my grandmother's life.

How can I forgive her? I can't. I feel my heart slam shut.

God wants too much from me.

"Good to see you, Lucy." Father Greg strolls up after Mass, vestments draped over one arm, a big smile for me. A tall, handsome man in his early fifties, with thick black hair graying at the temples, he was dubbed with the nickname *Father Hunk* by the ladies of our parish when assigned to our church last year. "I've missed you at Mass these past few months."

His words bring a quick flush to my face. Without Grandma around to remind me about going to church, I've turned into a rotten Catholic.

"Sorry, Father, I've been busy. They've got me working lots of weekends." The lie slips smoothly from my tongue.

"You're singing to the choir," he says, his face spreading in an easy smile. "I work weekends, too, remember? Saturday night Mass, plus two Masses every Sunday morning."

It's easy banter, and it horrifies me. I haven't been catching up on my columns, I've been sleeping in late. Now I'm guilty of a double sin. I've missed Mass, plus I've deliberately lied to a priest.

"When are we going to see you back up in the choir loft?" he asks. "God gave you a true gift with that beautiful voice of yours."

My face burns hotter than the fires of Purgatory. Lila's eyes boring into me feel like additional penance. "I didn't know Lucy sang in church," she says.

"She hasn't, at least not since Winnie got sick," Father Greg replies. "But I have faith she'll be back eventually." He flashes me a quick smile. "I've been praying for it. We could use a cantor at ten o'clock Mass."

"She was always singing when she was a little girl," Lila says thoughtfully. "She used to sing herself to sleep at night. She would lie awake for hours, singing in her bedroom. Do you remember, Lucy?"

I grip the handles of Grandma's wheelchair and hold on tight as a long-forgotten memory sweeps me away to another place and time. A warm bed, a soft blanket, and a child's voice—my voice—chirping away musical nonsense in the darkness.

Lucy, sweetheart, that's enough. Go to sleep.

My heart clutches, remembering the lilt of a woman's voice floating up from downstairs.

"Do you remember, Lucy?"

"No," I reply sharply. I force away the hazy memory, put it back to sleep.

Father Greg claps me on the shoulder. "Don't be a stranger. You know where to find us."

"Thanks, Father." There'll be no absolution for me today. Only loneliness and guilt. I feel like I'm at a funeral.

"Lila, thanks for all your help. As usual, you did a wonderful job." He glances at his watch. "I hate to ask, but would you mind taking care of things here before you leave? I'm running late for my pastoral meeting downtown."

She nods. "I'll make sure everything is taken back to church."

"The keys are in the usual place." He hands her a large, black leather case. "Your mother is a real treasure, Lucy. I can't tell you how glad we are to have her with us. It's hard to remember how we managed without her."

I bite my lip until I taste the rusty metallic tang of blood. Maybe Father Greg needs her, but Grandma and I don't. We managed on our own just fine all these years without any help from Lila.

Father Greg can have her.

"You ladies have a terrific afternoon. Enjoy the beautiful weather."

"Our parish is lucky to have a priest like him," Lila says as he disappears out the door.

Our parish? Since when has it become *our parish*?

Maybe since I quit going to church.

She hesitates. "Do you plan on staying awhile? I need to pack things up, but I would love it if we had a chance to sit and chat."

I stare at her, dumbfounded. Exactly what does Lila plan on us chatting about? Her drinking problem? Her job at the grocery store? How much both Grandma and I hate her?

Maybe Lila would like to talk about that.

"Sorry, but I've got to get back to the paper. I have an interview." Not exactly a lie. I *do* have an interview. The one I'm doing with Kris. Only today, I won't be the one asking the questions. I'll be answering them.

"Of course, I understand. You have work to do." Lila hesitates. "But someday, if you could find the time, it would be nice…"

I challenge her with a bold stare. She's lived in town nearly six months. If I wanted to talk to her, I would have already done it.

Her face flushes, as if she's somehow read my mind. "Lucy, I know I've made some terrible mistakes in the past. I'm sure it was very difficult for you. I know you must have been very hurt."

She doesn't know anything. I flinch as she touches my arm. Part of me wants to shake off her hand, slap her face, tell her she can go to hell.

But I'll damn myself if I do. Grandma raised me better than that.

Then again, Grandma also raised me never to trust this woman.

Lila searches my face. Her dark brown eyes are so like my own, it's like my own reflection staring back at me in a mirror. Much as I hate to admit it, there's no getting around the fact that she is my mother. She is the woman who gave me life.

And the thought of trusting her makes me want to vomit.

"Please, just think about it. That's all I ask." She hesitates. "I suppose I'd better pack up. They'll need this room soon."

I watch as she moves toward the altar. Her movements are practiced and reverent, as if she's done the same thing countless times. She blows out the candles, packs the chalice and ciborium for the hosts in the black leather case. Then she lifts her head, catches me watching her, and answers with a hesitant smile.

Why today? I can't help wondering. Why now? What does she want? Why is she being so nice?

And suddenly the truth hits me like a rock out of nowhere. Lila isn't interested in correcting past mistakes or forging a new relationship. She's interested in one thing, and one thing only.

The money.

She has to know I won. According to Kris, the story is spreading quickly. And Lila works at the grocery store, one of the few places in James Bay that delivers news faster than the *Journal* can print it. Even now, coming off so righteous and holy, Lila's probably busy thinking up some scheme on how to win me over, how to get me to give her some money. Maybe she hopes to dupe me by suddenly playing the role of the dutiful mother. Or perhaps she thinks it's better to play the role of Mary Magdalene, an admitted sinner who repents and turns to Jesus, sorry for her sins. Exactly how stupid does Lila think I am? I read the Bible.

Well, some of it. The important parts. Plus, I went to college. I know what she's after.

Lila halts in her folding of the altar cloth and eyes me with an uncertain smile. "Did you change your mind?"

Seventy million dollars. How much will it take to buy her out of my life?

"I have to go." I grab the handles of the wheelchair and spin out of the room so fast, Grandma's wheelchair nearly careens out of control. But I don't slow down till I've put half the length of the hallway between myself and Lila.

Damn the past and Rose Gallagher's hand-me-downs. Rose better be a good lawyer, because I intend to hire her today. Plus Sam Curtis, the accountant Max mentioned. I need the best legal and financial advice money can buy. It's been less than twenty-four hours since I won the lottery, but I can't afford to let things wait even another day. Not anymore.

Not with Lila already busy figuring out how much money, including interest, I owe her.

CHAPTER SIX

Instant fortune, I quickly discover, carries its own set of problems. Such as phone calls that do not stop.

"Who is this?"

"You don't know me, but I've got an idea I was hoping you might—"

I slam down the phone and swear under my breath.

Kris is seated across from me at my kitchen table. Her eyebrows rise slightly. "Who was that?"

"I don't know." I blow out a hot breath and swipe my bangs away from my eyes. What is it with people? Why don't they leave me alone? "I don't know, and quite frankly, I don't give a damn."

"Lucy Carter, I am shocked," she says, grinning. "What happened to that nice polite girl I used to know?"

"She decided to start cultivating some rudeness," I say darkly. "You have no idea what it's like. My phone hasn't stopped ringing since the interview was published. It's unbelievable, the people who are asking me for money. This morning, it was one of Grandma's buddies from the Rosary Altar Society. This little old lady I've known all my life hits me up for a five-thousand-dollar donation to buy new vestments for Father Greg."

"Tut-tut, better watch yourself, turning down the church. That sounds like it might be a sin."

"I didn't turn her down. I told her she could have a check once I get the money. But Sam Curtis is out of town on vacation and I'm not making one move before I talk things over with him. I have an appointment at his office first thing Monday morning."

"It will all work out," Kris assures me. "Besides, you're rich now, remember? What's five thousand dollars here or there?"

"I won't have five thousand left if this keeps up," I say. "Did I tell you the director of Whispering Pines called after lunch? I've never spoken to the woman before today, and suddenly she's lobbying me for a new recreational room, complete with plasma TV and commercial popcorn machine. Tax deductible, she told me—three times, in fact—not to mention that Grandma would benefit from my generosity."

I shoot Kris a doleful stare. "I told her I'd have to think about it. I said Grandma doesn't watch TV anymore, and she never did like popcorn."

Kris hoots with laughter.

"It's not funny," I add defensively. "How would you feel if everybody in town suddenly wanted to be your new best friend?" Even as I speak the words, I feel the day's tensions start to melt away. As usual, the sight of Kris in my kitchen is a welcome relief.

The sight of my landlady five minutes later isn't. Especially once I learn what Polly is after.

"I held off as long as I could," she says. "I knew you were having a hard time making a go of things, especially with your grandmother sick. But I just don't have a choice. After the special downtown development assessment they levied last spring, I need the extra money." Polly doesn't even have the grace to look embarrassed. "Besides, it's not like you can't afford it."

"Talk about ridiculous," Kris mutters as we watch her disappear down the back steps a few minutes later. "She can't raise your rent like that. Don't you have a lease?"

"I guess so," I say, slumping against the counter. "I think I signed something, but that was months ago."

"You *think* you signed something?"

"It's around here somewhere." The disbelief in Kris's voice automatically has me playing defense. "Even if I found it, I doubt it would do much good. Polly's a savvy businesswoman. She probably stuck a clause in there allowing her to raise the rent."

"A one-hundred-percent increase? Puh-leeze, I don't think so." Kris rolls her eyes. "It would serve her right if you moved."

"Break the lease?" A nervous flutter stirs in my stomach. "Is that legal? She might sue me."

Kris's eyes narrow. "And your point is?"

"I don't know. Besides, where would I go?"

"Anywhere you damned well please." She sighs, shakes her head. "Lucy, what is the matter with you? You're rich now, remember? You can buy anything you want."

Not necessarily. The money hasn't bought me dinner reservations at the James Bay Yacht Club. Tonight was supposed to be special, a once-in-a-lifetime-splurge. And who better to help me celebrate than Kris, at what supposedly is *the* most elegant restaurant in town. Not that I would know, since I've never been inside. Rumor has it they splurged on a decorator from Chicago, and they dropped a cool million on the chandeliers alone.

But we won't be checking out the chandeliers tonight.

The rule is firm, the hostess frostily informed me when I called for reservations. *Members Only.* Which, after a detailed search of the Yacht Club's roster, she assured me I most definitely am not.

Kris eyes me across the table. "You need to start thinking on a bigger scale. It's not like this apartment is anything special. The view is nice, but if I were you, I'd move in a heartbeat. Besides, it's not like you can't afford it."

"Just because I can afford it doesn't mean I want to move. I love it here." The sweeping view of James Bay from the living room window sold me on the place, and the downtown location mere blocks from the *Journal* couldn't be more convenient.

Then again, maybe a little too convenient, I think as yet someone else starts pounding on my kitchen door. Damn those back steps off the parking lot. Anyone can wander up and poke their nose into my life.

Kris peeks over my shoulder, then sighs. "Oh, joy. It's your favorite realtor."

I cringe at the sight of Didi Taylor peering at us through the kitchen window. For three days I've managed to avoid returning her calls, but there'll be no avoiding her this afternoon. Maybe Kris is right. Once I have the money, my first priority should be to buy myself some privacy.

"Where do you think you're going?" I watch warily as Kris downs the last of her coffee and pushes in her chair.

"Back to work." She snatches her keys from the kitchen table.

"And leave me alone with her? No fair."

Kris smiles politely. A little too politely. "She's your problem, sweetie, not mine."

"What about dinner? I thought we were going to celebrate." Kris is the closest thing I have to family, not counting Grandma and definitely not counting Lila. "Please, Kris?"

"What about dragon lady?" She nods toward the door.

"I'll get rid of her as fast as I can." I cross my heart. "Promise."

Her face softens. "I'll be down at the *Journal*. Call me once you're free."

"You're the best."

"Keep that in mind. You might not think so once the dinner bill shows up," she warns as I open the door. "I plan on ordering the most expensive thing on the menu."

"Congratulations!" Didi pushes past Kris into the kitchen and shrouds me in a layer of expensive perfume. "Such exciting news. Lucy, the thought of you winning all that money took my breath away."

I smile politely, trying my best to ignore the smirk on Kris's face. "It took my breath away, too." I leave out the throwing-up part. No need for all the messy details.

Didi flips her clutch purse on the table. "I told Richard—have you ever met my husband? Remind me, I must introduce you, you'll love him—that I knew you'd want to talk to me. Although I must confess, I'm a little surprised you haven't returned my calls."

"I know, I should have. I meant to. I'm sorry."

Why am I apologizing? And to Didi Taylor, of all people. Her wounded look is so pathetic yet so polished, I can't believe I'm falling for it. "It's just that since I won, my life has been a little…"

"Out of control?" Kris suggests. "Bye, girls. Have fun." She squeezes past Didi and out the door faster than a rat deserting a sinking ship.

And my ship is sinking fast. With Didi in my kitchen, I feel a certain empathy for how the captain of the *Titanic* must have felt when the White Star Line official urged him on: *Full Speed Ahead*. I rammed the iceberg when I let Didi in the door, and it won't be long before I'll be sucked under by her breathless enthusiasm. Death by Didi.

"Don't forget our plans," I yell out the door as my human life preserver Kris heads down the steps. "I'll call you."

"You're going somewhere?" Didi asks brightly.

"Just out to dinner," I say, instantly regretting the words as soon as they're out of my mouth. "A little celebration."

"Well, I should hope you would celebrate. Are you going somewhere special?"

I sit with a sigh. "We wanted to go to the Yacht Club, but we couldn't get in."

Didi's eyebrows rise nearly to the roots of her professionally enhanced strawberry hairline. "Did you tell them who you were?"

"I gave them my name, but they said members only."

"How utterly ridiculous."

The fact that Didi knows how to snort catches me by surprise. So does the rapidity with which she sinks into the chair recently vacated by Kris, flips open her cell phone, and hits a speed-dial number. "You want the Yacht Club? You've got the Yacht Club."

"But it's members only…"

Didi blows out a deep breath and rolls her eyes. "Lucy, what am I going to do with you? You are a sweet girl, but you definitely have some things to learn when it comes to how things work. And I am about to show you how it's done."

"But—"

She shushes me with a raised finger. "Jacqueline? Hi, it's Didi Taylor. Listen, I know this is last minute, but I need a table for tonight. Something nice, overlooking the water. Something very special." She pauses for a moment, then nods. "Yes, yes, that's right. For one of my very special clients."

Didi's fawning smile puts me on edge. If I'm one of her special clients, she needs to do some major advertising to increase her clientele. The only listing I've given her is Grandma's house. Which, as Didi herself reminded me last week, isn't worth much. *Damn little*, to quote her words correctly.

"Just a minute, Jacqueline, let me check." She covers the phone with one hand. "What time works best for you?"

"Six o'clock?" If Didi can pull off landing us reservations at the Yacht Club tonight, I'll take back every nasty thing I ever said about her, no matter what Kris thinks.

"Yes, make it for six o'clock. We'll need a table for three. Thanks, Jacqueline, you're a doll." She flips the phone shut. "We're all set. I hope you don't mind if I join you."

"Of course not," I hear myself reply, even as my brain screams *Lucy, are you crazy?*

"Very good. *Members only.*" She flashes me a quick smile. "I'm the member."

What am I supposed to say? I swallow hard. Looks like it will be a threesome for dinner tonight. Oh, God. Kris isn't going to like this. Not at all.

Didi glances at her watch, an elegant piece of wrist jewelry that flashes I'm-much-too-expensive-for-just-anyone-to-afford in the fading afternoon sun. "It's already past five. We should plan on leaving soon. Why don't I drive? I have the Mercedes. I'll phone Richard and let him know my plans while you change."

"Change?" I glance down at my clothes. "But I hadn't planned to…"

Her withering gaze sweeps me from head to foot.

"Is there something wrong with the way I look?" I venture.

"You might want to rethink the slacks." She clips out the words without missing a beat. "And the top is very nice, but it screams Walmart."

How the hell does she know where I shop? It's what I can afford. Besides, I could never compete with Didi in the looks or clothes department, even if I wanted to. She's wearing a suit of orange silk shot with gold that makes her look like a million bucks. Women like Didi are born knowing how to put themselves together.

I glance down at my narrow pants and simple, sleeveless shell. Isn't black supposed to be a timeless color that will take you anywhere?

Obviously not to the James Bay Yacht Club.

Didi's green eyes soften. "You don't have to change. You look perfectly acceptable just the way you are... if that's the impression you wish to make."

I've always wondered how beauty pageant contestants cope under constant scrutiny, and after being around Didi for five minutes, I'm even more clueless about how they manage to keep smiling. I think every one of them deserves a crown simply for having the guts to step on stage and allow themselves to be judged.

"I'm only trying to help," she says. "It's Friday night and the Club will be crowded. You do want to fit in, don't you?"

"Yes, of course." At least, I thought so. Now I'm not so sure.

"Good." Didi perks up with a bright smile. "I'll make myself comfortable while you change. And don't forget to phone your friend."

I groan to myself as I remember Kris, waiting for my call. She'll be thrilled when she hears we're headed to the Yacht Club. Especially since I have no intention of mentioning the Didi factor. Why spoil the party? Kris will find out soon enough.

"I'll call her right now. Thanks for reminding me."

"I had no choice. She never would have made it past the maitre d' in those khaki pants and that dreadful Hawaiian-print shirt she's wearing." Didi shudders. "Does the woman even own a dress?"

I head for my bedroom with a growing uneasiness about my dinner plans. What was meant to be a simple celebration between two friends has somehow blossomed into a full-blown affair that could easily end up in disaster.

Those million-dollar chandeliers better be worth it.

Money might not buy happiness, but it definitely helps when it comes to purchasing ambiance. The James Bay Yacht Club is a prime example. The lobby and dining room reek of understated elegance with crème-colored, silk-upholstered chairs and exquisite wall coverings. And, just as Didi promised, we have a prime table in front of one of the floor-to-ceiling windows offering a million-dollar view.

Not to mention the million-dollar chandeliers. I try not to gawk at the one centered directly above my head. I'm sure Didi definitely would not approve.

Though she obviously approves of her dinner. Didi spears another piece of the flaky red meat covered in a light dill sauce, pops it in her mouth, and sighs. "This salmon is to die for."

Who needs salmon? I felt like dying after one look at the menu and translating the no-dollar-sign, a-la-carte language. Whoever heard of a chunk of iceberg lettuce decorated with carrot curls costing *nine*? For that price, I could buy nine heads of lettuce at the grocery store and throw in a few cucumbers and tomatoes, too.

Didi points her fork at Kris's plate. "Is something wrong with your shrimp?"

"It's fine." The smile on Kris's face is as stiff as the collar of the ill-fitting dress she unearthed from some remote region of her closet. She pokes her fork through lobster-stuffed shrimp drizzled with Béarnaise sauce.

Poor Kris. I don't blame her for being confused. My Lobster Carbonara isn't exactly what I expected, either. The

Yacht Club has a reputation for superb food and exquisite presentation, but the selective menu and limited choices came as a surprise. Where's the lobster tail dripping with butter? Where's the king crab?

"Next time, order the salmon," Didi advises. "It's one of the house specialties. Tender, with just the right touch of dill and not too heavy a dish. Who needs the extra calories?" She dabs her lips with the linen napkin. "Lucy, you have no idea how lucky you are, being so thin. I'm sure you get away with eating exactly as you please."

"I wouldn't say that," I say, though food's never been a problem for me. I eat what I want.

"There's no need to be embarrassed," she continues. "Some women are born that way, with no need to worry about calories. Not that I would presume to speak for Kris, but I assume she's watching her waistline, just like me."

"Oh, I'm watching it all right," Kris replies as she hoists her beer, toasts us both, and downs a healthy swallow.

I feel like diving under the table as Didi stares her down. "You've quite the droll wit, don't you?" she eventually says. "I've never bothered with your columns, but perhaps I should give them a try."

Kris's eyes widen with an innocent look that would put Bambi to shame. "Oh, Didi, would you? Our managing editor will be thrilled. It would bring my readership count up to five. Or is it ten?" She shrugs. "Well, whatever."

Lord, I owe Kris big-time after tonight's fiasco. I throw a pleading look across the snowy tablecloth and she rewards me with quick wink.

Plus a swift kick in my shin, under the table.

I smile to myself and wince through the pain. It's good to be among friends.

Didi clears her throat. "Ladies, this evening deserves a toast."

"I'll drink to that." Kris raises her glass. "To Lucy."

Didi grabs her arm and pulls it down. "For heaven's sake, you don't toast with beer. This celebration calls for champagne." She swivels in her chair, her head weaving from side to side. "Where is that waiter?"

"I'm fine with coffee," I say. Why spend the extra money on something we don't need? I don't drink, plus we already have that bottle of sinfully expensive wine Didi insisted on ordering to go along with dinner. And no one—including Didi—will ever separate Kris from her beloved beer.

"Seventy million dollars deserves champagne," Didi says, looking offended.

"I appreciate the sentiment, but I'm thankful enough without champagne."

Her mouth droops in a pout, reminding me of a pert little Pekinese about to yip at being denied her favorite treat. "Being here at the Club is celebration enough," I add. "Thank you again for getting us in."

"My pleasure," she purrs, going from petulant Pekinese to pampered Persian in one second flat. "To Lucy." She lifts her glass. "May all your dreams come true. And of course, they will, since you can afford them now."

What does money have to do with dreams? I don't dare look at Kris, for I'm sure I won't like what I see. I tuck my legs under my chair, far out of kicking range.

"You are my favorite client," Didi continues. "If there's anything I can do for you, you only need ask."

"Try finding her another apartment," Kris mutters as she downs the last of her beer.

Didi perks up. "You're in the market for a new place?"

I hold back a sigh. Bad enough I signed Didi's six-month realtor listing for Grandma's house. I don't need her running interference when it comes to where I live.

"Lucy's landlady just raised the rent." Kris shoves aside her glass.

Didi rolls her eyes. "That sounds just like Polly Mitchell."

"Since she won the money, the whole town is banging on her door. Lucy needs privacy, don't you think?"

"I couldn't agree more." Didi's head bobs violently. "You never know what type of people could wander up those back steps. Not to mention she's right downtown near all the bars. Not exactly the best location for someone with lots of cash." She throws the waiter a gracious smile as he tops her glass with the last of the wine. "Lucy, you simply have no choice. You have to move. Staying where you would be dangerous."

Kris levels with me a steady gaze. "I agree with Didi. You need to be somewhere safe."

"I appreciate your concerns, both of you, but there's one tiny problem. I can't afford to move, even if I wanted to. I still don't have the money." I don't even have enough cash in my wallet to pay for tonight's celebration. But I do have a credit card stashed aside for emergencies. And tonight, no matter how revolting I find the thought, I plan to say *charge it*.

"I have the perfect solution," Didi counters, "and I guarantee it won't cost you a dime."

Perfect solutions, in my experience, have a way of costing plenty. "Thanks, but I don't think—"

"That's right, Lucy, you don't have to think… because I am going to do it for you." She snags her purse and pulls out her Blackberry. "By tomorrow night, you'll be sleeping in a brand-new condo."

"A condo?" I throw a helpless glance at Kris, who merely smiles and shrugs. I turn back to Didi. "But isn't a condo—"

"Exactly what you need," she informs me. "It comes fully furnished and has a view equally magnificent to—if not better—than this." She gestures toward the window where, in front of us, the sun is setting fast. Before us, the waters of James Bay glow as the last vivid hues of violet, red and blue slip against the horizon.

"It's the perfect spot. I don't know why I didn't think of it before." Didi beams. "Four bedrooms, five baths, designer kitchen, plus an outside veranda. It's right on the water and even comes with a boat slip."

She definitely has my attention. Evening sunsets, waves lapping gently against the shore. "Where is this condo?"

"Just down the street. It's the model we show people who are interested in joining the Club."

"And you think it might be available?"

"Everything is available, if you know the right people. Let me make a few phone calls. I'm sure you'll be welcome to stay as long as you like."

A chance to live at the Yacht Club, with James Bay straight out my front door? I fell in love with my tiny apartment because of the view. But that same view is blocked by heavy summer traffic and heavy noise from the downtown crowd.

I take another glance out the window at the sunset sinking beneath James Bay.

No noise. No people. Just me.

"And you're sure this place is on the water?" I say.

A little sigh floats from her lips. "I've showed this condo more than once. Yes, it's on the water."

I shake my head, awed by the thought. "No way."

"Fine, you're the client." She shrugs. "The Club is a gated community. I thought you might prefer the privacy. But I'm sure I can find something equally nice to make you happy. Give me a minute." She glances down, frowns at her Blackberry.

Is the woman insane? A condo on James Bay. Waking each morning to the sound of waves gently lapping against the shore. Drinking my morning coffee outside on the veranda.

"I'll take it."

Her head lifts, her eyes narrow. "But I thought you just said—"

"I'll take it." The firmness in my voice surprises even me. I don't care what the condo costs to rent. I can afford it. I have the money. Correction. I *will* have the money, once the lottery office and I get squared away.

Kris lays a hand on my arm. "Don't you think you should see the place first? Tomorrow is Saturday. I have the day off. I'll go with you."

"I don't need to see it." I turn back to Didi. "When can I move in?"

"All I have to do is clear it with the Board. I'll call you tomorrow." Didi slips her Blackberry into her purse, eyes focused, all business. "You'll love living at the Club, Lucy. The people here are simply marvelous. Richard and I bought our condo when the Club first opened and we wouldn't dream of living anywhere else. It's spoiled us forever."

I feel like scrambling to my feet, jumping up and down on the silk-upholstered chairs, leaping high, grabbing hold and swinging from one of those million-dollar chandeliers. That would certainly cause quite the commotion! But the hell with what people think. I won the lottery. I can buy what I want. I can do as I please. Who's going to stop me?

"Lucy? Are you okay?"

Kris's voice rolling across the table reminds me of waves tossed and turned in a summer storm. Exactly how my stomach feels. Am I okay? Hell no! I've never felt so geeked in my life, not even when I discovered I held the winning ticket.

God bless Didi for bringing us here tonight. All that talk I've heard for years about the Club is definitely true. It's by far the most elegant place in town. And I lucked up big-time when I hooked up with Didi.

Who would have believed it? By this time next weekend, plain old Lucy Carter will be living at the Yacht Club!

CHAPTER SEVEN

"You're firing me?"

Charles's abrupt order that I clean out my desk trumps me waltzing into the office intending to quit. *Good intentions never get anything done*, as Grandma always said. My letter of resignation is still in my purse.

"Don't take it personally," he says smoothly from his chair across from me in the conference room. "Try and see it from a broader perspective. With all the people running in here lately looking for you, no one's getting any work done. Especially me. I've got a newspaper to run, remember? The news waits for no man—"

"*Or no woman*," I mutter, finishing one of his favorite slogans. "No need to remind me."

But in my heart, I know he's right. My notoriety as *small-town famous* has rocketed since the public announcement that I won the lottery. Through the open door, I hear the overhead ding of the calls coming through fast and furious and the receptionist trying to keep up.

"I'm sorry, Ms. Carter is not available. I'm sorry, she's not in the office. I'm sorry, Ms. Carter is not giving interviews."

Since when did I become Ms. Carter?

Since when did the *Journal* start speaking on my behalf?

"You surprise me, you know that?" Charles folds his arms and gives me a cool, appraising look. "Anybody but you would have already quit. To tell you the truth, I figured that's why you showed up today. I half expected you to throw your resignation in my face."

"Give me a break," I scoff, and clutch my purse tighter. No need to haul the resignation letter out now. And that maddening smile on his face makes me want to scream. How would Charles feel if his life were suddenly turned upside down?

I never asked for any of this. I never even wanted to buy the damn ticket.

"What about my replacement? Have you already hired someone?"

He shrugs. "Not yet, but I don't anticipate any problems. Face it, Lucy. It's not like you were writing Pulitzer Prize material."

My lips twist in a grim smile. "Thanks for making me feel so special."

The fact that he finds it necessary to knock my writing irks me to no end. Why can't he simply be happy for me? Why does he have to rub it in my face? How would he feel if someone fired him? For one crazy moment, I contemplate buying the *Journal* and doing exactly that. That would show Charles who's in charge.

"Stirring up controversy about the parking-meter debate isn't exactly going to knock Wall Street off the front page. Besides," he adds, "it's not like you need the money."

"I know," I reply grimly.

"Someone else could use the job. Someone who *needs* it."

"I *know*."

A loud bell rings from behind a door, followed by the muffled roar of machines and a steady vibration beneath my feet. They're printing today's *Journal*. I swallow hard. It will be hard walking away from this. I gave it my best. I wrote my best. Parking meters or not, I'm going to miss this place.

I head for my desk. With Kris out on assignment, it won't take long to clean out my drawers. I'll pack up and go home.

I force down the nagging thought poking around my brain.

Home to what?

"I might have some freelance work from time to time," Charles says in an aside. "I've been tossing around an idea for a weekly feature section. People, places, things. You could work from home, if you're interested."

"What did you have in mind?" I hang a cool look on my face. Am I interested? The thought of being surrounded by empty space and no schedule has me scared silly. Never in a million years did I dream I'd be in a financial position like I am now. But what am I supposed to do with myself all day? Shoe shopping will never rank high on my daily agenda, no matter how much money I have in the bank.

"I assume you'll want to travel. Why not take our readers along? Let them see what it's like to fly first class, to vacation at a world-class resort. Let them experience it right along with you."

"You want *me* to write a travel section?" The word *vacation* might as well be part of a foreign language. I'm not exactly a world traveler. I've never been on an airplane, and I've only been out of Michigan once in my life, during a very long bus ride on our senior-class trip to Washington D.C.

"Think about it and let me know," Charles says. "Meanwhile, there is a freelance story I'd like you to write, but it's not about travel. I see it as a four-part feature, five thousand words. We could run the first installment next week."

"Next week?" That barely gives me any time to do research. "What's the topic?"

"Here's the working title: *A DAY IN THE LIFE OF A LOTTERY WINNER.*" A smile hangs on his face. "That ought to knock our competitors off their game."

Five minutes later I head for the door with my personal belongings crammed in two banker boxes and my dignity intact. Charles can write his own damn feature stories. I'm not about to throw away my privacy to beef up his bottom line.

I balance the boxes on top of one another, stumble out the door, and smack into Max.

"Whoa." He catches the top box before it hits the ground. He hefts it in his arms and peers over the box at me. "Pretty heavy stuff to be handling by yourself. What have you got in here?"

Three years' worth of dreams, but why bother him with all the messy details? I nod toward my VW. "Thanks for helping. My car is over there."

Between the two of us, we manage to shove the boxes into the trunk. I slam it with a grim satisfaction.

Max eyes me cautiously. "Bad day at the office?"

"More like *last day at the office*."

"You quit?" he says, grinning.

I slump against the front fender. "Actually, I got fired."

He whistles low and leans beside me. "You're kidding. They fired you?"

I shade my eyes against the noon sun. "The managing editor told me I was a distraction. He said if I stayed, I'd be taking a job from someone who really needed it."

"I suppose that's true," he says after a moment.

"Don't remind me." Pouting isn't pretty, but I can't hide the scowl covering my face. I hate this feeling that's burning inside me, like I've been cast aside, like I no longer count. "Even if it is true, he didn't have to say it. It's not fair."

Max shrugs. "He's jealous you won the money. Why waste your time or energy thinking about it? It's his way of getting even."

But it's more than that. Charles's taunting hit harder than I expected. Maybe I'm not the world's greatest journalist, but I've always taken pride in my work. I was a stickler for checking my facts. I always tried to deliver a good story to my readers.

"He made fun of my writing," I admit in a small voice. "He said anybody could do it."

"Stop it." Max grabs me by the shoulders and gives me a little shake. "You're a great writer. Don't let anybody— including your creepy ex-boss—tell you any different. The guy's a jerk."

I chance a small smile. "You really think so?"

"Yes, and so do half the people in town," he replies. "Or at least the ones who read his column. He comes across like a pompous ass."

121

Suddenly I feel better than I have in days. Kris is a great friend and champion, but she's been working overtime covering my old beat, and it's been awhile since we talked. In fact, it's been awhile since I felt like anyone was on my side. Knowing it's Max makes me feel even better.

"I'll miss reading your byline," he says.

"Thanks." The sun is hot, and so is my face.

"What about the Loon Lake rezoning? You've been covering that issue since day one."

My heart does a little flip-flop, diving right into my stomach. Loon Lake. Is that the only reason Max is sorry to see me step aside from reporting?

"Kris is an excellent journalist. She'll fill in for me until they hire a replacement."

"She might be good, but she's not you. You have a way of cutting through the b.s. and putting things in simple English that the public understands. I hope Kris can keep that going. If they approve that development out on Loon Lake, things around town are going to change… and not for the better," he predicts darkly.

"I'll talk to Kris," I promise. Though for all I care, the developers can go right ahead and turn Loon Lake into one big muddy swamp.

His face brightens. "Hey, I caught you on the news the other night, picking up your check at the Lottery office."

I roll my eyes. "The place was a madhouse." Jammed with pushy reporters shoving cameras and microphones in my face. *Over here, Lucy! Look this way, Lucy!* Hopefully I was never that rude or insensitive when I covered the news. Until this happened to me, I never realized what a terrible feeling it is to lose your privacy, to be jostled and treated like a commodity instead of a person with feelings. I wouldn't wish it on anyone.

"You looked pretty happy when they handed you the check for seventy million dollars."

"It wasn't really the check. The money was wire transferred as soon as I signed the papers. My accountant, Sam Curtis, said it ended up around thirty million once the government took its share."

"Glad to hear you've got Sam helping you out."

"Amen to that," I agree. My gut told me I could trust him at our very first meeting, and I know I made the right decision in hiring Sam. He's a sweet, steady guy who obviously knows what he's talking about when it comes to investments. More important, I like that he listens to me. He's sensitive to the fact that I'm cautious about money. He's not pushing me into anything, and I like that. I like Sam.

"He suggested I keep most of the money in treasury bonds. He said it would be safe there till I figure out what I want to do." And as far as I'm concerned, the money can sit there for years, collecting dusty interest. Thinking about it still makes me want to throw up.

"I'm glad I ran into you today," Max says. "I tried calling, but I couldn't get through."

"I had to get an unlisted number," I explain. "You wouldn't believe the calls I've been getting. People asking—begging!—for money. Some of them I don't even know. People wanting to tell me about some fantastic deal that's guaranteed to triple my investment."

He grins. "Welcome to the world of high finance?"

"I guess what they say is true, that money changes things. It's changed the way people behave around me."

"I'm still the same guy," Max says with an easy smile.

Thank God for that. "Did you hear that I moved?"

His eyebrows rise. "No more downtown apartment?"

"Too many people banging on my back door. I'm living in a condo at the James Bay Yacht Club. It's a gated community. Very private."

He squints against the sun. "You like it out there?"

"It's perfect. What's not to like?"

"I don't know." Max shrugs. "You just don't strike me as the Yacht Club type."

"And what makes you say that?" I shade my eyes and peer at him. Does he think I'm not good enough to live there?

"Just some things I've heard around town."

"That's the problem with this town." My words rush out like a blast of hot air in the noon heat. "People in James Bay talk way too much about things they know nothing about."

"Whoa, forget I said anything." He holds up his hands in surrender.

But just the way he says it makes me feel prickly inside. "The Yacht Club is a very nice place." I try to keep from sounding too defensive, but it's not easy. "I think I'll be very happy there."

He glances at his watch. "I've got to get going."

My chest suddenly feels bruised, like I've been kicked from the inside out, and I'm hit with the surety that if Max walks away, that will be that. Somehow, somewhere, things went wrong between us. But I don't want him walking away. He's just walked back in my life.

Do I owe him an apology? Even if I don't, maybe I can find a way to say it.

He touches my arm. "Look, Lucy, I'm sorry. I didn't mean to be short with you. Guess I'm just a little punchy today."

I take a hard look at him. Dark rims shadow his eyes and his clothes look rumpled, like he slept in them all night. I've been so wrapped up in my own little drama, I didn't notice until now. "Are you okay?"

"Nothing a few hours' sleep won't cure. I spent most of last night in the hospital's waiting room. One of our counselors had an emergency appendectomy."

I catch a breath. "Is he okay?"

"He'll be fine," Max assures me. "But that's the end of summer camp for him. We'll be short-staffed until we hire a replacement. That's why I'm here at the *Journal*. I came down to place an ad." He shifts on his feet, suddenly grins. "Sounds like you have some time on your hands. Maybe you'd like the job?"

"Me, work at Loon Lake? Ha! You've got to be kidding."

And suddenly I don't want to tell him good-bye. Saying good-bye means hopping in my car and heading back to my condo. The empty four-bedroom condo where I've rattled around by myself for nearly a week.

"Do you have time for lunch?" I try to keep the hope from creeping into my voice. My spirits sink as he shakes his head, but the tinge of regret I glimpse on his face softens the rejection.

"Sorry, I've got to get back to camp."

"No problem." *Slow down*, I caution myself. I'm not exactly the greatest conversationalist when it comes to dealing with men. The last thing I want is to scare Max off, or to come across as needy.

"How about the two of us have dinner together sometime?"

Maybe I'm not the only needy one in this relationship. Because, unless I am totally clueless, I think Max just asked me out.

"Saturday nights work best for me," he adds. "Camp's over for the week, the kids are gone. It's a good time to kick back and unwind."

"This Saturday night?" I ask.

"How about if we make it for seven o'clock? I'll pick you up."

I scribble down the address of my condo and hand it to him before he changes his mind. "You'll have to give the gatekeeper my name. I'll make sure you're on the list. I'm not hard to find. It's the first condo on the right, just past the Yacht Club."

"I figured," he says with a shrug.

"Have you been to the Yacht Club before?"

He shoots me a funny look.

I brighten. "It's a beautiful place. You'd love it, Max. We should go there for dinner. It's members only, but I'm sure that won't matter anymore, even though I'm not a member yet. I heard it's merely a formality. My membership will be approved at next month's board meeting."

"I don't—"

"You have to see this place," I insist. "The food is delicious and it has a marvelous view."

Max squints against the sunshine as he stares at the slip of paper in his hand.

"If you don't want to go, that's fine," I say. "I just thought you might like it."

He's so quiet. Have I said something wrong? "Or maybe you've already been there—"

Then suddenly I get it. Of course he's never been there. I've been blathering on about a fancy club, which is members only. But someone like Max would never be invited to join. Just like he'd never be able to splurge on a pricey dinner. Not on his salary.

"My treat," I quickly add. "That's only fair, seeing how I'm the one who suggested it."

His eyebrows lift. "Worried I can't handle the tab?"

"I didn't say that."

"You didn't have to." His voice holds a gentle rebuff. "Look, Lucy, I'm not exactly a Yacht Club kind of guy. Why don't we just keep things simple? I'll pick up a pizza, stop over, and you can give me the grand tour."

A few minutes later we say good-bye. Greasy pizza isn't on my list of top-ten foods, but if Max wants pizza, then I'll eat pizza.

Not to mention the slice of humble pie I'll be serving myself for dessert.

"How big is this place?" Max swings his neck from side to side as we wander down a hallway.

"Four thousand square feet. Four bedrooms, five bathrooms." I step aside as he peeks in one of the guest rooms. "Plus it has a three-car garage and boat dock."

He stares at me with a doleful grin. "You planning on buying a boat?"

"Who knows? Maybe." I laugh. It's fun showing Max my new place. He's my first official visitor since I moved into the condo. Kris helped me move, so she doesn't count; neither does Didi or her husband Richard. The two of them showed up the first night with a bottle of chilled champagne to toast my new digs.

I lead Max down the wide hallway and fling open another door. "And this is where the maid sleeps."

"You hired a live-in maid?" He looks a little shocked.

"Silly, of course not. That's just what my realtor called it. The room could be used for anything."

"Not much of a view," he says, glancing out the window. "The maid will be disappointed."

"She'll get over it." I pull the door firmly shut.

We end up back in the mammoth living room, which boasts a fieldstone fireplace, floor-to-ceiling windows, and a covered balcony just beyond the pair of exquisite French doors. Grandma's creaky Bentwood rocker looks miserably out of place amidst all the stark white designer furniture that came with the condo, but eyesore or not, I am not getting rid of that chair. It's the only piece of home I have left.

"Wow. Look at that view." Max stands at the windows, where the sparkling waters of James Bay are on display. "Now I understand why you like the place."

I join him at the window and we stand shoulder to shoulder, staring out over the water. "Sometimes I look around and think, is all of this real? Did it really happen? Three weeks ago I was struggling to come up with enough money to pay my rent, and now I own this. I feel like pinching myself. I still can't believe it's all mine."

"You bought it?" He seems stunned.

I nod. "Sam tried to talk me out of it, but I couldn't help myself. One look and I fell in love. So I made them an offer they couldn't refuse. I think they were surprised since it wasn't on the market. Plus, I paid cash. I guess most people don't do that."

"I'd say that's a safe bet," he agrees.

"Why not? I have the money." I push away the unpleasant memory of Sam trying to talk me out of making a rash decision. But I wasn't swayed, no matter how much his fiscal arguments made sense. Grandma worked hard all her life to make the house's monthly mortgage payments to the bank. I'm not being saddled with a one-million-plus debt. The condo is all mine. Two stories with an enormous kitchen and glossy granite countertops, a foyer bigger than my downtown apartment, and a home office featuring custom cherry cabinetry. Not to mention hardwood floors throughout. I feel guilty just walking across the polished wood. I can't help but keep thinking about how happy Grandma was when she finally saved enough money to carpet our house.

Max turns from the window. "You hungry? The pizza is getting cold."

I eye the dining-room table, a formidable expanse of gleaming mahogany that scared me silly the first time I saw it. I still haven't gotten up the nerve to eat a meal at that table. "I suppose I could set out some place mats," I say doubtfully.

"How about we eat out there?" Max nods toward the balcony directly off the living room. "Might as well take advantage of the million-dollar view."

Exactly what it cost me, I smile to myself. At least I'll get my money's worth. "You take out the pizza and I'll get some plates." A few minutes later, I'm on the balcony with a tray filled with plates, napkins, and cutlery. Max has dragged two of the spotless white chairs lined up in a tidy row against one wall and placed them near the railing. The harbor sprawls before us, alive with slow-motoring yachts and colorful sailboats. I settle into the chair beside him. One month ago, the thought of me living a lifestyle like this would have been filed under the heading *ain't-gonna-happen*. Yet it has.

"Isn't this perfect?" I balance my plate on one knee and take in the surroundings with a contented sigh. "I used to wonder why people with money always seemed so happy. Now I finally understand."

He shakes his head. "You never fail to amaze me."

"What did I say?"

Max grins. "Never mind."

"But—"

"Hey, I almost forgot. Be right back." He stands, leaves me sitting alone as he heads inside, and returns with a paper sack a few minutes later. He pulls out a six-pack of beer. "Pizza and beer are like hamburgers and French fries. You can't have one without the other." He rummages around in the sack and comes up with a six-pack of icy-cold pop. "I hope you like cola. I know you don't drink."

I'm touched by the gesture. "That was sweet."

"I stopped at the grocery on my way over." He cracks open a beer. "By the way, your mom says *hello*."

I feel the blood rush to my face. "You talked to Lila?"

"She was working the checkout counter and we got to chatting. I like your mom. She's a nice lady."

"No disrespect, but that's just your opinion." *And she's no lady, either.* I concentrate on picking off the little bits of spicy pepperoni spread out over my pizza. My lips sting like they've been burned, and so does my heart. Max and Lila together, talking about me? I don't like the idea. Not one bit.

"I know the two of you have had your problems, but who knows? Maybe if you give her a chance, she'd—"

"Forget it, Max. I don't want to talk about it." Lila had her chance twenty years ago, and she blew it.

"She made a mistake. Everybody make mistakes. It's part of being human."

My jaw clenches and I feel my heart turning to stone. "That's right. Lila made mistakes. Lots of mistakes. Now she has to live with them… just like we all do. I have my own problems, and my life to live."

"She's your mom. She only wants to help."

"I don't need Lila running interference in my life," I slam back. "I'm a big girl, and I can handle things just fine. I'm going to make it on my own."

If someone else had said it, I would have groaned out loud. I sound like an old rerun from one of those Nickelodeon marathons they run on Saturday afternoons. Mary Tyler Moore, twirling in the street, throwing her hat in the air. *Well, it's you, girl, and you can do it… you're gonna make it on your own.*

But I'm a Lucy, not a Mary, and my small list of attributes doesn't include a perky attitude. Not to mention I've always hated hats. Plus, the last time I looked, there was no benevolent Mr. Grant in my life, keeping me out of trouble.

Just Charles Kendall, lurking in the background, waiting for me to mess up.

"I didn't mean to upset you," Max says. "Roberta and I were talking last night, and she told me—"

"I hope you weren't talking about me." The hair on the back of my neck bristles. What gives people the right to feel they're entitled to discuss my personal life?

"Don't get so defensive," he says smoothly. "We were talking about Roberta and Bob, and how they know your mom."

"Lila," I say flatly. "Her name is Lila." I shove away my plate. My appetite's gone, and the one slice of pizza I gobbled down is churning in my stomach. I'm beginning to regret having eaten it. I'm beginning to regret a lot of things.

"Okay, they've known *Lila* for years. They both happen to think a lot of her."

I stare at him with dead eyes. "I assume you have a point."

"Just that people can change," he counters. "And they do change... if they have enough motivation. Maybe Lila's changed."

"Even if she has, it won't change what happened. It won't give me back my father."

"That's true," he admits. "But it's still possible to salvage your relationship with her. All you have to do is be willing to try."

My eyes narrow. "You think I should feel grateful Lila is around? That woman has done nothing but make my life miserable. I don't need her."

"She's family, Lucy," he answers softly. "She's your mother."

"Don't remind me." I hug myself in the darkening shadows. Did Lila put him up to this? Championing her case? Trying to get me to accept her? If she did, and he agreed, Max is sadly mistaken. He has no idea who she is, what she is, or how she operates.

"I'd give anything for a chance to talk with my mother," he says quietly. "She died a few hours after I was born."

I bite my inner lip so hard I taste blood.

"I never had a chance to know her," he says. "I never heard her voice, never held her hand, never felt her kiss me. I grew up feeling like a part of me—a big part of me—was missing. Do you ever feel like that?"

"No," I state flatly. Yet even as our eyes catch and hold, I glimpse something familiar, something I recognize in myself. A longing for family, for things I will never have. For all that was lost to me.

Max leans against the railing. "It's your life, Lucy. I'm just telling you how I feel... and what I would do, if Lila was my mother and I were you."

His words bring a torrent of feelings flowing through me. Feelings I've tried to keep buried deep inside, hidden under an umbrella of detachment that I'm always ready to pull out and snap over my head whenever I see Lila coming. Feelings of regret, remorse, and—to be honest—revenge.

Why do we always want things we can't have? Max longs for his mother, while I have a mother I long to have out of my life for good. The last time we spoke, Lila admitted she'd made mistakes, that she regretted the past. She mentioned wanting to talk. She wants a future that includes me. Is that really what she wants?

Is it me? Or my money?

Seagulls swoop overhead and sail ever closer to the railing. I stare at my plate. The pizza is cold, the tomato sauce congealed in a slippery mess. Just like my life. Do I really want to spend the rest of it trying to avoid Lila and running from the truth? How long can a person run? How long can a person hide? I'm tired of hiding. Maybe Max is right. Maybe it's best to get it over with. Maybe I should sit down with Lila and talk it out. I'll never know until I try.

Max upends the beer can and drains it in one long thirsty swallow, then sighs. "Look, forget what I said. I haven't got any business telling you what to do about your mother. Hell, I don't even talk to my own father."

My gut feels like it's been hit by a sucker punch. "What do you mean?"

"He lives downstate. We rarely talk, by mutual agreement." He rolls the empty beer can between his hand. His eyes scan the horizon, now merely a rosy red glow. "He doesn't approve of my lifestyle, of me living up here, working at camp. He hates the place. He says I'm wasting my degree."

I hesitate. "I didn't know you went to college. I thought—"

"I've got a master's in business from the University of Michigan." Max throws me a hard stare. "You look like that's a surprise."

I swallow down my embarrassment. U of M is one of the toughest schools in the country, and his MBA gives Max some serious credentials. Not to mention he would have had to pull down serious good grades to qualify for a scholarship from such a prestigious school.

"My father prides himself on being a man of high standards. He took it as a personal offense that I was born crippled. Not to mention my birth robbed him of my mother, the only person he ever loved."

His jaw is set like granite, his face like it's chiseled out of stone. But his voice cracks with little faults of pain. "It took a long time before I learned to walk. The doctors insisted on waiting until I was five years old before they would operate. When I was a kid, I spent a lot of time in bed. Even after they did the surgery, I still had a limp. My father turned his back on me, and that's when LC got involved."

"LC?" I ask quietly.

"My grandfather." Max leans against the railing, stares off into the growing darkness. "I spent every summer up here with LC. He was my mother's dad. They called him LC, short for Lloyd Christopher Colley. He lived at the camp. He loved that place, Lucy, and he taught me to love it, too. LC died of a heart attack when I was a freshman in college, and they shut down the camp shortly after that. The Board resurrected it and we opened up again last spring. Camp Call of the Loon is LC's legacy."

I feel sick at the thought of what Max has been through. He's fighting for his grandfather, who took care of the camp. I'm fighting for my grandmother, who took care of me. Max and I are two of a kind, both of us survivors of unhappy childhoods. Both of us grew up with parents who didn't love us.

And grandparents who did.

"Maybe now you understand why it's so important to me to keep the developers out." His face and knuckles are ghostly white as he turns to face me. "If that PUD is approved, the development will totally surround the camp. They intend to build houses on lots that run about a half acre in size. Plus, they'll fence in the property. Our nature trails wind around that property. Those trails will disappear. The developers also plan on putting in a golf course. Know how they intend to allow us access to camp? They're running a cement driveway straight through the fairways."

I think of the curvy road winding through the woods and the trees that provide a natural green canopy as campers and parents make their summer journey into childhood. Max is right. The camp itself will remain untouched, but everything surrounding it will scream of money. Of entitlement and prestige. Of adults and their toys.

"I can't let it happen, Lucy. I have to fight for it. If I don't, it will all disappear."

Max braces himself against the rail of the deck. His shoulders bow under the weight of what yesterday, today and tomorrow might bring. I know that feeling, of holding your breath, squaring yourself, waiting for the inevitable blow. I join him at the railing and lay a hand on his arm. It's cool to the touch and I feel his muscles rippling under my fingers. It's a man's arm, strong and steady, just like Max's heart.

He turns to face me, and the look in his eyes takes my breath away. I'm nearly as tall as he is, and we're standing nose to nose. But for the first time in my life, I feel fragile and achingly feminine. His eyes are warm and dark and questioning. A woman could get lost in those eyes. They hold honesty and truth and a yearning for something that remains unspoken. The warm night air hums with electricity. My breath catches and for one wild moment I actually believe Max is on the verge of taking me in his arms and...

"Help me?"

I stumble slightly, and he catches me. Not exactly the kiss I expected.

"I need help, Lucy. Your help. You've got the resources. You're the only one I can ask."

I feel the bottom drop out of my stomach. I wasn't wrong about Max. He does find me attractive. Seventy million dollars' worth of attractive.

Money goes a long way toward buying rose-colored glasses.

"You want me to give you a loan?" I say flatly.

"I don't want your money." His eyes are harder than glass marbles and his jaw clenches. "I want you to help me fight them."

The butterflies take over, lifting my heart into my throat. "Fight who?" I ask in a weak voice, though we both know the answer.

"We can't let them win. If they do and the Loon Lake development goes through, I'll lose the camp. It will be like losing LC all over again." A lost, lonely look sweeps across his face. "I know it's not fair, bringing you into this. But sometimes it feels overwhelming. Sometimes I feel like I'm in it all alone."

I'm helpless to stop myself. "You're not alone, Max. But I'm not sure exactly how I can help. I don't know much about any of this, just background information. Some of it's already been printed, some is confidential."

"I understand."

Does he? Journalists walk a fine line every day between reporting the news and creating the news. I don't intend to start questioning myself about where I draw the line. I wouldn't do that for anyone. Not even Max.

He claps his hands on my shoulders, looking me square in the eyes. "I'd never ask you to do anything that goes against what you believe. That's one thing people love about you, Lucy. You know who you are, and they respond to that. They trust you to tell them the truth."

If only he knew. How can people trust me when I barely trust myself? "I'll do what I can," I promise.

"You have no idea how much it means, knowing I have your support." He takes me in his arms. His breath is soft against my ear. "Thank you."

The smell of fresh air and pine needles cling to his shirt. I close my eyes and try to block out the thought of evergreens hugging the shoreline. Loon Lake has haunted a good deal of my life. Damned if I'll let it interfere with my love life.

"I had a feeling about you the night we met," he says softly.

"Good or bad?" I whisper.

"Definitely good." He tips my chin with one finger and bends his head toward mine. "But this is even better."

His lips are warm as they meet my own, his breath a sweet mixture of desire, spicy herbs and a faint taste of beer. Sparks jump between us.

I flinch and rub my lips with a smile. "Talk about an electrifying kiss."

Max laughs and pulls me closer. "Opposites attract. More proof we're meant for each other."

I eye his feet, clad in leather sandals. "Or maybe it means you ought to wear some other shoes next time you visit."

He pulls me back against him with a low laugh. "I could skip the shoes and show up barefoot."

"Shirt and shoes required," I murmur. It's difficult to talk with his lips showering me with delicious little kisses. I shiver in delight. "The Yacht Club does have certain standards to uphold."

"Screw the Yacht Club," he says softly in my ear. "What about Lucy Carter? Does she have certain standards?"

"Absolutely. Anything to keep out the riffraff."

He answers by kissing me again.

If I had any doubts this lottery business has screwed up my thinking, tonight is all the proof I need. I'm falling hard and fast for a man that lives and breathes Loon Lake. I've known all my life the lake is cursed. It has a way of twisting good into bad, life into death.

Nothing good can come of this. I must be crazy, promising to help Max in his quest to save the camp. It's doomed to end in disaster. Perhaps it will destroy us both.

"You're shivering," he says. "Want me to get you a sweater?"

"No, just hold me closer," I tell him. But even within the shelter of Max's arms, I can't stop trembling. Nothing will help. Not with Loon Lake waiting.

I can't shake the sudden certainty I've just sealed both our fates.

CHAPTER EIGHT

"Lucy, I am so glad you changed your mind and decided to join me. Isn't this just the perfect way to start the day?"

I open an eye and squint across the dimly lit room. I've had my doubts about Didi from the beginning, but if she thinks being pulled and pummeled in all directions like this is anything remotely resembling fun, the woman is in desperate need of therapy. She was vague on the phone last night when inviting me to join her at the Club for an early-morning session and I showed up not sure what to expect. Breakfast, at the very least. Certainly not to end up like I currently am, laying on a heated table, naked.

"You're right, it is perfect." Perfectly horrid, I think to myself.

She sighs happily from her spot on a nearby table. "I knew you would love it."

The soothing sound of oriental music floats across the room. I wriggle on my back, close my eyes, and order myself to relax. The light scent of lilac hangs in the air, thanks to Ron the masseur and the little spray bottle he keeps spritzing above the narrow table where I'm lying. I sneeze once, twice, as tiny droplets of lilac mist gently assault my nose.

Ron bows. "Sorry, miss. You turn now, on stomach, please."

I flip over and settle down as Ron methodically manipulates the towels draping my body. I feel like a mummy, swathed in hot towels from head to foot on a table warmed with heated water pads underneath even more towels. No wonder services at the Yacht Club are so expensive. A person could get rich around here merely owning the laundry concession.

Ron's hands in my hair work their way through the strands, pulling at the roots.

"Ouch, that hurts." Gingerly I put a hand to my head, which is tender and greasy. Even my hair has been shown no mercy, subjected to Ron's heated massage oil.

"You no like, miss?"

"Not in my hair." What I'd like to do is escape to the locker room and shower area where I surrendered my clothes. The room was stocked with little wicker baskets brimming with designer lotions, deodorant, and toothpaste. Hopefully shampoo is also included.

I shut my eyes as Ron's hands stroke the length of my legs, back, and each of my arms. Every minute is sheer torture. I hate massages. I will never do this again. How can women enjoy this? As usual, I'm in a minority of one.

Something hot and hard hits my shoulder. "What the—?" I bolt upright, managing to grab my towel and cover myself before I embarrass us both. "What are you doing?"

"Hot rocks." Ron shuffles around to face me and holds up two stones smaller than my fists. "Very nice. I rub..." He makes quick circular motions. "All over your body. Feels good."

"Feels hot," I correct him. "Sorry, thanks anyway, but no hot rocks for this girl today." I swing my feet over the side and search with my toes for the rubber sandals he gave me when I surrendered my shoes. Ron bows low and discreetly holds the thick terrycloth bathrobe open. I wrap myself in it and cinch the belt tight.

"Done so soon?" Across the room, Didi opens one eye but doesn't budge.

"I'm going to hit the shower." And scrub the gooey gunk out of my hair.

"Take your time. I won't be long." Her voice isn't convincing.

Fifteen minutes later I hit the salon with squeaky-clean hair and an appetite screaming for coffee and breakfast. The morning has been a monumental waste of time, and given the threatening skies outside, the day doesn't show signs of improving. So much for soaking up sunshine. Maybe this would be a good day to spend doing research in the public library. I need to bring myself up to speed on PUDs and current zoning law if I intend to make good on my promise to Max.

Didi is still a no-show. I perch on the edge of an impossibly soft velveteen chaise lounge to wait. Everything about the salon whispers elegance, thanks to a team of interior designers who have made it their life mission to find just the right furniture in just the right shade of pale moss green. Antique pink tea roses blossom in potbellied vases gilded with gold. Lush carpet so thick underfoot that, for a brief moment, I actually consider kicking off my shoes and going barefoot.

Who am I kidding? This is the Yacht Club and my toenails aren't polished.

"There you are." Didi breezes into the salon. "I adore morning massages."

"Let's have breakfast," I say as she air-kisses my cheek. "I'm hungry."

Her green eyes soften. "You should have said something sooner. Run along and find us a table." She pushes me toward the dining room.

I hang back. "I thought we were having breakfast together."

"We are, and we will. But my nails need a little touch-up." Didi waves a hand toward the manicure area just off the salon. "I'll be ten minutes, tops. Order me an orange juice and a croissant."

I glance at the exit, then the salon's cash register in plain view.

"It's already taken care of," she says with a smile.

She paid for my massage? I don't particularly relish the thought of being in Didi's debt. "Are you sure?"

"Lucy, you worry far too much." She cuts me off with a look that tells me people do not regularly—if ever—dare to question Didi. "This is your day. I suggest you relax and enjoy it. You deserve it."

But I haven't done anything to deserve it. Nothing at all. Three weeks' worth of nothing, to be precise. If this is how the rich and famous live their lives—by perfecting the art of doing nothing—I might want to rethink my definition of happiness.

"Thank you."

"No worries. That's what friends are for." She pats my arm and heads for the salon.

The restaurant is crowded for a weekday morning, but the hostess has an instant smile for me. I'm beginning to learn that being an *Almost-Member* of the Club has its rewards. She seats me at a cozy banquette table. A waitress approaches before I even have a chance to scan the menu. I glance up, then do a quick double take.

"April?" I take a closer look at the familiar face behind the coffee pot. "Hi. I didn't know you worked at the Club."

My former classmate pours my coffee with a tight smile. "I've been here a few years." She nods at the table. "The cream and sugar are right there." Her voice is chilly in the sun-splashed room. "Are you ready to order?"

Her no-nonsense look and let's-get-down-to-business tone catch me by surprise. Not at all what I expected from one of the chattiest girls in high school. I'd been waiting for a cheery hi-how-are-you-it's-been-awhile, followed by a wow-I-hear-you-won-the-lottery-that's-wonderful-news.

She shifts on her feet. "I can come back if you need a few minutes."

"I'm all set." I hand her the menu, sight unseen. "Scrambled eggs and toast, please."

"I'm sorry, but we don't serve toast."

"Excuse me?" Grandma taught me it is rude to stare, but I can't help myself. What kind of a restaurant doesn't offer its customers toast for breakfast?

"We have a nice basket of freshly baked muffins and rolls. I'll bring one out. We also have croissants. Our English muffins are quite good, too."

I take a deep breath. This place definitely needs to revamp its menu. I'm not much of a cook, but even my kitchen has a few loaves of bread. "Muffins will be fine. And I have a friend joining me. She'd like the croissants. Plus, two orange juices, please," I add, followed by a polite smile. *Kill them with kindness*, Grandma always said. The no-toast policy isn't April's fault, but she definitely needs to do something about that semi-scowl plastered across her face.

I sink back in the cushions and watch my former classmate work the room with her coffee pot, remembering how I always envied April... especially the day I interviewed her for the school newspaper after she was crowned homecoming queen. I thought she was so daring, with those short little skirts, brassy attitude, and the way she had of flirting with the boys. Today she's a picture of absolute decorum in a slim black skirt and trim white blouse. Times certainly have changed.

Or maybe not. I catch the sound of the same low, throaty laugh I remember from high school. It echoes through the room as she makes a brief stop at a table of men finishing their breakfasts. Their heads swing in unison as April and her coffee pot stroll away, followed by their stares.

I stare, too. One of the men is Charles Kendall.

"Whatever possessed you to let them seat you back here?" Didi sinks down beside me in a breathless rush and a not-so-pretty pout. "What a horrid table."

My brain races to multitask as I try to keep up with Didi while my eyes, ears, and brain are focusing on Charles. What is he doing here at the Club? Last I knew, he wasn't a member.

"You don't like this table?" I murmur.

"If you prefer sitting in no-man's-land, it's perfect."

But as far as I'm concerned, this table *is* perfect... for Charles-watching, that is. Four other gentlemen are with him. *Turn around and let me see your faces*, I send the silent message zinging across the room. Unfortunately, mental telepathy has never been my strong suit. They just keep eating and talking.

"You have to learn to be more assertive," Didi says as she laces her coffee with a generous amount of cream. "You're a little too nice for your own good. People will take advantage if you're not careful. But don't you dare let them get away with it. Remember, soon you'll be a member of the Club. These people work for you. Don't let them seat you in the back of the room. Next time, tell them you want a table at the window. Tell them you *insist*."

"I'll try," I promise, sneaking another glance over her shoulder. Charles and his friends are finally on their feet, giving me a good view of all five men. While I don't recognize the fifth man, something about him looks vaguely familiar. I watch as he picks up the tab, slaps Charles on the shoulder, and glad-hands the other three men. Men who live and work in James Bay. Men who are all members of the Bay Township planning commission.

What business could Charles Kendall possibly have with any of them?

"Hello? Lucy?" Didi waves a hand in my face. "Are you still with me?"

"Sorry." I muster up a polite smile and shrink back into the plush cushions of the velveteen banquette as Charles and his friends stroll out the door.

"Did you even hear what I said?" she demands. "Never let them seat you in the back of the room again. If all else fails, give them my name. They know who I am. They have their instructions."

I breathe easier as the staff briskly clears the table where Charles and his friends were sitting. A prime spot. Even Didi would approve.

"If you want to move, I can call the—"

"It's too late now," she said with a sniff as our food approaches. "We might as well stay where we are. Besides, there's no one interesting here this morning."

I nod meekly. Didi's correct. Charles and his cohorts are already gone.

An older waitress with a quiet smile and quieter demeanor serves our breakfasts. My friend April is nowhere to be seen. I sigh and chalk it up to human nature. Perhaps she decided any tip I might leave isn't worth the humiliation of having to refill my coffee cup.

"Aren't you working today?" I ask Didi.

"I'm working right now." She splits her croissant and spreads a thin layer of orange marmalade inside the flaky crust. "It's called networking. You never know when or where you'll meet someone. I sold a house one day while I was having a manicure. And that, Lucy dear, is how deals are made."

I lift my napkin, dab my lips, cover my smile. Leave it to Didi to make million-dollar deals over bottles of Baby Doll Pink or Moonlit Mauve.

"If you want to be successful, you have to look successful," she continues. "I owe it to my clients. When you look good, you feel good. People naturally like you if you like yourself. It's a proven psychological principle."

Funny, I've always liked myself, and I've never had a manicure. Up until now, my fingernails wore ink stains rather than polish. And as for my cuticles? I curl my fingers around my coffee cup. My days in the newspaper business might be over, but I've no desire to join the ranks of women who live for the newest shade of Ravishing Red. There's got to be more to life.

"You're too hard on yourself. You need to learn how to relax. Pamper yourself a little." Didi's laugh tinkles against the sparkling clean windows reflecting the Yacht Club harbor. "You should make this a weekly treat. After all, you'll soon be a member of the Club."

"I'll think about it." Though I don't intend to spend much time on the subject. The last thing I need is to be pummeled and pushed and subjected to hot rocks. I'll heat up my own and save myself some money.

"You have so much to learn." She peers at me over her coffee cup. "Has anyone mentioned your skin tone? It's a little uneven under the tan. A good concealer would do wonders. And then there's your hair…"

I touch a hand to my head. "What's wrong with my hair?"

"Nothing. Absolutely nothing." She has the courtesy to smile. "It's just that it's so… so brown."

I shift on the bench. She makes it sound like brown hair is a bad thing.

"Have you ever considered having it highlighted? Perhaps a simple shade of auburn…"

"You want me to dye my hair red?" I sit back, horrified. For the first time in months, I'm glad Grandma isn't around. If she was in her right mind and could hear Didi, guaranteed she'd throw one big hissy fit.

"We should get you to a stylist. A professional can help bring out the best *you* inside."

I put down my coffee cup and spread my hands on the table. Who cares what my cuticles look like? This is my skin. My hair. My life. "I don't think—"

"I'll call Renaud's. I'm sure Jackie will be able to fit you in." Her words are more a command than a suggestion. "You will absolutely love Jackie. The woman works miracles."

I don't have time for miraculous interventions. The library and my research beckon. The fact that I spotted Charles enjoying a leisurely breakfast on a weekday morning with three of the five Bay Township commissioners doesn't sit right with me. None of them are members of the Club. And who was that fifth gentleman at the table with them, the one who looked vaguely familiar? That's an intriguing thought. Even more intriguing is contemplating what they were discussing. Somehow I doubt it had anything to do with Yacht Club boat slips.

Didi pops the last of her croissant into her mouth and delicately dabs away the crumbs. "I didn't invite you here to chat about your skin. We have more important things to discuss."

"We do?"

"Richard and I belong to a small group of local investors. One of them is going through a nasty divorce and has to divest his interest in the group. Naturally, I thought of you right away. It's the perfect opportunity: a chance to make some serious money. That is, if you're interested in investing."

I eye her carefully. "What kind of investment?"

"Real estate. Is there anything else?" Didi smiles. "Businesses come and go, but they'll never make more land. It's the best investment money can buy. You have the money. You should put it to work."

I rub my forehead. "I don't know. I planned to sit tight for a while until I figured out what to do."

She shrugs. "I just thought you might be interested. There's virtually no risk. Our manager takes care of everything."

"You have a manager?" Having and spending money is one thing, but managing it properly is a totally different matter. I've never had a head for business, and I don't intend to start now. The lottery money is cumbersome enough, even with Sam watching over it. Overseeing investments isn't something I'm keen on buying into.

"Our group portfolio is quite diverse," she continues. "We hold a few condos here at the Club, as well as some downtown properties and some local investments. The rest is involved in downstate developments, though don't quote me on that. Our manager handles the details. Bottom line, it's proved very lucrative for Richard and me. We have a sizeable investment."

"You buy and sell real estate?"

"Not all the listings are for sale. We offer rental properties, too. Those units turn a very nice income. Again, our investment manager takes care of everything. You don't need to worry about how or where it's being handled. Once you make the initial investment, you merely sit back and watch your bank account grow."

"Exactly how much money are you talking about?" Sam will want the details.

"That's entirely up to you." She pushes away her plate and dabs her lips with the linen napkin. "Most of us have invested at least one million dollars. Some have contributed a little less and some a little more."

"One million dollars?" I suck in a sharp breath that whistles between my teeth as I sign for the breakfast tab. "That's a lot of money."

"You paid more than that for your condo." A smile curves around her lips and she pats my hand. "By the way, thank you for breakfast."

I slide from my seat and follow her out of the restaurant. Didi is full of surprises this morning. First she has me sprawled on a masseuse table, naked, and now she's eyeing my bank account. No doubt about it, the woman lives and breathes money. She earned a hefty seven-percent commission when I purchased the condo. Still, I can't begrudge her the money. I love the place... even if I do tiptoe through the rooms.

Black thunderclouds and pelting rain greet us as we step outside. We huddle together under the portico as the valet runs for Didi's car.

"So?" She throws me an inquisitive look. "What do I tell our group? Are you interested in joining?"

"Let me think about it for a few days." I'm not stupid. The Internet is filled with horror stories about lottery winners that blew their winnings in one fell swoop. My money won't last if I keep up the spending. Not that I begrudge the Rosary Altar Society ladies or the donation I made of a new MRI machine when the hospital came begging. Or the new plasma TV and popcorn machine at Whispering Pines, either. But sooner or later, I have to start saying *no*.

I've barely said *yes* to myself.

"Don't wait too long, or you'll lose the opportunity." Didi laughs and squeezes my arm. "Not to mention, the returns can be very nice." She nods as the valet returns with her car. "I'm driving one."

"Your Mercedes?"

"What else is money for, except to make life more pleasant?" A faint blend of lilacs and roses lingers in the rain-soaked air as Didi's cheek touches my own. "We'll be in touch."

She tucks herself behind the wheel of the luxury sedan. I catch a colorful glimpse of Caribbean Coral as she throws me a quick wave. "Don't forget about Renaud's," she calls through the open window. "Tell Jackie I sent you."

I mull her words as she pulls away. For once, something Didi's said actually makes sense. Rental units turn a healthy income. Maybe I should think about becoming a landlord myself. Grandma's house is just sitting there empty. I pulled it off the market when I won the lottery. But with the neighborhood in transition, maybe now is the perfect time to get into the real estate game. Grandma will never go back, and neither will I. Still, I'm reluctant to let the place go, even though it's not home anymore. No place is.

I shove down the thought. That's not true. I do have a home. A very nice home. A nice *big* home. Four thousand square feet of condo.

The rain comes down in sheets as the valet chugs up in my VW bug and holds open the door. I smile and slip him a five-dollar bill. He reminds me of someone who might be interested in Grandma's house. People need a decent place to live, and her house would be the perfect spot. It was good enough for Grandma. It would be good enough for someone like him. Grandma never complained. Well, not much. Besides, how much money does someone make shuttling cars back and forth from the parking lot? It can't be much. I bet he'd be grateful someone cares enough to provide him with a nice place to live.

The windshield wipers slap full speed as I pull into traffic. My mind is made up. When I get home, I'm calling Didi. She'll know the name of a good local contractor who can fix up Grandma's house without eating up all my profits. As Didi said, rental income is a good thing for all parties concerned. I'll be giving someone a decent place to live while earning a nice return on my investment.

Grandma's old house, an investment property. I can't stop grinning as I drive toward the library. Even the rain-soaked streets can't dampen my spirits. *Lucy Carter, Landlord*. It has a nice ring to it. Grandma would be proud of me.

Five minutes later, the heavens have opened up and the rain beats down with the strength of something akin to Noah's flood. Rivers of water gush through the street. I've got no choice but to wait it out. Reluctantly, I pull over to the curb. It's hot and steamy inside the car. I crack the vent window and peer through the sheets of rain pelting the windshield. The storm has wrought considerable damage in just the short time since I left the Club. Things are blown around, branches litter the streets. Some poor soul, caught in the downpour without an umbrella, struggles down the sidewalk just a yard or two away. She heads for the intersection where a traffic light swings like a crazed pendulum. I watch as she tries to navigate the swirling waters. The crosswalk is flooded, and the gutters churn with ankle-deep water. She'll be drenched before she makes it to the other side. *If* she makes it to the other side.

No one deserves to be caught out in weather like this.

Not even Lila.

My heart pounds in my ears. It takes another second or two before my hand finally hits the horn. "Get in," I shout through the open window. "I'll give you a ride."

Her hand is on the door, but Lila doesn't move. "Are you sure? I don't want to put you out."

"Get in the car, would you? You're letting in all the rain."

A faint, not-unpleasant scent of citrus mingles with the smell of wet clothes as she struggles into her seat. I resist the urge to crack the window further. Am I crazy? Why did I offer her a ride? Why didn't I just sit here and let her walk by? No hassle for me. No problem. So much simpler.

But *keep it simple* has never been my style. Making things difficult for myself seems to be my motto. Am I ever going to learn?

The sheets of rain hit with violent force and a clap of thunder rocks the air. Jagged lightning streaks across the sky, followed by resounding thunderous booms that rumble through the street and the car.

"That was close," Lila says with a shaky laugh.

"I hate thunderstorms," I mutter. My hair feels like it's standing on end. I cringe and press against my seat as vivid sheets of lightning shoot across the sky.

"We're safe enough in the car," she says in a quivering voice.

That's debatable. I won't feel safe until the seat beside me is empty.

"Where are you headed?" I grip the wheel in grim determination. As soon as the rain lets up, we are out of here.

"To the grocery store where I work. My shift starts…" She glances at her watch and I watch her face fall. "Ten minutes from now."

154

"We'll make it." I peer up at the sky and send a silent prayer zinging up to heaven. *Please make this rain stop.* Grandma taught me we're not supposed to pray for selfish things, but I'm hoping God will understand. With Lila close in the seat beside me, my *Gimme-Prayer* qualifies under the category of an emergency.

"Thank you for rescuing me." She flashes a quick smile. "The grocery isn't far and I always walk to work. I suppose I should have listened to the weatherman's warning. Now I'm a mess." She glances around at the wet puddles on the floor and upholstery, and her face falls. "Look what I've done to your car. I'm sorry."

I shrug. "Don't worry about it."

She finger-combs her hair. "Your father had a car like this when we were dating."

My mouth tightens in a thin line. Grandma used to talk about my dad's VW, but I never figured Lila into the equation, much less put her in the front seat.

And if she dares say one word about the back seat...

"It was bright orange," she muses. "And it had a tricky starter, if I remember correctly. He used to tinker with it and cuss like crazy."

My foot itches to hit the gas. If we sit here much longer, I'll be crazy, too. Max has no idea how lucky he is, despite his *my-mother-died-when-I-was-born* guilt-inducing scenario. At least he's able to pick and choose a fantasy mother of his own making. I don't have the same luxury. Lila is alive and well, sitting right beside me, chattering away like a squirrel who's unearthed a buried trove of long-forgotten peanuts. I've got better things to do than sit around listening to her dusted-off memories, courtesy of some alcohol-induced fog. Grandma filled me in long ago

155

on our family history. I don't need Lila around, messing with the details.

She's already messed up enough of my life.

"He finally traded it in for a used blue Mustang the year after we got married. Of course, a new car would have been nice, but we never had much money."

Money. I knew she'd eventually bring up the subject, it was just a question of when. Well, if she thinks I'm just going to sit here and listen to her beg me for a handout, she's got another think coming. The water swirls and rushes through the street as I put the car in drive and edge away from the curb.

"We can sit here awhile longer." Lila hesitates. "I don't mind if I'm a little late."

And blame me when she gets fired? No thanks. Not my problem.

The windshield wipers barely beat back the rain. It isn't even noon but it might as well be night.

"Are you sure it's safe to drive?"

Her questioning tone sets my nerves on edge. I jam my foot on the gas and whip down the street. What business does she have, telling me how to drive? She doesn't even have a driver's license or own a car. The State of Michigan revokes driver's licenses for drunks.

I drive faster, eager to get her to the store. We fly through puddles, spraying water. Suddenly the car goes into a nauseating spin and we start to hydroplane. I whip the wheel but I've lost control. There's nothing I can do but watch in dizzy horror as the same trees fly past us—once, twice, three times.

"Look out!" Lila throws herself toward me.

We slam headlong into a tree.

CHAPTER NINE

Kris and I huddle together under her umbrella. Flashing emergency lights reflect vivid red zigzags against the wet pavement as the ambulance crew loads Lila on the gurney.

"Thank God you're okay," Kris repeats for the umpteenth time. "We heard on the scanner that the National Weather Service reported a possible tornado touching down not far from town. You're very lucky."

Kris has it wrong. I'm not the lucky one. Lila is. She's lucky to be alive. I can't stop trembling as I view the ruins of my car. The passenger side is completely smashed in. My poor little VW is headed for the scrap pile, but thank God Lila is headed for the hospital. No matter what differences lay between us, I never could have lived with myself if my rash behavior cost my mother her life.

My mother.

Like it or not, Lila is family.

I squeeze Kris's arm as the rain pelts against us. "Thanks again for coming. I don't know what I'd do without you."

"Do you honestly think I'd let you go through something like this alone? When we heard the ambulance call come across the scanner, Charles told me to sit still, that I was on deadline. But I told him to screw it, that I was going to be with you." She grins. "Let him finish the damn story."

"How did you know it was me in the accident?"

"How many old VWs do you think there are in this town?" she answers with a cheeky grin.

Despite all that's happened, my spirits inch up a notch. I am blessed to have such a friend.

"What did they say about your head?" Her gaze darts to the scrape at the top of my forehead.

"I'm fine. I'll live." No blood involved, though at first I was woozy. Maybe it was the shock of hearing Lila's moans and seeing my car twisted at a crazy angle. I take a deep breath. The hot humid air is still heavy with rain. I shake my head. "I still can't believe I walked away from this and that I'm okay." I don't deserve it.

"What about your mom?"

"I don't know. It took a while to get her out of the car." My gut twists as I replay the scenario over and over in my head, and I blink back hot tears that spring from nowhere. I refuse to cry. This is no time for tears. This is a time to be strong. But there's no excuse for what I did. No matter how angry I was with her, I should have sat there and let Lila rattle on as we waited for the storm to blow over. Instead, like a fool, I took off and churned up a storm of my own. One rash act on my part, and I nearly blew both our worlds apart.

One of the EMTs approaches. He's sweating, I'm shivering.

"We're leaving for the hospital."

Kris and I exchange glances. "I'll take you," she volunteers.

I hesitate. For some reason I don't understand, I don't want to be separated from Lila. "Would it be okay if I rode in the ambulance with her?"

He shrugs. "You can ride in the back."

"Are you sure you want to do that?" Kris says.

She sounds and looks worried, and I give her a little hug. "I'll be fine. Go back to work and finish your story."

"Call if you need anything." She squeezes my arm. "I'll swing by once I finish and take you home."

They've already loaded Lila into the ambulance. I climb in the back, take a seat on the bench beside her gurney. I swallow hard. I always thought my first time in an ambulance would be a ride-along for reporting purposes, not something personal like this. I wince at the sight of the IV line hooked up to Lila's arm. Her eyes are closed. Even if I wanted to hold her hand, it's tucked under a blanket.

Lila grimaces as we pull away from the curb and bounce along the side streets, but she never cries out. Not even when we reach the hospital and they roll her into the ER. The bright lights are blinding, and the horrible astringent smell turns my stomach. I stand there, feeling helpless, quickly answering questions, watching Lila as they examine her. And then she is gone, on her way to x-ray before I can say *Good-bye. Good luck. I'm so sorry.*

A hefty nurse sails into the waiting room adjacent to the ER staffing desk. "You're next."

I shake my head. "I'm fine. The ambulance crew already checked me out."

She rolls her eyes. "You should be seen by a doctor. Scale of one to ten, how's the pain?"

"About a one-point-five, I guess," I say. "I'll be fine." But it's far from the truth. My heart is breaking. Seeing Lila whisked away to x-ray rated a full-blown ten.

"Are you refusing treatment?" She shoots me a do-you-really-want-to-argue-with-me-because-we-both-know-who's-going-to-win look. Obviously she aced nursing school. Plus, she's got at least one hundred pounds on me.

"Lucy? What are you doing here?"

The sight of Father Greg Kozminski strolling through the waiting room is comforting beyond words. He claps a hand on my shoulder as his eyes stray to my forehead. "Are you all right?"

The nurse scowls and points a finger at me. "You stay put. The doctor will want to see you." She huffs out of the room.

"What happened?" Father Greg asks.

Somehow I manage to sob out the story of our accident and Lila's injuries without breaking into tears.

"Sure you're all right?"

"My head does hurt, but only a bit," I admit. Mostly it's my heart and soul that feel out of whack. No medicine they give me can take away the guilty feeling that my stubbornness could have killed us both.

"Any word about your mother?"

"She's down in x-ray. I'm waiting for the doctor."

"Feel like some company?"

The compassion in his voice threatens to bring on the tears. I sniff them away. "I'd like that."

"How about we go somewhere more comfortable?" He glances at his watch. "I just finished my hospital sick calls.

Come on, I'll buy you lunch. The cafeteria is just down the hall. They'll find you."

I trail him out of the waiting room. Having someone else take charge is a blessing I hadn't counted on. Especially when that someone is wearing a Roman collar and clutching a prayer book.

Lunch is almost over and the cafeteria is nearly empty. Father Greg orders a cheeseburger. My stomach does a flip-flop at the sight and smell of the greasy burger as he slides it on his tray.

"I'm not hungry."

"How about some soup?" he suggests. "It would do you good to eat. Shirley here makes the best soup in town."

The short lady with the hairnet behind the counter waves a serving spoon at him. "Shush, Father, you know it's a sin to be telling lies."

My legs feel like mush, and I don't have the energy to argue. Plus, the vegetable soup looks thick and homemade, just like Grandma used to make. "All right."

Shirley ladles the rich, steaming broth into a deep bowl and hands it to me with some crackers and a smile. "Enjoy."

We head for a table by the window. The rain has stopped and the sky is a steely gray that looks more like October than July. Waves beat against the shore and whitecaps crash against the break wall guarding the harbor entrance. The beach is empty.

I nibble the edge of a saltine. "Thanks for lunch."

"My pleasure." Father Greg decorates his burger with catsup and the trimmings. "Besides, I think I'm the one who should be thanking you. Connie phoned yesterday and told me about your donation for the new altar vestments. That was very generous of you, Lucy."

I bow my head, praying that the steam from the hot soup will cover the flush heating my cheeks. "She shouldn't have told you. I wanted to stay anonymous."

"I don't think Connie could have kept that secret if her life depended on it," he says with a quick smile. "She's been lobbying for weeks to get someone to kick in enough money to purchase those vestments in time for Advent. Thanks to you, we're set."

"All I did was write a check," I mumble. "Anyone could do that."

"But no one else did," he says with a smile, then bows his head and clasps his hands. "Shall we pray?"

I drop the half-eaten saltine I've been nibbling as Father Greg blesses our food. It's a quick prayer. Our priest has an appetite. He takes a big bite out of his burger. I drag my spoon through the thick soup.

"I never meant for this to happen," I hear myself suddenly saying. "It was an accident. It was raining, and the car went into a skid, and…"

He glances up in surprise. "No one blames you."

"But I am to blame, Father. It was my fault." I swallow hard. "I felt sorry for her. It was raining hard, and she was wet. But after she got in the car and we were sitting there, then she started talking about my father and bringing up things from the past. Things I didn't want to hear. I just wanted her out of my car. I wanted to get her to work, to get her far away from me. I shouldn't have done it. I knew it wasn't safe to drive. It was still raining really hard, but I didn't care. I was mad. My foot hit the gas and then the car spun out and then…"

I hang my head, ashamed, afraid to admit the fear sticking in my throat. "What if she's badly hurt? What if—"

The *What If* is beyond comprehension.

"She never should have come back to James Bay. This never would have happened if she'd stayed away," I blurt out. "I don't want her back in my life. I don't need her."

Father Greg puts down his burger, wipes his mouth, sits back in his chair. His gray eyes are sober and serious. "Did you ever stop to think that maybe she needs you?"

Me? Or my money?

I don't dare voice the thought out loud. Father Greg and Lila are friends, and he might take offense. Bad enough Lila and I are barely on speaking terms. I don't need a priest as an enemy.

"She's a gentle soul, Lucy, with a gentle spirit."

"With all due respect, Father Greg, are we talking about the same person?"

His eyebrows lift. "Sounds like you and Lila have some communication issues."

"Communication issues? That's an understatement. We don't even speak the same language." The language Lila values probably involves a bank book with her name on it, and a dollar sign with some numbers followed by lots of zeroes.

"There's one language everyone understands," he says. "The language of the heart."

His words cut deep but my heart toughens. Father Greg has no idea what my life was like. Grandma took care of me, not Lila. What kind of mother dumps her own child? It was hard, knowing she'd abandoned me, that she was out there somewhere, that she didn't care. "She's not exactly Mother of the Year."

"I'm sure Lila agrees with you, from everything she's told me." He rescues his burger from his plate and calmly resumes eating.

Suddenly I am furious. With Lila, with Father Greg, but mostly with myself. Grandma always said I was stubborn and bullheaded whenever I was mad, and she was right. Just look where it's brought me. If I hadn't reacted so fast, I wouldn't be sitting in a hospital cafeteria lunching with a priest. I'd be at the library doing research for Max. And Lila would be at the grocery store ringing up orders.

"Why are you trying to make her out to be such a saint?" I ask him.

"I don't remember saying Lila was a saint." His mouth wears a hint of a smile and a bit of catsup. He dabs it away with a napkin.

"Naturally you'd take her side. The two of you are friends." My head is beginning to throb and I rub my forehead with the heel of my hand. I shouldn't argue with him. Father Greg is a priest. He has God on his side.

"We all have our personal demons. I know I do, and I assume you do, too—not that I'm trying to take your inventory. Why should Lila be any different? She's no better or worse than any of us. She's simply trying to do the best she can. You might want to cut her a little slack." He eyes me across the table. "Have you ever heard me talk about my Uncle Jerry? I mention him every now and then at Mass."

"Maybe," I say uneasily. "I don't remember." I haven't been in church for weeks. Months. At the rate I'm going, it could end up years.

"Jerry was my mother's baby brother. He came to live at our house after my grandmother died. I was probably about six years old then, and Jerry was eight years older than me. We went to the same catholic school. I was in first grade and Jerry was in high school. My mother made him walk me to school every day. I would have been better off walking alone. Jerry took my lunch money and bought himself cigarettes. He threatened to beat me up if I told my mother. Of course, I never did. I was too scared."

I hang on his words. I can't imagine Father Greg afraid of anyone. He's well over six feet tall and towers over most people, including me. He's the kind of man who fights for what's right. He's a champion for those who are lonely, afraid, beaten down.

Maybe he learned to be their champion because he was beaten down himself?

"The longer Jerry lived with us, the more I hated him," he continues in an easy voice. "As far as I was concerned, he was going straight to hell. And well deserved, I might add."

I blink hard and straighten in the plastic chair. A priest, confessing to sitting in judgment of people like everybody else? Maybe there's more to Father Greg than that Roman collar around his neck.

"The nuns rued the day my mother enrolled him in our school. Jerry ran with a wild crowd. He had a couple of minor skirmishes with the law. Petty stuff... loitering, breaking curfew. But it was enough to break my mother's heart. One day I saw him lifting money from her purse." His eyes narrow. "What kind of man steals from his own sister? She had a hell of a time trying to keep him under control and in school. But all of that changed his senior year. Two months before graduation, Jerry's past caught up with him."

My spoon halts midway to my mouth.

"He was out with a girl, a nice girl from school who knew better than to hang around with a guy like him. It was late at night. Jerry was speeding."

Suddenly I have a bad feeling about where this story is headed. "Alcohol?"

"Nope, he never touched the stuff. He was just being Jerry, trying to show off. He took a curve too fast, they crested a hill, and the car went airborne. The girl wasn't wearing a seatbelt, and she was thrown from the car. They pronounced her dead at the scene. She never had a chance."

My spoon clatters as it hits the table. "What about Jerry?"

Father Greg shakes his head. "He was arrested for vehicular manslaughter. He walked away in handcuffs, without a scratch on him. Eventually Jerry ended up pleading guilty. He did eighteen months in the county jail." He sits back in his chair, pushes his plate aside. "Turns out, jail was the best thing that could have happened to him. God offered him a chance to turn his life around by putting him exactly where he needed to be.

"Jerry was in jail the day his classmates graduated. The girl's parents weren't at the ceremony, either. They chose to spend the time with Jerry. He was having a rough time of it, coming face to face with himself. *Why her and not me*, he asked anybody that would listen—including me. Sitting in jail, Jerry had lots of time to think. And lots of people to love him. Including my mother. Including the girl's parents. It changed his life. He earned his GED while he was in jail, and he planned to go to college after he was released. He wanted to work with high school kids and try to help them so they wouldn't make the same mistakes he did."

"What's he's doing now?"

"He's dead." Father Greg's face sobers. "Leukemia. Jerry got sick shortly before his release from jail. He died six months later. He never had a chance to work with those kids."

I swallow hard. "That's horrible. It's so unfair."

"No one ever said life was fair," he gently counters. "Jerry lived his life the way he wanted, but he died the way he wanted, too. Reconciled with God, reconciled with his family. He taught me a lot, Lucy, especially from the way he died. He asked for forgiveness for what he'd done, from the people he'd hurt. The girl's family. My mother. Even me."

He sighs, then smiles, but it's a sad smile, a bittersweet smile, of what is gone and will never be again.

"My mother was with him at the end. She was holding his hand as he took his last breath and went home to God. I was there, too. It was one of the greatest blessings and most powerful moments in my life. Jerry turning his life around, then watching him die, surrounded by people who loved him and being able to witness that profound healing love he found through the grace of God."

He pauses, swallows. "Uncle Jerry is why I became a priest."

My eyes hit the table and my heart feels as if it's been split in two. It's a tragic story, a terrible tragedy for all involved. But it is Father Greg's story, not mine. And Lila is not Uncle Jerry.

"Sorry, I didn't mean for this to turn into a sermon," he says. "But all of us have family members we're not especially proud of. For you, it's your mom. For me, it was my Uncle Jerry. But who are we to question the wisdom of God? Who knows why things happen?"

"Certainly not me," I mumble. Why is he telling me this? What does Father Greg expect me to do? Throw my arms around Lila? Bless her? Forgive her? I don't want her to die, but I'm not looking for a reconciliation. I want her out of my life. I want things the way they used to be. Is that so much to ask?

If Lila sues me for causing the accident, I'll pay her off by writing a check. But in a way, that feels wrong. It feels like I'd be taking the easy way out.

And I have a sinking feeling it will take more than donations to the church to make things right between me and God.

Father Greg's gray eyes pool with compassion. "Don't be too hard on your mom. She loves you very much."

A doctor in a white lab coat approaches our table. "Lucy Carter?"

I swallow hard over the unsmiling face, the solemn tone. Am I ready for news that will not be good? I look to Father Greg, whose face is grave, but his nod is reassuring. Despite his not-meant-to-be-a-sermon, I'm suddenly very glad for his company.

"Yes, that's me."

"I'm Dr. Singer. You're listed as Lila Carter's emergency contact and next of kin."

My heart catches in my throat. Lila listed me as her next of kin?

The doctor eyes me with a keen look and I wonder if he can see right through me. I am not the typical anxious daughter, one that weeps and wails and worries over her mother. Lila and I have never pretended between ourselves. Why should I pretend for her doctor?

"She has a slight concussion. We're keeping her overnight for observation."

"Is she going to be all right?" I ask. Lila was white as the sheet covering her slender frame when they wheeled her down to x-ray.

"Her ribs are badly bruised, but the radiologist didn't see any breaks. We'll fix her up with a rib protector."

I hesitate. "But what if there is a break?"

He shrugs off my concerns. "Bruises, breaks, we treat them the same. She can wear the protector until she feels better, but she'll recover. That ankle of hers is a different matter. It's a clean break, but she needs to stay off her feet until the swelling goes down. Then we'll cast it."

Dr. Singer flips the chart shut with a pointed stare for me. "Does she live with you?"

I have a bad feeling about this. "She has her own apartment."

"She won't be able to manage on her own," he warns. "You'll have to make other arrangements."

I feel my face blanch as our conversation takes an unexpected direction.

Straight down the road to my condo at the Yacht Club.

"Check with the nurses when you're finished with lunch. They should have your mother checked into a room by then." Dr. Singer turns and strolls away.

"Lucy, you look a little funny. You okay?"

"I'm fine." Somehow I manage a brave smile for Father Greg, despite the fact that it feels like my world has been flipped upside down. Wherever I landed, I'm not in Kansas anymore. I stare out the window over the lake. At this point, I wouldn't be surprised to see winged monkeys headed my way or ominous words in black smoke scrawled across the sky.

Surrender, Lucy.

I feel like surrendering. I feel like laying my head down on the table and crying. But tears won't solve anything. They'll only make my eyes puffy and turn my nose an ugly red. Tears won't make the problem go away.

A problem that will soon be living with me.

I manage a deep breath and shudder. The effort costs me. My ribs hurt like hell, but I need all the oxygen I can get.

Father Greg reaches out and squeezes my hand. "Let's get you back to the ER. Might be a good idea to have them take a couple x-rays of your ribs. Maybe you need one of those rib protectors, too."

I think about what the doctor said. Then I think about Lila living in my condo, twenty-four seven.

Forget the rib protector. I need something to safeguard my heart.

How does she do it? Even flat in a hospital bed, Lila is beautiful. Her short blond hair frames the pillow and her cheeks are dusted with the perfect blend of pain and prettiness done up in a rosy hue. If it weren't for the all-too-real anguish pinching her face, I'd think I'd stumbled upon a room with an actress filming an advertisement for regional hospital health care.

"Did the doctor talk to you?" I take a seat at her bedside.

"He said I was lucky I only broke my ankle."

Guilt rushes through me. "You're being released tomorrow and he doesn't want you staying alone." I take a deep breath. "He thinks it's a good idea that you come home with me."

"He mentioned that." Her eyes are wary. "And you? Do you think it's a good idea?"

"I do." I bluster my way through. "At least for a while. Until you feel better."

She touches her head. I see the bewilderment in her eyes. The nurses warned me about the symptoms of concussions. Dizziness, headache, pain, confusion.

"My condo has lots of room. You'll be quite comfortable," I add, pushing away the nagging worry that even four thousand square feet might not be enough room between the two of us. I glance out the window. The high summer afternoon sun beckons. But with my car out of commission, I'm stuck here until Kris is finished working. I resist glancing at my watch and turn back to Lila with a brave smile.

The troubled look in her eyes makes me wish I'd looked elsewhere.

"I don't know if staying with you is such a good idea," she says haltingly. "I don't want to put you to any trouble."

"Don't be silly." I plaster a smile on my face. "You won't be any trouble."

I am such a good liar.

Her chin wavers slightly. "The doctor told me I'll have to wear a cast."

"Look, Lila, I just want to tell you... I'm very sorry this happened." The words spill out of me, but it's the truth. I *am* sorry. Deeply sorry. Sorry to see her in such pain. Sorry I caused the accident. Sorry I messed up her life.

And I'm especially sorry she's coming home to live with me.

She winces.

"Does it hurt much?" I grew up lucky without suffering any broken bones. Only a broken heart, courtesy of Lila. I push away the thought. If I'm laying blame, then it's my fault she lies immobile in bed, with pillows cradling one leg. "What did they give you for the pain?"

"Nothing." She sighs and closes her eyes.

"That's crazy. Why should you suffer?" I look around for the call bell. "I'll get someone in here to help you."

"Don't bother. They already asked, but I refused the drugs."

The thought of handling pain without medication leaves me horrified. "Do you think that's wise?"

"I don't want anything." Her voice is firm and her eyes stay shut.

Then it is quiet between us and after some moments I realize she's fallen asleep. I slump back in my chair, grateful to close my eyes, grateful there's no need for more talk between us. I've got a feeling that won't be the case in the coming days.

Two hours later, I'm stiff and sore from napping in the hard plastic chair. Dr. Singer has returned and so has Kris. We leave the room and wait outside the door while he examines Lila.

"How many times do I have to say *no*?" Lila's voice rings into the hallway. "I am a recovering alcoholic and I will not use narcotics."

"Sounds like she's not having any of what he's offering," Kris says with an uplifted eyebrow.

I shrug. Lila has guts, I'll give her that much. How many people would be as honest as she's being about their addictions? It takes guts to label yourself like Lila has done, and even more guts to push through the pain without using pills. More guts than I have. Like it or not, I'm impressed.

Dr. Singer does not look impressed as he joins us in the hallway several moments later. His brow arches in a disapproving scowl. "I suggest you speak with your mother. She's being rather stubborn."

I bite back a tiny smile. Lila, stubborn? No need for a medical degree to make that diagnosis.

He scrawls some lines on an embossed pad and hands me the slip with a curt nod. "Make sure you get that filled. I'll guarantee you come tomorrow morning she'll be howling for something to take away the pain. Recovering alcoholics, they're all the same."

I stare at the indecipherable prescription. Feel-good pills are such an accepted part of our society. He's probably unaccustomed to people turning down free offers. But what gives him the right to judge my mother? I don't care how many years he's been practicing medicine. Dr. Singer could use some better bedside manners.

He could use better manners, period.

"Call my office to make an appointment. Once the swelling goes down, we'll cast the ankle." He peers at me over his glasses. "You can take her home tomorrow. She'll be discharged around noon."

"Asshole," Kris whispers as he strolls down the hall.

"Ditto," I mutter.

"And what's all this about you playing nurse?" she hisses. "Lucy, are you crazy? You faint at the sight of blood."

"There's no blood involved. She broke her ankle, remember? Besides, I don't think I have much choice."

There's no point in trying to explain things to Kris. Her family is nice and normal, at least from what I saw when they toured the *Journal* offices a few months earlier. Her mother is plump, a gentle soul with a shiny face and kind eyes that crinkle in a smile. The kind of mother I always wanted. The kind of mother you wouldn't be ashamed to introduce to your friends.

The kind of mother Lila never was and never will be.

Kris eyes me skeptically. "How long do you plan on her staying with you?"

"I don't know. Until she's better, I guess." I rub my head, which is suddenly throbbing. My life and Lila's ankle blown to smithereens, simply because I let off steam while driving. I make a silent vow to myself. Never, never, never again will I allow myself to vent behind the wheel of a car.

Which won't be a difficult promise to keep, since I no longer have a car.

Kris grabs my arm as I start for Lila's room. "We should go. You look like a wreck."

"Thanks a lot." Leave it to Kris to put things in perspective.

"What are friends for?" She gives me a gentle hug. "Come on, let's go say good-bye and then I'll drive you home."

Home. No stink of disinfectant, no doctors being paged, no nosy nurses chattering in the hallway. *Home.* Peace and quiet and a soft king-sized bed with fresh sheets changed on a daily basis, courtesy of Didi's housekeeper Betty, currently on loan to me until I find my own. No wonder women with money manage to look like they have it all together. It isn't hard to do if you have the resources to hire a legion of hardworking people like hairdressers, masseurs, and housekeepers to back you on a daily basis.

Lila sits propped up in bed. My heart lifts at the sight of the rosy tint on her cheeks and the Jell-O on her tray. She looks better. She's eating. Maybe this won't be as bad as I think. Maybe she'll only stay with me a few days. Maybe then I'll get my life back.

A life without her in it.

"Kris is taking me home, but I'll be back tomorrow. Meanwhile, is there anything I can bring you that would help you feel more comfortable?"

I'll do whatever she wants. I'll wait on her night and day. I'll be the best damn nurse she's ever had, right down to the last detail. Whatever it takes to get her back on her feet.

And out of my condo.

Lila sighs. "I don't know. I haven't thought about it."

"We can run by your apartment and pick up what you need," I say, glancing over at Kris, who gives me a brisk nod. "And we'll stop at the grocery. Would you like more Jell-O? I'll stock up on your favorite."

Lila lifts her spoon and contemplates the quivering lime green Jell-O. "I've never been much of a fan of wiggly food."

"So why are you eating it?" Kris asks. "Ring the bell and tell them you want something else."

The hint of a smile hovers on Lila's face. "Maybe I'll do that." She puts down her spoon.

"All right, scratch the Jell-O," I say, with a pointed glare for Kris and a mental note to myself. *No bedside bell for Lila.* "Anything else?"

Lila thinks for a moment, and suddenly her eyes blink wide. "Suzy-Q!"

Now it's my turn to blink. I begged for Suzy-Q snack cakes in my lunch sack when I was in school, but Grandma always scoffed. Too much sugar rots your teeth and dentists cost money, she said. And why would Lila settle for a plastic-wrapped, crème-filled chocolate snack cake when I'm offering to buy her deli bagels, gourmet ice cream, or thick juicy steaks? She's definitely suffering from confusion caused by a concussion.

Do they even make Suzy-Q snack cakes anymore?

Lila struggles to reach the bedside stand. "Where is my purse? I need my purse."

Obviously Suzy-Q sales are still going strong. And Lila is addicted.

"Keep your money," I say as Kris hands her the purse. "I'll buy the Suzy-Qs."

"You must hurry." Lila shoves her keys at me. "She's been cooped up in the apartment all day."

"Excuse me?" I'm not psychic, but I have the sense we are no longer talking about devil's food dessert cakes.

"Suzy-Q is my dog."

Kris drops me off and hunts for a parking space. I head into the building alone. Lila's apartment is on the third floor of an older housing complex and just what I expected—small. What I *didn't* expect is how it looks— immaculately furnished in a modest, tasteful style that speaks to the tiny space. I move through the rooms, eyeing the surroundings. Lila must have a friend with a flair for interior design.

Smack-dab in the middle of the vinyl kitchen floor sits one of the cutest dogs I've ever seen. With her curly white hair and long, crinkly ears, Suzy-Q definitely isn't a hound dog, though her timid look and soulful brown eyes remind me of that breed. She looks so sad. Is she missing Lila?

I spy the puddle near the back door. Mystery solved.

"Oops. Looks like someone had an accident."

Suzy-Q whimpers and crouches low on the floor.

I drop to my knees. Poor little thing, she's scared of me. Not to mention she's been cooped up for hours, all but forgotten. Instinctively I extend a hand. "Hey there, Suzy-Q, it's okay. I won't hurt you."

Where has that sing-song voice come from? I never even cooed at my dolls.

She thumps her tail but doesn't move.

Something about this little pup suckers me in, though I've never been one for animals. "Come on, sweetheart. That's a good girl."

Her curiosity and loneliness finally get the better of her. A few tentative sniffs and she licks my hand. By the time I hear the front door open, I'm on the kitchen floor with Suzy-Q in my lap, and we are fast buddies.

"Cute, Lucy," Kris says dryly from the doorway. "The two of you make a very nice couple."

"Very funny."

"I thought you hated dogs."

"Who told you that?" I bury my face in soft puppy fur. "Hey, Suzy-Q, want to come home with me while your mama is in the hospital?"

She answers with puppy-dog kisses, and I laugh and wrinkle my nose. Perhaps I've missed out on a few things in life.

"Hey, check this out." Kris's voice echoes through the apartment.

"Give me a minute." Suzy-Q winds herself around my feet as I give her fresh water, refill her bowl with kibble, and wipe up her mess. The living room is empty when I wander in. "Kris? Where are you?"

"In here."

I follow her voice down a narrow hallway and into a woman's bedroom. Lila's bedroom. Creamy white walls, peach-colored bedspread, sparsely furnished, neat as a pin. Kris stands near the bed, a small silver picture frame in hand. "Recognize anybody?"

I squint at the black-and-white photo. I don't recognize the picture, but I know the three people in it. I haven't worn my hair in pigtails for years, and the woman in the photo looks much younger than she did today, lying in her hospital bed. As for the tall, lanky man? Grandma's house was like a shrine, filled with photos of her son.

"Look at you, Lucy. You were such a cute kid."

My heart clutches as I scan the twenty-year-plus image of me caught between my mother and father. With that toothy grin, I couldn't have been more than a toddler. Three years old, tops.

"Check out your dad. He is a major hunk. I don't blame your mom for looking so happy, married to a guy like him."

I study the photograph closer. One of my mother's hands clutches my own and she shades her eyes against the sun with the other. But the radiant smile on her face is in plain view. Lila glows like a woman in love. In love with her husband, her child, her life.

Why have I never seen that look before? Why have I never seen pictures from this time? Where were they? Did Grandma keep them hidden?

"Why did she come back?" I whisper.

"Because she's your mother, silly," Kris says. "She missed you. Mothers always miss their children."

"Not my mother. Lila's not like that."

"Let me tell you something about mothers. No matter how old their children are or how far away they go, their mothers still miss them. It's this funny habit mothers have. They're all the same. It's a little thing called love."

I drop the frame face-down on the bureau and turn away. Kris has no idea what she's talking about. "Let's get out of here," I say. "I'll grab some clothes and stuff out of the bathroom. It won't take long."

"Take your time." She wanders around the room, scans the small bookshelf, eyeing other photos lining the dresser. "I'm in no hurry."

Maybe she isn't, but I am. The sooner I am out of Lila's apartment, the better.

I head for the bathroom when a sudden bark stops me in my tracks. Suzy-Q sits in the doorway, gazing at me with those big brown eyes. Her tail thumps.

"What's her problem?" Kris asks.

Suzy-Q tells us all about it with a series of rapid barks. Unfortunately, neither Kris nor I speak *dog*. "Maybe she needs to go out," I finally guess. "Do you mind walking her? It will give me a chance to pack."

"The things I do for friendship." Kris heaves a long sigh. "Come on, pooch." She heads for the kitchen, Suzy-Q scampering at her heels.

I blast through Lila's closet and bathroom, cramming things in a bag. She won't need much. Slippers, nightgown, toothbrush, comb. I yank open the bottom drawer and find it lined with cosmetics. Who is there to impress? Just me and a little dog. Suzy-Q already loves her, and as for me…

I slam the drawer shut, leaving the makeup behind.

For once in her life, Lila will have to face things *au naturel*.

CHAPTER TEN

"What would you like for dinner? A steak? Salad? An omelet?"

"I'm not a picky eater," Lila says from her throne on the couch. Her crutches are close at hand and her foot is propped up on cushions. Suzy-Q is on her lap, enthroned like a queen on yet another heap of pillows. Two days ago I was living like royalty, and now I'm reduced to waiting hand and foot on Her Majesty and the Royal Pooch.

"Whatever you feel like fixing," she says. "I'm not very hungry

I head into the kitchen and scan the refrigerator's contents. If it was up to me, I'd scarf down a bologna sandwich and call it good, but I doubt bologna is the best food for mending broken bones. With Lila under doctor's orders to stay off her feet, I've been appointed head cook for the foreseeable future. And forget the idea of hiring someone to come in and cook. Bad enough having Betty underfoot every morning when she comes to do the beds and bathrooms. I hate having people around me, touching my things, doing what I would normally do for myself.

Hiring a cook would only be a further invasion of privacy. I can't shake the feeling that I'm not alone, even in a four-thousand-square-foot condo.

I'm not used to living with someone. I'm not used to playing nursemaid.

I'm not used to being someone's daughter.

Slamming the refrigerator door, I march back into the living room and stare her down. "I'll make whatever you like. Just name it." It's already past seven o'clock and my stomach is growling. If she doesn't order off the menu soon, I'm going to hand her a jar of peanut butter and a spoon. "We've got everything. The kitchen shelves are stocked."

"Truly, it doesn't matter." She pauses. "Although I think we both know you can rule out Jell-O."

Her self-deprecating humor catches me off guard, and I feel myself smiling in spite of everything as I head back to the kitchen. "How about grilled cheese?" I call out after a moment.

"Perfect."

Ten minutes later the three of us are feasting on grilled cheese sandwiches. I sit cross-legged on the floor, facing the couch. Suzy-Q munches daintily from her perch on her pillow as Lila hand-feeds her snippets of crusts. The dog might as well be royalty, for she's successfully succeeded in reducing me to servant status.

No dogs allowed on the bed, I sternly informed Suzy-Q the first night she took up residence, introducing her to a nice folded blanket on the kitchen floor. Five minutes later, I hauled her back downstairs with a stern warning to stay put. Fifteen minutes later, the whimpering and scratching at my bedroom door broke down my defenses. Suzy-Q settled at the foot of my bed where we both slept soundly—until the break of dawn, when her highness woke me with a few quick barks, signaling it was time for another potty run.

"Thank you again for taking us in." Lila fingers her sandwich. "I didn't expect it. It was very kind of you."

One look at her conciliatory smile, tucked inside a hint of pain, has me zooming straight down the guilt highway. Why is she complimenting me? Both of us know why she's here. Though truth be told, I must admit that she sounds sincere enough. Maybe she's not angling for something. Maybe she really means it.

Then again, Lila has always been a wonderful actress.

"And what a lovely home you have."

"I'm glad you like it."

"So inviting and comfortable."

Just so she doesn't get *too* comfortable. Once the doctor casts her ankle, Lila should be able to manage on her own.

I push away the nagging thought of all those stairs leading up to Lila's third-floor apartment. Surely her building has an elevator. If not, maybe I could spring to have one installed. Her apartment complex is federally subsidized low-income housing. I'll bet a donation would be tax deductible.

"And the bedroom is so spacious," she says. "Such a nice view. Did you know you can even see a bit of Lake Michigan from the window?"

A wave of guilt equal to the ferocious gales of the lakes in November crashes over me. The bedroom I gave her, with its partially obstructed view of the Yacht Club parking lot, is the worst one in the condo. But it's not like I had a choice. Lila can't climb the stairs, and that's the only bedroom on the first floor.

Hopefully Lila won't find out she's sleeping in the maid's room.

I watch as she hand-feeds Suzy-Q a tiny bit of crust. "She's a smart little thing."

"Isn't she?" Lila's face lights up. "Roberta got her for me shortly after I moved to James Bay. She knows how much I love dogs, and she knows how lonely I've been."

Way to go, Lila. Rub it in that I'm not the perfect daughter. One who drops by to visit on a regular basis.

Make that a *never basis*.

She strokes Suzy-Q's head. The little pup yawns and stretches, then tucks her head against her paws and decides to take a nap.

I stifle a yawn myself, remembering last night and Suzy-Q curled against my feet. I wonder if Lila knows her little dog snores?

"Do you remember Brownie?" she asks after a moment.

"Brownie who?" I say, frowning.

"No, I suppose you wouldn't," she muses softly. "How could you? You were just a baby. Brownie was such a sweet little dog. Everyone loved him." She throws me a smile. "He certainly loved you."

A faint memory surfaces from somewhere deep inside. I finger my sandwich. Suddenly, I've lost my appetite.

"He used to curl up on the floor beside your crib when I put you down for your nap, and he never budged until you woke up. We used to laugh about it. God help anyone that went near your carriage when Brownie was around. He was tiny, but he had a mighty bark. No one messed with his baby." She smiles fondly. "Do you remember?"

"No, I don't," I lie, putting down my plate. For the truth is, I *do* remember. Lila's words have brought back the ghost of a small dog with stubby legs, a high little bark and a rough tongue constantly covering me in kisses. I'm haunted by vague, unsettling memories of a long-forgotten place and time, of a long-forgotten dog, of a long-forgotten life.

It is not a place I want to revisit.

Lila glances around the vast room with an uncertain gaze. "Funny, but I expected you would have some dogs of your own. You loved Brownie so much."

I shrug. "I guess I never thought about it." Animals were more mess than they were worth, Grandma always said. I suppose that after years of cleaning up other people's messes, the last thing she wanted at the end of her day was to come home and clean up after a dog. "Our house was too small," I add coolly.

"That sounds like an excuse Winnie would make," Lila says with a knowing smile. "She always was a mighty stubborn woman."

Exactly who does she think she is, criticizing Grandma? Lila is talking about things that she knows nothing about. I haul myself to my feet and point at her partially eaten sandwich. "Are you finished?"

"Yes, I guess I am." She eyes me uncertainly as I snatch her plate. "Did I say something wrong? Are you upset?"

"No," I state flatly, fighting back the surge of pure venom rushing through my veins. I feel like flinging the plates against a wall. Is the woman an idiot? Does she have no sense? Of course she has upset me. What does she know about my family? My grandmother? My life?

Not one damn thing.

I storm into the kitchen. Inviting Lila to stay in the condo while she recuperates was a dreadful mistake. Maybe it's time to regroup. There's no reason for her to stay here. I could hire a nurse, rent Lila a hotel room. James Bay is a resort town. There are plenty of empty rooms if you can afford them.

And I've got the money.

"Poor Winnie. She's such a good person and I know she means well, but she's always had a hard edge." Lila's voice trails me into the kitchen. "Though I suppose it's no wonder she turned out like she did. She's certainly had her share of tragedy."

I busy myself loading the dishwasher, trying to drown her out. If Lila dares say one word—even one word—about my father, I will throw her out on the street. I jam the forks and knives in the silverware compartment, cram the plates and griddle in the bottom rack, slam the door shut. Swear to God, not one word.

Then I am out of dishes. But Lila is not out of breath.

"Winnie has a big heart, but she always found it difficult to let people know how much she cared. I think she's one of those people who find it hard to say those kinds of things out loud." Lila pauses. "In fact, come to think of it, I don't believe I ever heard her telling your grandfather she loved him."

A stinging retort flies to mind, but I bite it down. Some—okay, a good deal more than some—of what Lila says is true. Grandma never was much of one for cuddling, or telling me I was special. I was expected to do my best, without complaint. And as for Grandpa Carl? He died when I was six. How am I supposed to remember if he and Grandma were affectionate?

I push the buttons, bringing the dishwasher to life. Hopefully the machine will drown out the rest of Lila's nonsense. But the expensive model barely makes a sound, just a quiet, steady drone as it cleans away the food. I lean heavily against the machine, listening as Lila dishes dirt in the living room.

"She doted on you, though. Your father told me she cried on the phone when he called to tell her you'd been born and that we'd named you after your Aunt Lucille. Of course, she never said anything to me about it, but that's Winnie for you. Stubborn on the outside, sentimental on the inside. It's hard digging through that outer crust."

My feet carry me back into the living room against my better judgment. "Excuse me? I don't have an Aunt Lucille."

"Well, technically I suppose you're right. She wasn't your aunt; she was your great-aunt." Lila blinks. "She was your grandmother's sister."

I fold my arms against my chest. "Grandma didn't have a sister," I staunchly counter.

She watches me for a long moment, then sighs. "Winnie never told you about Lucille?"

I stare at her in stony silence. Lila will have to do better than that.

"Lucille was three years younger than Winnie. The two of them were very close." She cocks her head, regards me with a thoughtful air. I have the sudden notion that we're pitted against each other in some silent version of one-upmanship, and that I should prepare myself. For I am about to lose.

"Lucille died of a ruptured appendix when she was eighteen. I'm guessing the reason Winnie never told you about her is because losing Lucille broke her heart."

I take a step backward, brace myself against the wall. It's true? Hearing the story breaks my heart. I've hated my name all my life. I always assumed my mother was the one who picked it out. I'd grown up blaming Lila, resenting her for sticking me with the ugly name of Lucille. I wanted to be an Amanda. A Tiffany. Or better yet, a Susan. Everyone loves a little girl named Susan. Instead, I got stuck with Lucille.

And now I know the reason why.

Poor Grandma. Why didn't she tell me? If only I'd known, I'd have worn my name—her sister's name—with loving pride.

I'm still berating myself as the doorbell chimes.

"Hi, Lucy."

Hearing the way Max says my name makes me feel instantly better.

"Hey." A familiar face peeks around him on the doorstep. "We dropped by to see your mom." Roberta tosses me a package big as a football done up in aluminum foil. "Here you go, kiddo. I brought you some bread."

"Thanks. That was nice." I step aside as she brushes past me with a quick glance around.

"Where's your mom?" She gawks up into the soaring three-story foyer, then leans back with a cocky grin. "You didn't stick her way up there, did you? I've heard the two of you don't exactly get along."

"She's in the living room," I say, ignoring Max's fit of coughing. "Straight down the hall," I point, "and to your right."

"Sorry about barging in like this," Max says as she disappears from sight. "Roberta insisted on coming and I volunteered to drive."

"No problem. Lila will be glad for the company." And so am I. Max in my foyer is a welcome sight. He steps closer, though a good foot still separates us. I wish it was inches. No, I wish we were closer than that. I wish I were in his arms.

And suddenly, I am.

He hugs me close, kisses me gently, thumbs away my tears. "I've been worried about you. Sure you're okay?"

"Just a few bumps and bruises," I assure him. "Nothing to get upset about." The truth, especially now that he's here. I hide my face against his shirt, embarrassed by giving in to such a girly-girl whim as dissolving in a man's arms.

"This doesn't look like nothing." His fingers lightly trace the scrape on my forehead.

I look up into warm brown eyes that hold care, concern, and something else, too. Something that takes my breath away.

"How are things going with you and your mom?"

I shrug gently. "We'll survive."

Max searches my face. "You sure? If you need help, give us a holler. Roberta will be right over, and so would I."

God bless the man. I can always count on him to say just the right thing. "I'm okay, Max, thanks."

Seconds later, he gives me even more reason to thank him. The soft brush of his lips against mine makes my legs feel like that wiggly Jell-O that Lila despises. I hang on tight, fearing they might give way beneath me.

"Sorry we can't stay long," he says with regret. "I've got to be back before campfire time starts. We have a special ceremony planned for our first-time campers."

"Like what? Walking on coals?" Though I honestly believe I would walk on coals if it would make Max stay. Besides Kris, he's the most genuine human being I know. Max is thoughtful, considerate, and unlike so many others I've recently met, doesn't seem to want a thing from me. I trust him. He lets me be me, and there's no need for any pretense when he's around. For that, I am grateful.

I lean in closer and show him exactly how grateful.

Minutes later when we meet up in the living room with Lila and Roberta, I'm stunned as Max drops an easy kiss on Lila's cheek. If I didn't know him better, I would accuse him of ulterior motives. But Max knows how I feel about my mother. There's no need for him to do any schmoozing.

He catches me watching and sends me a wink that has my feet curling with pleasure. Maybe I should let Max schmooze as much as he wants... especially when it comes to schmoozing with me

"Lucy is doing a wonderful job, taking care of Suzy-Q and me." Lila beams at our visitors from her throne on the couch. "I feel so blessed, being here with her. And isn't her condo beautiful?"

"Nice digs," Roberta agrees. "How big is this place, anyway?"

"Big enough," I say. Three stories, a lofty foyer, huge bedrooms with floor-to-ceiling windows overlooking the lake, and a bathroom off my bedroom with a spa tub so large, it's embarrassing. What were the designers thinking? It's not like I plan on throwing a party in my bathroom.

"Doesn't it drive you crazy, having everything so white?" Roberta adds. "I bet it's the dickens to keep clean."

"I bought it furnished," I inform her coolly. Why do I suddenly feel so defensive? Especially since I agree with her. Being surrounded by stark white is a bit overwhelming. But now isn't the time to be making changes, not with everything I've got going on in my life. Besides, I'm not the one who keeps it all clean. And Betty, my housekeeper-on-loan, hasn't complained. At least not yet.

"Roberta's right," Lila says. "It wouldn't take much to liven things up. A touch of color here and there would help."

I keep quiet, but privately I'll admit all the white at the Yacht Club borders on boring. Don't any of these people have imaginations? White walls, white furniture, white deck, white flowers. Mrs. Richardson, my next-door neighbor, appears on her balcony every morning at precisely nine fifteen and waters an array of gorgeous white petunias. I waved at her once over my morning coffee, and we chatted a bit over our railings… until I mentioned some pink and purple blooms would add a nice variety. She froze me out with a thin-lipped stare and we haven't spoken since. Not that I'm offended, especially after Betty told me that Mrs. Richardson is a terrible gossip. Who needs a neighbor like that? Let her keep her white flowers for all I care.

The soft peal of a distant chime brings me to my feet. More visitors?

My heart sinks as I round the corner and catch sight of a perfectly coifed Didi Taylor waving at me through the glass entryway. You'd think an expensive door would offer some protection, but I'm wholly exposed. All I can do is smile at her and open the door.

"Lucy, how are you? I've been so worried."

"I'm fine, thanks," I say as we exchange air-kisses. Being around Didi, suddenly I don't feel so fine. I'm wearing blue jeans and a t-shirt, but she makes me feel grubby compared to that power suit with the white piping that reminds me of blueberries and cream.

"I came over as soon as I heard the news. Richard and I were downstate in meetings and we got home late today."

She nods at my scratched forehead with a cringe. "Ouch. Poor Lucy. Are you sure you're all right?"

"I'll survive. Unfortunately, my car didn't."

"Don't tell me you're driving that dreadful thing?" She shudders as she nods toward the driveway.

I glance over her shoulder, then grin as I catch sight of Max's Jeep parked close to Didi's Mercedes. "No, that belongs to a friend who dropped by to visit my mother." I step aside. "Everyone is in the living room. Would you like to come in?"

"No, no, I don't want to bother you. You're busy. And I know how it can be with people like that."

"People like what?" My eyes are bleary from lack of sleep, but I catch the tone in her voice and I don't like it. Is Didi making fun of my mother? Of Max and his Jeep? Neither of them can help where they live or work. The grocery store pays an honest wage, and so does Max's camp. At least I assume it does.

Didi has the grace to look embarrassed. "I only meant people that drop by unannounced. I know, I know, I did the same thing, but I was worried about you. And you're sweet to ask me in, but you don't need more visitors at a time like this. I'm sure you have your hands full."

"Well, I am rather tired," I admit. "My mother is staying with me while she recovers."

"That's right; I heard she was in the car with you." Didi leans closer, eyes wide with concern. "How is she?"

"Her ankle is broken. She'll be with me at least until they cast it."

"Smart girl, keeping her close," she says with a shrewd nod. "At least this way, you can keep an eye on her. It sounds as if she has a good case."

"Case?" I blink.

"You *have* spoken with your attorney, haven't you?" she interrupts.

I shift on my feet. "I was thinking that maybe—"

"Don't *think* about it, Lucy. *Do* it. You need to protect yourself. Legally, as well as financially."

Finally I'm starting to understand exactly what Didi is inferring. "She wouldn't sue me. She's my mother." Yet even as I say the words, my mind is whirling. Haven't I thought the same thing myself?

"What difference does it make if she's your mother or not?" Didi's eyebrows lift. "You have no idea how people can be when money is involved. They resort to all sorts of terrible things, regardless of who they are or might be. Who knows what your mother might do?"

My thoughts are crashing through my mind just as fast and hard as my car crashed into that tree. I have insurance, plus millions in the bank, while Lila has bruised ribs and a broken ankle. She has the classic hallmarks of a lawsuit in the making. I was the one driving. She was the one injured. By all rights, I should have gotten a ticket, even though I didn't. Lord knows I deserved one, driving too fast for conditions. Maybe it had something to do with me being on a first-name basis with the cops since I covered the police beat while Kris was on vacation.

But Lila knows the police, too. She rings up their groceries when they pass through her check-out line. How long will be it before she's back on her feet again and working a cash register?

How long will it be before she contacts a lawyer?

"What about your car?" Didi asks.

As if I need to think more bad thoughts. "It's totaled."

"You've got to get that taken care of. You need a car."

"I know." All I can think about is the potential threat of Lila suing me. Settlement value? We could be talking millions. I hug my arms across my chest, pull in a deep breath. "Maybe I'll rent something until I figure out what to do."

She rolls her eyes. "Honestly, Lucy, sometimes I wonder about you. Rent a car? Why on earth would you want to throw good money away?"

"But I don't—"

"Never forget the first rule of real estate: why rent when you can own? It applies to cars, too." Didi sizes me up with a distressed gaze that makes me suddenly feel as if I'm a disappointment to her, that I've let her down. "So, what are you waiting for?" she asks. "Buy yourself a new car."

"I suppose I should do that." I can't depend on Kris forever to shuttle me back and forth between the doctor, the hospital, the grocery store.

"You have the money. Buy what you want."

"But—"

"Everyone has a dream car," she interrupts. "What's yours?"

I don't need to think twice. "A Jaguar convertible."

Summer must be near when the Jaguars appear. A sleek, black Jaguar convertible, the luxury car of choice for the James Bay summer elite. Merely thinking about it puts a smile on my face, which quickly disappears as I picture myself behind the wheel. Who am I kidding? Me, Lucy Carter, driving a Jag? No way.

"A Jag? Perfect," she replies. "I knew you had excellent taste. There's a Jaguar dealership in Grand Rapids."

"But that's three hours away." Didi makes it sound so simple, like I can just hop in my car—what car?—and drive down there. "Maybe in a few weeks, once my mother is gone—"

"This is why God invented telephones," she says. "Why are you waiting? Call the dealership tomorrow morning and tell them what you want."

Idly I wonder if Didi's brain is addled from spending too much time in the spa. Sometimes she is so far out of the loop, it's scary.

"Buying a car isn't like ordering a pair of new shoes on the Internet," I patiently explain. "I can't just pick up the phone and order a car. People don't do things like that."

"Yes, they do. People do things like that all the time... people with money, that is. And you now have the money. Money opens doors. Car doors. Just pick up the phone and tell them exactly what you want. If they have it on the lot, they could have it delivered by tomorrow afternoon."

The possibility of a Jaguar convertible in my driveway in less than twenty-four hours leaves me speechless. Could Didi be right? Could I really make this happen?

"I've kept you too long." She opens her bag and pulls out a thin sheaf of papers. "These are for you. I picked them up while I was downstate."

I eye the paperwork she's handed me. "What is it?"

"The partnership agreement to join our investment club. Remember what I told you about my Mercedes? You invest in this club, and the money you'll make from the interest alone will pay for that new car before it's delivered."

I scan the document, which runs over ten pages of single-spaced sentences and numerous clauses, Whereas, and Herewith. A sticky tab on the last sheet indicates where I should sign.

"I'll think about it."

"Don't think too long," she warns. "This opportunity won't last long. I'm speaking to you as a friend, Lucy, as well as someone who's invested in the Club. I'd hate to see you miss out."

I toss the paperwork on the hallway table a few moments later as Didi's powder-blue Mercedes purrs down the drive. Her argument for investing in the Club makes good sense. Financial sense. She and Richard wouldn't be involved if they didn't believe in what they were doing. She's a savvy professional when it comes to real estate. If it was the stock market, I'd dump the papers in the kitchen trash. But land is a good investment. *They can't make more land*, Grandma used to say when she made the mortgage payment. Having your own land is a good thing.

I head for the living room. Now I have money, I should let it start making money for me. Isn't that the hallmark of a true entrepreneur?

"Everything okay?" Max comes to his feet.

"A friend stopped by. She heard about the accident and wanted to make sure I was all right." I feel the beginning of a smile tug at my face. "She told me I should buy myself a new car."

"Good idea," he replies. "If you need some help shopping the dealerships, give me a holler."

Won't Max be surprised when he sees the car? My mouth twists in a fresh smile as I imagine myself behind the wheel of my new Jaguar convertible, and him beside me in the passenger seat.

"Sorry to break things up, ladies, but I promised I'd get back before campfire starts." He turns to Roberta. "Ready?"

"Two more minutes," she promises.

Max and I leave Roberta and my mother to say their goodbyes. We share our own private goodbye in the foyer. I feel myself relax against him despite the faint scent of pine lingering on his shirt as his arms draw me close. He showers my lips, my neck, my throat, with soft butterfly kisses, leaving me tingling, wanting more. Everything inside me tells me this is the man I've been waiting for.

And I didn't even know I'd been waiting.

"Call if you need anything," he whispers softly against my ear.

"I will." His gentleness gives me sudden courage, and I lift my hand and brush his cheek.

"Thank you, Max."

He catches my hand in his own and brings it to his lips. "For what?"

"For being so sweet. For being you. For being…" I hesitate. Do I dare say what's in my heart? "For being so kind," I finish lamely.

"Kind?" His eyebrows lift, then knit together in a slight frown. "Well, you're welcome."

I pull away before I betray myself. My emotions are too tender, too fresh and new to me to share, even with him. I swallow hard and try to concentrate. Not an easy task when you realize you *might* be in love. You *could* be in love. You *are* in love.

For the first time in your life.

I clear my throat. "I owe you an apology."

His eyes hold a hint of surprise, then a swift smile breaks across his face. "What did you do now?"

"It's not so much what I did, but what I haven't done… at least not yet. I've been meaning to start on the research I promised do to for you about the Loon Lake rezoning. Believe it or not, I was headed to the library when we had the accident. But now with Lila here, I'm not sure when I'll be able to—"

He holds up one hand. "You don't have to explain. I know you're busy."

But I gave him my word. Keeping a promise is important, and I don't want to disappoint him. I want Max happy with me.

Just as happy as I am with him.

"I'll swing by the library tomorrow," I promise.

"In what?" He shakes his head, chuckling softly. "You plan on buying a car that quick?"

I smile to myself. I can't wait to see the look on his face when he sees me in my new Jaguar. Won't he be surprised?

"Maybe Kris can give me a ride. If not, there's always Didi."

"Who?"

"Didi Taylor. She's a local realtor. In fact, she's the one who stopped by tonight. She's also the one who found me this condo."

"That explains it." His eyes narrow. "I wondered how you ended up living here at the Yacht Club."

"Have you met Didi?"

"I've seen her around," he says, shrugging off the question like it's a pesky mosquito.

Something odd in his voice, something I don't understand and I'm not sure I want to, gives me pause. "Do you know her?"

197

"I know her type. That's enough," he states flatly. "Women like that drive me crazy."

"*Women like that?* Women like what?" I feel my face flush and the irritation surge through me, though I've got no clue why. It's not like Didi and I are best friends, but we *are* friends. "What are you talking about?"

"Come on, Lucy, you know what I mean." He pulls away with a hard stare. "Frankly, she doesn't strike me as the type of woman you'd choose for a friend."

"Exactly what kind of woman would that be?"

"I don't know." He shrugs. "Someone like Kris, I guess. Someone normal."

I size him up with a cool stare. "Are you saying Didi's not normal?"

"Why are you getting so defensive?"

"You're the one who brought it up. And I don't see where you get off, telling me who I can and can't have for friends. Didi heard about my accident and came over to see how I was. She was concerned."

"I'll just bet she was," he says darkly. "Concerned about her number-one client."

"I'm not a client anymore. What she's going to sell me? I already bought the condo."

"She's a business woman. They're always selling something."

"You're wrong. She just dropped by to make sure I was okay." I don't like the contemptuous look in his eyes or the direction this conversation is headed.

"Whatever," he says with a shrug. "I'm just saying you'd be wise to watch out."

I take a few steps to stand in front of the hallway table, effectively shielding the paperwork Didi dropped off from

Max's view. I've got no intention of sharing anything more with him about her visit tonight. I already plan on talking things over with Sam. He's a professional. He'll advise me on the right thing to do. Besides, it's none of Max's business what I do with my money.

"I'm a big girl, Max. I can take care of myself."

Let him stew on that for a while. I think I've been doing a decent job of taking care of myself so far… taking care of me, and everyone else, too.

Maybe it's time I started thinking more about Lucy.

What Lucy wants.

What Lucy needs.

"Where's Roberta? I've got to get going."

My eyes narrow as I catch him glancing at his watch. It's a fancy chrome display with all the bells and whistles. That watch on Max's wrist didn't come cheap. Who does he think he is, telling me what to do with my money?

He blows out a long sigh. "I didn't mean to make you mad or insult your friends. You can do as you please."

Damn right.

"I just don't want to see you get hurt," he adds.

I am slightly mollified. Only slightly. My mood doesn't improve even after Max and Roberta leave, and I find myself once again alone with Lila.

"There's something I've been thinking about, Lucy. Something that I want to say to you."

I sink into a chair and take a good hard look at her. Lila's face is pale, with dark circles rimming her eyes. She must be hurting; if not her ribs, surely her ankle. She still hasn't broken down and asked for a single pain pill since I brought her home from the hospital, but now she finally wants the medicine. Can't say I blame her that she's finally caving. I doubt I would be so brave. "Is it your ankle? Do you want me to get you something for the pain?"

She waves off the suggestion with a tired smile. "No, thank you. I told you once that I don't take pills. What I wanted to talk about is that new car you mentioned."

"What about it?" I say, frowning. My VW is beyond repair, and no way she's talking me out of the Jag.

"I hate to think of you spending all that money on a new car. Why don't you use mine? It's not like I'll be driving it anytime soon."

The news floors me. Good thing I'm already sitting down or I would be flat on the hardwood floor. "You own a car?"

"Most people do," she points out mildly.

But Lila isn't most people.

"You're welcome to use it. It's nothing fancy, but it's clean and it runs. The keys are in my purse."

I sit in silence, my mind still trying to wrap itself around the ridiculous notion that Lila actually drives. "I guess I just didn't realize. You walk everywhere," I finally say.

Her eyebrows lift in a slight, uncertain smile. "I like to walk. It's good exercise."

My heart pounds at the thought of Lila loose on the road behind the wheel of a car. Then suddenly I'm nauseous, my world spinning in a crazy revolution as I remember the accident, how I lost control, how fast it all happened.

And I don't even drink.

"Do you even have a driver's license?" The words rush out before I can stop them.

She blinks. "Of course I do. It's against the law to drive without one."

"But—"

Her eyes narrow. "But what?"

"I thought you couldn't drive." I blunder on, though I already sense I'm about to make a big mistake. If I was smart, I'd shut up right now. But I never took the Mother-Daughter Relationships 101 class. Not my fault, seeing how Lila wasn't around to participate.

"I thought you lost your license... that they took it away."

Her cheeks instantly redden, and she looks as wounded as if I'd slapped her. "Why would you think that?"

But there's no use pretending. Both of us know she understands exactly what I mean. "Because..." I stammer, swallow, stop, as I come face to face with the ugly truth I grew up with.

The truth that ruled my life.

The truth that made me hate her.

"Go ahead and say it." Her lips press together in a thin white line. "It's because I'm a drunk, right? Isn't that what you want to say?"

My heart slams in my chest, and despite the room's air-conditioned comfort, I break out in a sweat. Lila suddenly looks ten years older. Pain does not make for a pretty face, and I'm the one who withheld her makeup. What made me think I had the right to do that? Where has this notion come from, this belief I've held all my life that her license was permanently suspended? Anyone in their right mind knows that drunks are a menace behind the wheel of a car.

Obviously, when it comes to Lila, the State of Michigan does not agree.

"I suppose your grandmother filled your head with that nonsense."

"Excuse me?" What does Grandma have to do with this?

"I can't say I'm surprised." Lila's eyes narrow. "Winnie always had to have the final say. I'm not saying she was all bad, but she could be a cold, bitter woman when she chose. God help anyone who got on her wrong side."

"You're wrong," I shoot back, though I'm all too aware that some of what Lila says is true. I grew up with Grandma. She could be sweet, but downright sour, too. I lived with her bitterness. I know how much she hurt. But Lila wasn't there. What gives her the right to talk about Grandma? She has no right to criticize or judge. That's a privilege reserved strictly for family. Only if you love them. First, they have to be yours.

"You don't know what you're talking about. You don't know anything about Grandma."

"I know she had a special touch for making people miserable."

"She wasn't like that."

"No?" Lila's eyes glitter. "She certainly made me miserable."

I stare right back. "Maybe you deserved it. Grandma did the best she could. She was there when you weren't. And at least she loved me."

"I loved you, too. I've always loved you."

"No, you didn't." I push back as hard as I can. I want to see her hurt. I want to make her feel as bad as I did, growing up without her, living with the knowledge that she didn't care, that she'd abandoned me. "Mothers who love their children don't leave them behind."

Lila opens her mouth to speak, then clamps it shut. Her eyes are huge, hollow, and empty. My zinger landed exactly where I intended... in her very soul. But I don't feel joyous, or proud, or giddy at what I've done.

More like sick and ashamed.

Especially when she turns her head. But not quick enough to hide the tears.

"Sometimes I think you have no idea how hard I try," she says softly. "And I'm still trying, Lucy, believe it or not. Sometimes I wonder why I keep trying…"

Her voice is sad and flat, but it slices its way through my heart, leaving a deep cut. Dragging Grandma's name into this is a low blow, even for Lila. This woman caused me pain my entire life. It isn't fair that I should be the one making all the sacrifices. It's not my fault she's a drunk. It's not my fault I spoke the truth. People make their own choices. Lila made hers long ago.

I close my heart to the grief on her face. If she thinks she can guilt me into feeling something I don't feel, into doing something I shouldn't do, then Lila is dead wrong.

Grandma taught me better than that.

"Never mind, it doesn't matter." She winces, and her eyes flutter shut. "I'm tired. I think I'd like to go to bed."

This is my cue. Until the doctor sets her cast, Lila is helpless and so am I. The two of us are stuck with each other, whether we like it or not.

"I would appreciate it if you would walk Suzy-Q." Her tone is cool and my acquiescence equally frosty, unlike the night air which hangs hot and heavy as I take her dog outside. By the time Suzy-Q finishes her evening routine of perusing my side yard, my sandals are soaked. I lead her inside, unsnap the leash, and Suzy-Q abandons me, heading straight for Lila's room without so much as a *Thank You* yip.

Ungrateful little dog. Just like her mother.

Upstairs in my room, I fling open the French doors, throw off my clothes, and tumble into bed. But neither the fresh sheets nor the waves lapping outside my window work their usual magic tonight, lulling me into sleep. The hurt floods through me and my stomach churns. I feel wired, naked, alive. The central air kicks on with a sudden whoosh and settles into a comforting drone. I think about getting up and closing the French doors. My electric bill will be sky high. I probably should close them.

I should do lots of things.

Quite the difference from my tiny apartment in downtown James Bay, where the steady beat of a bass drum often made sleep impossible until the bars finally closed. Funny, how money has a way of insulating you from the noises and messes of everyday life.

What's keeping me awake tonight?

Lila's words of earlier vibrate in my head faster and louder than the grinding thump of a big bass drum.

Do I really want to spend all that money on a new car?

I flip on my back and stare at the ceiling shining above me, reflected in the moonlight. White, just as Roberta pointed out earlier. Everything around here is white. It hadn't seemed to matter, up until tonight.

I haven't noticed lots of things, up until tonight.

I've got money now. I can do what I want. I can buy what I like. I can buy that brand-new sports car. But who is going to sit beside me in the front seat? No one told me it would be such a lonely ride. Without Grandma along, it feels like I lost my roadmap.

I think of Lila's offer to let me use her car. She didn't have to do that.

She didn't have to do a lot of things… like drink herself to madness and my father to his death.

Father Greg's words from a few days earlier while we had lunch join the steady thump-thump-thump pounding through my head. Grandma taught me to cherish our faith, to respect priests, but lately she's taking to wearing her rosary around her neck.

And as for Father Greg's suggestion I cut Lila some slack? The two of them might as well be playing in the same rock band.

No, he's a priest. It's his job to help people reconcile. To help them make things right with themselves and with others.

Then I think of Lila asleep downstairs in the maid's room. Isn't she just trying to do her job? Her job of being a mother? *My* mother?

My heart clutches and I shove the thought away. It's a little late for her to try and start acting like a mother now. About twenty years too late. Things are fine the way they are. I don't need anyone interfering in my life. I'm a grown woman. I can pay my own way. No one has the right to tell me what to do.

Not Lila, not Max. Not even a priest.

My money.

My house.

My rules.

CHAPTER ELEVEN

"You mean to tell me that snazzy car out front is yours?" Pete's whistle ricochets off the walls of his convenience store.

"It is." I sneak a proud peek through the station's front window at the sleek black convertible parked at the nearest pump. "Pretty sharp, don't you think?"

"Never thought I'd see the day that Lucy Carter would be driving a Jag." He throws me a wide grin. "You're definitely moving up in the world. Next thing we know, you'll be too good to pump your own gas and start using that new full-service station down the road."

"Come on, Pete, you know I wouldn't do that," I tease back. Though I have to admit I've toyed with the idea. It would be nice to simply relax in the comfort of the sleek leather interior while someone else pumps my gas, cleans my windshield, and check-the-oil-for-you-miss? But Pete needs the business and it wouldn't be fair to desert him now.

Especially since he's the one who convinced me to buy the lottery ticket. Without that ticket, there'd be no Jag.

"All set?" Pete peers over the cash register, fingers poised above the keys.

"Thanks, just the gas." I scan the shop for Kris. Her car is in the shop and I'm playing chauffeur today. But the aisles are empty. "Kris? I'm ready to go."

"Hold on," comes a mumbled response, somewhere from the direction of the beer coolers.

"That'll be thirty-eight fifty." Pete rings open the till.

"Ouch," I say, handing over my two twenties.

He cocks an eyebrow. "No complaints out of you, miss. That's something reserved for us working stiffs. Even if gas hits six bucks a gallon, you can afford it."

My mouth hangs open a split second, then I snap it shut. There's no sense arguing with him. Pete's right. Wealth brings privileges, but it also takes some away. When I won that money, I lost the right to whine about things the way I used to do.

Money changes things. It's even changed the way people around town look at me lately. It's like they think I've changed, that I'm different, that I'm no longer the same Lucy Carter that grew up in James Bay. Sometimes I feel like my reputation is balancing on the edge of a thin dime. If I gripe about something, suddenly I'll turn into *that ungrateful Lucy Carter who won all that money and doesn't know how good she's got it.* Like I'm not nearly appreciative enough for the sudden windfall that landed in my lap. People I've known all my life… Grandma's friends, former classmates, the downtown merchants. Even people like Pete. Then again, he's got nothing to complain about. In fact, he should be thanking me. If I hadn't bought that winning ticket from him, Pete wouldn't have an extra four hundred thousand dollars sitting in his back account.

I'm starting to understand why the rich and famous choose to isolate themselves behind high walls and gated estates. Everybody wants a piece when you have extra to spare. And I've got plenty to share. But shouldn't I be the one who gets to decide the who, what, when, where and why?

When I won the lottery, I even lost my platform in sharing my views. Churning out a weekly column could be a grind at times, but at least I had an opportunity to voice my opinion. That's gone now. No one's interested in what I have to say unless it involves will-you-write-me-a-check? I might have plenty of money, but I also have plenty of questions. Such as why gas prices are consistently ten cents higher in James Bay than ten miles down the road. Why the city fathers haven't settled the downtown parking-meter debate. Why Jaguar messed up a good thing.

That distinctive emblem I've always loved—the jaguar crouched atop the hood, ready to pounce—is no more. My new car showed up minus the unique status symbol. The salesman from Grand Rapids did his best to soothe down my ire when I called to complain, but I wasn't buying his excuses. That car came with a ninety-thousand-dollar price tag (plus, I paid cash!). You'd think I'd be able to get what I want. I listened with one ear as he stumbled through some inane explanation about the company's strategy to modernize their image and streamline the car. Who cares why they did it? What matters most is that I still feel cheated every time I glance at the hood. Without that emblem, the Jag is just like any other fancy sports car.

A car that guzzles gas. *Lots* of gas. Yes, it's sleek, luxurious, and fun to drive, but it's easy to waste a tank merely tooling around James Bay. The Jag is like a thirsty teenage boy in front of an open fridge, chugging gasoline straight from the carton.

My old VW had the good sense to politely sip a few gallons here and there.

Not to mention this car is born for speed. Yesterday the police clocked me doing twenty miles above the limit. I fumed behind the wheel as I received the first traffic ticket of my life, compliments of my brand new Jag.

"Hope you've got something else in mind to drive once winter hits." Pete lounges against the counter as we wait for Kris. "A car like that isn't exactly made for snow."

"I hadn't thought of that." The Jag probably won't get much traction on icy roads or be much good in the kind of deep, heavy snow we get around here. Northern Michigan winters would easily bottom out a sports car. And even with the top up and heater working overtime, I doubt the Jag can compete with a wind chill of twenty below.

"Shame about the VW," he says. "Word around town is you wrapped it around a tree and totaled it. That true?"

I nod, still in mourning for my old VW. Poor little car. It's probably scrap metal by now. I do a quick spot-check for Kris, who has yet to emerge from the cooler.

"Too bad. Those kind of cars are classics."

"At least nobody was hurt," I say, then redden. Lila's cast is pretty-in-pink, but there's no way anyone could label the bulky plaster encasing her leg from knee to toes a feminine accessory.

"Hear your mom's staying with you. How's she doing?"

"Better every day." Thank God.

Lila and I have silently agreed to a grudging truce since we quarreled a few nights ago. She hobbles on her crutches while I waltz around the edges of our differences, yet the whole polite dance makes for cramped living quarters, even at four thousand square feet. But with Didi's words still ringing in my ears, I'm determined to keep Lila close. I have no desire to end up being hauled into court. Sued by my own mother. That would definitely make the front page of the *James Bay Journal* and set the town buzzing.

"You're a good girl, Lucy, taking your mom in," Pete says. "Not everyone would do it. People nowadays are too wrapped up in themselves. Can't be inconvenienced. But I'm sure she appreciates it. Lila's a good sort."

I merely smile.

"Like mother, like daughter. Ya know, there's truth to that old saying… the apple doesn't fall far from the tree."

Pete comparing me to Lila churns me up inside so I'm feeling like a mushy bowl of applesauce. I'm not at all like my mother, but obviously she has Pete duped. I start to set him straight, then decide to keep my mouth shut. Let Pete think what he likes. Give him enough time, and he'll reach the same conclusions about her that I did twenty years ago.

"Thanks for waiting. Let me just pay for this beer." Kris breezes up to the counter with a six-pack. She thumbs through her wallet, jammed with credit cards. She plucks one from the stack, swipes the card, then frowns. "I think something's wrong. It didn't go through."

"Damn machine, always getting jammed. Why they make me use this junk…" Pete grabs the box and peers at it, stabs a few buttons, then shoves it back toward her. "Try it again. I think that cleared it."

Kris flashes us a smile as she runs the card through the scanner again. "Sometimes I think the whole world runs on plastic. What would we do if things didn't work? One glitch in the system and everything crashes down around us."

Not everything or everyone. Only Kris. Her face heats up, redder than the ugly glowing *DECLINED* flashing accusingly across the digital screen. "What the hell?" she mutters. "Why isn't this working?"

"Is it debit or credit?" I ask.

"Debit." She scowls at the machine. "Damn it, I know there's money in my account."

Pete shifts on his feet behind the cash register. I feel a nervous crawl headed through my stomach, starting for my throat.

"That'll be ten fifty," he says.

Kris makes a quick search of her wallet. Long enough for me to notice there's only a five-dollar bill.

"Let me get it." I gently nudge her aside and hand Pete a fifty.

"Put your money away. I don't want you buying my beer."

"No problem." I pocket my change and slide the beer toward her.

"You don't even drink," she murmurs.

Good thing, too. I eye the imported lager I just purchased. Gas or beer, whatever we're talking, whether it's premium versus regular or imported versus domestic, better quality always means a higher price. Does Kris really need European beer? Why not simply drink a good cheap American beer? Why doesn't she simply quit drinking beer, period?

Especially if she can't afford it.

"I promise I'll pay you back," she says, trailing me out the door.

"Forget about it. It's no big deal."

"You'll have the money tomorrow," she insists.

I shrug. She's been in a snit since I picked her up after work. Something to do with her girlfriend Toni, who's been in Florida the past several months. Toni's mother is ill and she's been helping out down in the Sunshine State. I know Kris misses her, though she rarely mentions Toni. Maybe things aren't working out between the two of them. But it's not my place to intrude. Kris's love life is none of my business. Neither are her finances.

Though I can't help wondering how much of her weekly paycheck she blows on things like beer. If she's strapped for cash, she should think about what she can live without. Some people do the stupidest things with their money. Kris needs to get her priorities straight.

I sink into the driver's seat and take the wheel. The leather is cool and supple under my hands, but damn, I wanted that hood ornament. Without it, I feel like I wasted my money.

"Where to now?" I muster a smile for both of us. "How about dinner? My treat."

"I need to get home."

She's giving up on me so soon? "It's Friday night. I don't want to go home yet."

Her lips are set in a grim line and she doesn't answer.

I swallow down a surge of resentment. I've spent the past few evenings at home tiptoeing around Lila. Now I've finally busted loose for a few hours, my friend deserts me. "Please, Kris? We can drive around and—"

She shakes her head. "I have to call the bank."

"Can't you do it tomorrow?" I check my watch. "It's almost six. They'll be closing soon."

"Just take me home, okay?" She stares straight ahead.

The silence is awkward as we head out of the parking lot, but it gives me time to think. I know she's mad, embarrassed, upset. Still, I can't help wondering who made the mistake. Kris or the bank? But this is no time for rebukes. "I'm sure you'll get everything straightened out."

"Easy for you to say. You're not the one whose account is frozen."

Her voice is dark, and her face is an even darker shade. An ugly crimson shade I've never seen before.

I hang on to the wheel and my patience. She needs a friend right now, not me sniping at her with an I-told-you-so. "I know you're upset, but—"

"Damn right I am." She snaps her head around to face me. "I can already tell you exactly what's going to happen. First I'll call the bank and we'll bicker over who's at fault. Then, no matter what happens, I'll still end up paying the penalty fees." She folds her arms across her chest and scowls. "Like I can afford that."

Her soliloquy stops me flat. It sounds as if Kris has been through this before.

"And there's no need to look at me like that," she adds in a hot tone.

"Like what?" My fingers clench the wheel.

"You know what I'm talking about. Like you think I should have a better handle on my money."

"Did I say that?" I squirm behind the wheel.

"You didn't have to. It's pretty obvious." She blows out a heavy sigh. "Never mind, Lucy. You wouldn't understand. Not in a million years."

Ouch. "That's pretty unfair."

Especially coming from a friend. My best friend.

I force my eyes to stay on the road, but I can feel her staring. The glare she throws me is hotter than the sun blazing overhead.

"Have you ever bounced a check?" she demands.

"No, but what does that have to—"

"Have you ever maxed out your credit cards?"

The knot in my gut twists in a messy entanglement of self-righteousness and guilt. Why are we fighting? And why is she twisting things around, making me feel like I'm the one at fault? After all I did for her, why is she suddenly turning on me? Besides, I'm the one who bought her the beer.

And I'm not the one whose card was declined.

I pull my eyes off the road long enough to sneak a quick peek at her. Her arms are folded in a tight embrace across her chest, and she's tuned me out, staring out her window as the streets fly by. Obviously, as far as Kris is concerned, our conversation is finished.

Moments later, we pull up in front of her apartment. "Thanks for the ride." She hauls her beer and bag from the back seat. "And don't worry about your money. You'll have it tomorrow."

The passenger door vibrates as she pounds it shut with an extra-hard slam.

My heart ricochets against my chest as Kris storms up the walk. What is her problem? I get it that she's angry, embarrassed, humiliated. But was it really necessary to slam the door that hard? Plus, it's not my fault her stupid debit card didn't work. Kris needs to get her issues under control—and fast. If she isn't careful, she'll turn into someone I don't recognize.

Money will turn her into a monster.

I pull in my driveway ten minutes later and find Bob and his rusty pickup parked outside. He's just finished unloading two gleaming fuchsia-colored rockers. He parks them side by side on the hot black asphalt.

"Are you sure these are for me? I didn't order them."

He shrugs. "Told me they were a housewarming present."

I circle the chairs, give them a once-over. "But who sent them?"

"Don't ask me." Bob slams the tailgate. "I'm just the delivery guy. Roberta told me to bring them over." He wipes the sweat from his face and squints at me. "Where do you want 'em? The porch?"

I stand back and eye the chairs for a minute. "Actually, I think they'd look perfect on the deck. Would you mind carrying them through the house?"

"Makes no difference to me."

The chairs exhibit the mark of the same superior craftsmanship as the ones I saw on the lodge's front porch at Camp Call of the Loon.

"Are these your chairs, Bob? Max told me about your woodworking."

"Yep."

"You did a wonderful job," I tell him. "I've never seen anything as nice as this, even at the local summer arts and craft fairs."

"Just a hobby. Keeps me busy." He shrugs off the compliment, but I catch the fleeting smile.

I can't help smiling myself. "This is no hobby. You're a real artist."

Mr. DaVinci grunts, grabs the first chair and hauls it up the porch steps. I trail behind him into the house. Housewarming present? The chairs must be from Max. Talk about a sweet guy. And I still haven't researched the zoning issue. Tomorrow, I promise myself, before the guilt engulfs me further. Tomorrow I'll swing by the library and get Max some answers.

Lila opens the door and the two of us follow Bob through the rooms as he heads for the balcony.

"They're absolutely beautiful," she breathes.

For once in our lives, my mother and I are in complete agreement. I hurry onto the deck and show Bob exactly where to put the first chair, then stand back and admire it. Maybe I'll add a small table. And perhaps some tubs of flowers would be nice, just like Mrs. Richardson's next door. A curtain flutters in her window. It's only her fat white Persian cat, but I wouldn't be surprised if Mrs. Richardson is watching, too. Good. Maybe once she sees these colorful chairs, she'll realize how nice things can look merely by adding a little splash of color here and there.

Bob heads back through the living room for the second chair. Suddenly the possibilities seem endless. What am I waiting for? I've got tons of money I can spend on things like flowers and deck furniture, but until these chairs arrived, I never had a clue.

Clever Max, knowing exactly what I needed. As soon as Bob leaves, I'll phone and thank him. Maybe if I ask nice, he'll slip away after campfire so I can thank him in person. We can try out the chairs, rocking in the moonlight. Different than the original plans I'd made for this evening, but so much better.

Then I remember Kris, and how things ended with her tonight, and suddenly I feel ashamed. Kris isn't having the kind of evening she planned, either. She's probably stuck on the phone with her bank right now. Hopefully she's managed to persuade them to forego the penalty fees.

Bob pushes past us, lugging the second chair.

"They certainly are bright," Lila says.

"True, but I like them," I say. Max made a good choice.

"You really like them?" She eyes the chairs cautiously. "They're so… *pink*."

It's obvious she's trying. Well, I can try, too. Plus, I'm in more than a generous mood, seeing Max's gift on the balcony. "The chairs are perfect. The pink is perfect. Absolutely perfect."

"You have no idea how happy I am to hear you say that." A tiny whoosh escapes her lips. "First I thought maybe I should check with you. But then I decided, no, I'd let it be a surprise."

"Excuse me?" Grandma taught me it's rude to stare, but I can't help myself. Just like I can't quash the pounding of my heart as it slams against my chest. "*You* sent me these chairs?"

Lila nods and beams. "I'm so glad you like them."

How would she know what I would like? And how did she afford them? Even if Bob gave her a discount, they must have cost a good chunk of her weekly paycheck.

Not to mention, Lila currently isn't working—thanks to me and my rash decision that put us both in danger and that bulky pink cast on her leg.

"I do like them. I love them." I clear my throat, swallowing down the sentiments. "Tell me how much you paid and I'll write you a check."

Lila's eyes widen. "I don't want your money."

She's got no business buying things that she can't afford. I have no wish to be the reason her checking account is overdrawn. It's bad enough I feel guilty every time I see her hobbling around on those crutches with that cast. "I insist on paying you."

"Please don't." Her eyes are round, serious, sober. "If you pay me, it doesn't count."

"What are you talking about?"

"I meant them as a peace offering."

We're outside on the deck, but it feels like all the air has suddenly been sucked out of the space surrounding us.

Lila takes a deep breath. "I'm sorry for what I said. I had no business talking about your grandmother the way I did the other night."

My eyes widen, hearing Lila making amends.

"Winnie is who she is. I've always known that, and I have to accept it, whether I like it or not." Her voice is soft but firm, and it never wavers. "She took you in when I couldn't, and I'll always be grateful for that. I know how much she loved her rocking chair. And I thought maybe, if you had these chairs from Bob, you'd remember Grandma and all she meant to you."

The mention of Grandma's name fills me with a wild, sudden loneliness I haven't felt in weeks. I steal a glance at the creaky Bentwood rocker tucked away in one corner of the room. I would give away everything I have, all my lottery money, if it meant I could have Grandma with me... right here, right now, rocking away in her chair. Or in one of Lila's chairs on the balcony.

Grandma would know what to do. What kind of flowers to buy, how much water they needed, what kind of tubs to plant them in. I listened to her all my life. Grandma always had the answers. But not anymore. Nowadays she can't even remember her name or what she ate for dinner. She's left me alone to search out my own answers.

Alone, except for Lila.

A high flush rides her cheeks, and the day's heat has twisted her hair into golden curls that frame her face. Part of me yearns to trust her. She looks the part of the perfect mom. The one I always wanted. I want so much to believe that she's telling the truth. I want so much to believe that she bought these chairs because she's truly sorry for what she said.

Why is it so hard to trust her? Why is it so hard to have faith in her? Why is it so hard to let go, to let her in?

Bob strolls in off the deck. "All set."

"Lucy loves the chairs." Lila gingerly hobbles to his side, rewarding him with a fragile hug. "Thank you for bringing them over. You were wonderful to deliver them."

"They're perfect, Bob," I echo her words. "Thank you."

"No problem. Glad to do it." He shrugs off my sentiments and eyes Lila. "I'll be taking off now."

"I'll see you to the door," she says.

"You go sit down," he says. "Didn't the doctor tell you to stay off your feet?"

"He also said it was good for me to be up and around a little more each day. Did Roberta happen to mention that, too?"

He chortles. "You know my wife. That woman has a mouth on her that won't quit. She's worried about you, Lila."

"Worried that I won't be available for our euchre game," Lila says with a quick smile.

He pats her on the back. "Best thing you can do right now is take care of yourself. Let Lucy help. After all, isn't that why you're staying with her?"

So far I've managed to quash Lila's talk of returning to her apartment with a nonchalant *no-problem-stay-as-long-*

as-you-want. But I'll admit I haven't exactly played the part of the world's best nurse these past few days. And Bob is right. Lila's ribs are on the mend and she's on her feet more, but she still needs time to heal. And with Susie-Q constantly playing tag with her crutches, it's a miracle Lila hasn't tripped. She'll end up with her other leg in a cast if she isn't careful. Someone needs to watch out for her.

Like it or not, that someone is me.

"You go sit down. I'll walk Bob out." I start for the hallway, trailing behind Bob.

"Lucy?"

Something in her voice makes me stop. I glance back over my shoulder. The look on her face shakes me to the core. A haunted look. A hopeful look. A look I vaguely remember from somewhere in the distant past. "Do you really like the chairs?" she asks.

I don't trust myself to speak. I don't dare voice the thoughts buried in my heart. If Lila believes I'll be thinking about Grandma when I look at those chairs, then she's sadly mistaken. It won't be Grandma I'll be thinking about. Instead, it will be Lila herself.

I'll be thinking about her gift. Her generosity.

And the life lesson she taught me tonight.

It takes guts to be the first to say *I'm sorry.*

CHAPTER TWELVE

"I'm sorry about the other night." Kris's sigh floods across the telephone. "Sometimes I wonder why you put up with me."

"Because we're friends." I plump my pillow, nestle the phone under one ear and stretch out in bed. What a luxury, just being able to lie here, relishing a day of luxurious nothingness sprawled out before me and the knowledge that I can do as I please.

"I didn't mean to go off the deep end. I know that sounds like an excuse, but you know how I get sometimes. I get going and there's no stopping me."

"Don't worry about it," I say, smothering a yawn. "You've been under a lot of stress."

Unlike me, who no longer has to work for a living, or worry about sleeping through the snooze-alarm like I used to do.

"You shouldn't let me off so easy," she warns. "I had no business talking to you the way I did. I don't want you mad at me."

"I'm not mad," I assure her, even though I still am a little miffed. But Kris sounds contrite. Why add to her misery? Our little tiff wasn't that important. "Did you get everything straightened out with the bank?"

"It's all cleared up," she confirms. "So, we're still friends?"

"Of course we are, silly."

"You're the best, Lucy."

"Ditto." I miss her. We haven't connected much in the past couple weeks, and it's good to hear the sunshine back in her voice. Just like the bright morning sun streaming through the French doors. I snuggle deeper under the blanket as the central air kicks on with a whoosh. The temperature outside must be in the mid-eighties, but my bedroom feels as cool and crisp as a late autumn morning.

"Gotta go. I'm at work and our esteemed editor is giving me the evil eye. I better get my butt in gear if I want to keep my job."

"Charles Kendall would be a fool to even think about trying to put out a paper without you."

She chuckles. "Be sure and tell him that next time you see him. Maybe then I'll get that raise he keeps promising. I could use the money."

I hang up, happy for myself that I got rid of him, sorry for Kris that she's still stuck with Charles. At least she's got a sense of humor to keep her company. I throw back the covers and toss the phone aside, only to have it promptly ring again. I grab it with a grin. Kris is on a roll. It's already her second call of the day. I connect and greet her with a cluck of my tongue. "So much for you being worried about getting fired."

"Excuse me?"

"Oops." Wrong voice, wrong friend. "Hi, Didi."

"Who got fired? Anyone I know?"

"I don't think so." Even if I did, Didi would be the last person I'd tell. I'm beginning to think the woman has her own agenda. I swallow down my growing desire for a jolt of wake-up coffee and try to churn up some interest in what she has to say. "What's up?"

"Actually, I'm calling with good news. We have an offer on your grandmother's house."

Good thing I'm still in bed because her words would have knocked me off my feet. "How can that be? I thought I told you to pull the house off the market last month. It's not for sale."

"Anything is for sale, if the price is right," she counters. "It's a good offer. Buyers are in the driver's seat today, with the economy the way it is. The neighborhood is in transition. Properties aren't exactly the hot commodity they were a few years ago."

"But why are they making an offer now?"

"I'm sure they have their reasons." Didi's words are slow and patient, as if she's speaking to a child. I resent the implication. I might not know much about the real estate market, but I'm not stupid. A downturn in the market, and the wolves start circling. I'm fortunate to be a position where I don't need the money. Grandma struggled all her life to keep a roof over our heads. If and when I decide to sell, the house won't come cheap. I owe Grandma that.

"Tell them I'm not interested."

"Don't say no right away. You really need to think about this." Her voice is cool and placating, laced with an edge of steel.

"I don't want to think about it. At least, not right now." I can be just as stubborn as Didi. "Besides, once they see all the work it needs, they'll change their mind and pull the offer."

"They didn't seem too concerned when I showed the house this morning."

Without asking me? I bolt out of bed. Forget the coffee. Our conversation has me wide awake. I grip the phone and stomp to the window, staring stonily through the sheer gauze curtains at the yachts slowly cruising the bay. "Why the sudden interest in Grandma's house? It sat on the market for months with no takers."

"This is a serious offer. These people have already purchased some of the neighboring properties surrounding your grandmother's house."

I didn't know any of the other houses on the street were for sale. "What are they doing with all that land?"

"I don't believe their plans have been finalized yet."

The hedging in Didi's voice puts me on edge. "It sounds pretty final, seeing how they're buying up land up and down the street. Come on, Didi, what's going on?"

"What makes you think I'm privy to their plans?"

I meet her words with stony silence. Didi is a detail person. I've got to believe that she knows more than she's letting on. And until she spills it, I'm not budging one inch. We're talking about Grandma's house.

"Lucy? Are you still there?"

"I'm here," I say. "And I'm waiting for an answer."

Didi's sigh trickles over the phone like a stream of dirty water headed down a sewer drain. "Fine, if you insist. But you're not going to like it."

"Try me," I say, though I have a sneaky suspicion that she's probably right.

"They intend to build a housing development."

"Condos?" I groan inside, thinking about Grandma's street going upscale. What will happen to all the normal people who need affordable housing? Property values are climbing and people's incomes are falling. Where will they all go if places like Grandma's house and her street are gobbled up by hungry developers looking to make a quick buck?

"If you must know the truth, it will be low-income housing."

Even worse than I thought. Grandma spent her days on her hands and knees cleaning other people's floors. It wasn't an easy life, but she did the best she could. Too many people look to the government to bail them out, but Grandma never asked for assistance. Now I'm supposed to let them turn her house into a low-income project?

No way in hell.

"Call them back and tell them it's not for sale."

"But you haven't even heard how much they're willing to pay. It's a fair price, Lucy."

"I don't care." I stare out the window at the sparkling blue waters of Lake Michigan. The waters are tranquil, unlike my thoughts, which churn like storm-tossed waves in a November gale. The gall of some people, thinking I'd sell Grandma's house just to turn a quick profit.

"You might not get a second offer," she warns.

"I don't care," I repeat. "The house is not for sale."

"Fine, I'll tell them," Didi says. "All right, that's enough business talk for one day. Meanwhile, since I have you on the phone, I want to ask you about the hospital benefit fundraiser. I haven't heard you mention anything about it. You *do* plan on attending, correct?"

"Hospital fundraiser?" My brain feels foggy, but not from lack of caffeine.

"The Northern Nights dinner-dance-charity auction. You must have received your invitation. They were in the mail last month."

My gut knots like back in seventh grade when the birthday party invites went out to every girl in the class but me. "I'll have to look," I say slowly, though I already know the search will be fruitless.

"Never mind. Edie Phillips is in charge of the invitations. I'll call and tell her to send you another one."

"Maybe my name wasn't on the list," I venture softly.

"I can't imagine why it wouldn't be."

Maybe Didi can't, but I can. The bank president's wife has had it out for me ever since I won the lottery. The woman can't stomach someone else's good fortune.

"Let me handle this. I'll set Edie straight." Her voice bristles in a way that cheers me up immediately.

"Thanks, Didi, I appreciate it." She might be a little rough around the edges, but Didi's heart is in the right place.

"I hope Edie has her cell phone. She told me she was planning to go shopping for her dress when we chatted earlier today." She pauses. "I'm so glad you're planning to attend."

"Me, too. It should be lots of fun." And a great way to extract revenge for poor Grandma. She never attended a charity fundraiser in her life, except as the hired help.

"Since you're definitely going, would you be interested in hosting a table? It's tax deductible. Last I heard, they still had a few left."

"Why not?" I close my eyes, imagining myself presiding at the head of a table, smiling politely, dripping in elegance. Edie Phillips isn't the only woman in town who can afford to show off in style.

"Wonderful." Didi's voice swells with enthusiasm. "I'll tell Edie you've agreed to sponsor a table and to watch for your check."

"How much do I write it for?"

"I assume you'll want a table for ten?"

I swallow down my indecision. How am I supposed to know what size table to purchase? I've never been to a charity fundraiser, except with my camera in tow when covering the benefit for the *Journal*.

"Ten is the smallest table available," Didi adds after a moment. "A table for ten runs five thousand dollars."

I clear my throat. "Five thousand dollars?"

"It's only five hundred dollars per guest."

Only? I swallow hard. But why am I surprised? When Didi talks money, it's inevitable that numerous zeroes will be involved.

"I suppose it's this terrible economy. People don't want to admit it, but I know that many of them are having problems. Even my husband decided against buying a table this year. Normally Richard writes it off as a business expense, but he said with the housing market down, he felt he like he couldn't justify the expense. And it does seem such a waste, spending all that money on just the two of us. Our close friends who usually join us are out of the country this year. It's rather sad, actually, to think we'll be there all alone."

I roll my eyes as we say goodbye. Who is she kidding? Didi knows everyone in town. It's hard to imagine her alone on any given day, let alone in a ball room filled with five hundred people.

The downstairs doorbell chimes and the muffled sound of Suzy-Q barking and Lila chatting with someone gets me moving. Betty must have showed up to start her cleaning.

Soon she'll be up here, knocking on my door. I scurry out of the bedroom and head for the shower. I like the way Betty leaves things neat and tidy, but sometimes I wish she would simply do her work and leave. I don't know how Didi puts up with her. Betty has a penchant for puttering and a tongue that doesn't stop. All well and good, but I'm not paying her to stand around and chat. I twist the shower knob nearly all the way left, waiting for the water to heat. God bless whoever invented indoor plumbing, plus the makers of shampoo. I finger my hair in the full-length mirror. It's a mess.

The phone rings again. I glance wistfully at the steaming water, then snap off the faucet. My hair will have to wait.

"Hello?"

"Good morning, Lucy. Is this a good time to talk?"

I grimace at my reflection in the mirror. Sam Curtis came highly recommended, and in the past few weeks, I've learned exactly why. Sam is focused and very good at what I hired him to do—protect my financial interests. But chatting about money issues with Sam isn't on my list of priorities this morning. I haven't had my shower. I haven't brushed my teeth. I haven't had my coffee. Not to mention I have a sinking feeling in my gut what he's going to say. And I don't especially want to hear it. "Do you mind if I call you back?"

"This is important." He clears his throat. "There's a problem with your account."

I stare forlornly at my toothbrush, then sink down on the toilet seat. "What's wrong?"

"I'm looking at your latest statement from Financial World Services." Papers rustle over the phone. "It shows a substantial withdrawal. One million dollars."

"I'm aware of that." I take a deep breath, and try to remember that he is not the big bad financial boogeyman. Sam is a professional. He's only looking after my best interests, which is exactly what I hired him to do.

Though I didn't exactly seek his advice before I forked over one million dollars to Didi's investment group.

"No worries," I assure him. "It's a legitimate transaction. I requested the money be transferred."

"That's a lot of money, Lucy. Mind telling me what you did with it?"

My gut tightens, and I try to shake off the feeling that's pulling me down into the toilet. The feeling like I've been called on the carpet, that I've done something wrong. But it's too late now. The paperwork is signed, and the money wire-transferred. Plus, this is my money we're talking about. Shouldn't I be able to spend it as I please?

"I made an investment. A private investment."

"One million dollars is a big chunk of change."

"I'm not worried," I say, hoping I come off breezy and more confident than I feel. One million dollars *is* a lot of money, but it was worth every penny to get Didi off my back. I pull in a breath, bite my lower lip. "I probably should have talked to you about it first, but there wasn't time. And it *is* my money," I add.

"I understand that." Sam chooses his words carefully, his voice slow and smooth. "I'm sure you made a wise investment. But we should sit down and discuss it soon. I want to make sure we're on the same page. The tax ramifications could be significant."

Taxes? Something I hadn't thought of. Something Didi never mentioned.

"Fine. We can do that." Why was I so worried? Dreading discussing things with him? "The papers are here at the house. I'll bring them in to your office soon."

"I look forward to it."

Suddenly the day seems brighter and I'm feeling generous. "Actually, Sam, I'm glad you called. I'm going to be writing another check. Do you know anything about the hospital's charity fundraiser? I think it's called Northern Nights."

"It's next weekend."

"That soon?" My heart flutters. Yikes! How am I supposed to fill a table for ten in merely seven days? But I can't back out now. Didi is probably on the phone with Edie Phillips this very minute. She'd never let me forget it if I pulled my offer to buy a table. "Are you going?"

"We usually do," he says, "though I'm not sure if we've bought our tickets yet. My wife Patty is in charge of those things."

Relief floods through me. "I'm hosting a table this year. I'd love it if you and your wife would be my guests."

"Well, thank you." He hesitates. "That's very generous."

"It's my pleasure." Hearing the surprise in his voice puts a smile on my face. Sam has drilled me on the benefits of philanthropy. I can start by letting this invitation be a tribute to him. I can afford to be generous. This is business. Tax deductible. Not to mention I need to fill those ten chairs.

"I'll call Patty and tell her right now. I'm sure she'll be very pleased."

"Wonderful. Thanks, Sam." I hang up feeling immensely satisfied with myself. I haven't even had my coffee yet, but I've already made significant progress for the day. Kris and I are no longer on the out-and-out, Didi finally knows exactly who is boss, and I've managed to successfully divert any criticism from Sam about the way I'm handling my financial affairs. This definitely calls for a celebration. I toss my cell across the room. It lands with a soft thud on my bed and I shut the bathroom door on any more distractions. I have a busy day ahead. Topping the list is my promise to Max.

It's time I paid a visit to the library and find out what I can about the developers eyeing Loon Lake.

I sink back in the hard plastic chair and rub my eyes. They feel grainy and tired from scrolling for hours through microfilm. It was bad enough sitting through the planning commission meetings and zoning board discussions when I covered them for the *Journal*, but the board minutes read as dry and dusty as corn fields in July after two weeks of no rain. Plus, I have yet to come across anything remotely interesting that could make a case for Max. The rezoning application has worked its way through the complex approval process for months, and from what I've read, it appears the township and county will have no choice but to approve the PUD sometime soon. Maybe by autumn. Surely before winter.

The new development could break ground early as next spring.

The devil is in the details, my favorite professor in my college journalism classes always said, but I feel like I'm trying to flush out Lucifer himself. Up North Business Ventures, the corporation listed on every piece of paperwork, is a valid Michigan business. Whoever owns it, the developers have protected their identities well. A highly respected downstate law firm serves as the corporation's registered agent.

Poor Max. How do I tell him we've hit another dead end?

The realist in me aches for him. He's fighting for a way of life, for the chance to give city kids something he was lucky enough to have growing up. A chance to experience a little magic in their lives for one week each summer. The same kind of magic his grandfather gave him. Max and his camp provide kids with opportunities they wouldn't have elsewhere. A place where they can fish, canoe, hike, swim, dive off the docks. A special way of life.

A way of life that will disappear for good if the rezoning bid goes through. But not if Max can help it.

And I promised to help him.

The irony isn't lost on me. The rezoning is a complicated issue, but my feelings for Loon Lake aren't complicated. I hate the place. And my feelings for Max aren't complicated, either. I think I love him.

And I know I have to help him. I have to try.

But why does it feel like I'm wasting my time?

I turn back to the microfiche with a heavy sigh and a heavier heart and keep on scrolling. Finally I reach the agenda and last month's meeting minutes. Names flash across the screen. Faces I know, people I remember. Names and faces of men I saw with Charles Kendall at the Yacht Club the day Didi and I had breakfast.

The screen blurs before my eyes, and I blink hard once, twice, three times. Up until this moment, I'd forgotten about that morning and how strange it seemed. Why would three members of the planning commission be having breakfast together?

Stranger still that Charles would be with them.

The devil is in the details.

A chill shudders through me and goose bumps pop on my arms as a horrible suspicion starts to crawl through me. Good Lord, could the truth be that simple? I covered municipal meetings for years and learned a few things about the way our government functions. Such as, a majority of members gathered together constitutes a quorum. A quorum constitutes a public meeting. And all public meetings must be properly noticed and attended.

Was there a quorum at the James Bay Yacht Club that morning?

I grab my laptop and pull up the township's website, clicking through into the planning and zoning department. God bless the government for insisting taxpayers have access to names, addresses, and phone numbers of their duly elected officials. Everything is posted, including information on members making up the township planning commission.

All five of them.

I'm no good at math, but even I can manage the simple division... and the implication behind what I've stumbled upon leaves me reeling.

Deliberations. Discussions. If challenged, let them call it whatever they want. But the truth is simple: if the three commissioners, Charles Kendall, and the other man discussed anything besides blueberry pancakes that morning at the Yacht Club, then their being together constituted a meeting. An illegal meeting. A flagrant violation of the Open Meetings Act.

Depending on what was said, every one of those board members and even the township itself could be sued.

That still doesn't explain Charles's presence at breakfast. Much as I don't like the guy, Charles isn't stupid. He knows he has an ethical duty to protect the *Journal* from potential conflicts of interest.

And what about the fifth man? The stranger I didn't recognize? Is he the face behind Up North Business Ventures? I slump back in my chair and close my eyes, trying to conjure up a vision of him in my head. Tall, tan, casually dressed in an up-north style distinctly at odds with his demeanor. That man was someone who looked, talked, and smelled like money.

When it comes down to it, it's always about money.

I vow to myself, right then and there, to order a title search. At least I'll be able to follow the chain of title and figure out who owns the property. It's a long shot, but I owe it to Max. I promised him I would do everything I could to help save his camp. And a promise is a promise, even though the irony of the situation isn't lost on me. If not for that stupid promise I made to Max, I could walk away from this mess right now. Let the township board make its decision. Let the developers win. Let the camp disappear. What do I care? I declared Loon Lake my sworn enemy twenty years ago, yet somehow I ended up fighting for its survival. It would be so much simpler to simply stand back, take my revenge, and let Loon Lake suffer the same fate it showed my father.

No mercy.

My hand reaches out and my fingers fumble through another drawer. I swore to myself years ago I would never do this again. Why torture myself? Yet I'm helpless to stop. Within moments, I have the aging microfilm loaded. I crawl through the pages, skimming the headlines, stopping only when I reach the date carved deep in my heart.

234

LOCAL MAN LOSES LIFE IN LOON LAKE

The James Bay Journal

John Carter, 35, drowned in Loon Lake Sunday, July 17, 1988. Carter's body was recovered by divers from the lake shortly after 4 PM, roughly two hours after the incident occurred.

Carter, a native of James Bay, was fishing with his wife, Lila, and five-year-old daughter Lucy when they encountered difficulties shortly after 2 PM. Strong winds were reported on the water, but it is not known at this time if they contributed to the accident. Witnesses on shore said Carter was not wearing a life jacket.

"This is a downright tragedy," said Bob Campbell, a local EMT who worked the scene. "John Carter and I grew up together. He fished that lake since he was a boy, and he knew those waters like the back of his hand. Something happened out there that he didn't expect. Something bad."

A full investigation of the accident remains under way.

Carter is survived by his wife, Lila, daughter, Lucy, and parents, Carl and Winnie Carter, of James Bay. Funeral arrangements are pending.

I sit in stunned silence. Though I've read the article countless times over the years, it always leaves me with the same sense of emptiness and numbing loss. This afternoon is no different.

Except for the one name that leapt off the screen.

A name that, until today, carried no significance for me.

Bob Campbell, a local EMT, was at the lake the day my father drowned.

Roberta's Bob.

Why didn't he tell me? Why didn't he say anything? Max introduced us. Bob knows who I am. He must understand how important this is to me. Why hasn't he ever stepped forward and told me that he was my father's friend... and that he was there on the beach that day.

My spine tingles, like a bony finger just tapped me for a ghostly game of *Tag, you're it.*

Maybe Bob hasn't said anything because someone begged him not to. Someone who was also out at the lake that day.

My eyes narrow and I can no longer stomach facing the screen.

Both Lila and Bob have some explaining to do.

CHAPTER THIRTEEN

"This is a nice surprise," Max says as I climb out of the Jag. "You're the last person I would expect to see here at camp."

The quick kiss he plants on my lips makes me instantly hot, but it's not desire... rather embarrassment. We've got an audience. I eye the scraggly group of campers trailing behind Max into the parking lot. "We have company," I whisper.

"Aw, don't mind them," he says with a grin. "We're good. Right, guys?"

An answering chorus of catcalls and cheers greet his words, but it's not good enough to convince me. Little boys are a mysterious breed I'm not sure can be trusted. Especially those two little guys dragging sticks behind them. I plant myself in front of the Jag, standing guard just in case either of them is tempted by the gleaming paint job.

"All right, guys, the show is over. Head on back to whatever you were doing." Max folds his arms against his chest and fakes a scowl. "Move it!"

The young boys laugh and scatter, taking my skepticism with them, and I end up laughing, too. It's obvious he loves kids, and the feelings seem to be reciprocated. Max will make a great dad someday.

"Kind of rough on them, don't you think?" I give him a playful poke in the ribs.

"They'll get over it." He pulls me into his arms and warms my lips with another kiss, this one slower, softer, and utterly more sweet. "I'm glad to see you. I've missed you."

"I missed you, too."

"Did you?"

I give him another hug and kiss to erase any doubts he might have. We haven't seen each other for nearly a week, and I've forgotten how good he smells. It's a welcome scent, that unique blend that is pure Max. Sunshine, fabric softener, the fresh outdoors, plus a faint whiff of bug spray. He holds me close. His arms are a safe place. I feel like he could waltz me through anything.

Including dancing under the stars at the Northern Nights benefit. I'm going, and so is Max He just doesn't know it yet.

He brushes the bangs out of my eyes, then gently tugs the pair of brand new sunglasses from my face. "Much better."

"Why'd you do that?" I squint against the glare of the noonday sun and swallow down a twinge of annoyance. My designer shades cost over three hundred dollars, but the mirrored lenses make them worth every penny. I can stroll down the streets of James Bay watching people watching me while they don't know I'm watching. It's quite the kick. Almost like being invisible.

"You have beautiful eyes, Lucy. Why hide them?"

I sniff and grab my sunglasses from his hand. His compliment leaves me slightly mollified. But only slightly.

Max laughs and hugs me close. "So, 'fess up. What are you doing out here? I thought you hated this place. Or did you decide you missed me so much, you're facing your fears about bugs, dirt, and snakes to pay me a visit?"

Ugh. Just the thought of snakes slithering silently in the nearby grass makes me wish I'd remembered to grab my new rubber boots. "Actually, I'm here to see Bob. Is he around?"

Max frowns. "I think so." Then a slow grin lights his face. "But I think he's wiped out of pink chairs, if that's what you're after."

"The two I already have are plenty," I assure him. "Believe me, if they didn't know before, no one will ever mistake which deck is mine. Not with those chairs on it. They're definitely pink. But I love them. I even put out some pots of purple petunias yesterday. My neighbor hasn't said anything yet, but I saw her eyeing them. I'm hoping she'll take the hint."

His eyebrows rise.

"She's into the all-white thing," I explain, "just like everybody else at the Yacht Club."

"And you're not?"

The hint of a smile lurks around one corner of his mouth, and I can't help returning the smile. Sweet Max. I might as well admit the truth. "White is nice, but it's also rather boring."

"Good for you, Lucy. Go get 'em! You'll put some color into that place yet." He tucks my hand in his own. "Bob is probably down at the dock working on the sailboats. I'll show you."

We follow a gentle, grassy incline down toward the water. Loon Lake is a brilliant blue today. The wind has picked up, and the sun catches and dances against each wave lapping against the shore. Bob stands on a sailboat tied up to one of the docks, his back to us, busy working.

"Could you wait a minute?" I tug Max's hand, halting at the tree line before we hit the beach. "I want to ask you something."

Briefly I fill him in on the details of the Northern Nights benefit. Max looks rugged and handsome in his camp uniform of khaki shorts and white polo shirt, but I'll bet he looks even better in a tux. "It's next Saturday night, at the Yacht Club. Everyone who's anyone is going to be there. I'm hosting a table," I quickly add, as if this makes a difference.

Max shifts on his feet. "I don't know. You know how I feel about that place. The Yacht Club isn't exactly my kind of—"

"It will be fun." I don't want to hear him say *no*. The doubtful look on his face isn't encouraging, and neither is the frown hovering on his forehead. And I can take a good guess about what's troubling him. That whole *I'm-a-member-of-the-Yacht-Club-and-better-than-you* attitude some people have.

But doesn't Max realize that those are exactly the kind of people who scare me, too? I'm not sure I have the courage to face them alone. I never would have joined the Club if it wasn't for my condo. You have to be a member in order to purchase. But first you have to purchase, in order to be voted in as a member.

It's a wonder people with money don't go crazy, living under all those crazy rules they vote in upon themselves.

"Please, Max? At least just think about it?"

"I told you once, Lucy, that I'm not a Yacht Club type of guy."

"But this isn't about the Yacht Club." I am not giving up. I refuse to go to this party by myself. "It's about raising money for the hospital."

He shoots me a hard look. "Why this sudden interest in the hospital? You've never mentioned it before."

"The hospital is a worthy cause. Why shouldn't I be interested in supporting it?" I ask, trying to sound as innocent as possible, knowing I'm guilty as hell of everything he's accused me of. Thank God Max can't read my mind, for he'd surely think I'm crazy. And who knows? Maybe I am. But I am determined to go to that party, though I'm not sure why. It's not at all the kind of thing I would normally do.

Maybe it has something to do with showing the Edie Phillipses of the world that I'm as good as they are. That I deserve a spot at the table, just like everyone else.

Or maybe it's something else entirely.

Maybe, just maybe, for once in my life, I want the chance to feel like other women do. To be dressed in a beautiful gown and on the arm of the man I love.

Why can't Max understand that? Maybe it's because he's a man. Or maybe it's because he doesn't feel the same way about me... which makes it a whole different ball game.

And I don't want to play games. I never learned the rules.

"It's a free meal," I add. "A gourmet dinner, delicious food. Plus dancing under the stars."

His jaw tightens. "In case you haven't noticed, I'm not much of a dancer."

I bite my lip. I've grown so accustomed to Max's limp, I never gave it a thought. "I'm sorry. I didn't mean to..."

He shrugs off my apology. "I know you didn't."

"The hospital needs our help," I say slowly. "How can that be a bad thing? I can afford it. I don't see what's wrong with doing something good for the community."

What am I supposed to do if he won't come? Who will I dance with if Max tells me *no*? How am I going to fill those ten chairs?

"Lucy Carter." His frown deepens, but I catch the glimmer of a smile. "Since when did you become such a philanthropist?"

"You, of all people, should understand. Isn't that what you're doing here at camp? Supporting the community? Being of service to kids who need help?"

He runs a hand through his hair and sighs. "You really know where to stick the knife, don't you?"

I throw him a semi-triumphant smile. While Max hasn't said *yes*, he hasn't said *no*.

"I suppose it's black tie." He sounds even more dejected.

"You'll be the most handsome man at the party," I assure him.

"Who else is coming? Anyone I know?"

"Kris Henderson. You remember Kris, don't you? Plus, Sam Curtis and his wife will be there, too." I decide right then and there not to mention Didi. Max hasn't seemed particularly keen on meeting her, but he'll get over that once we're seated around the table together.

He won't have a choice.

"What about your mom?"

"I invited her this morning."

The open surprise on his face is slightly annoying. Just because Lila and I don't exactly get along is no reason for me not to invite her. Grandma always said good manners will take you anywhere. Being kind and decent works to your advantage. And right now, more than anything, I need Lila on my side. I don't want us to end up *Plaintiff v Defendant*.

"I'm glad you invited her. It was the right thing to do."

I wave off the compliment. Preening under flattery I barely deserve seems a bit pretentious. "I'm not sure how much good the invitation will be, seeing that she's still in a cast and using crutches."

Plus, it would have been an insult not to invite her. Especially since she's living with me. Not to mention I'm haunted by the thought of those ten empty chairs. People will think I don't have any friends.

"If you know anyone who would like to join us, let me know. I'm sure we can find room," I add generously.

"How about Bob and Roberta?" Max nods toward the sailboat tied up at the dock. "Roberta loves to dance. She does a mean polka whenever we host Polish Night at camp."

I shudder slightly. "I hope you're not serious."

"What if I am?" He cocks an eyebrow and stares at me. "Something wrong with that?"

Men. Some things are beyond explanation. Bob and Roberta at the Yacht Club? Talk about a fiasco in the making. They wouldn't fit in, plus neither of them would have the slightest clue what to wear. Roberta is addicted to her hideous sweater-vests, and I've never seen Bob in anything but grungy blue jeans. Better to let two chairs go empty than invite them.

"You know, Lucy, sometimes I wonder about you."

I'm not sure if he means it as a compliment or criticism. "Is that a yes or a no?" I ask in a small voice.

"Yes, I'll be there," he says with a long sigh. "Though I'm not sure why. I hate this kind of stuff." He shakes his head, but I ignore his slight look of disgust and give him a big hug. Max is coming, and that's the most important thing. I won't be alone.

A bell clangs in the distance. Max nods toward the hall. "Want to stay for lunch? Roberta's got macaroni and cheese on the menu."

"No thanks." I glance at Bob, still on the sailboat. There's a reason I'm out here today.

"I've got to go. Lunch duty calls." Max plants a kiss on the tip of my nose and heads back toward the lodge.

I slip on my sunglasses and take off my sandals, wiggling my toes in the hot sand as I slowly shuffle toward the dock. Loon Lake today makes a perfect picture of tranquility. Blue skies, blue waters, a light breeze. But this lake has always been a ballet of sadness for me, a place of endings rather than beginnings.

Hopefully after I talk with Bob, I'll have some peace of mind about what happened in the middle.

He lumbers to his feet as I near the water's edge. "Well, if it isn't Miss Lucy herself."

"I hope I'm not interrupting."

He shrugs. "The work will be here after lunch." He climbs out of the boat. His hands are covered in grime, and he wipes them on a dirty rag he fishes from his pocket. Idly I wonder if I was a bit too hasty in my decision not to invite him to the benefit. It might be worth it just to get a look at how Bob cleans up in a tux.

"Have you got time to talk?"

"Talk about what?" He squints against the noonday sun reflecting off the water and plants himself on the narrow dock. It rocks slightly against his weight.

I hold my ground in the sand shifting beneath my feet. I saw the movie *Jaws*, along with everyone else in America, but I'm not as stupid as that chief of police. He was scared of the water, too. Plus I remember that shark. At the end of the movie, someone lost their life.

I do not swim. I do not go near water. And I'm not stepping one foot on that dock.

I nod behind me at the empty shoreline. "Do you mind if we sit on the beach?"

Bob shrugs. "All the same to me."

I dig my toes in the sand and am plowing back toward the trees when I hear a sudden heavy oof. Turning, I see Bob has already chosen his seat. I head back a few steps and sink down beside him, turning my back on the water. His stomach growls, loud enough for me to hear over the sounds of the waves lapping against the shore. "So, what's this all about?" he asks.

I pull my legs close to my chest and hug them tight. Turning my back on Loon Lake is unnerving enough, but facing Bob is even more daunting. He doesn't look particularly inclined to talk. More like he's ready to bolt for the lodge and dig into a big bowl of Roberta's macaroni and cheese. I take a deep breath and dive into the conversation. "It's about my father."

He stares at me a long moment. "That's what you want to talk about? Your dad?"

"Yes." My mouth feels as gritty and dry as the sand we're sitting on, and I send a silent prayer flying upward to God and my father for a heavenly intervention. The stern glare, the squint in his eyes, has me scared, but I know Bob has the answers. I want to hear them. I need to hear them.

But am I ready to hear them?

A gust of wind blows in off the lake, like an eerie reminder that, even now, twenty years later, Loon Lake is trying to protect itself. But I have to do this. If I don't, I'll never screw up the courage again. "I understand you and my dad were friends," I press.

"The best."

"I barely remember him."

He peers at me with hooded eyes, rubs the back of his neck, then shrugs. "What do you want me to say? We grew up together. He was a good man. I miss him."

"I do, too," I say quietly. "You were there the day he died."

"If that's what you're here to talk about, you can just forget it." Bob starts to his feet. "I don't talk about that day."

I grab his arm and pull him back down. He's got a good hundred pounds on me, but I don't dare let go. "Please, Bob? I need to know what happened. You know the truth. You were on the beach."

His face screws up in a dark scowl. "Lots of people were. Go talk to them."

"You were one of the EMTs."

"*Was*," he confirms. "I quit the department the very next day. I lost one of my best friends."

"And I lost my father," I softly remind him. "Please, Bob? I was only five years old. I barely remember anything. But you must remember. I read the newspaper article. You thought something happened out on the lake. Something my father didn't expect."

My mirrored sunglasses protect me as I watch his face undergo a cacophony of surprise, sadness, and finally, resignation.

"I really want to know," I beg softly. "I *need* to know."

Bob stares at his feet, then brings his head up to scan the lake, searching the horizon. Finally his gaze finds its way back to land and eventually to my face. "I was home that day watching the baseball game when the nine-one-one call came across the scanner," he says slowly. "I ran down to the boat ramp. I didn't know it was your mom and dad out on that boat. Not until they brought the three of you in. It was… it was a horrible thing."

He rubs his forehead with the heel of his hand, and a swift rush of guilt floods through me. Bob's done his best for twenty years to drown the memories, but now they're back, thanks to me.

He nods at the beach, toward the public boat launch farther down the lake. "We tried our best to bring him back, but it was too late. John was already gone when they got him on shore."

I'm silent, lost in my own thoughts. My memories are waterlogged and bleary. A hot day. The wind in my face. My hat is gone and a rush of water. My mother's screams. My father's cries. Wet, cold sand. Sirens. People. So many people.

And one other memory… the smell of alcohol.

Her fault. All her fault.

Do I pry the bandage off little by little, or simply rip it loose and pray the wound has healed, that the blood won't start gushing? Either way, it's going to hurt, and I'm in it too deep to stop. I can't stop. I have to know the truth.

"It was Lila, wasn't it?" I prompt softly. "She was drunk and fell out of the boat. Or did she jump?"

The muscles in his jaw tighten and I know I hit a nerve. I rush to finish before I lose my nerve. "Did she say it was an accident? Or do you think she did it on purpose?"

"What the hell are you talking about?" Bob staggers to a stand, his features a dark thundercloud rumbling across his face. "How the hell should I know?"

I scramble to my feet. "Because the two of you are friends. You just admitted you were on the beach when they brought us back to shore." I opt for the *rip-the-bandage* method. Fast and quick. "She turned to you, didn't she? She told you what happened. Why are you trying to protect her?"

"Why are you so goddamned determined to blame her?"

"Because it's her fault he died!" The blood roars through my brain and my heart slams against my chest so hard my ribs ache. "She was drunk. They were arguing." I struggle to finish, fighting for each breath. "She was angry, she was screaming at him. And then…"

My voice drops to a whisper. "…And then he was gone."

"Lila told you that?"

His look is so fierce, I feel as if I've been slapped. I stagger two steps backward. "She didn't have to," I answer softly. "I remember."

But that's all I remember. Precious little. Crying. Being scared and wet.

I lost my hat. I lost my father.

"You're talking to the wrong person," he says roughly. "You need to talk to Lila."

"Why? So she can tell me again how guilty she feels? How sorry she is? How it was all her fault? Why bother? I've heard it all before." My eyes narrow, and I feel myself go cold inside, despite the day's heat. "Why should I care how she feels? She never cared about me or my father, either."

Grandma's words flash to mind. *She's nothing but a drunk.* Poor Grandma, whose entire world slipped under the waves one Sunday afternoon while Bob watched baseball on TV.

"Why should I care anything about her?" I repeat stubbornly. "She's nothing but a drunk."

I turn my back on him and stare stonily across Loon Lake, daring it to defeat me. What a waste of time. I never should have bothered to come out here. What made me think I'd learn anything from Bob? Trying to talk to him was a terrible mistake. The man is immovable, with a mind and heart harder than one of those rocks in the break wall along the Yacht Club's pier.

I might as well be talking to a rock, for all the good it would do me.

"You're a mighty harsh young lady, you know that?" His voice rises behind me, hard and flat. "What kind of a daughter talks about her mother that way? You ought to be ashamed. Your mother is a wonderful person and she deserves better. Everything she did, she did for you."

The tears aren't far away, but neither is my anger. It breaks the surface with the fierce intensity of a summer squall.

"I might be a rotten daughter, but she was a rotten mother," I spit out. The wound is open, gushing blood, but I don't care. It's time things were finally out in the open. "No, she was worse than that. She wasn't a mother to me at all. My grandmother raised me, remember? After Lila fell apart. Grandma told me all about it. About Lila's drinking, how she couldn't take care of herself. How she couldn't take care of me. How she didn't even want me."

Now it's my voice that's hard and flat.

"She never even tried."

"Your grandmother tell you that?"

The air hums between us with unspoken tension like electric lines vibrating through the summer heat. But I refuse to give him the dignity of a reply. I bite back my tears. I will not cry. Crying is for wimps, and I am not a wimp. I can take care of myself. I've had a lot of practice, especially this past year.

"For your information, Miss Lucy-High-and-Mighty, your mother is one of the bravest women I know. I can't think of any other woman who would have had the courage to do what she did."

"I should have known better than to think you would help me." I bend and grab my sandals. As far as I'm concerned, our conversation is finished. "I don't know why I even bothered. You don't know anything. You don't even know what you're talking about."

"Don't I, now?" He hisses through his teeth. "Funny you should say that, seeing how you're the one who showed up here today, wanting to talk to me."

His eyebrows pinch together, forming a stern arch. "And while we're on the subject, that grandma of yours isn't such the fine woman you seem to think she is. Those churchgoing women can be the most righteous and unforgiving of all. You might ask Lila about that when you have your little talk. If I recall right, she was on the receiving end of your grandma's tongue plenty. So don't you go telling me I don't know what I'm talking about. There's only one person who knows what happened out there on the lake that day, and that person is your mother.

"I'm going to go get me some lunch." He points a crooked finger in my face. "As for you, I suggest you get your butt in that fancy car of yours and go home. Talk to your mother if you're looking for the truth. Maybe it's time you finally heard it. But not from me."

Fury engulfs me. How I hate this man. I hate him with a passion. How my father and Bob could have ever been friends is beyond explanation.

"And one more thing." He levels me with a stony glare. "I'd be careful if I was you, going around calling someone a drunk. Your mother's been sober for nearly twenty years. She goes to A.A. meetings regular, just like me. Don't you go pointing a finger at someone unless you're ready to take a good hard look at the three fingers pointing right back at you."

Bob stomps away through the sand, leaving me alone on the beach. I am shaken and upset by what I've learned... but even more so by what I haven't. I came here today hoping to find the truth, but our conversation has left me burning with resentment. And more questions than answers.

I'm frustrated and angry. Angry with myself. Angry with Bob. Angry with Lila.

And for once in my life, angry with Grandma.

CHAPTER FOURTEEN

The officer salutes me with a curt nod as he snaps his ticket book shut. "Have a nice day."

Is he kidding? Sarcasm 101 must be a required course at the police academy. I sit steaming behind the wheel of the Jag as the black-and-white cruiser pulls away from the curb. My second speeding ticket in less than two weeks. Have they got me on speed-radar down at the station?

Damn cop. Damn ticket. Damn car.

I'm having serious regrets about buying the Jag. It guzzles gas, it sits too low, and it won't be any good come winter. I should have known I was headed for trouble when it showed up in my driveway minus the signature Jaguar ornament crouched on the hood, ready to leap. But even without that, this car leaps. Straight into overdrive.

Sometimes, the things you wish for aren't as great as you think. I'd give anything to have my old VW back. I keep a close eye on the speedometer, my foot barely tapping the gas as I crawl toward home. My mood only sours as other cars zoom past me, but I don't dare chance another ticket. By the time I reach my driveway, I'm surprised the

National Weather Service hasn't issued a severe thunderstorm warning. I blow through the door and find Lila waiting in the foyer. The look on her face instantly deflates me. She looks more miserable than a puppy about to pay a visit to the vet.

I throw my purse on the hall stand. "What's wrong?"

"There was a phone call for you while you were gone." She hands me a slip of paper, refusing to meet my eyes. "I took the name and number. You need to call back."

A phone call? I take in Lila's swollen eyes, her red nose, and my stomach rolls in a slow one-eighty. A phone call. *The* phone call. The one I've expected and dreaded for months.

Oh, God. Not Grandma.

I swallow hard, breathing deep, trying to brace myself. It was inevitable. She's an old woman. She lived a good life. It had to happen eventually. But even when you see it coming, who is prepared to face a loss?

Not me. Not today.

My hand trembles as I glance at the note, begin to read. The words blur as my brain absorbs the familiar name. I scan it briefly, trying to make sure there's no mistake, that my eyes aren't playing tricks on me.

No tricks. No mistake.

Not Grandma.

But what does the president of the Yacht Club Condo Association want with me?

I frown over the paper and glance at Lila. "Did he say what it's about?"

"You're supposed to call him." She dabs her eyes with a sodden Kleenex. "The sooner, the better."

Whatever she thinks the problem is, it's certainly nothing to cry about. Anything has got to be better than what my imagination conjured up in the last five minutes. Cleaning out Grandma's room at Whispering Pines. Making funeral arrangements. Meeting and greeting people at the wake service with Grandma's body laid out in a coffin behind me.

I dial and wait through four rings. The Yacht Club president picks up on the fifth.

"Hi, Mr. Harris, this is Lucy Carter," I say, fully aware of Lila's eyes intently trained upon me.

"Thank you for returning my call."

"No problem." I relax against the kitchen counter with a thumbs-up for Lila. Whatever her problem is, she can forget the tears. Bill Harris sounds calm, pleasant, and happy I called. As for me, I'm happy that I'm not talking with our local funeral director.

"I hope you're finding life at the Yacht Club a pleasant experience."

"Absolutely. Things couldn't be better," I confirm. This has definitely been the best summer ever. A condo on the lake, a housekeeper to clean up the messes, and central air conditioning. Who couldn't love this kind of life?

"Glad to hear it. We like to keep our members happy."

"You'll hear no complaints from me."

"Fine." He clears his throat. "Unfortunately, Ms. Carter, we have received a complaint. Several, actually, but I'm sure it can all be easily straightened out. That's why I decided to contact you directly, rather than getting the full board involved."

"Someone complained? About me?" I throw Lila an uneasy stare. I'm starting to understand her tears. "What's wrong?"

"Nothing serious. Just a little matter pertaining to the bylaws."

His voice is smooth. Rather too smooth for my liking. Suddenly I remember I didn't like Bill Harris much the one and only time I met him. The Yacht Club president is one of those older gentlemen with a shiny bald head, tasseled shoes, and a polished attitude. A little too polished. Too pretentious. Too patronizing.

Funny how his attitude changed once he learned I intended to pay cash for the condo.

"Since you've just moved into the Club, you may not be aware of certain things. That's what prompted me to make the call today. We have rules in place, which all our members must follow. Certain things, of course, we can overlook. Minor details. But in this particular instance, I'm afraid that the bylaws are very specific. There would be chaos at the Club if they were not enforced. Naturally, that would be unacceptable."

"Naturally," I agree, trying not to interrupt, trying to push down my irritation. I still have no idea what he's talking about. And Lila still refuses to meet my eyes. But whatever it is, she knows. And it's bad. Bad enough to make her cry.

She didn't even cry when we crashed into that tree.

"I knew we could come to an amicable agreement." The relief in his voice is evident. "You seem like an intelligent young woman. I told her you weren't intentionally trying to cause trouble."

"Told who?" I frown over the phone.

"I'm afraid that's confidential."

"Now wait just one minute," I say firmly. "Someone lodged a complaint against me, yet I'm not allowed to know who?"

"Our members' privacy is at issue. They need to feel that they have a right to present a potential problem to the board without fear of reprisal."

"But what about me?" I feel my face growing hotter. The longer he talks, the more unbelievable our entire conversation seems. "I'm a member."

"Not quite," he corrects me. "Not until the board votes next month."

"All right, next month then." I swallow down my annoyance. "But I'll be a member soon enough. Don't I have any rights?"

"You'll have your say," he answers smoothly, "if it should come to that."

I resent his implication that I'm somehow at fault. I haven't done anything wrong. Not one damn thing. "Mr. Harris, I think you had better tell me exactly what this is all about."

"I should think that would be obvious. For one thing, those chairs."

His edgy retort stops me cold. "What chairs?"

"Frankly, Ms. Carter, I must admit that I, too, was rather surprised when I saw them on your deck. You were provided with a copy of the bylaws when you purchased your unit. Article six deals with restrictions. You should have known those chairs would be completely unacceptable."

Lila's chairs? Our gorgeous fuchsia-colored chairs? "Please explain to me exactly what the hell is wrong with those chairs."

"There is no need for profanity."

What a pompous, arrogant man. I find myself disliking him even more. He even made my mother cry. Suzy-Q whimpers at her feet, which seems to add to Lila's tears.

"Unfortunately, it is not only the chairs. I understand you recently put out some flowers. They are also in violation of the restrictions."

My jaw drops. "Are you saying I'm not allowed to have flowers on my deck?" How could anyone in their right mind object to some petunias?

"White ones, yes. Purple ones, no."

"That is ridiculous."

"Check the bylaws." He clears his throat. "I have a copy in front of me."

I storm past Lila, down the hall, through the living room, and out onto the deck. The flowers he finds so offensive are splashes of brilliant purple nodding in the lake breeze. The vivid pink chairs are pulled up close against the railing to take advantage of the full sun. It's beautiful. Comfortable. Peaceful. Inviting. How could anyone object?

"No unsightly conditions shall be maintained upon any deck or balcony," he drones on. *"Only furniture and equipment consistent with ordinary deck or balcony use shall be permitted on any deck or balcony,"* he concludes triumphantly.

"Unsightly conditions?" I glance around the deck. Everything is perfect. "I beg to differ."

"The flowers and chairs will have to be removed." His voice tightens. "To quote further from Section six, *anything seen from any portion outside the condominium from any position or angle must be white.*"

My fingers curl around the phone, but what I'd really like to do is wrap them around Bill Harris' neck... and squeeze really tight.

"Just so that I understand correctly, you object to the color of our flowers and chairs," I say, barely managing to keep my tone civil. What an odious little prick of a man. "Is there anything else?"

"Unfortunately, yes," he states. "There is another matter, one which is rather sensitive. But I feel it is my duty as a board member to bring it to your attention. I understand your mother is staying with you."

The hair on the back of my neck prickles at his mention of Lila. Certainly the bylaws don't contain provisions against overnight guests.

"What does my mother have to do with any of this? We had a car accident and she's staying with me while she recuperates. I assume that is not against your bylaws and regulations."

Northern Michigan is known for its hospitality, but I'm beginning to have my doubts about the Yacht Club.

"Certainly not," he assures me. "Guests are allowed. But I understand your mother has a dog. And according to Section six of the bylaws, we do have restrictions when it comes to animals."

"Excuse me?" I sputter.

"The dog will have to go."

"Hold on a minute," I say. "Suzy-Q is not the only dog in this place. I've seen people walking their dogs. I've seen their droppings."

How dare someone complain about me? I'm very careful to use my pooper-scooper.

"We've had numerous complaints about the dog. I'm told it barks continuously, at all hours of the day and night. That cannot and will not be tolerated. Your mother's dog is causing a disturbance to our members."

"Who?" I demand. "I want to know who."

"I have already told you that I am not at liberty to discuss that. Suffice it to say, she has complained on numerous occasions."

"She who?"

"It doesn't matter," he snaps. "The dog barks. I've heard it for myself."

Suddenly I've got a sneaky suspicion exactly who's been behind the complaints. I stare across the grassy green area at the only other unit directly facing my balcony and my *unsightly* deck furniture.

My nosy neighbor might have a green thumb, but everything else on her balcony is white. Her petunias, her wrought-iron set of table and chairs. Even her Persian cat that sits in the window is nothing but a fat ball of fluffy white fur.

"Mr. Harris, if I didn't know better, I'd wager a guess that it's your sister, Mrs. Richardson, behind these complaints." Didi mentioned once that the two of them are siblings. It makes perfect sense. Mrs. Richardson took her complaints directly to him, rather than me.

"That information is confidential," he informs me coldly.

No need for him to confirm it. I know I'm right. I feel it in my gut. Talk about rude. I couldn't care less if she doesn't like my flowers or chairs, but at least she could have had the decency to tell me to my face rather than go running to her brother, the president of the board. And complaining about Suzy-Q is flat-out ridiculous. That sweet little puppy barely yips, let alone growls at strangers. She's so friendly, she'd probably help someone break into the condo. The only time she does whine and carry on is when she sees that silly Persian cat sitting in the window. A typical feline, hissing and spitting on cue, taunting our poor little puppy.

"Your sister's cat isn't exactly a little princess," I remind him.

"Her cat is not the issue," he replies heatedly. If a voice can blush, I think I caught him. "And while pets are allowed under the bylaws, what is *not* allowed is for an animal—any animal—to cause unnecessary or unreasonable disturbance to other members."

I roll my eyes. "We're talking about a puppy."

"Puppy, dog, call it whatever you like. Regardless, it has to go."

Over my dead body.

"I don't like your tone," I say. "Or your attitude." I don't like *him*, period.

"That is certainly your prerogative. But meanwhile, let me remind you that the board has every right to assert its authority. It would be in your best interests to comply."

My heart gallops like I'm running with the bulls in Pamplona. But I'll be damned if I will allow this man to cow me. I refuse to be intimidated by him, his board, or his sister, either.

"You can tell the board that perhaps they need to amend their bylaws," I say. "Personally, I see nothing wrong with my chairs or my flowers, either. I am sick to death of white. It's stark, it's boring, and it's everywhere."

"We have our rules."

"To hell with your rules."

"As I mentioned once before," he bristles, "profanity will not be tolerated."

I snort. In my world, *intolerance* will not be tolerated. What is wrong with people in this place? Does having money automatically stifle people's creativity and imagination? There must be someone besides me here at the Club who's tired of living in a world devoid of color. If not, I'm in big trouble. I happen to like my purple flowers. I like Lila's pink chairs. And I've fallen in love with Suzy-Q.

"We will expect you to comply with the bylaws immediately."

"And if I refuse?" My chin tilts upward. Just let him try to knock me off my feet. I dare him.

"There will be consequences," he warns.

"Such as?" My chin tilts higher. I double-dare him.

"Ms. Carter, may I remind you that your membership in the Yacht Club has not yet been formally approved?"

"Is that a threat?"

"To the contrary," he coolly replies. "I am merely stating the facts."

"I doubt anyone even reads those stupid bylaws, let alone pays attention to what they say." Spouting off kicks up my heartbeat, kicks up my adrenalin, kicks my voice into high gear. I am so mad, I could just spit. My fingers tighten around the phone. "And if you think for one damn minute that I have any intention of knuckling under just because your damn sister decided she doesn't like my deck or my dog, then you'd damn well better think again."

"Young lady, you have made a serious error in judgment. As far as I'm concerned, this conversation is finished."

A dial tone buzzes in my ear. I stare at the phone. He hung up on me?

"Three damns in a row. I'm impressed."

I whirl and see the long, lanky form of Father Greg Kozminski leaning against the French doors. His arms are crossed against his chest, and his eyebrows are raised in a holier-than-thou look.

Oh, God. How long has he been standing there? How much did he overhear? Grandma taught me to respect those who embrace the religious life, but cursing in front of a priest hardly qualifies as respectful. I'm not versed in canon law, but swearing in the presence of a priest must rank as a worse sin than swearing in private.

"Sorry, Father. I thought I was alone."

"Lila let me in. She needed a little time to herself, so I thought I'd see how you were doing." He eyes me with a questioning look. "Everything okay?"

"Fine." The word slips out harsher than I intend, consuming me with more guilt. Bad enough he overheard me swearing. I'm sorry about that, but not sorry for what I said. The anger still consumes me, ugly and monstrous, feeding my outrage, worse than the fire and brimstone of hell. But I'm not about to confess. Confession means admitting you're at fault. Taking possession of your sins. Cleaning up your life, making amends. Saying you're sorry.

Admit to Bill Harris that I'm sorry? I'd rather choke and die. I have no desire for absolution.

I want revenge, and I want it now.

"Feel like talking about it? I'm a pretty good listener." His gray eyes hold me with steady concern.

"Believe me, Father, I doubt you want to hear this. It's not a pretty story."

"Try me."

Can't he take a hint? He and Lila are friends. Telling him what happened will only make him feel bad. Plus, there's nothing he can do. Father Greg doesn't live at the Club. He isn't forced to abide by some archaic set of rules.

Lucky him.

I can no longer stomach the view from my deck. Mrs. Richardson's unit taunts me, the all-white surface glaring triumphantly in the heat of the afternoon sun. A curtain flutters. Maybe it's the breeze, or maybe she's hidden herself from view behind the drapes, watching Father Greg and me even as we speak.

"Let's go inside." I say abruptly. "It's hot out here."

The cool, air-conditioned comfort of the living room welcomes us as we step inside. Unfortunately, so does Suzy-Q, waiting patiently at the door. Her tail thumps, her nose quivers, and her brown eyes are pools of such absolute trust that they nearly bring me to the breaking point. I sink onto the floor and pull her into my arms, burying my face in soft puppy fur. How can people be so petty and cruel? How could someone be so mean as to want her banished?

Losing Suzy-Q will break Lila's heart.

"Lucy?" Father Greg stands before me, a tall sober shadow. "What's wrong?"

No wonder they call him *Father*. He has such a caring, compassionate voice. I know he'd be on my side, if only I'd let him. And I can't hold back any longer. The dam bursts, bringing forth a flood of angry tears. "That was the Yacht Club president on the phone. He knows Lila has been staying with me." I hug Suzy-Q tighter. "He said we broke the rules, and he ordered me to get rid of her."

"Get rid of Lila? Good Lord, what has she done?" Father Greg looks as confused as some poor lost soul left to wander the vast wilderness of purgatory.

"Not Lila." I swipe at my tears. "Suzy-Q is the culprit. She's been barking at a neighbor's cat."

"Ah, the eternal battle between canine and feline." He taps Suzy-Q's head affectionately. "So, you're the one who has this place in an uproar. Don't you know it's impolite to bark at kitty cats?"

"Not just any cat," I tell him. "And not just any neighbor. She happens to be the sister of the president of the board."

"Ah, mystery solved. That explains Lila's tears." He nods. "You think this nosy neighbor tattled to her brother?"

"Who else?" I say. "Plus, she lodged a complaint with him about my deck. Supposedly, it's an eyesore and against the bylaws. Too much color."

Father Greg's eyebrows lift. "An eyesore?"

"Can you believe it?" I shake my head and sigh. "If you ask me, the woman has way too much time on her hands. All this grief over some flowers and chairs."

"Lila told me about the chairs when she ordered them from Bob. I know how excited she was about giving them to you." His face is etched with compassion. "I'm sorry about this, Lucy."

"I'm sorry, too" I say softly. "And truly, Father, if I have to, I could handle losing the flowers and chairs. But Suzy-Q? Poor little puppy. I don't know what we're going to do." I stroke her head softly. "She's had her run of the condo since day one, but she can't stay. And Lila's in no shape to move back to her apartment, not while she's still on crutches. Plus, even if she did, taking care of herself would be hard enough. How could she take care of a dog? It would be impossible."

"I see your point," he says thoughtfully.

"It's not fair," I add sadly. "Why should Suzy-Q have to leave? Too bad it's not the other way around. I'd love to get rid of Mrs. Richardson and her nasty old cat."

"What are you going to do?" Father Greg asks.

I sigh as Suzy-Q squirms out of my arms and off my lap. "Call the vet and arrange to have her boarded, I suppose. It doesn't look like I have much choice."

The president of the Yacht Club made himself perfectly clear. Either the dog goes, or I do. I'm already in violation of their stupid rules, and I haven't even been voted in as a member yet. And you have to be a member in order to live here. It's a catch twenty-two and it's breaking my heart.

"Boarding her won't be necessary. We're going home."

Lila stands in the doorway, leaning heavily on one crutch. Suzy-Q wiggles happily at her feet.

"You can't leave yet," I say.

"Of course I can," she firmly replies. "I'm an adult. I can do anything I want."

Suzy-Q sits on her haunches, barking rapidly, as if on cue. Is she backing Lila, or pleading with me to make a good case? "You can barely manage on your own," I say. "How do you expect to manage with a dog?"

"I'm stronger than you think. We'll get by."

I'm not about to put Lila's theory to the test. "You know what the doctor said. It was a bad break and it needs time to heal. You can't afford to rush it."

"I can't afford to stay any longer," she replies in a steady voice. "Lucy, let's be honest. Look at what's happened since I moved in. You're in trouble with your friends, and it's all because of me."

"These people are not my friends." I blurt out the words, surprised to hear them spilling from my mouth. Surprised even more as I realize it's the truth. I don't have any friends here at the Club. I barely know anyone except for Didi. I've never been invited to their homes, or any of their parties. Even with all my money, I'm still an outsider.

And so is Lila.

Suddenly I realize I don't want her to go. Not yet. Not like this. She shouldn't have to. Neither of us has done anything wrong.

You can't choose your family but you can choose your friends, Grandma always said. And while I didn't choose to call Lila family, that's exactly what we are. *Family.* And then I remember something else Grandma taught me. *Families stick together when things get tough.*

"You can't go home," I repeat stubbornly. "I won't let you."

Lila stands her ground and doesn't look convinced. Am I supposed to beg? I swallow down a sigh. The things you do for family. "Please don't go."

"Lucy's right." Father Greg straightens to his full height. "It's better you stay put."

"I am not boarding my dog," she insists.

"That won't be necessary," he says. "I have a solution. Why don't I take Suzy-Q home with me?"

"To the rectory?" Lila and I join voices in surprise.

"Why not?" He shrugs. "It's a big old house with just me in rambling around all by myself."

"But what will people say?" Lila says.

Exactly what I'm thinking. Our Lady of the Lakes Parish has enough controversy without Father Greg and Lila's dog adding to the gossip.

"Who cares what people think? Besides, who is going to tell me *no*? Certainly not the parish council." A slow grin spreads across his face. "Plus, last I heard, the diocese hadn't issued restrictions against priests having pets."

Though she hasn't agreed, I know it's already a done deal. Relief spreads across Lila's face as she glances back and forth between the two of us, blinking a silent thank you.

"But that still leaves the flowers and chairs," I suddenly remember. "What do we do about those?"

Father Greg throws up his hands in a count-me-out gesture. "I'll take the dog, but I don't have a deck. Besides, I'm a priest, not a florist. Send the flowers home with me, and it's guaranteed I'll forget to water them. They'll be dead in a week."

"We can pull the pots inside," Lila suggests. "If we put the flowers in the living room by the French doors, they should be fine. They'll still get the full morning sun."

I nod slowly. "And if I pull the chairs away from the railing and push them against the far wall, that might appease Mrs. Richardson. Besides, I don't think she'll be complaining again. At least, not anytime soon."

I'll bet a million dollars Bill Harris already spoke with his sister. No doubt she got an earful of what I had to say. But I meant every word. Just let her try and cause us any more trouble. Bad enough Suzy-Q is being banished to the rectory. I've had enough of playing martyr, of feeling guilty, of chanting *mea culpa.*

My fault, my fault, my most grievous fault.

This is *not* my fault.

And if Mrs. Richardson doesn't like it, let her sue me.

"Great, I'm glad we've got that all settled. And don't worry about the dog. She'll be fine." Father Greg reaches down and scratches between her ears. "I could use the company."

"I'll bag up her food and dishes." I swallow over the lump in my throat. It's going to be hard seeing Suzy-Q go, but it seems like the best solution. And knowing she's going home with Father Greg makes it easier to say good-bye. He'll take good care of her.

"She'll need to be walked every few hours," Lila reminds him. "Lucy's been so good about doing that."

"And make sure you brush her every morning," I add. "She loves the attention."

"Don't forget she's still a puppy," Lila warns. "She likes to chew. I suggest you hide your shoes."

"Would the two of you please quit worrying? I don't anticipate problems." His eyes crinkle in a smile. "If I lose a few shoes, who cares? It's not like I'm going dancing soon."

My heart skips a beat as the strain of music suddenly starts waltzing through my head. Why not? It's worth a shot. "Father Greg, do you have any plans next Saturday night?"

"Same plans I have every week. I'm saying the five thirty Mass." He pauses. "Why?"

"What about after Mass? Would you be interested in going to a party?"

"That depends. Will there be food?"

I break out in a wide grin. Father Greg might be a priest, but he's still a man.

"There'll definitely be food," I confirm. "Lots of food. The most delicious food you'll ever taste in your life."

"Count me in," he says.

"Wonderful." My table for ten is filling up fast. I still need to find that killer dress, but suddenly I can't wait for this party.

Just like I can't wait to see the look on everyone's faces when they get a glimpse of my colorful group of friends sitting at my table.

CHAPTER FIFTEEN

Cinderella herself couldn't have wished for a more perfect evening. Me in a black, strapless knock-em-dead dress, and Max in his tux. We waltz to the strains of a moonlight serenade in a room that's been magically transformed from everyday elegance into a twinkling fairyland of glitter and romance.

But who am I kidding? I'm Lucy, not Cinderella.

And Didi is *not* my fairy godmother.

I really need to stop listening to that woman. I knew the knock-off designer dress was wrong for me even before the saleswoman somehow managed to zip me into it, but Didi convinced me to buy it anyway. *You never go wrong with black*, she said, though I notice she hasn't taken her own advice tonight. Her swirling concoction of blue and sea foam-green silk complements her copper curls. Didi looks sexy, comfortable, and completely the vamp.

Whereas I can barely breathe, barely sit, barely dance in this dress that's strangling me. I would rip the damn thing off right now, but I'd probably get arrested.

"What's wrong?" Max asks as he leads me around the dance floor. "You've been fidgeting all night."

"My dress is too tight," I admit after a moment. "And my feet hurt. These new shoes pinch."

He glances down at my feet. "Why did you buy them?"

"Because they matched my dress," I admit, remembering Didi's rapture over the sequined heels. The ones she liked. The ones I bought. The ones with the three-hundred-dollar price tag. Right now, I'd gladly fork over a thousand dollars for a pair of cushy slippers or my usual flip-flops.

"As long as I live, I'll never understand women," Max says, rolling his eyes.

I wince as he leads me through a complicated series of dips and twirls. Somewhere in some previous lifetime, Max must have taken dance lessons. Or maybe they give them at camp? "I wouldn't expect you to understand. You're not the one whose shoes pinch."

He blows out a deep sigh. "You know, Lucy, some people have lots more things pinching them than expensive shoes."

I bite my lip, deciding then and there to keep my mouth shut. Max is dealing with some big problems, and he has every right to be upset. It's been a difficult week for him, since the Bay County planning commission has recommended the PUD be approved. The *Journal*'s editorial announcing its support for the project ran in yesterday's paper. Now all that's needed is the township zoning board to follow the county's recommendation and rubber-stamp the final plans. The PUD will be approved. The developers will win, and Max will lose his camp, his home, his grandfather's legacy.

It will all disappear. Everything he's been fighting for, everything he cares for. And I know how that feels, losing the only family you have. It leaves you empty and alone inside, like heaven itself has turned a cold shoulder on your very soul.

The music heads into a slower rhythm and I use the chance to move closer in his embrace. Regardless of how I feel about Loon Lake, it's all Max has left. "I'm sorry about everything," I whisper. "I wish it had turned out different."

His arms tighten around me and I know he's gotten the message. "Thanks. That means a lot to me. But at least we tried to stop them."

"Maybe there's still a chance the zoning board won't go along with the vote," I offer. But both of us know it's a fruitless wish and I'm merely trying to cheer him up. There's virtually no way the PUD won't be approved.

"I don't want to talk about it anymore, okay?" he says. "Tonight's meant for celebrating."

I play along, though it's obvious neither of us is in any mood to celebrate. I close my eyes and do my best to concentrate on the music. But guilt is an excellent dancer and waltzes along, beat for beat, taunting me with its endless melody.

You could have done more. You should have done more. You didn't even try.

Max asked for my help in beating the zoning ordinance and I promised to help him.

You didn't even try.

"Tonight wasn't a total loss." He nods toward the other end of the dance floor. "They look like they're having a good time."

I follow his gaze and see Lila *almost-dancing*. For once, she is without her crutches, allowing her partner's arms to carry her instead. He holds her loosely, barely an embrace, as they move about the floor. He laughs and she laughs, and it is sweet to watch. Dear God, forgive me, but I can't help thinking they make the perfect couple.

Too bad priests can't marry.

"Father Greg's a lucky guy." Max runs a finger around his neckline, giving himself a little breathing room. "He doesn't need to wear a tux. That Roman collar outfit of his goes anywhere."

"Don't complain. Trust me, you look very handsome tonight." I run my hand along the rich, smooth edge of his shoulder. I'm so used to seeing him in chinos and deck shoes, but Max looks splendid in his tux. I brush a light kiss upon his lips. "This tux fits perfect, like it was made for you."

He throws me a grim smile as he twirls me in his arms. "Probably because it was."

"Very funny." I barely catch my breath as he spins me around the dance floor. If he's not careful, he'll spin me right out of my dress. That would make quite the story at the Club. I haven't checked the bylaws, but I'm sure there must be some restriction against exposing your breasts.

And if Edie Phillips isn't careful, she'll be the first to find out. She's displaying a lavish show of cleavage in that salmon-colored chiffon dress she's wearing. If Kris were here, she'd turn it into a quip or two. Such as suggesting Edie could easily turn a G-rated evening into an X-rated spectacle.

I swallow hard as a sudden swift longing for my friend tugs at my heart for the umpteenth time tonight. Kris had an invitation and promised she'd be here, but she's a no-show. I miss her. I miss the old Kris. The Kris I could count on. The Kris who always made good on her promises. What happened to her? Somewhere along the way, she disappeared. And the new Kris didn't even have the decency to phone and tell me she couldn't make it. Nothing left for me to do but grit my teeth, suck in my gut and throw Edie a smile as I sail past her on Max's arm.

He stops mid-dance. "Mind if we sit down?"

"Fine by me. I think I'm getting a blister."

He takes my hand and leads me off the dance floor, limping noticeably by the time we reach our table. I bite my lip, wishing I'd bitten my tongue as well. Max made it clear he didn't want to come and he didn't want to wear a tux, but he did both, simply because I asked him. He's danced with me all night, and his leg must ache, yet he hasn't complained once.

Maybe because I've been doing such a great job of it myself.

"This is just the perfect evening." Lila hobbles to the table, leaning heavily on Father Greg's arm. "Thank you again for inviting me, Lucy. I was afraid to come, but I'm so glad I did. The food was delicious, but mostly it's the company I'm grateful for."

"Sure it's not the music?" Max teases gently as she sinks into her chair. "Lucy and I were watching you out there on the dance floor. You've got pretty good moves, even with that cast."

"Why, thank you, Max." A radiant smile beams across her face.

It's good seeing her happy again. Since we lost Suzy-Q to the religious life, Lila has been so quiet. The Club's restrictions have caused her remorse, and she rarely sits on the deck anymore, even when I'm out there. And though she hasn't said it, I feel like she's made the decision to spend the rest of the time she has left at my condo living in the shadows.

Just like the pink chairs we tucked away from prying eyes underneath the awning. Hidden in the shadows.

"This is some party." Father Greg's gaze sweeps the room. "Looks like everyone in town is here."

"Not everyone," I say. "Just those who can afford the five-hundred-dollar-a-plate ticket."

"Five hundred dollars? Good Lord, is that what this cost?" Lila's horrified voice matches her expression. "If I'd known, I never would have come."

"It's no big deal," I mumble.

"You're already much too generous as it is," she insists. "But buying me a ticket for five hundred dollars so I could come to the party? It's simply too much. It's—"

"It's a tax write-off," I blurt out before she embarrasses me further. Leave it to Lila to call attention to what I've done. But I don't want people getting the wrong impression. No matter what she thinks, my altruism had nothing to do with decency or kindness. Still, there's no way I'm going to admit the real reason behind the invitations I gave out tonight. Plus, I never did fill those last two empty chairs.

"Wonder how much they rake in on this kind of event," Father Greg muses.

Max glances around the room. "From the look of this crowd, probably a couple hundred thousand."

"Well, at least we know it's going toward a good cause." Father Greg shakes his head. "Don't get me wrong. I know the hospital needs money. But I can't help thinking what our parish could do with that kind of financial support. Our collections are down, and with the economy the way it is, people—even the ones with money—aren't as generous as they used to be."

I know he hasn't meant his words as a personal

accusation against me. Father Greg isn't like that. Still, I can't help feeling guilty. I make a silent vow to double my contribution next time I go to church.

Or maybe it would be simpler if I just mail a check. It's been a long time since I graced a pew with my presence. I don't want to mess up my track record and get both me and God confused.

All of us sit quietly, content for a moment to enjoy the company and the people moving about the dance floor. The music is loud and the dance floor is crowded. Sam Curtis and his wife Patty sway to the music, eyes only for each other. She's heavily pregnant, and he moves her gently around the room. It's obvious he adores her. I sneak a glance at Max. Will he ever look at me like that some day? Our relationship is too new, too fresh, but a girl can always hope.

Didi and Richard work opposite sides of the room. She's barely spoken to me tonight except for a few sentences during dinner. I suspect she wasn't too thrilled to be sharing a table with a priest. Or with my mother and Max, either, though Didi is much too polite to say it to my face. But it's obvious my friends sitting around my table aren't the sort of people she and Richard usually run with. I suppose she thinks we're a motley crew.

Then again, I'm not entirely off the hook myself. How Bob and Roberta managed to swing the five-hundred-dollar-a-plate tickets on their camp caretaker and cook's salaries is beyond me. But the two of them are here and there's no escaping them. Especially with Max and Lila seated at my table.

"Nice to see you all tonight," Bob says as they make the rounds. He glad-hands Father Greg and Max and kisses Lila's cheek.

Bob nods in my direction. Barely.

My cheeks redden at the deliberate snub.

"Who are you sitting with?" Max peers toward their chairs, two tables to the left.

"A couple new young doctors from the hospital and their wives." Roberta shrugs. "Never met them till tonight, but they seem nice enough."

"It would have been wonderful if we could have sat together," Lila says with a wistful glance in my direction. "I wish there had been room."

I sink low in my seat. Leave it to Lila, the saint, to rub in the fact that I didn't invite them. Though I've got to admit that Bob cleans up good, even if his tux is a bit snug. And the gold flecks in Roberta's sparkling brown eyes match the glitter of her gold gown.

Did I honestly believe she'd show up wearing a sweater-vest?

I slide even lower in my seat, thoroughly ashamed of myself. I should have asked them to be my guests, numbers nine and ten. It wouldn't have hurt me or cost me a thing. Why didn't I do it? My selfishness, my guilty conscious and the shame I feel pinch sharper than these expensive shoes.

Plus, once the PUD is approved, Bob and Roberta, just like Max, will be homeless.

My tight dress prevents me from sinking even lower.

"Too bad we don't have more people like them in James Bay," Father Greg says as Bob and Roberta head toward the dance floor. "They're the kind of people that make up the heart of this town. We've been blessed by their generosity. Take Bob, for example. Every year he donates a few of his pieces to the silent auction and they always fetch a high price. This year, it's his chairs."

Bob, a philanthropist? I throw Max a doubtful glance. Why didn't he tell me?

Father Greg smiles. "Who knows? Maybe if enough people bid on them tonight, Lucy's pink chairs will be in vogue and she can move them back out on her deck."

"God, my feet hurt." Didi slides into her seat and refills her champagne flute with liquid golden bubbles. She sips, then turns to me with a sweet, frothy smile. "What pink chairs?"

"Just some furniture that Bob Campbell gave me." I shoot Father Greg a warning look. Is it a sin to kick a priest? I've managed to keep Didi out of the loop about my latest debacle here at the Club. She's sponsoring my membership and I don't need her on my case. Bad enough that Bill Harris and Mrs. Richardson are after me. I have no desire to face Didi's wrath.

"Bob Campbell." The name lingers on her lips as she turns to Max. "Isn't he that man who works at your camp?"

"He's our caretaker. His wife Roberta is our cook."

Didi's eyebrows lift slightly. "Frankly, I'm surprised that the camp's board of directors would allow him to work around children. Isn't there some law against it?"

Max's fists clench in hard balls against the snowy white tablecloth. "What exactly is that supposed to mean?" he says, his voice low and dangerous.

I glace from Didi to Max, then back again. I'm confused, too. Bob and I might have our differences, but I've never heard the slightest hint of controversy about him. If he was a child molester or convicted sex offender, everyone in town would know it, including me. Especially me. I'm a reporter. Being in the know is my business.

Correction. It *used* to be my business. I'm not a journalist anymore. Now I'm merely Lotto Lucy.

"You would think the camp director would have more sense than to keep a man like him around. Everyone in town knows Bob Campbell is a drunk."

"For your information, I'm the camp director," Max says. "And who or what Bob Campbell is or does is none of your business."

Max comes to his feet and gives his chair a violent shove. "Excuse me. I need some air." He storms off, leaving us all to sit there in stunned silence. If this is supposed to be Cinderella's ball, then my Prince Charming just limped away, leaving me alone to deal with a slightly tipsy and extremely rude Fairy Godmother.

"Well, that man is definitely not in a party mood." Didi pours herself a little more champagne, then lifts the bottle. "Anyone else?"

Lila shakes her head. Father Greg's large, tanned hand covers his empty glass. "None for me, thanks."

Didi eyes him over the rim of her flute. "Don't tell me you'd allow a lady to drink alone?"

"I don't drink," he says flatly.

"I thought all priests drank," she says. "You use wine in church."

"Not in my chalice."

I draw in a sharp breath, suddenly realizing without being told exactly what Father Greg, Bob, and Lila all have in common, and how they know each other.

Am I the only person who doesn't attend twelve-step recovery meetings these days?

"The reason I don't drink is because I'm an alcoholic." Father Greg lifts his chin, and his eyes contain a stubborn glint. "I use a sacramental grape juice known as mustum in my chalice when I say Mass." He rises to his feet and shoves in his chair. "I think it's time I went home."

"I'm sorry if I offended you. I didn't mean anything by it." But Didi doesn't look sorry. Her face wears a practiced pout that I'm sure has seen plenty of use. But there's a big difference between pretty and petty, and it's not just the lack of an *r*.

"I've got an eight o'clock Mass tomorrow morning." Father Greg nods abrupt goodbyes around the table. "Thanks again for the invitation, Lucy. I'll see you in church."

Lila hesitates. "Would you mind dropping me off at the condo? My leg is hurting."

"No problem." Father Greg offers his arm and assists her to her feet. "I'll pull the car around."

Father Greg is stopped by people at nearly every table as he and Lila thread their way toward the door. He seems to know as many people here as Didi herself does. I never realized how much a priest is always on display. Good thing he doesn't drink. He can't afford to let his guard down... especially since he's leaving with Lila in tow. Knowing this town, the rumors could be flying before tomorrow morning's Mass.

Didi slips into Max's chair. "My God, how archaic—a priest, no less," she hisses in my ear. "Whatever possessed you to invite him tonight?"

I do not bother to grace her with a reply. She wouldn't understand.

"Men like him drive me absolutely insane. Exactly what hole did he climb out of?"

"Our Lady of the Lake Parish... and it is not a hole," I add hotly, inexplicably miffed by the situation in which I suddenly find myself. Miffed at Max for abandoning me. Miffed at Lila and Father Greg for leaving me alone to face Didi's interrogation tactics. Miffed at Didi herself. What gives her the right to criticize Father Greg? He isn't here to defend himself, and she's not even Catholic.

Not to mention, Didi isn't the one who spent five thousand dollars for the privilege of hosting this table tonight. I did.

And I can invite anyone I damn well please.

"He's quite attractive, you know." She settles back in her chair, fingering her champagne flute. "Such a waste, a man like that, stuck as a priest."

"I doubt Father Greg thinks of himself as being stuck. This isn't the Middle Ages," I remind her. "No one forced him into the priesthood. He made a conscious choice."

"Yes, but was it the right choice?" She offers me a Mona Lisa smile. "Think what you like, but priest or no priest, he's still a man. They're all alike, with one thing on their minds. Did you notice how many women he danced with tonight."

"Didi, he's a priest!" The mere implication that a devout man like Father Greg might harbor sexual longings is more than my Catholic mind wants to contemplate. I wipe the notion away faster than you can say *Amen*.

"Don't be so naive," she counters calmly. "Just because a man is a priest doesn't automatically make him an asexual creature. Just pick up the newspaper. The church has spent millions—perhaps billions—on the clergy sex scandal." She smiles pointedly. "Maybe once upon a time, Father Greg might have chosen to look and not touch, but things are different now."

"You're wrong," I insist.

"Am I?" She eyes me with a kind of smug smile that suddenly makes me want to reach out and slap it right off her face. "I notice he didn't refuse when your mother asked him to take her home."

The fire on my cheeks rages hotter than the fires of Purgatory. Didi must be drunk, for there's simply no other excuse for her to talk this way.

"Nothing is going on between my mother and Father Greg."

Yet, hadn't I toyed with the same thought earlier this evening?

"Absolutely nothing," I add with a burning emphasis and shake my head so hard a few diamond-studded hair pins tumble loose, falling on the table.

"Let's be realistic. Your mother is an attractive woman, even with that cast on her leg. Plus, they left in the same car. Pretty damning evidence, if you ask me."

"You have it all wrong."

"Do I?" Didi merely says with an enigmatic smile.

"You said it yourself. Father Greg danced with lots of women tonight."

"But he left with only one." She lifts her glass in my direction and smiles. "Go ahead and think what you like. You're still young. You'll learn."

If Max were here, I'd insist he take me home. I'm still blustering through my outrage as the Club's hostess appears at my side. "Miss Carter, I'm sorry to disturb, but there's someone in the lobby who insists on talking to you."

Why do I continue to doubt God always provides? I slip from my chair, grateful for the chance to escape. I don't care who's waiting for me in the lobby. Anything will be better than arguing with Didi.

NOT.

My gaze sweeps over Kris, standing before me in wrinkled brown slacks, brown t-shirt, brown sandals.

"Where have you been? And why are you dressed like that?" The longer I look at her, the madder I get. She promised she would show up, and now she finally has, she looks like the UPS guy out for delivery. "I told you this was a formal party. You can't come in here in jeans. People are staring."

"So what?" She shrugs. "I don't give a rip. Let them stare." Her jaw clenches and her fists knot in hard balls at her side.

I refuse to allow her to see my hurt and dismay. Not to mention my embarrassment. Never in a million years would I have done this to her. What kind of friend leaves another friend stranded? Kris didn't used to be so inconsiderate.

"Decent of you to show up, now the party's almost over."

"I didn't want to come anyway." Kris sways unsteadily on her feet and rubs her forehead with the heel of her hand. Her eyes are bleary and red-rimmed. Has she been crying? Then I catch the smell of something else, a smell I've always associated with Lila.

My eyes narrow. "Have you been drinking?"

"I might have had a couple beers," she says in a loud voice. Her eyes hold a challenge. "But so what? You're not my boss."

I grab her by the arm and haul her into a small hallway off the valet entrance, away from watchful eyes. "What is wrong with you?" I hiss. "You're making a scene."

"Is that so? Well, la-di-da. I certainly don't care. And you didn't used to, either, Lucy. You never cared what people thought," she mutters. "You've changed."

"Damn right I have. At least I learned some manners," I shoot back, trying to take away the sting of her words. Kris has it all wrong. I'm the same person I've always been. She's the one who's changed. She's different. Her attitude is different. Her attitude about me, about our friendship. And the reason is so obvious. Kris is jealous. She's just like everyone else. She resents the fact that I have money and she doesn't. But that's not my fault. It's not like I did anything to deserve it. All I did was win the lottery. The only difference between us is a little bit of luck.

"You knew tonight was important to me. You knew it was formal. If you didn't want to come, at least you could have called. But you couldn't be bothered."

"I tried your cell, but you didn't return my call."

A lame excuse, a little too late. "I left my phone at home," I say crossly. This dress doesn't have pockets, and my little black clutch barely has enough room for a Kleenex and my lipstick. But it doesn't matter. I don't have to explain myself to her.

"Typical," she mutters. "Thinking you're too important to be bothered by people's calls."

"That's unfair, and you know it. Besides, just look at you. When you finally bother to show up, you're drunk and dressed in jeans. Well, if you think I'm putting up with this, you're wrong. I have enough problems to deal with tonight."

"Problems?" She blows out a snort. "Lucy, you don't know the first thing about what real problems are."

"Don't I? Right now, *you* are my problem. The last thing I needed tonight was you showing up like this, humiliating me."

She flinches, staggers backward. Even through the beer haze, my words connected with a punch. Then she recovers. "Well, excuse me," she drawls. "I'm so sorry to have embarrassed you. Trust me, it won't happen again."

I struggle to rein in my temper before I slap her with a stream of words that I'll end up regretting... before I kill our friendship for good. "Whatever."

"Whatever," she mimics, then slumps against the wall with a scowl and a heavy sigh.

I eye her carefully. Granted, she's drunk, but this is not the Kris I know and love. Something's not right. Something's definitely out of kilter.

"Kris, what's wrong?"

She shuffles slightly, rolling her eyes. "Like you care."

"Come on, you just told me you didn't want to come, yet you still showed up. Something must have happened. What's going on?"

She shakes her head, stares at the floor.

"Tell me."

Her head shoots up and she fixes me with a hard stare. "Okay. You want the truth? I came here tonight to ask you for some money."

Money. My stomach twists in a tight knot. I should have known. If you've got it, people want it. Eventually it always comes down to that.

"I need a loan." Her words come hard and fast. "And I need it tonight."

Something deep inside me starts to shut down, and a numbing cold settles in, freezing out the love I have for a friend. The trust I placed in her. Of all the people in my life, Kris is the only one who's never asked for a single dime.

I can't stomach the sight of her. I close my eyes, blocking her out. "How much?"

"Five thousand dollars."

I bite my lip, taste the metallic tang of blood. The pain is a welcome distraction from the hurtful truth. I now know the exact cost of the price tag Kris has placed on our friendship.

"I'm in a hurry." Her voice slurs slightly. "Do I get the money or not? A simple *yes or no* will suffice."

I feel like bolting, and there's no place I'd rather be than home. But unlike my mother, there's no Father Greg to rescue me. And my so-called-Prince-Charming, AKA Max, has also disappeared. He needs to get his story straight. Cinderella was the one who fled the ball.

"Five thousand dollars is a lot of money. What do you want it for?"

Her face tightens. "That's none of your business."

"Excuse me?" It's rude to stare, but I can't help myself. Forget the loan. If Kris truly needs the money, I'll gladly give it to her… but not like this, not given the shape she's in. She won't even tell me why she wants it. God only knows what she might do with it.

"I haven't got all night." She straightens, weaving slightly on her feet. "Are you going to give me the damn money or not? If not, just say so, and I'll find someone who will."

Enough. Kris knew this party was important to me. A true friend never would have abandoned me. A true friend would have known that I needed her support. A true friend never would have left me alone to face all these people.

If Kris wants my money so bad, then let her at least tell me why. She's the one who came begging.

"I think I have a right to know," I insist. "After all, it's my money, remember?"

Her eyes glaze over, and for an instant I think she's on the verge of admitting the truth. Then she glances over my shoulder and suddenly draws in a sharp breath. Her eyes narrow.

"You're right. It *is* your money and everyone knows it. You remind us often enough." She takes a deep breath. "Forget I even asked."

Turning her back on me, she stalks toward the lobby door.

"Kris, wait!" My dress rustles, silk against skin, as I move to dart after her. But a warm hand from behind clenches my bare shoulder, keeping me from following.

"Don't go begging after her. You are so much better than that."

I shudder, and slowly turn to face her. If I see the merest hint of an I-told-you-so-look, I intend to slap it right off Didi's face. I am in no mood to be trifled with.

Her eyes shine with sympathy. "Trust me, I know exactly what you're going through. But you won't be doing her any favors by chasing after her. You've moved on with your life, and your friend needs to learn to do the same. It will be hard, but she'll get over it eventually."

Maybe Kris will, but what about me?

I can't remember a time when my heart's ever felt so heavy. Not even the day I moved Grandma into the nursing home. At least I'd had sufficient time to prepare myself for that. Kris was right there with me, holding my hand, seeing it through. Tonight, her betrayal stings like nothing else. I trusted her. I thought we were friends. Best friends. And now we are…

Nothing.

I no longer have the stomach for a party. My feet hurt, my head hurts, but most of all, my heart hurts. My heart *aches*.

I shrug away from Didi's grasp. "I'm going home."

"No, you're not." She grabs me by the arm. "This is a party, remember? And it's not over yet." She steers me toward the banquet room door. "There's someone I want you to meet."

CHAPTER SIXTEEN

A tall gentleman in a well-cut Armani tux stands at the edge of the dance floor as Didi leads me near. He's huddled in deep conversation with another man, and though they have their backs to us, one voice is all too familiar.

"Hello, Charles."

"Well, look who's here. Lotto Lucy herself." He rolls a fat, unlit cigar between his fingers while he scans me up and down. "You clean up nice. Amazing what money can buy."

Being publicly ogled by my former boss makes me feel like diving into a tub and scrubbing myself from head to toe. That, or slapping his eyeballs right out of his head. Either way works for me.

But if Charles can play the snob, I can, too. "Money definitely does have its advantages. I'm hosting a table tonight. What about you? I wouldn't think you could afford a ticket on your salary. Or maybe you got a big raise?"

It's rude and nasty, but he deserves it. Charles is so cheap, it wouldn't surprise me if he blew a good deal of the *Journal*'s advertising budget on his ill-fitting tux. "Are you here as a private citizen or a member of the press?" I add sweetly.

"He's my guest," the other man says, extending his hand. "Bill Graham."

"Bill, this is Lucy Carter. She used to work for me." There's a catch in his voice. Fawning, compliant, pandering. And that look on Charles's face is familiar. It's the one he wears when he glad-hands business owners with big bucks to spend on advertising campaigns.

"It's a pleasure to meet you, Lucy."

Something about him as we're introduced seems vaguely familiar. More than familiar. I've seen him somewhere before. He clasps my hand, presses my fingers lightly. "Congratulations on winning the lottery. Smart girl."

And suddenly I remember. I know who he is.

"All I did was buy a ticket," I stammer as I shake hands with the mysterious fifth member of Charles Kendall's breakfast group that day at the Club.

"You did more than that," he corrects in a rich baritone. "You bought the winning ticket."

"Lucy covered the municipal beat," Charles adds quickly. "The city and the townships."

"I remember you mentioning that," Bill says. His gaze never leaves mine, and he still has hold of my hand. My palm is sweaty, while his is cool and dry to the touch. I want my hand back.

"Ah, I see you've met Bill. I'm so glad the two of you finally have a chance to meet." Didi steps between us. "Bill is the mastermind behind our investment group. He's the one you'll have to thank when your million-dollar investment turns another million in profits."

"You've got a million dollars tied up in this?" Charles stumbles backward slightly. Scotch splashes down the front of his tux.

"I don't think I can promise any guarantees on a million-dollar profit, given today's economy," Bill replies with a smooth smile. "But I promise to do my best to get you a decent return on your money. Our goal is to keep our investors happy."

I finally manage to tug my hand away from his with a weak smile. Something about the man bothers me. The shift in his eyes, the expression on his face.

Charles brushes off his tux and glares at me. "I need another drink."

Didi's withering look follows him as Charles stomps off toward the bar. She turns to Bill. "I still don't understand why you thought it was necessary to invite him tonight."

"He's harmless enough," he says with a shrug.

For the first time in my life, I feel sorry for Charles. It sounds like he's gotten himself involved in something way above his pay grade. What does he think he's doing, hanging with people like the man facing me? I've seen Charles go off in a snit when things upset him, but this man doesn't look like he would ever lose control. Smooth, suave, urbane, he is as opposite Charles as two men could get, and there's no way I can envision a scenario that would bring them together... not unless it involves money.

Didi touches his arm. "You and Lucy have something in common besides our investment club."

"Is that right?" His eyebrows lift as he regards me with a curious smile. "And what would that be?"

"Max. He's here tonight as Lucy's guest."

He zeroes in on me with keen interest. "You and Max are dating?"

And that's when I suddenly make the connection. No wonder Bill Graham looks familiar. He shares the same jaw line, same cheekbones, and same last name as his son.

"This isn't normally Max's kind of party." His eyes sweep me appreciatively from head to toe. "You must be very special."

"Where is Max?" Didi scans the room. "Did he leave?"

"Yes, where is he?" Bill Graham echoes. "I'd like to talk to him."

"I... I think he's outside." Somehow I manage to choke out the words, though it's hard with my mouth dry as sandpaper. I'm talking to his father, a man Max despises. Has he seen his father yet? Does Max know he's here? "I'll see if I can find him."

I dart away and slip through the crowd before either of them have a chance to protest. I hurry past the silent auction items on display, past Bob's chairs, and into the lobby, where I spot Max striding in from outside through the valet entrance.

"Max!" I wave him over.

"There you are." He grabs me by the arm. "Good. At least you saved me the trouble of hunting you down."

His jaw is clenched tight, his voice barely civil. His fingers dig into my flesh.

"Stop, you're hurting me." I struggle to pull away.

He instantly takes his hands off me, but his eyes lock on mine like radar. "The two of us need to have a little chat."

For the first time since we've met, I'm leery about being alone with him. I don't like the look on his face. Clenched jaw, flashing eyes, stern brow. He's never looked at me like that before.

"Let's go back inside," I suggest. "We'll find a quiet table and talk."

"I'm in no mood for a party." Grabbing my hand, he drags me halfway down the service hallway. Finally he halts, pinning me against the wall, blocking my exit with a hand on either side of shoulders. We are eyeball to eyeball, his breath hot and heavy against my face. I shrink against the damask-covered wall, cowering at the sight of his anger. This isn't the Max I'm come to know and love. This man is a stranger. "Is something wrong?" I ask meekly.

"Damn right something's wrong. Tell me why you did it."

"Why did I do what?" My voice squeaks like a mouse. Right now I wish I were tiny like a mouse. I'd scurry down some hole near the carpet and hide.

"You know what I'm talking about. What kind of woman treats a friend like that?"

My heart sinks as I realize it's too late. I don't blame Max for being mad, now he's seen me talking with his father, a man who's caused him nothing but grief and pain. I catch the anger, the betrayal in his eyes, and I steel myself for what's sure to come. Max is furious, but things are going to get much worse when he learns what else I've done. Investing my money with Didi's group was a big mistake. A gigantic mistake. A colossal mistake. And I have to tell Max before it's too late. If I don't fix this, it is finished between us.

There will be no more *us*.

"I never met him before tonight. Didi just introduced us."

The glint in his eye hardens. "What are you talking about?"

I throw him an uneasy stare. "Your father."

"What the hell does he have to do with this?" He shoves away and plants himself in the center of the hallway, arms folded against his chest, and levels me with an icy glare that tells me anything that was once between us is already gone, frozen in his anger.

"I thought you were different. Looks like I should have known better," he says. "It happens every time. It's always about money. It changes things. It changes people. Winning the lottery changed you, Lucy. And not for the better."

"That's not true," I whisper. "I'm the same person I always was."

"No, you're not."

His words carry a powerful hurt, yet I recognize the truth behind what he's saying. The Lucy Carter I used to be, the zealous reporter who prided herself on doing the research, on getting the facts straight, never would have invested one million dollars without thoroughly checking the company before she proceeded. Instead, I couldn't be bothered. I did the unthinkable. I broke the golden rule of reporting.

The devil is in the details. If only I'd taken time to check things out. If only I'd asked Sam to review the paperwork. If only I'd invested a little time and patience instead of investing one million dollars. All of this could have been prevented. But I chose to blunder on like a stubborn fool. I insisted on doing things my way. The easier, softer way. One little phone call bought me a membership in Didi's investment club. One little phone call shut her up and got her off my back.

"You don't think the money's changed you?" he presses. "Look what you did tonight, turning your back on Kris."

I drag in a deep breath at the mention of my friend's name. "What has she got to do with this?"

He shakes his head in disgust. "I thought the two of you were friends."

"Kris and I had a private conversation. I didn't think you were the type to eavesdrop."

"What makes you think I eavesdropped?" he challenges.

My heartbeat takes off. "You and Kris talked?"

"What do you think?" He blows out a hard breath. "And if the way you treated her tonight is any indication, then God help all your friends. The Lucy I met months wasn't like this. That woman had a big heart." He stares at me with cold, hard eyes that glint like high-glossed steel. "I bet it never occurred to you to ask why she needed the money."

"I did ask, but she wouldn't tell me." I feel the anger rising in my throat. I'm not the coldhearted monster he's making me out to be. And what gives him the right to criticize or judge me? No one has that right. Not Max. Not Didi. Not even my mother.

"It's time you faced facts. The world doesn't revolve around you and your money."

I feel my face burning. "That's not fair."

"You want to talk fair?" His eyes narrow. "Maybe Kris wouldn't tell you why she needed the money, but I will. Her friend Toni's mother died this afternoon. Kris needed help so she could fly down to Florida and be with her friend. She needed the money to help Toni cover funeral expenses."

I stagger backward and lean against the wall. That's why Kris didn't show up for the party tonight? That's why she came, begging me for money? Max's words sicken me and sink my heart. What a fool I've been. A fool and his money are soon parted, but instead, I held on to it, denying a friend in need. Money that I never would have missed.

"I would have given her the five thousand dollars if she'd only told me why," I say quietly.

"You should have thought about that sooner. It's too late now."

"No, it's not." I start for the door. "It's never too late. I can fix this. She's probably back at her apartment by now."

"Don't bother. She's gone."

Max's words stop me. I'm nearly at the door, but I turn to face him. "She won't get far without money."

"She has the money. I gave her a loan."

"Five thousand dollars?" My eyes widen. "How did you come up with that kind of money?"

Max doesn't flinch. If anything, my words seem to make him more defiant. "I gave her everything I had in my wallet: seven hundred dollars. And I wrote her a check."

"But you barely know her."

"You still don't get it, do you?" His eyes narrow. "Friends help friends. Kris and I are friends. And I thought she was your friend, too. Your best friend."

I shudder at the thought that Max is willing to spend that much money on someone he barely knows. Money he needs. "You might not get it back," I warn.

He shrugs. "She seems like a good risk. Plus, it's only money. I don't need it. I've got plenty."

I've got plenty.

Then I remember why I came looking for Max. I remember who his father is, and what line of work he's in. Real estate development takes money. A great deal of money.

Bill Graham bought Charles Kendall's ticket tonight.

And Bill Graham is wearing a very nice tux. An Armani tux.

"You come from money, don't you?" I guess, stringing out my words in a long quiet sentence. "Your family has more money than you know what to do with."

Max's silence and stony glare is all the confirmation I need.

The betrayal rocks me. All this time, I thought Max was someone who grew up just like me. Someone who lost a parent at an early age. Someone who, except for the shelter of a grandparent's love, would have grown up empty and broken.

Instead, Max grew up in luxury, leading a life of privilege and ease.

"You lied to me," I say through clenched teeth. Hot, stinging tears bite behind my eyes, but I blink fast. I refuse to cry. I am not going to let him see how much this hurts.

"I never lied," he said. "You never asked."

"You should have told me," I insist.

"Why? It doesn't make any difference. I'm the same person I was when we met."

"What about your grandfather? Or was that all a lie, too?" I blink away more tears, staring him down in the same accusing way he's eyeing me. "Was he or wasn't he the caretaker out at camp?"

"I never said he was the camp caretaker."

"You did," I insist. "You told me you spent summers with him. You told me your grandfather lived at camp."

"He lived there because he owned the place."

The truth roars through my brain. I am not the only one who was careless with my facts.

"You said having money changes everything," I say bitterly, "that it changes people. It does." It's changed Max and me.

"The camp property has been owned by my family for years," he says. "It's in a trust. My grandfather controlled it till he died, then my father took over as trustee until I turned twenty-one. I manage the trust now."

The betrayal is devastating, and I can't face looking at him for even one more second. I turn my back, close my eyes, drag in a deep breath. I've had to learn some hard lessons these past few months when it comes to dealing with people and money, but at least I had an excuse. I'm not the one who grew up protected by a trust fund. Maybe I messed up, but at least I've been honest.

Max has no excuse. He should have known better.

He should have known you can't base a relationship on lies.

"Speaking of my father, exactly what did you mean earlier?"

"He's here at the party. Didi introduced us." I swallow hard. "He sent me to find you. He wants to talk to you."

Max's jaw clenches. "He's in for a long wait. I haven't spoken to him in over a year, and I have no intention of starting tonight."

"But…"

He holds up a hand, effectively silencing me. "Let me give you a piece of advice. Don't get tangled up with people like my father and Didi. You'll be in way over your head, and you'll be sorry."

Good advice, but a little too late. I'm already sorry. Way beyond sorry. Sorry for everything I've done. Sorry for the *couldas, wouldas, shouldas.*

Max turns away.

What's the point in pretending? He's going to find out sooner or later. I feel like I've been sucker-punched, like something deep inside is broken that can never be repaired.

And it's the truth. Something is broken. Max and I are broken, and there's no going back.

"There's something you need to know." With a deep breath, I admit what I've done. Admit I threw common sense out the window. Admit I threw care and caution to the wind. Admit I threw cash into an investment portfolio managed by his father.

Saying the words out loud is hard.

Facing Max is harder.

Facing myself is hardest.

I see the question blazing in his eyes.

Why?

I feel the answer seared across my heart.

Money.

"I'm sorry," I finish quietly. "I wish things were different, but I can't change what I've done. And I'm sorry. Very, very sorry."

Can money buy true happiness? I can afford thirty million dollars' worth of love and happiness, but I've never felt more miserable or alone in my life.

Correction. I hit that bottom as I watch Max's face slowly crumble. As I watch the fight die in his eyes.

As I watch him walk away.

I slump against the wall and let it take my weight. People warned me to be careful, not to let the money turn my head, not to be dazzled by the things it could buy. And they were right. The money bought me nothing but misery and heartache, plus a huge heaping of selfishness. I've never felt more ashamed of myself than I do right now, despite the jewelry, the makeup, and the fancy gown. Deep inside, I'm an ugly mess. I've turned into someone Max no longer respects. Someone I no longer respect. I've turned my back on the people that mattered most, and what have I gained?

A healthy balance in my bank account. A spotless condo, a flashy sports car.

But the balance sheet doesn't add up, and I'm left calculating what I lost.

A good job. Good friends. Purpose in my life.

Most important, I lost me. And if tonight is any indication, I'm in danger of never finding myself again.

I stumble back into the room and thread my way through the crowd. What's the point in staying? Everyone is gone. Max, Lila, Father Greg. I find Richard alone at our table, sprawled in his chair, drumming his fingers in time to the music.

"Leaving so soon?" he asks as I grab my black clutch.

"I'm tired. Tell Didi I had to go, will you?" But even as the words slide from my mouth, I realize I could care less where she is, what she thinks, or if I ever see his wife again. It's the Didis of this world that got me in this mess. When did I start listening to all of them?

More important, am I ready to quit?

Richard eyes me thoughtfully. "You look a little down."

Tears spring up as I hear the unexpected sympathy. I reach up, try to finger away the tears, but they don't stop. My two-hundred-dollar makeup job from the salon visit this afternoon is probably ruined, but I've ruined so much more than that tonight.

I've ruined my life.

He pats the chair beside him. "Have a seat. You look like you could use a friend."

No doubt he means well, but the man is clueless. He married Didi, didn't he? But Richard's eyes are kind, and when it comes to sympathy, I could use some support. Currently I'm flat broke when it comes to the friends department.

I sink onto the chair's soft cushion.

"So, what's the problem?"

My tears flow freely as I eye the littered remains of our dinner table. I poured so much hope into tonight, but there's nothing left but empty glasses and crumpled napkins smeared with lipstick stains. I grab one of the napkins and dab at my tears. Mascara, lipstick—stains are stains. At this point, who cares? My sobbing increases.

"Poor Lucy. It's been hard, hasn't it?"

I hiccup, and nod, furious with myself for being such a girl, furious with Richard for being so nice. "I'm not usually like this," I sputter. "I don't know what's wrong with me."

"Well, I do," he says. "In fact, it's pretty obvious."

I draw the napkin away from my face and eye him uncertainly.

"You care too much." He swirls the champagne in his flute. "You've got a big heart, and they all know it."

"Excuse me?"

He leans forward, elbows on the table, face near my own. "You're in way over your head, trying to run with this crowd. Take it from me. I know what I'm talking about. I've been married to Didi for over twenty years."

"But I…"

"Want some advice?" he says bluntly. "Take your money and go home, before you get hurt. You're no player, Lucy."

Where has Richard been all this time? I could have saved myself a lot of heartache if we'd talked weeks ago. "It's too late," I admit. "I already invested quite a bit of money."

"Well, good luck to you, then. Still, it was worth a shot." He pours a second flute and slides the glass in front of me.

As if I'll find the answer to my problems in a glass of liquid bubbles. "No, thanks."

He clucks his tongue, chiding me gently. "Listen to Dr. Richard. Champagne cures everything. Especially heartache."

I offer him a halfhearted smile. "I don't drink."

"You don't drink champagne? Or you don't drink alcohol?"

"I don't drink, period. I've never had a drink in my life."

"Well, there's your problem, kiddo." He sprawls back in his chair and lifts his glass in a semi toast. "If you ask me, now would be the perfect time to start."

Who knew champagne could make you feel like this? What a strange, disoriented feeling, this sidestepping reality with an I-couldn't-care-less attitude.

I don't know why I took the first sip. Or the second, or the third. Maybe if everyone hadn't deserted me, I'd have ended up drinking decaf coffee. Maybe I'd have gone home. All moot points, but one thing is guaranteed. Champagne or no champagne, Max and I are finished. That much I remember.

I drain the last bit from my glass and hold it up for a refill.

"Maybe you should slow down. We already killed the second bottle."

Richard's voice floats from somewhere close, but my mind is blank, my tongue feels thick, and I can't respond. I'm lost in a fog... a fog that's left me feeling blissfully numb. Exquisitely numb. No wonder people drink. Thanks to Richard and his two bottles of Möet, the pain of knowing I've destroyed my friendship with Kris, of knowing I've lost Max, is not as sharp. I welcome the numbness of not caring, not feeling the feelings. If this is what's meant by being drunk, then I embrace it. At least my head is still up. At least I'm still breathing.

I drag in a deep breath and suddenly wish I hadn't.

"Are you all right? You look a little pale."

Richard's voice floats somewhere near my ear.

"I think I need some fresh air." I grasp the edge of the table and wobble to my feet. When did the room start spinning?

"Let me help you."

"No." I shake off his arm and his concern. "I'll be fine."

I stand, praying my legs will hold me, praying I won't throw up. At least not until I make it outside. The faint sound of a soothing waltz accompanies me as I stumble onto the terrace, a dark, quiet haven. The chairs have been pushed aside into the shadows for the evening, and I sink into one, a cold mesh of wrought iron that offers no comfort. The Yacht Club should buy some decent cushions. It's not like they're hurting for money. They rake in plenty from membership fees.

I rest my head against the wall and stare up at the sky, which is spinning as fast as the ground beneath me. The faint ping of diamond hair pins hitting the flagstone doesn't move me. Who cares what my hair looks like? Nothing matters anymore. Somewhere in the not-too-far distance, the waves of Lake Michigan crash upon the shore. Above me, the night sky is brilliant with stars. I close my eyes and shut out the memory of the last time I witnessed a sky like this. It was the night I found out I won the lottery. The night I was with Max, at Camp Call of the Loon.

A door clicks open, and the rustle of dresses and raucous laughter spills onto the terrace.

"My God, Edie, did you ever see so many women in black? It's worse than a funeral. You'd think someone died."

I shrink back in the darkness, my heart pounding loudly at the familiar female voice not more than ten feet in front of me tittering through the inky blackness.

"Obviously, none of them have heard black is the new gray. Some women have no sense of style."

"Speaking of style, I love that dress. Where did you get it?"

A tinkle of laughter floats through the night air. "You like it?"

"Edie Phillips, you know you look gorgeous. No man here can take his eyes off you."

"Good. I wanted to teach Kent a lesson. He should know not to take me for granted. Nothing like a little competition to keep your husband interested."

"Remind me to keep you away from Richard." Didi sighs. "I suppose I should go rescue him. Last time I checked, he was with Lucy Carter, spoon-feeding her champagne."

I shrink further into the shadows at the mention of my name. Grandma always told me not to snoop in other people's business or I'd end up sorry. She was right about that. It's too late to make my presence on the terrace known, and I'm dreadfully sorry about that.

And I have a sudden feeling that sooner, rather than later, I will be dreadfully sorry I drank all that champagne tonight. My stomach rumbles and lurches slightly to the left, and my head begins to throb somewhere just above my right eye.

"I never liked her, even before she won the lottery." Edie's voice wafts on the night breeze. "Do you notice how she uses every chance she gets to flaunt her money? That in-your-face attitude of hers makes me want to vomit."

I clutch my stomach. For once, Edie and I are thinking along similar lines.

"You should have seen the look on her face tonight when I introduced her to Bill Graham. It was precious. Obviously Lucy had no clue that Bill is her boyfriend's father."

An unladylike snort explodes somewhere to my immediate left. "You mean to tell me someone is dating her?"

"You must have seen them dancing together. The whole room was watching."

"No, I did not. Women like her live for moments when they know the world is watching, and I'm not about to give her the satisfaction. Lucy Carter's head and ego are already big enough."

I close my eyes and fight back the waves of nausea. Is that what people really think of me? What other women think of me? How will I ever show my face in this town again?

"You must have seen them," Didi insists. "Max—he's Bill's son—is the one with the limp." She pauses. "Actually, he's not bad-looking, if you prefer that type. The rugged sort. All that fresh air out at camp probably gives him stamina. I wonder if he's any good in bed?"

"Some women have a thing for cripples," Edie says with a sniff. "She strikes me like that type."

I am definitely going to throw up. Definitely tonight. Perhaps right out here on the terrace. What a way to put an end to their discussion and announce my presence in grandiose style. Guaranteed it will be a moment none of us would ever forget.

"He must be after her money. Money always brings them sniffing round. God knows it can't be her looks or personality."

"No, Max has plenty of money. Millions, in fact, though not as much as she does."

Max has millions. The pounding in my head increases. He has millions in the bank, and never a word to me. Not that it matters. Max and I are through. We're a casualty of my ignorance and arrogance, and there's no hope of recovery for us.

"Though, even if she wanted to, she couldn't get her hands on his money. Bill told me it's family money and tied up in trusts."

"Serves her right."

"Thank God Richard and I never had children. Look how they treat you. Bill gave that boy the best possible life, an excellent education, and for what? To have him throw it away out at that camp on Loon Lake. Well, that's about to end. The two of them have been estranged for years, and Bill says that young man is about to get everything he deserves. He told me tonight that since the planning board made their recommendation, everything is set. He has the newspaper's support, plus he's met privately with some of the township commissioners. They've already assured him that the vote next week will go exactly the way we planned. Thank God. It's about time. People in this hick town move like mud. We've been waiting forever to get approval."

"It's finally a go?"

"Mmm, and don't you love the irony of it? Lucy was the last investor to come on board, and it was her money that put us over the top. Enough so that Bill was able to convince the right people it would be to their advantage to make sure the development passed."

Quiet, feminine laughter ripples through the darkness. "I thought bribing people was illegal."

"Who said anything about bribes? No one broke any laws. No cash was exchanged. Besides, it's not as if someone got hurt."

I choke back the bile rising in my throat. Didi's talking about me, about my investment, about the investment that will destroy Loon Lake.

"Richard and I will have the listings for the properties through our agency."

"I'd love to live out at the lake. I've been after Kent for years to buy out here at the Club, but you know how he is. He absolutely refuses to live in a condo. Says he doesn't like all the restrictions. And you know how I feel about living in this town. I am so sick to death of all the people."

"We'll talk Monday," Didi promises. "I think you'll be very impressed by the preliminary plans Bill has drawn up."

"What about the camp?"

"What camp? By next summer, all those rustic little cabins will be gone. There'll be beautiful one- and two-acre lots available for sale." Didi laughs softly. "So much for Max Graham teaching kids how to canoe. Do people even own canoes anymore? Everyone I know is into jet skis."

"Maybe I could talk Kent into buying us a new boat…"

A rustle of dresses and the click of high heels sounds against the flagstone terrace as they sweep past me. Their voices fade in the distance as they disappear inside.

I bolt to a stand but don't even clear the bushes. Champagne and the remains of my dinner explode through the night, straight down the front of my designer gown.

Damn Edie Phillips, for being such a pretentious snob.

Damn Didi Taylor, for pandering to me, for pretending she was my friend, for using me for her own selfish gain.

But most of all, damn me.

Most especially, damn me.

I've turned into exactly the kind of woman I've always despised. The kind of woman who cares only for herself. The kind of woman who turns her back on friends. The kind of woman who keeps score, who expects to be repaid for every kindness. How did I sink so low? How did I slip so far away that I quit paying attention to the things that matter most?

Friends. Family.

When was the last time I even visited Grandma?

I've turned into someone I barely recognize, and I've only myself to blame. Bad enough I destroyed my own dreams. How can I live with myself, knowing it is my money, my carelessness, that will destroy Loon Lake... and Max's dreams, too?

CHAPTER SEVENTEEN

"Personally, I always found saltine crackers and club soda helped."

I pull the pillow over my head. My stomach churns at the thought of eating anything, even something bland. "Please do not mention food," I beg.

"You'll feel better tomorrow," Lila assures me.

"As God as my witness, I will never drink again." I groan into my pillow. I'm never leaving my bed. How can I face anyone? I've shamed myself and shamed our family in a public display of drunken debauchery that's sure to be the subject of talk at the Club for months to come. Too bad the champagne didn't wipe out the memories of me vomiting all over the flagstone terrace, the wrought-iron chairs, the bushes. The memories of being ushered home by Richard. Being helped upstairs by Lila, despite her clumsy cast. Spending the night on my bathroom floor, praying to the toilet.

When I finally awoke from a restless sleep, it was to find my eyelids crusted shut, a satin comforter covering me, and Lila perched on the toilet seat, sipping coffee and reading her A.A. morning meditations as she waited for me to wake up from my drunken stupor.

Like mother, like daughter.

And somehow during the time she was in the kitchen rummaging up my breakfast of saltines, I managed to crawl from the bathroom to my bed. And while the slightest movement is torture, even through my headache hangover, I'm intently aware of Lila at my bedside.

"You don't have to sit with me. I'll be fine." I squint against the morning light breaking through the window. It burns the back of my eyelids, but the pain isn't nearly as bad as knowing Lila has witnessed my disgrace. Dimly I remember vomiting in the bathroom, but the floor is clean, the toilet shines. She cleaned up my mess and took care of me when I couldn't care for myself.

"There's no sense in two of us feeling miserable," I add. "You can leave."

"Actually, I am leaving," she says. "Right after lunch."

I peer at her uneasily over the sheet. "What?"

"I'm going home to my apartment."

"But you can't do that." I sit up in bed, wincing as a jarring pain slams through my head. Last night's champagne is extracting an ounce of revenge for each ounce I drank.

"It's better this way, Lucy."

"But why now? Why today?" I swallow hard. My brain isn't up to speed, but Lila's logic is simple enough to follow. "It's because of me, isn't it? You're leaving because I got drunk."

"I'm going home because it's time," she replies gently. "I need to go home. I've been leaning on you, and it's time I

309

stopped doing that. Last night showed me how much I've been babying myself. I can't afford to do that."

"There's no need for you to worry about money," I say quickly. "I have plenty."

"This isn't about money." She smiles softly and shakes her head. "This is about me. About taking care of myself. About my recovery. I need to get back to my own life. Back to work. Back to my A.A. meetings."

I bite my lip and shut out the sight of her. If Lila wants to go, I can't stop her. She's getting around well enough without her crutches and there's no reason for her to stay. No reason for me to make her stay. The fears I had weeks ago that she might sue me now seem ludicrous. Lila would no more sue her own daughter than I'd think to sue Grandma.

Lila sat beside me on the bathroom floor as I groaned my way through the night. Not once did she play the martyr, the *I-know-it-all-and-I-told-you-so* recovering alcoholic. Not once did she lecture me about the dangers of overindulgence. And hideous as I felt last night, hideous as I still feel now, her presence was—and is—a comfort. Lila said I would feel better in the morning. She knew what she was talking about. She's been through it herself.

Talk about ironic. The first time in my life that I turn to my mother for comfort and support, it's because I was drunk.

"Thank you for everything you did last night," I say slowly. "For staying with me, and for not judging me. If anyone has a right to do that—"

She raises a hand and cuts me off. "I'm not exactly a saint myself. Who am I to judge?"

God help me, but isn't that exactly what I did to her? I've spent my whole life sitting in judgment of Lila. And now, when she finally has every justification in the world to criticize me, instead she lets it pass.

Would I be so decent and gracious if the situation were reversed? I have a lot to learn from this woman.

This woman who is my mother.

"You'll be fine. You're stronger than you think. Winnie taught you well." A smile plays around her mouth as she rises to her feet. "You'll probably feel bad most of the day, but just remember—this, too, shall pass. By tomorrow, you'll be back to normal, ordering takeout pizza."

"Please, please, no talking about food," I groan from my bed.

"Oh, honey, I'm sorry. I forgot."

I prop myself up on one elbow. There's so much I want to know, so much left to discover, so much I want to ask her. But the words catch in my throat. "When are you leaving?" I finally settle for asking.

"Soon. I'm nearly packed and I already called the cab. Larry is down at Penny's Restaurant. He said he'd drive over and pick me up as soon as he finishes lunch."

No surprise. James Bay is a one-cab town. People either flag Larry down as he cruises by, or flush him out at the local diner.

"I'm going downstairs and finish my packing. I put the mail on the kitchen counter. Did you know we forgot to pick up Saturday's mail? And Betty should be here soon. I'll write her a note and tell her you're not feeling well, that she shouldn't bother you."

"I'm sure Betty already knows what happened," I reply glumly. Word travels fast in this town. I'll bet by now, the recounting of my sins last night have been recited more times than a dozen Hail Mary's. But somehow it doesn't matter. I'll get through this. Lila is right. Grandma Winnie raised me well.

Thanks to Lila.

"It's going to be quiet here without you," I mumble over the lump in my throat, finding it suddenly difficult to breathe. She's leaving me again.

"You'll have Betty," she reminds me. "If things get bad, ask her to move in. She can have my room." Her face lights up in a playful smile. "That would be rather fitting, don't you think?"

My cheeks flame. The cramped little room off the kitchen was originally designed for the hired help. Yet even with three spacious bedrooms empty upstairs, Lila never once complained about being stuck in the maid's room. "You knew all the time?"

Her smile broadens. "It's fine."

My heart melts at how quick she is to forgive. "It's not that I thought you deserved to be... I mean, I didn't think that—"

"You don't need to explain," she chides gently. "Where else were you supposed to put me? You don't have an elevator, and I couldn't climb the stairs."

And my heart softens further.

"If I don't get moving, I won't be ready when Larry gets here." She reaches across the bed and touches my hand. "Please don't be a stranger. You're always welcome. I'd love the company." She hesitates. "Plus, I have something I'd like to show you."

"What?"

"Just something," she says, with the hint of a smile.

And then she is gone, leaving me alone with saltine crackers and an ache in my heart that is all too familiar.

I am mourning another loss.

Later in the day, after the distant roar of the vacuum quiets and I'm certain Betty has left, I crawl out of bed. I throw on a pair of shorts and t-shirt and pad down the stairs. The kitchen tile is cool against my bare feet as I open a cupboard, grab a bowl, and pour myself some cereal. Four thousand square feet of silence surrounds me. Lila is gone and the condo feels empty without her.

I grab the mail she's left on the counter, tuck it under my arm, and carry my breakfast onto the deck. I rescue one of Lila's pink chairs from underneath the awning and drag it into the sunshine. I'm way beyond caring what Mrs. Richardson thinks. Let her complain to her brother. I munch on granola and glance through the mail. Mostly bills, plus a bulky envelope from my friend Rosa at the title agency. I rip it open and briefly scan the contents of the title search I ordered for the Loon Lake property. Pointless now. I pick out the invoice and throw it on the mounting stack of bills to be paid. The rest of the paperwork I stuff back in the envelope. It belongs to Max, not me. Not that it will do him much good. Too little, too late. My money provided his father with the necessary cash to fund the project. But it's all I have left to give him.

And better that he doesn't know it came from me. If he did, he probably wouldn't open it. I hunt for the telephone book, scrawl the camp's address on a brand new label, leaving the return address blank.

Maybe it's time I found a place where I'm proud of the return address label. God knows I haven't found it here at the Yacht Club.

A few months ago, when Kris accused me of living my life on the sidelines, I thought she was crazy. Now I realize how right she was. This is *my* life, and the only one I have. Do I really want to end up like Grandma? Shackled by the past and fading memories. Tortured by thoughts of what should have been, what could have been.

No matter how painful things might be, it's better to live in the present. It's better to keep my eyes open, to take a long hard look at what is now and what can be.

It's time I take control of my life and figure out what I want to do.

It's time I take control of my money and figure out the right thing to do.

It's time I quit being afraid... of who I am, of the money I have.

Being rich doesn't take any particular courage. Courage is knowing you don't have the money, that you'll never have the money, and still hauling yourself out of bed, showing up for life.

Something Lila manages to do every day, even with a cast.

It's time I took a lesson from my mother.

I head for the kitchen, rinse out my bowl, pop another aspirin. I'm not sure if a hangover can be conquered through sheer willpower, but I've got places to go and people to see. Just like Lila said, it's time to quit babying myself. I'm an adult. It's high time I started acting like one.

The parking lot is almost full. Sunday afternoons at the nursing home are premium visiting time, with reluctant relatives stopping by for a hurried visit. I'm no better than any of them. When was the last time I checked in with Grandma?

I find her parked next to her bed, slumped in her wheelchair, fast asleep. The other bed is empty, mattress stripped, fresh linens stacked at the end of the bed. No sign of Grandma's roommate. I thought Grandma and Mary Margaret were rooming together again. I made a mental note to stop by the office when my visit is finished and find out what happened.

The television drones in a corner of the room and I snap it off. It's merely background noise, or in Grandma's case, noise to sleep by. The room is stifling and I fiddle with the air conditioner controls, but there's no comforting click resulting in a cool breeze. The machine is broken, just like so much of what I see in this place. Broken faces and spirits of the elderly, confined to their wheelchairs, lining the hallway as I pass. Calling from their rooms, crying like children, begging for help I can't give.

I can't help everyone. But I *can* help Grandma.

I crouch down beside her. She's lost weight since my last visit. Her skin is faded and her face wears a brand-new set of liver spots. My eyes take them in, trying to memorize each one on the map that is Grandma I carry in my heart.

"Grandma?" I rub her arm gently. "It's me, Lucy."

She stirs slightly and her eyes finally open. The light in them looks faded, too. I lean forward and brush my lips against her forehead. Her skin is dry and tissue-paper thin. Old-people skin.

"Well, hello." A chunky nurse I've never seen before breezes into the room with a hurried smile for me and a paper cup of pills for Grandma. "I see you've got a visitor today, Winnie. Lucky you."

The nurse's sing-song voice is one you would use with children and it sends the hair on the back of my neck bristling. "My name is Lucy. I'm her granddaughter."

"Nice to meet you." She bustles around the side of Grandma's bed, smoothing down the sheets.

I point at the other bed. "Where's Mary Margaret? Is she back in the hospital?"

"She's no longer with us," the nurse says matter-of-factly. "She went home this morning."

I cannot fathom that Mary Margaret's family would have taken her home in the state she was in. They aren't wealthy people, but she had a stroke. Who will care for her?

"When is she coming back?"

"Never." The nurse frowns, then gives me a pointed stare as if I've asked a stupid question. Then my gut twists, and my heart knots, and I get it.

Mary Margaret has gone home. Permanently home.

"Winnie's getting a new roommate today. I heard they're transferring someone over from the hospital before dinner." The nurse's voice raises three notches as she pats Grandma's arm. "You'll like that, won't you, Winnie?"

Knowing Mary Margaret has died leaves a hollow hole in my heart. She was nowhere near Grandma's age, and now she's gone. Grandma's beaten the odds by making it to eighty. My father didn't even make it to forty.

"Was it her heart? Or did she have another stroke?"

"I'm sorry, but I'm not allowed to give you that information. HIPPA laws." The nurse's tone borders between polite and dismissive. "Winnie, I'm going to take your vitals," she says, her voice louder and plainer, "and then it's time to take your medicine like a good girl."

Grandma is not a child, nor is she deaf. I stand back and watch as the nurse fumbles for Grandma's wrist, checks her pulse, then grabs a stethoscope and listens to her heart. "You're sounding good, Winnie. Looks like we'll keep you around for a while."

Why does she make it sound like Grandma is some broken-down piece of machinery? And why does she find it necessary to talk so loud?

"There's no need for you to shout," I say as she finishes taking Grandma's vitals. "She can hear just fine, especially now that she has her new hearing aids."

"You're right." The nurse shakes a few pills from the paper cup and points to the nightstand. "If she wore them, she'd hear just fine."

I stare at the little plastics orbs that should be inside Grandma's ears. "Why isn't she wearing them?"

"Probably one of the aides forgot to put them in, or they didn't have time."

"They didn't have time, or they didn't make the time?" Suddenly I'm the one who's nearly shouting. "I pay over seven thousand dollars a month for my grandmother to live here. You'd think for that kind of money, someone would make sure she's wearing her hearing aids every day."

The nurse pauses and takes a good look at me for the first time since she entered the room. "I understand how you feel," she says, "but your grandmother is not the only patient in this facility. I suggest you speak with the administrator if you have a problem with the way things are run."

I lift my chin and scan her name tag. "Good idea, Linda. I think I will do just that."

She snatches up her stethoscope, turns her back on me, and flounces out of the room without another word or a backward glance.

I look over at the empty bed next to Grandma's. Mary Margaret's death has rocked me in a way I cannot understand. This morning she was alive, and now she's gone. None of us know how much time we have left. Yet how many of us take each day for granted, never believing it could be our last?

There's no time to waste. I only have today. I drag a chair close beside Grandma. I've come searching for answers. It's time I asked the questions.

I snatch Grandma's hearing aids from the bedside table and carefully insert them in her ears. I take her hands in mine. "Hi, Grandma. It's Lucy. I need to talk to you."

She squeezes my hand with feeble fingers and her touch brings tears springing to my eyes. "I want to talk about Daddy. Do you remember, Grandma? Your son John was my daddy."

A vague light appears in her eyes.

"And Lila. Remember her? John and Lila married, and they had a little girl. A little girl named Lucy." My throat tightens but I force myself to continue. "That's me, Grandma. I'm that little girl. I'm Lucy. And Lila is my mother."

Grandma nods softly. Her arthritis-swollen fingers pick at the folds of her blouse. "Pretty girl."

Is she talking about Lila or me? All my life, we tiptoed around the truth. Grandma kept vigil over the sacred memory of her son, spewing venom at the mention of my mother's name. It was an evening ritual. My mother never wanted me. My mother gave me up. My mother was a drunk. My mother couldn't be trusted.

Who loves Grandma's little Lucy? God loves Lucy, and Grandma loves Lucy. Always trust in God. And always trust in Grandma.

Everything this frail woman in the wheelchair insisted that I believe flies contrary to Bob's words to me on the beach that day when he told me about my mother, my father, my grandmother. Where is the truth in all of this? Somehow I have to find it. Somehow I have to keep going. Before I lose my nerve. Before I lose hope. Before I lose heart.

"Can you tell me about John and Lila, Grandma? Did they love each other? Do you know the truth?" I'm breaking her code of silence by speaking of the past and the day my father died. But it's time the rules were broken. Even Grandma herself can't keep me quiet anymore.

"John and Lila went fishing one day. They took me with them. We went fishing on Loon Lake."

Grandma's face grows still and her gaze wanders across the room. My breath is shallow, watching her lost in time. Perhaps my parents are in front of her, packing up the boat, waving their goodbyes.

I swallow hard, force myself to continue. "There was an accident." I pause. "John drowned."

Her fingers move restlessly across her lap, climb up her chest, pluck at her throat. I hate myself for pushing her into the past, for calling back memories she's kept repressed for years, for forcing her to confront the things that I always understood were never to be discussed.

"What happened, Grandma? Was it Lila's fault, or was it an accident? Did she want me? Did she leave me?" I hug myself close, picking at the truth. "Please help me, Grandma. I can't remember."

Her eyes open wide and a smile suddenly lights her face. She strokes her cheek thoughtfully, staring at me. And I think, I hope, I pray she will finally tell me about Lila. About my father. About our family.

About who I am.

Grandma pulls at her ear, fiddles with her hearing aid, passes a hand in front of her eyes. She blinks and I wait.

And wait.

And the moment passes.

"Pretty girl," she says finally, nodding.

My heart sinks and my hopes fade at the sight of nothingness behind her faded blue eyes. There'll be no return to the land of the living for Grandma. No magic ending. No amount of money can buy back her mind.

Her memories are long gone, claimed by a shadowy, stealthy disease that's claimed them as its own. Stolen away from her as surely as my family was stolen away from me.

I blink back the tears, stoop and give her a gentle hug. "It's okay. I just thought I would ask." I pat her hand. "Would you like some water?"

The Styrofoam cup is filled to the brim with tepid water. How long has it been since anyone thought to refill it? I hold the cup under her chin and stroke her thinning hair as she sucks greedily through a straw. Someone needs to take care of our old people. Someone needs to take care of the people we love when they can no longer take care of themselves.

For better, for worse, she did it for me when Lila couldn't, and now it's my turn to do the same for her. No matter what she did, no matter what she told me, I'll always love Grandma. No matter what. People want to believe their own truths and Grandma was no different. She lost her only child and she lived her life caught up in the past. But I can't do the same. I refuse to do the same. I thought Grandma was the only one who knew the truth, but maybe I've been wrong. Grandma created her own version of the truth and lived her life accordingly. It's time I figured out what the truth is for me. It's time I shaped my own future. And hopefully someday, I'll be able to tell my own children the story of the way it really happened. The story of my mother and my father.

The story of Loon Lake.

Grandma's eyes start to droop, and I gently pull the straw from her mouth. I drop a light kiss on her forehead. "Sleep well, Grandma. I'll be back tomorrow. I won't leave you alone again, promise."

That is one promise I intend to keep.

The parking lot is nearly empty by the time I finish the paperwork and make it back to my car. I sink behind the wheel and pop another aspirin. Have I got enough stamina for the next round of *mea culpa*? But putting it off won't make things easier. No more living in the past. From now on, my life is about moving forward. I fish out my cell phone, and punch in the numbers.

"Hello?"

The voice is so clear, it's hard to believe Kris is thousands of miles away.

"Hi, it's me."

There is a long silence. "What do you want?" she finally says.

"I called to say I'm sorry."

More than miles separate us. Her fears and my stubbornness have forged a deep chasm between us and things aren't what they used to be. But nothing changes if nothing changes. I close my eyes and pray my words come out right. Apologies have never been my strong suit, but I need to make amends.

"You were right, Kris. I was a fool, and I'm very, very sorry. Will you forgive me?"

I'm sorry. Two simple little words are all it takes to melt things between us. I hear a sudden rush of breath from her end, followed by a racking sob.

"Please don't cry," I beg her as I wipe away my own tears. "Just tell me you're not mad anymore and that we're still friends."

"Are you kidding? Of course we're still friends. Oh, Lucy, I'm the one who should apologize to you. I never meant what I said. I know being drunk was no excuse, and I was wrong to talk—"

"You told me the truth, which was something I needed to hear." I swallow hard. "Besides, if your best friend can't tell you that you've turned into a jerk, who can?"

A shaky laugh explodes over the telephone. "You mean that?"

"The part about telling the truth? Or the part about you being my best friend?"

"Both?" she whispers in an uncertain voice that tugs at my heart.

"Both," I vow.

Kris sobs openly over the telephone and I do, too. I'm sure it looks odd to the couple approaching the car beside me. They eye me cautiously as they get in their car. I'm still wiping away tears as they drive away. They probably think someone died. And in a way, someone has.

But if I do this right, a new Lucy will be reborn.

CHAPTER EIGHTEEN

"There's someone here to see you."

I peer at Betty from where I sit cross-legged on the deck. I'm hot and dirty, still suffering from jet lag and in no mood for visitors except those with a green thumb. I glance crossly at the flower boxes and tubs surrounding me. Transplanting is more work than I bargained for.

"Who is it?"

"I don't know. Some guy I never saw before. He's waiting in the foyer. He looks a little scruffy." She shoots a look over her shoulder at the living room and sniffs. "I'm surprised they let him through the gate."

"If that's the case, why did you let him through the front door?"

Her mouth drops open, and for once she's speechless. And for once, I don't care. Betty is as much of a snob, maybe even more so, than Didi and her crowd. She's wrapped herself with that same smug sense of entitlement that seems to go hand in hand with an address at the Club. But I don't need Betty giving me attitude. If I had any regrets earlier this morning when I told her today would be her last day, I no longer do. I'm glad I made the decision to let her go.

And I'm glad I made the decision to let me go. I don't belong here. I've never belonged here. If I had any doubts, that night at the Club was the clincher. It turned everything—including my stomach—inside out. If I'm going to save myself, I've got to get out of this condo and this place before I turn into a bigger snob than any of them... Betty included.

"Hello, Lucy."

I smell him before I see him: a mingled fragrance of pine and sunshine that I know nearly as well as my own scent.

"Hello, Max." My heart flip-flops at the sight of him. Betty's right. He does look scruffy in his t-shirt, shorts, and scuffed leather sandals. There's an eight-day growth on his chin and he's in desperate need of a haircut. But he looks fine. Better than fine. So fine that I'm torn by the crazy notion to jump up, pitch myself helter-skelter into his arms, and smother his face with kisses. To reassure myself things will be okay. To reassure myself that we can make this work.

Then I remember everything that happened. I swallow hard, force myself to regroup. We *can't* make this work. It will never work.

His gaze darts from me to my pathetic gardening attempts. "You busy, or can we talk?"

I squint up at him, think one last time about jumping up and throwing myself in his arms, but can't drum up the nerve. I stay put on the floor. If Max wants to talk, we'll talk. Although about what, I haven't a clue. The weather? The price of oil? The current sad, lonely state of Lucy's heart?

How she's tremendously, utterly, *forever-and-a-day* sorry, and will always be in love with him?

Guaranteed that's one conversation Max isn't interested in having.

I'm loathe to take the hand he offers as I struggle to my feet. Dirt clings to my fingers, grime is jammed beneath my nails. But he doesn't give me much choice. The electricity snaps between us as his fingers wrap around mine and he pulls me to a stand. My senses are on red alert, and I move to put some space between us. My chest is tight and it's hard to breathe. I lean against the railing, unsure if it's the heavy humidity and relentless sun that have left me dizzy and weak. Or is it the sight of Max Graham in front of me again?

"I've been trying to call you for over a week," he says. "Your voice mail is full." He leans against the railing and eyes me warily. "I dropped by Lila's apartment. She told me you were in Florida."

My heart is in my throat. Did he go just to visit Lila, or did he go looking for me?

"She said you went down for the funeral."

"That's right," I admit.

"How's Kris doing?"

"A little better every day," I say carefully. The subject of Kris is a sore spot between Max and me, and I've no wish to reopen that wound. "She's staying in Florida for another week and then she and Toni are flying back to Michigan. She wants Toni to move to James Bay."

"Sounds like a good plan." Max gestures toward the flower tubs littering the deck. "What's up with that? Looks like you could use a hand."

Riotous colors of pinks, purples, yellows, and blues explode in a tangle of late summer finery. Transplanting them is more work than I bargained for, but it's time I started doing things for myself again. Things like transplanting flowers. Doing my own laundry. Answering my own front door. I grew up that way and I want it back. I need it back.

I need *me* back.

"Thanks, but I can manage. Besides, you'd get dirty."

"I work at a kid's camp, remember? My life revolves around dirt."

Then he grins, and I laugh, and for one sweet moment, everything feels light and easy between us… just like it was before that night.

Max glances around the deck. "What's the deal with all the flowers? The Club finally decided to enforce the restrictions?"

I sigh and shrug. "They're too beautiful to leave behind."

"You're going somewhere?"

Max doesn't know? "I'm moving."

His eyebrows lift.

"Back home," I explain.

His eyebrows arch higher. "Downtown to that apartment?"

"Back to Grandma's," I say. "It's a good, solid house and there's no sense in letting it sit empty. They started the new roof and inside remodeling last week."

The hint of a smile flits across his face. He approves of my decision. I jam my hands in my pockets before I do something reckless and crazy, like grabbing him and kissing him good and hard on the mouth. Not that it would do much good. It's far too late to try and convince Max that I should be a part of his life. Plus, I never was a very good kisser.

I lick my lips, swallow hard, push away the desire.

"When are you moving?"

"Sometime next week. I want to wait until the handicap ramp is built and the downstairs bathroom outfitted with everything she'll need. "

He throws me a hard stare "Lila's going to live with you?"

"Not Lila," I say. "Grandma."

We talk over iced tea, rocking away the minutes in Lila's chairs. Above us a gorgeous blue sky is filled with puffy white clouds, and before us the lake is adrift with sailboats. Mrs. Richardson's curtains flutter in the breeze. If she's watching, things must appear normal, but it feels downright eerie to be sitting on the deck chatting with Max.

Especially since I still don't know why he's here.

Until a few minutes later when he stands and pulls a thick sheaf of papers from his back pocket. Paperwork I recognize. Paperwork from my friend Rosa at the title agency. The paperwork I mailed Max before I left for Florida.

"I still don't get it, Lucy. Why didn't you bring this out to camp yourself?"

"I don't know." I clink the melting ice in my glass and stare at my bare feet. What does he expect me to say? I'm no masochist, and I doubt he is, either. Me showing up at camp would only have caused us both more pain. And even though it was unintentional, I'll always be ashamed of what I did. That impulsive investment I made with Didi and her group provided Max's father with enough ready cash to destroy the camp. My money destroyed Max's dream. I'm sure he doesn't need any reminders of how much damage I've done.

I blow out a little sigh. "How did you know I sent it?"

"It wasn't hard to figure out. There was no invoice in the envelope, so I called the title company and asked who ordered the search."

I mull over his news in silence. Rosa's always been too chatty for her own good. But at least I know what brought him here today. I'm surprised Max hasn't already pulled out his checkbook. Then again, he could have popped a check in the mail. That would have been easier. It would have saved him a trip and the need to see me again.

"You don't have to pay me back. It was just a favor I did for… for a friend."

He gives me the oddest stare, and I'm not sure if it's bewilderment or bemusement I see captured in his eyes. "Is that what you think?"

Now I'm the one who's bewildered. "I don't understand."

"When was the last time you read the paper?" he asks.

"Yesterday morning." A crowded airport, a three-hour delay, a long winding line at the coffee stand. Five dollars for a cup of bitter dregs and the last newspaper available. "The *Miami Herald*. Cover to cover."

"You should have been reading the *James Bay Journal*," Max informs me. "It was front-page news all last week."

"The *Journal*? What happened?" Only a sensational local story would rate front-page coverage five straight days. "Was someone murdered?"

"Not someone. Something." He waves the title work in his hand, creating a slight breeze between us. "You honestly don't know what happened?"

I shrink further in my chair. Do I admit the truth and confess that I'm clueless, and that our conversation has me flying by the seat of my pants? Or do I take the easy way out, trying to bluff my way through? I don't know if I'm the story's heroine or villain.

Then I remember this is a new Lucy. No more living on the sidelines. No more pretending to be someone I'm not. I might have a nice, fat bank account, but I'm flat-out broke when it comes to options. If I'm going to move forward, then I've got to be honest. I cringe and hope for the best. This *being honest* stuff isn't easy. "Sorry, Max, you'll have to tell me."

"It was in this paperwork you ordered." He crouches down in front of me and unfolds the sheaf of papers. "You found the missing key."

We're nearly nose to nose, and I get a faint whiff of suntan lotion and bug spray, of sunshine and satisfaction. My senses spin and it's hard to concentrate with him so close. I take a deep breath. "What key?"

"The answer to everything," he patiently explains. "The one we didn't know existed. But we do now. Everyone knows... thanks to you."

The smile on his face wipes away my frown. I still have no idea what he's talking about, but I'm starting to get the funny idea that maybe—just maybe—I've done something right.

"It might help if I explained a few things." He sinks into the chair beside me and scoots close. "It's about the camp property. My great-grandfather, Maximillian Colley, bought the land back in the early twenties. He earned his fortune in the furniture business, and he built a huge summer home on the shore of Loon Lake. He also created a summer camp for his employees and their families. A place where they could escape the steamy heat of the city for a week each summer. His wife died of influenza a few years later, and sometime after that, the house burned down. He let the property go to seed and abandoned the idea of the company summer camp.

"After he died, his son, Lloyd—my grandfather, LC—decided to start up the camp again. He created the family trust and deeded the property over to the camp. A boy's camp. LC ran the place for years and funded scholarships that would allow city kids to spend a week or two at Loon Lake. My mother was LC's only child. After she died, he moved north and lived here at camp year-round. He—"

"Wait, you've lost me. What does any of this have to do with the title work?" I ask, then suddenly catch myself. If I aspire to be a kinder, gentler Lucy, I have a lot of work ahead of me. Starting with patience and better manners. "Sorry I interrupted you."

Max chuckles softly. "You'd never make it writing fiction, Lucy. You're too interested in the *who, what, when, where, and why*. Okay, I'll show you the *how* and *why*."

He thumps the paperwork in his hand. "When I took control of the trust, I discovered all the property was gone, except for those few acres with the camp buildings and beach. I assumed the rest had been sold off throughout the years. But at least I had the camp. That was enough for me. I decided to reopen the place, to try and get things back to where they were when my grandfather was alive. But just when things started to pick up, we got slammed with the news of the Loon Lake Development."

Max leans forward, eyes guarded, jaw clenched, and grips his knees so hard his knuckles turn white. "I couldn't figure out how it got so bad, so fast. The camp was doing great, our summer roster was up, and I'd met this girl I liked. Then things did a one-eighty. Suddenly the rezoning seemed like a sure thing, and it started to look like this might be the camp's last season."

My heart clutches. Max's talking fast, but all I can focus on is *this girl I liked*. Did he really say those words, or was it my imagination?

"I felt like a failure. Like I'd let the kids down, and that I'd let LC down. I couldn't face myself. I couldn't even face the girl. Want to know how much of a jerk I am?" He pauses, throws me a hesitant glance. "I purposely picked a fight with her so I wouldn't have to admit the truth. I'm not proud of what I did. And someday, if I'm lucky, I'll be able to make things right with her again. But in the middle of all this, when I'm at my lowest, feeling pretty much like pond scum, I get an envelope in the mail with papers that hold the answers. Papers this girl that I loved cared enough to send me."

My heart beats so fast, I fear it might fly straight out of my chest, soaring like a seagull as it swoops across the bay. Who cares about those stupid papers? I want to hear about Max and that girl. That girl that he loved.

He stabs the documents with his finger. "None of the property was ever sold. After LC died, my father deeded everything over into the names of his corporations. He did it all before I turned twenty-one and gained control of the trust."

I struggle to understand. "But isn't that illegal?"

"Who was going to prosecute him? My father was the trustee. But he didn't get away with it. There was something he didn't count on. Let's call it the secret weapon." Max's eyes gleam. "I'll give you three guesses what it was."

"I'm no good at guessing games," I whisper. Those words *the girl I loved* have me in a tizzy.

"It was you, Lucy. Your perseverance was the thing that saved us. We'd be shutting the camp for good if it wasn't for you."

"Me?" Now I'm really confused. "What did I do?"

"You found this." He flips through the documents until he reaches a tabbed copy of an old black-on-white legal-sized document. He points out a paragraph toward the bottom. "That is the reverter clause. If the property is transferred or sold for any other purpose than intended, it automatically reverts back to the original owner... which in this case is the family trust. And since I'm the trustee, that makes me the owner."

Max slumps back in the chair with a wide grin even his scraggly beard can't hide.

I'm happy he's happy, but things still don't make sense. "I thought there wasn't a problem with the camp being sold. You told me once before that the property was safe, that the camp's land couldn't be touched."

He chuckles softly. "For a reporter, you can be a little dense. I'm not talking about the camp. I'm talking about the rest of it."

"You mean…"

Max nods. "No more worrying about the PUD being approved. It's hard to sell real estate lots for a development when you don't own the land."

My mind whirls so fast, my brain can't begin to process. "And you discovered all this—"

"Through the title work you ordered."

"But how did your father manage to do this without anyone finding out?"

"Who was going to stop him? His development companies had possession of the properties. If a bank had been involved, everything would have been different. A bank would have insisted on a title search being done. But my father, through the trust, already owned the land. And he funded the development using private investors."

"People like me, you mean," I say soberly. I threw away one million dollars in a capricious move that nearly provided the impetus to destroy Max's dream.

"Don't be so hard on yourself. If you hadn't done your research, the camp would be finished. Instead, every piece of property reverts back to the family trust. And just like my grandfather intended, every piece will be owned by the camp. Thanks to you, we'll be opening next summer for another season."

The devil is in the details. My old journalism professor would be proud.

"And this is the story that's been running in the *Journal*?"

Max nods. "Now the Loon Lake development is dead in the water, the people who put down earnest money to buy those lots are threatening to sue. Not to mention the court might be bringing possible criminal charges of conspiracy and collusion. Didi Taylor's realty company is in trouble, and some township officials are going to be plenty sorry before this is finished. I still have Friday's paper, if you want to read it. I think you'll find the lead story interesting." He flashes me a confident smile. "They caught Charles Kendall taking kickbacks in return for throwing his editorials and the *Journal*'s support. He was fired Thursday night."

My jaw drops on hearing the news. "Wait till I tell Kris. She'll never believe it."

Max drains his iced tea. "What about you, Lucy? What happens now?"

"Grandma's coming home to live with me, remember? I'm going to be busy."

Don't get your hopes up, I chide myself. Max mentioned that girl, but he hasn't made a move to touch me. Men in love don't act like that.

"Do you plan on taking care of her all by yourself?"

"I hired twenty-four-hour nursing care. Grandma has more medical needs than I can deal with. This way, someone will always be available."

"Glad to hear it. You don't want to be alone through something like this."

A bittersweet smile tugs at my face and my heart. "I won't be alone. I'll have Grandma."

"It's still a big job, even with the nursing care to help out. There aren't many people that would do what you're doing."

I catch the gleam of admiration in his eyes despite the fading sun, but I shrug off the compliment. I tuck his words away, hoarding them for some cold, lonely night when I can pull them out again and bask in the warmth of the knowledge that, once upon a time, Max admired me. Once upon a time, he loved me.

"I'm only doing what Grandma deserves. Why not give it to her? Besides, what else am I supposed to do with all my money?"

He shakes his head thoughtfully. "I've been doing a lot of thinking since that night at the Club. All my life, I thought I was such a great judge of people. I had opinions about everything and everybody. My father, his friends, the whole lot of them and the way they lived their lives. Know

334

what I am? I'm the worst kind of snob you'll ever meet. I'm a reverse snob. I prided myself in thinking I was better than all of them because I didn't need the money." His brown eyes narrow. "Talk about grandiosity. I'm a jerk."

"No, you're not, Max." He's being way too hard on himself. "Not at all."

"I'm afraid I am," he responds with a self-deprecating smile. "Maybe I never said it, and maybe I did a good job of hiding it, but it was in my head."

His willingness to confront his weakness, to analyze his behavior, to not cut himself any slack, sears through my nerves like those hot rocks scorching my back that day at the spa. And if what Max says is true, then I'm guilty of the same thing. Didn't I revel—even a tiny bit—in feeling superior and smug about Didi and her crowd? About Kris? Even about Charles Kendall?

No. The last thought I shove out of my mind. Charles deserves everything he gets. He broke every rule, every ethical code a journalist lives by. It's time he paid his dues... even if it includes jail time.

"Maybe that's why I like working at camp around kids." A small smile flits across Max's face. "Kids are just kids, out to have a good time. At camp, they're learning to sail and swim. Learning who they are, learning to be themselves. Know what I mean? The money stuff doesn't matter to them yet."

I nod silently. It seems so long ago since I was a kid. Everyone grows up. It's inevitable. But is there ever a way for people to find their way back?

"What happens now, Max? What are you going to do?"

"Once camp closes for the season, I'm going downstate and concentrate on the family affairs. I want to make sure things are in order and that my father didn't do more damage in the years he ran the trust. I owe it to LC to make sure things are properly managed."

I think of the tangled legal mess facing Max. The property, the PUD. It isn't a job for the fainthearted. But if anyone can set things straight, it will be Max.

"I need to spend some time figuring things out," he adds. "It's time I quit running from the money and faced my responsibilities. I have to learn to grow up. How can I hope to help kids if I can't help myself?"

The fleeting look in his eyes breaks my heart. I'm responsible for putting part of that sadness there. I have no clue what will happen to the money I invested, or if I'll ever see it back. But that doesn't matter. I've got more money than I'll ever need.

But what I *don't* have is Max.

"Max, about that money I invested with your father—"

He lifts a hand, cutting me off. "It's over and done with. Let it go."

His words bring a dead silence between us, and I feel the whoosh of air settle in the pit of my stomach. Max has spoken. I have my answer. It's over and done between Max and me.

He rakes a hand through his hair as he rises to his feet. "Anyway, that's why I came over today. To thank you for what you did. You saved the camp, Lucy. You saved us all."

I don't feel like a heroine. Rather, I feel like I'm drowning in my own sadness, knowing that he's leaving. This might be the last time I see him. "Do you really have to go?"

" 'Fraid so. This is our last week of camp and dinner starts soon. Plus, I'm in charge of campfire activities tonight." He cocks his head and eyes me with an uncertain look. "You're welcome to come out, if you like. Roberta makes a mean meatloaf."

My breath catches. Is this merely a pity invite, a *feed-her-a-hot-dog-and-chips-to-let-her-know-how-grateful-we-are*? Or does Max really mean it?

He must, or he wouldn't have asked.

Then I remember my promise to Lila. Maybe I could call and cancel? She knows Max. She would understand. Plus, it's not like I'm looking forward to our conversation. Truth is, I've been dreading it. But Lila and I need to talk. We need to clear the air between us.

This is the new Lucy. I promised Lila I would be there, and I won't renege on a promise. "Sorry, but I already have dinner plans."

"I understand." His face falls, and the blood roars through my brain. Maybe it's not as late as I thought.

"Lila invited me for dinner," I quickly add. "We haven't seen each other since she moved out. I don't want to disappoint her."

But he's already turned away.

"Max, wait." I lunge forward and grab his arm. "There's something I have to ask you."

His eyes cloud over and my breath catches, and for a moment I falter. What if I read him wrong? What if he doesn't care? What do I do then?

But what do I have to lose?

Nothing. Plus, everything to gain. This is my life and I'm betting it all.

I'm betting on Max.

"That girl you mentioned earlier?" I let the words tumble out of my mouth before I can think. "She made a mistake.

Lots of mistakes. She's young, she's stupid. But she's learning, Max. And she wonders… no, she *hopes*, that somehow, someday you'll find it in your heart to forgive her."

His eyebrows narrow. I have his attention. I swallow over the lump in my throat and push on before I lose my nerve. "And that girl wonders if… if despite everything she did and everything she said, if someday, you might love her again."

Max's face is sober, his eyes solemn, as he meets my gaze square-on. "You want the truth?"

Oh, God. He's going to say *no*. This won't be pleasant, and he's offering me a way out. Maybe I should take it. It would be simple.

But not easy. Nothing in life is easy. Not the things that matter most. And I have to know the truth. Cringing, I prepare myself for what he's going to say.

"Could I forgive her?" he questions. "I already have.

"Could I forget her?" he wonders. "I never will.

"But as for loving her again…" His voice trails off.

I can't speak. I'm too busy crying as Max opens his arms.

"Could I love her again?" he whispers softly against my ear. "I never stopped."

CHAPTER NINETEEN

The doorbell buzzes rather than chimes, catching me by surprise. I assumed Lila would prefer music. Then again, low-rent apartment complexes probably don't offer tenants a choice. I hear a dog yipping through the thin front door, which suddenly opens. Lila stands there in shorts and a sleeveless blouse, rosy and flustered, like she's been cooking.

"Hello, Suzy-Q, you sweet little thing!" I sink to my knees right in the hallway and surrender my face to a barrage of insatiable puppy kisses.

"Poor little Suzy-Q, banished to the rectory," Lila says, laughing. "I was so happy when Father Greg brought her home. I know he took good care of her, but she belongs with me."

I eye Lila's bare feet, her painted toenails. "I see they took off your cast."

"I begged the doctor, and he finally agreed a few days ago. My leg itched terribly. But please, come in." She opens the door wider. "We don't have to talk in the hall."

I follow her into the living room, immaculately furnished in the modest, tasteful style I remember from the one time I was here before. The night Lila spent in the hospital. The night Kris and I were sent on our mission to rescue Suzy-Q.

"Would you like something to drink?" she asks brightly. "I made iced tea."

"That sounds great." A flat-out lie. I already drank enough iced tea today to float myself across James Bay, but I haven't the heart to tell her no. Not to mention I could use a cool drink. Her apartment is sweltering. Lila disappears into the kitchen, and Suzy-Q scampers at my feet as I wander around the room, giving it a once-over. No air conditioner, only a single floor fan in one corner that barely stirs the air. No wonder the place is stifling.

And the view from her living room doesn't compensate. Her tiny balcony overlooks the parking lot, with a garbage dumpster in plain view. Similar to the view from Lila's bedroom window while she stayed with me. Except the Club parking lot's dumpster is hidden behind a tall fence and beautiful shrubs.

Rich or poor, there's no getting around the garbage in your life. It's merely a question of being lucky enough to afford decent landscaping.

Lila returns with tall glasses of tea and nods me into a wooden rocker. I sink into the seat, grateful to turn my back on the view. But *out of sight, out of mind* doesn't work anymore. The only thing stirring in the tepid air are my thoughts. How do people live like this? How can Lila live like this? Then again, I lived like this, too, just a few months ago. That tiny downtown second-floor walk-up was sweltering in the summer.

How could I have forgotten?

There are real lemon slices in the iced tea and I drain half the glass in a long, thirsty swallow. It tastes different than the canned tea I normally drink. Softer on the tongue. It stirs a memory. I take another sip. "What brand is this?"

"It's sun tea. I made it this morning." Lila sits carefully on the couch. Suzy-Q jumps up, circles twice, then settles comfortably in her lap. "Do you like it?"

No wonder it tastes familiar. "Grandma used to make sun tea."

"Yes, I know. Winnie taught me how to make it that summer we lived with her."

I nearly drop my glass. "You lived with Grandma?" I can barely wrap my brain around the thought of Lila and Grandma cooped up in a room together, let alone sharing a house.

"We lived with your grandparents for a short time."

"Why don't I remember?" I say, frowning.

She offers a slight smile. "I wouldn't expect you to. You were very young."

I stare uneasily at my glass. If only my mind dripped memories as easily as the tumbler was sweating water in my hand. "Was this some sort of vacation?"

An odd combination of remorse and regret flits across her face. "Living with Winnie was no vacation."

The trust between us is melting faster than the ice in my glass. Maybe Grandma was right about Lila after all. The reporter in me takes over. "If you didn't like it, then why were you there?"

Lila stares at me a long moment, as if she's carrying on some internal debate, figuring out whether to admit the truth. But I'm having my own debate as well. Do I want to know the truth? Am I prepared to hear it?

If not, then what am I doing here?

"Your father couldn't find a job," she finally says. "We were living downstate and the auto plant where he worked shut down. He was one of the first to be let go."

"Daddy got fired?"

"Back then, they called it being permanently laid off," she says softly. "It was a tough time for the auto industry. Foreign cars were flooding the market and we didn't have much money. You were only a baby, and we didn't know what to do. John decided we should move to James Bay. He was sure he could find a job back in his hometown."

"So you came north and lived with Grandma and Grandpa?" My thoughts whirl faster than the fan droning in the corner. *Why didn't Grandma tell me this story?*

Lila strokes Suzy-Q's head, kneads her behind the ears. "We lived with them for two months."

Except I have no memories of living in James Bay. Not until after the accident, when I moved in with Grandma.

"But you didn't stay in James Bay. Couldn't Daddy find a job?"

"He found one right away," she says. "A friend he went to school with owned an auto-parts store. He gave John a job working the counter."

"If he had a job, why did you end up leaving?"

Lila draws in a deep breath.

"There must have been a reason," I press.

She bows her head for a moment, then finally lifts her gaze to meet my own. "I told John I wouldn't stay. I told him I was leaving, and he would have to make a choice." Lila does not flinch, does not glance away. "I'm not proud of myself, Lucy," she says softly. "I was very young and very unhappy. I wasted so much time wishing things were different. But I finally decided that I couldn't and wouldn't put up with it anymore. I told your father I was leaving, and that I was taking you with me."

My head pounds and my heart races faster than the questions flying through my mind. Why did she want to leave? What got her so riled up? Was it money? The summer crowds? Post-partum depression? Finally I manage to find a voice. "Why did you want to leave?"

"It was Winnie," she says with a wooden smile. "It's no secret we didn't get along. She never liked me, from the day I married your father. Your grandfather Carl was sweet and acted like a buffer, but once we moved in with them, things went from bad to worse. She criticized everything I did. I wasn't good enough for her son. John wasn't making much money and we couldn't afford our own place. I finally told your father he would have to make a choice, that it would be Winnie or me. I said this town was too small for both of us, and I refused to live with his mother."

I draw in a sharp breath. No wonder Grandma hated her. Lila gave my father a choice, and he chose the wrong woman.

He chose his wife.

"Winnie was furious. She said I was selfish, blamed me for stealing her family away. Looking back, I can see how she was right. I was very young and very selfish. She told me I'd be sorry… and it turns out that she was right about that, too." Lila's voice falters. "I've been sorry for so many years, Lucy. I am sorry to this day."

Finally, after all these years, Grandma's bitterness makes sense. Grandma always was a sore loser. To her way of thinking, she lost everything to Lila. And in a way, she did… except for one thing.

Grandma got me.

"When John told her we were leaving, Winnie swore she would never speak to me again. And she didn't. Not until the day of your father's funeral."

And there it is between us.

Loon Lake.

My gut twists, my heart sinks, and there's no getting around it. Grandma talked around the subject as if she knew the truth, but there were only three people in the boat that day. One of us is dead, and one of us doesn't remember. My mother is the one who holds the answer, and it's time I faced the truth.

"I need to ask you something."

"You can ask me anything, Lucy. I'll do my best to answer."

I swallow over the lump in my throat. She might not be so sure, once she hears what I have to say. "It's about the day Daddy died."

Lila's face goes white and she stares at me a long time. But if the two of us have any hope for a decent relationship, then she needs to tell me about that day and what happened at Loon Lake.

"I suppose I always knew this day would come." Some of the blood returns to her cheeks. "You were just a little girl. Do you remember anything?"

"I'm not sure." My memories are a tangled mess, and it's impossible to separate what might be true from the stories I've read and the things Grandma told me. I squeeze my eyes shut, trying to bring back that day. "We were in the boat, out on the lake. Daddy was teaching me how to fish." *One, two, three, four little fish. Silver, gold, and green.* "But I didn't like the worms." *Icky worms.*

My eyes blink open. "He bought me my very own fishing pole when we bought the worms." It's a new memory, a good one that puts a smile on my face. "He baited it for me. It was the first time I ever caught a fish."

"Sunfish and perch," Lila says, nodding.

"They weren't big fish."

"It wasn't a big boat," she softly replies.

"He bought me a hat, too. He said it was important to wear a hat on the lake, to keep the sun out of your eyes."

A hot day. So windy. So hot. So hot. My hat is gone.

I blink, thinking hard. *Wet. Cold. Crying.*

The memory silences me.

"That's all you remember?" Her eyes hold mine fast.

I remember something else, too. Something Grandma said, but I don't dare say it.

She's nothing but a drunk.

The rest is a murky blur. How they found me in the boat. Lila was in the water, clinging to the edge. My father dove in to save her. But did she jump or fall?

"I remember you were mad at Daddy. The two of you were fighting."

Lila cocks her head and frowns. "No, that's not true. We weren't fighting."

"Yes, you were." The memory of her screaming at him is the one memory I'm certain of, the one memory I've clung to my whole life. "You were screaming at Daddy. I remember you screaming his name over and over."

She stares at me with haunted eyes and slowly shakes her head. "We weren't fighting, Lucy. I screamed when you fell out of the boat."

I suck in a ragged breath. I'm the one who fell out of the boat? I'm the one who went in the water? No!

345

Her face has turned ghost white despite her seasonal tan. "One minute the sky was blue and then it turned black. It was a summer squall, and it came up fast. Your father started the boat, and we tried to beat the storm to shore. We headed in, but the waves got bigger and the wind was blowing. And then your hat blew off, and you tried to catch it. We screamed at you to let it go, but you leaned over the side." Her voice catches. "Then you fell overboard."

I stare openmouthed as the memories rush over me, courtesy of my mother. And finally I remember.

Bobbing in the water, waves sloshing over my face. The wind howls. Scared, shrieking, coughing, spitting water.

Mama! Daddy! Come back, come back! Don't leave me! Cold. Wet.

But not because of the storm.

I was wet because I fell in the water.

Lila's face is pinched and her voice strained. "John tried circling the boat around, but we couldn't reach you. The winds had picked up and the waves kept crashing against the boat, pushing us farther away. He cut the engine and tried to turn the boat around, but then the engine stalled. He couldn't get it started again, and he couldn't reach you. So, he jumped in the water.

"He tried to grab you by your life jacket. John made sure you had one on. He made me wear one, too. I couldn't swim, and he knew how much I hated the water. I didn't want to go out in the boat that day. But I refused to stay home alone with Winnie."

Lila's face contorts in an anguished sheet of memories. "He fought against the waves and the wind and somehow he managed to snag you before you went under. He had you with him when he started swimming for the boat. He screamed at me to start the engine. I tried, Lucy. I tried and tried." Her voice suddenly falters. "I pulled the cord over and over, but it wouldn't catch. I couldn't get it going."

Wet. Cold. Scared. Mama screaming. Daddy's face looks like when the tornado siren blows.

Seeing Daddy scared is worse than a tornado.

"He wasn't wearing a life jacket, was he?" I guess softly.

Lila shakes her head with a little moan. Tears stream down her cheeks.

"He nearly made it to the boat. He was so close. I screamed at him, begged him to grab my hand, to grab the side of the boat. But the wind was too strong and the waves were too deep. He couldn't keep his head above water. I didn't want to lose him and I didn't want him to lose you. And then... and then..."

A soft whoosh escapes from somewhere inside her and I watch as she deflates before my eyes.

And I know that my father has drowned again today.

"But somehow he got me back in the boat. I was in the boat when they found me." My face is wet, and I am crying, too. "Daddy got me back in the boat."

She sits silent, openly weeping.

"Didn't he?" I press.

Lila buries her face in her hands.

I stare at her in horror, realizing I've broken the primary rule drilled into our heads in journalism school: always check your facts.

The devil is in the details.

The biggest story of all, the story of my life, and all this time, I had my facts wrong.

My mother didn't cause my father's death. In fact, she saved my life.

Lila finally emerges from the bathroom. Her face is tear-stained and pale, her hands still shaky. I take in her slim shoulders, her small frame. How she mustered the courage to face her fear of water and jump in to save me, how she got me into the boat, then somehow managed to cling to the edge and hold on herself until help arrived, is truly a marvel.

No. It is a miracle.

I can't think of any other woman who would have had the courage to do what she did. Bob's words that afternoon on the beach when he gave me an old-fashioned tongue lashing flood back to mind. *Your mother is one of the bravest women I know.*

For once, Bob and I are in complete agreement.

"Bob Campbell knows the truth, doesn't he?" I say. "He was on the beach when they brought the boat in. You talked to him afterward and told him what happened."

"Lots of people were there, Lucy. The beach was crowded."

"Then how did he know?" I wrap my arms against my chest. Lila's story has wiped away the truth I've lived with all my life, and I'm desperate for a hug.

"I've shared the story at my A.A. meetings. It's a safe place to talk."

"But why didn't Bob tell me?"

"To protect my anonymity. What you hear at those meetings stays at those meetings. Bob works a strong recovery program. He knew eventually I would make my amends to you."

"There's no need for you to make amends," I say softly. "You saved my life, remember? I think that pretty much covers it."

"You're wrong, Lucy. I do need to make amends… for what I did afterward." She chews softly on her bottom lip. "I fell apart when you needed me the most, and for that I am dreadfully sorry." Her voice drops low. "Watching your father drown killed something inside me. I needed time to find myself again. After the funeral, when Winnie and Carl wanted you, I didn't try and fight them. The doctors had me on medication, and I couldn't cope. How could I care for a child when I could barely care for myself? So I agreed and let them take you home."

The adult Lucy gets it, but the sulking five-year-old buried deep inside me suddenly springs to life, wishing she could kick something. It's a horrible, empty feeling, knowing you're alone. That your father is dead, that your mother let you go. That your mother turned her back on you.

"I thought you didn't want me," I finally say. "I thought you forgot all about me."

"How could I forget you? You're my baby." Her words are barely above a whisper. "I wanted you with me so much, but I knew you'd be better off with Winnie and Carl. But I never forgot you, Lucy, not for one day. A mother never forgets her child. I was in no shape to care for you. I'd fallen apart. Physically, emotionally, mentally." Tears stream down her cheeks, but she doesn't seem to care, she doesn't try to hide them. "It's an ugly story, and one I'm not proud of."

I sit, silently watching her. Is Lila right? Did she make the right choice? Was I better off growing up without her around? Some of the other kids' parents were divorced, but at least they had parents. They had families. All I had was Grandma.

"I never meant it to be forever," she adds abruptly. "I knew they would take good care of you and give you a good home until I could get back on my feet. And no matter what I thought of Winnie, I knew how much John had loved his mother. But most of all, I knew how much Winnie loved you. She loved you when I couldn't even love myself."

"You never called." I bite my lip, bite back the hurt rushing through my heart, the hurt I've held back all these years, knowing I'd been left behind. "You could have come and seen me."

Lila falls silent, then finally sighs. "Maybe you're right. I should have tried harder."

If we're being honest, I might as well get it all out.

"Grandma told me you were a drunk."

"That's true," Lila admits. "My drinking did get out of control. I'm an alcoholic. You know that. When your grandfather died, I hadn't been sober very long. I came to his funeral, and I tried to see you, but Winnie refused to budge. She could be a cold, hard woman when it suited her. She threatened to take me to court, and she told me she'd win." Lila shudders slightly. "The thought of going up against Winnie and maybe losing you forever left me terrified. So I didn't try and fight her. And as the years went by, I started to think it would be more hurtful if I tried to take you away. The two of you had made a life together. I didn't want to rip you away from your grandmother. She'd already lost John. If I somehow managed to win you back, Winnie would have been all alone."

I draw in a breath that fills up all the empty space inside that I never had a name for. Why didn't Grandma ever tell me all of this? All my life she let me believe that Lila didn't want me, that she'd forgotten me. Grandma never once told me that Lila wanted me back.

"I tried to keep in touch." Her face wears a soft, uncertain look. "I sent you letters and birthday cards, but most of them came back unopened, marked *Return to Sender*. As for the others, I don't know. Maybe she threw them out."

"I did get one," I admit after a moment. *"To Lucy on her twelfth birthday from Mama. I love you very much."*

A card addressed to me with no return address. I got the mail before Grandma came home. I devoured Lila's card, memorized every word, stared at the twelve crisp, new, one-dollar bills tucked carefully inside.

Then slowly, deliberately, I ripped the card to shreds... just like Lila had ripped apart our lives. I thought about ripping up the money, too, but Grandma had drilled me on the value of a dollar. And despite knowing the source, I couldn't convince myself to tear up good money. Finally I stashed it inside a pair of winter socks in my underwear drawer and stuffed the shredded pieces of card in the bottom of the trash. Where Grandma would never find it. Where I wouldn't have to see it ever again.

"I tore it up."

"I'm sorry, honey." Lila wipes away the tears spilling over on her cheeks. I know she wants to touch me, to reach out and hug me close, because I feel the same. For so many years, I've longed to feel her arms around me, to know a mother's touch.

And now the moment is finally here, neither of us moves.

Memories flood through me, washing away the uncertainty. So many years wasted, living in fear. I was afraid of being left behind, and Lila was afraid she would never be a good enough mother, that she might fall apart again.

Grandma was the only one who wasn't afraid.

Or was she?

She's nothing but a drunk.

"You weren't drunk that day in the boat, were you?" I guess quietly.

Lila stares at me from her perch on the couch. "No, of course not. Why would you think that?" Then her eyes suddenly widen and her face goes flat. "Oh. I see."

Poor Grandma. From my five-year-old's perspective, she was a powerful source of strength and comfort, a strong woman with arms that scrubbed kitchen floors, that cuddled me close when I cried. Hands that often held a Bible, searching for answers. Unfortunately, Grandma preferred Old Testament scripture, with revenge as its guiding law. *An eye for an eye and a tooth for a tooth.* Lila took Grandma's son and Grandma took me. Each of us paid the price for Grandma's revenge.

"She told me they put you away in a sanitarium." I push away the nagging guilt, the feeling that by speaking the words aloud, I'm being disloyal to Grandma. But truth isn't betrayal. Truth is truth. And only truth will set you free.

"No, I was never in a sanitarium, although I did spend some time in treatment. I never drank much before the accident, just an occasional glass of wine. I didn't start drinking seriously until after your father died."

Her face is sober and she doesn't try to hide her grief or the pain in her eyes. "I couldn't deal with the guilt of knowing I couldn't save him, of watching him die. I fell apart and it wasn't pretty. I was out of control for a year or two. Vodka was my favorite. It worked fast. I liked feeling numb. You don't remember things. I got lost in a bottle, and I lost everything... including you."

"There's something I still don't understand," I say slowly. "Grandma is still alive. If you hate her so much, why did you come back to James Bay?"

"Hate is such a strong word. I never hated Winnie." Lila smiles sadly. "I think now I'm older, I understand her better. Why she acted like she did. But I never hated her, Lucy. That's not why I came back."

"Then why?"

Her face softens. "I heard Winnie was sick and that you'd put her in the nursing home. I thought you might need my help. I didn't want you to go through it alone."

Too little, too late. I could have used some help while Grandma was still at home, wandering the house all hours of the day and night. But I snuff out the resentment as quick as it flares up. Even if Lila had been willing, even if I'd been willing, Grandma never would have agreed. Grandma was the one who kept the hate alive. But it no longer matters. Even Grandma doesn't care anymore, now her mind is gone.

I clear my throat, smooth away a wrinkle in my shorts, stare at my feet, my unpainted toes. "And that's all?"

Lila's voice drops, catches. "Did you want more?"

I swallow over the lump in my throat, the one cultivated through years of feeling sorry for myself. A big lump of resentment. Of course I want more. A child always wants more. And I still haven't grown up.

"I thought you understood," she says. "I came back because of you. I missed you, Lucy."

I hang my head. None of this is turning out the way I expected.

"Remember that night you spent on the bathroom floor?" she reminds me. "You said something to me that night that I can't forget. You told me I didn't love you, that I'd never loved you."

My cheeks flame, hearing her words. Good God, did I really say that to her? I was drunk that night, and I can't remember. What else did I say?

"Wait here. There's something I want to show you."

Lila stands and without another word disappears down the hallway. I sit in stunned silence. A full-blown confession of maternal longing and she leaves the room? But soon she is back with a sealed plastic bag in her hand. She draws out a worn, folded tissue with faded blue writing. Slowly she unwraps it, handling it as if it's some fragile treasure that belongs in a museum rather than in her hand.

She offers it to me. "This is for you."

I eye the miniature white chunk resting in her palm. "What is it?"

"Your baby tooth," she says softly. "The first one you ever lost. I kept it, including the note you had me write to the tooth fairy. You probably don't remember. You'd just turned five, and you were playing outside when the tooth finally came out. You'd been wiggling it for days, and you were so excited when you finally had it in your hand. But then you dropped it in the grass. We looked all over, but we couldn't find it, so there was no tooth to put under your pillow. You were heartbroken and wouldn't quit crying. So, we wrote the note and put it under your pillow instead of the tooth. The next morning, you found a dollar under your pillow. You were so excited. Daddy said the tooth fairy made a special exception, seeing how it had been your first tooth and all. But I'm sure you don't remember."

But she's wrong. I remember everything about that night. The first tooth I ever lost and then I *really* lost it. How I threw a fit and cried, and she wiped away the tears. How I sat on Daddy's lap and sucked my thumb while she wrote the note. How Daddy teased me that the rest of my teeth would fall out of my head if I didn't stop sucking my thumb.

I remember every word. The timber of his voice, the rich baritone, how he sang out my name in that special way of his. The one that made me feel all lit up inside.

The same way I feel staring at my first baby tooth in my mother's hand.

"If I lost it in the grass, then where did this come from?"

"I found it a few days later when I was outside weeding flowers," she answered. "But I couldn't give it to you. The tooth fairy had already paid a visit, remember? So I wrapped it up in the note I'd written and tucked it away for someday when I could finally show it to you." Lila smiles softly. "Looks like someday is finally here."

How many moves did she make throughout the years? Treatment centers, apartments, making do with what she had. What kind of rough spots did she face? Life is hard when you go it alone. You keep what matters most.

You keep what is precious.

I kept my memories and a few photographs. Lila kept my baby tooth.

"You're all grown up now, Lucy. We can never get those years back. But you'll always be my little girl. That's why I came back… because it was time. I missed you and I loved you. I've always loved you, Lucy. I always have, and I always will."

And finally, I hear the words I've been waiting for all these years.

Lila didn't come back because of the money. She didn't come back because of Grandma.

She came back for me.

"I'm so glad we're finally talking about this." Her voice carries an edge of relief. "I've wanted to for so long. I tried once before, remember? That day we saw each other at the nursing home. I said something to you after Mass, but you made it very obvious you wanted nothing to do with me. At least, not then."

That day was months ago, but the memory of how fast I shot her down still leaves me cringing. How could I have been so cruel? So unforgiving? So unwilling to listen?

Maybe I'm more like Grandma than I thought.

"I knew you weren't ready, and I didn't want to force you." She ventures a tiny smile. "Want to know the real truth? I was scared."

"You? Afraid?" Lila just admitted to jumping into a lake in the middle of a storm and saving my life. She lived through hell on earth in a bottle and made it to the other side. She faced Grandma's wrath and survived. "I find that hard to believe."

"Just ask Father Greg," she says. "That poor man. He spent hours talking with me when I first moved to town, helping me figure things out. I was convinced that you hated me, but he kept saying I should give it some time, give you some space, and that things would turn out fine.

He thinks very highly of you. He told me you are a kind, generous, decent woman. And he was right. You are."

Talk about a priest being clueless. I'm not a nice person. Just thinking how I acted toward her those first few months after Lila moved to town makes me wince. I turned my back on her. I traveled miles out of my way just to shop at another grocery store in order to avoid her. I wouldn't take her phone calls. When people asked me about my mother, I pretended she didn't exist, that she was nothing to me.

But all along, I was the world to her.

"I'm sorry." I'm surprised to find my face wet. "I'm sorry for everything. I treated you horribly and I'll always regret it."

"No regrets," her voice rushes at me. "Lord knows I spent a lifetime regretting what I've done. But I'm learning that it's better not to live in the past. Though I'll admit I'm not very good at it yet. Some days it seems like two steps forward and three steps back. But I aim for going forward. That's where the future is. Going forward."

I smear away my tears with the back of my hand. "I get stuck in the past a lot."

"Baby steps," she says with a shaky laugh, wiping away her own tears. "That's what we call it in recovery: taking baby steps. But eventually, those baby steps all add up and get you where you want to go."

Lila taught me how to walk once upon a time. Maybe she can help me learn this time, too.

"You have to be patient with me," I say. "I'll need some time. And lots of practice."

"It's the things we're not good at that we have to practice." There's a soft catch in her voice. "Maybe we can practice together."

Max told me earlier today that he still had some growing up to do. He's definitely not alone. I've got plenty of growing up to do, too. But unlike the first time around, this time things will be different.

This time, Lila will be there to help me.

EPILOGUE

Some nights like tonight when I can't sleep, I brew myself a cup of tea, pull one of Max's old sweaters over my pajamas and sneak out on the deck. I snuggle in one of Lila's chairs. Above me the night sky is brilliant with stars. I stare up at the heavens and think about Grandma. It's been nearly a year since she died, and I still miss her. Grandma took care of me when Lila couldn't, and no matter what, she loved me. Right or wrong, Grandma did what she thought was best. I pray for her every night, and I hope she's at peace.

The night air is cool, blowing in off the lake, and I cuddle deeper in Max's sweater. Autumn is here. Soon the lake will freeze over, the snow will start. We need to get things winterized, store the deck furniture, put up the storm windows. Lila's way ahead of us. She pruned back her garden last week, and Max and I helped her cover the bushes in Grandma's backyard.

It seemed fitting that Lila should have the house where my father grew up. I deeded it over shortly after Grandma died. I'm sure Grandma would be shocked by the colors Lila used, but I like how she redecorated. The house has an airy, peaceful feel and a wonderful lived-in look, especially the kitchen. The mingled fragrances tempt your nose to linger, and Lila's Sunday-night dinners are not to be missed. Even Father Greg is becoming a frequent guest.

Lila has lots of time to garden, cook, and putter around the house since I convinced her to quit her job at the grocery store. Why should she work? I've got plenty of money for both of us. She cried when I bought her the baby-blue Mercedes, and she told me it wasn't even her birthday. I said it was to make up for all the birthdays we missed, though truth be told, I planned on buying it anyway. Just because.

Kris choked up when I signed the title for the Jaguar into her name and handed her the keys. I love my new convertible, a sporty little VW. It's not as fast or luxurious as a sports car, but it gets great gas mileage and gets me where I'm going. First-class passengers on an airplane arrive the same time as those who sit in coach. Why spend extra money on things you don't need? Why not use it on the things that matter most?

The people you love.

People like Lila.

Kris.

And Max.

He's been walking around for the past few weeks with a peculiar smile on his face. My birthday isn't far off, and I'm not sure what he's got planned. Maybe a surprise party? Maybe a diamond ring is involved. Either way is good. I know I'm loved and I know he feels the same. We're a good match, Max and me. We're healthy, happy, and we lead busy lives doing what we love. I have my work and he has his camp.

Camp Call of the Loon's survival is guaranteed. After transferring the various properties from his father's corporations back into the family trust, Max deeded them over to the camp. We pooled some funds and established the Lloyd Christopher Colley Scholarship Fund in honor of his grandfather. LC was a smart man who knew that summer camp is a wonderful place to break down social barriers as kids grow, learn, and play together, no matter what their family background. Max and I are determined that money will never be an issue. Our scholarships ensure there's a place at Camp Call of the Loon for any boy who wants to attend.

Max held back five acres of land and we built a little cabin nestled above the shores of Loon Lake with a wraparound porch and huge fieldstone fireplace similar to the one in the main lodge. The cabin is cozy and perfect for the two of us, with room for expansion. Maybe someday we'll need it, but I'm learning not to look ahead. Lila and her recovery talk has taught me a few things.

Keep it simple. Easy does it. One day at a time.

I burrow deeper in my chair, sip my tea. Before me, Loon Lake shimmers in the moonlight. An eerie cry splits the night silence, and a long, dark shadow circles low across the lake, skims the surface, and lands. The long plaintive cry of the loon is one I've come to recognize and it no longer scares me. I've made peace with the lake and peace with the past. Peace with my mother. Peace with myself.

The Didi Taylors have their place in the world, but so do I, and it's not on the sidelines. I'm writing my own future. Since winning the lottery, I've learned a lot about people, about life, but especially about myself. Wishing for something and having something are two very different things, for reality has its limitations. Sometimes dreams are better left at that... something to dream about.

Investing with Max's dad was a costly mistake, but I don't regret a single penny. It taught me a valuable lesson. When it comes to money, I need help. Thank God I've got Sam at my side. We've set up various trusts to manage the funds. Now before I sign documents—legal, financial, or otherwise—I pass them by Sam and my attorney. Why ask for trouble? I've got more important things to do.

Like a newspaper to run.

Sam tried his best to talk me out of buying the *Journal*. He said I paid too much, especially when the downstate conglomerate balked at selling. But my gut said it was the right thing to do. And I prefer to think of it as money well spent. Plus, Kris and I make a great team. I'm the owner and publisher and she's managing editor. We're committed to restoring the *Journal*'s status as a hometown newspaper. No more printing stories hinging on gossip and innuendo, no more smearing people's reputations. We want the *Journal* to be a newspaper James Bay can be proud of; a newspaper that provides its readers with fair and accurate reporting, focused on community rather than advertising space.

Though Sam keeps insisting our financials should reflect a profit, breaking even is okay with me. Because this isn't about the bottom line. It's about people's lives and telling the truth. It can't be about the money. Never again.

Money might buy a fancy sports car and nice toys, but it won't buy happiness. That's an inside job and one I'll be working on for the rest of my life. As Lila says, it starts with baby steps. Slow going at times, but I'm learning if I keep on taking those baby steps, they eventually get me where I need to go.

Except when it comes to snakes. Living here with Max at camp, I still encounter the occasional snake.

And then I run like hell.

ABOUT THE AUTHOR

Kathleen Irene Paterka has never won the lottery, except when it comes to life and love. She is the author of numerous novels which embrace universal themes of home, family life and love, including *FATTY PATTY* and *HOME FIRES*, part of the Women's Fiction series, "*The James Bay Novels*". Kathleen is the resident staff writer for Castle Farms, a world renowned castle listed on the National Historic Register, and co-author of the non-fiction book *FOR THE LOVE OF A CASTLE*, published in 2012. Having lived and studied abroad, Kathleen's educational background includes a Bachelor of Arts degree from Central Michigan University. She and her husband Steve live in the beautiful north country of Michigan's Lower Peninsula. Kathleen loves hearing from readers. You can contact her via her website at

http://www.kathleenirenepaterka.com

or follow her on Facebook at

http://www.facebook.com/KathleenIrenePaterka.

If you enjoyed **LOTTO LUCY**,

check out these other titles in *The James Bay Novel series* by Kathleen Irene Paterka:

The James Bay Novels

FATTY PATTY (#1 – available now!)

HOME FIRES (#2 – available now!)

LOTTO LUCY (#3 – available now!)

FOR I HAVE SINNED (#4 – coming soon!)

Non-Fiction:

FOR THE LOVE OF A CASTLE (available now!)

Coming in 2013:

ROYAL SECRETS

Turn the Page for a free bonus read!

FOR I HAVE SINNED

Book #4 in The James Bay Novel series

FOR I
HAVE
SINNED

A James Bay Novel

KATHLEEN IRENE
PATERKA

FOR I HAVE SINNED

A James Bay Novel

KATHLEEN IRENE PATERKA

ISBN-10: 0985512180
ISBN-13: 978-0-9855121-8-7

CHAPTER ONE

Maybe the nuns lied.

Year after year, with us kids cooped up like prisoners in stuffy, overheated classrooms that smelled like dirty socks, they drilled the rules into our heads about the need to repent. Confession, they warned, and receiving absolution for our sins was the only way to enter heaven and be with God.

So where is everybody?

Every Saturday afternoon for the past two years I've spent as priest in this parish, it's been pretty much the same thing. I sit alone in this tiny afterthought of a room, tucked away in the back of church and wait for someone to show up. From four o'clock to four thirty when my confessional is open, I've got time enough to say one rosary plus count the stained-glass panes adorning the window; two rosaries, if I skip the window. It's my regular routine and I've got it down to a spiritual science.

Obviously, people nowadays have better things to do on Saturday afternoons than visit my confessional.

Or maybe not. There's a creak as the door opens, then a slight rustle as someone kneels, a shadowy figure behind the linen screen.

"Hello? Father? Are you still here?"

The voice—young, female—comes as a surprise. The occasional penitent tends to be elderly, but she sounds barely out of her teens.

"Go ahead." I shove my rosary in my pocket, shift in my chair as the church bell tolls four thirty. First—and last—customer of the day. Mass starts at five.

"Bless me, Father, for I have sinned. It's been *years* since my last confession." The voice rushes through the screen. "Ohmigod, Mama would kill me if she knew. When I was growing up, she always said you had to confess at least once a year, or it's considered a sin. And she would know. Mama went to Catholic school. She knows all the church rules."

I can't help chuckling to myself. Sounds like her mama and I might know some of the same nuns.

"Let's not worry how long it's been," I suggest. "Instead, give yourself some credit for showing up today. That's a good first step, and I'm sure God agrees."

"You think so?" A sigh filters through the screen. "I don't think He'll like the other part." She hesitates. "Can you go to Hell for hating people? Especially if one of them is a priest?"

Did I hear her correctly? I'm fifty-four years old and thought my hearing was fine.

Until now.

"Could you repeat that?" I lean closer to the screen.

"I know it's a terrible sin to hate someone." Her voice drops, barely above a whisper. "Do you think God will forgive me?"

Forget about God. I'm curious which guy she's talking about. Our diocese in Northern Michigan has over forty priests, and I can think of a few I don't like either without too much trouble. So, which one is it?

My gut tightens. Good Lord, what if it's me? All those jokes I tell from the pulpit; I should have known they'd get me in trouble someday.

"God forgives everyone if they are truly sorry." I tug at the Roman collar tightening around my neck. When did the room get so stuffy? Who the hell installs a stained-glass window that can't be opened?

"I'm not sure about the being-sorry part, but I'm working on it," she says. "It was hard enough getting up the nerve to come in here and admit the truth to you. I sat in that pew for what seemed like forever. In fact, five minutes ago I nearly lost my nerve and walked out. But then I remembered your sermon from last Sunday, how you laughed all the way through it…"

Oh, God, she *is* talking about me. And I'm guilty as charged. But this is the first time anyone has complained about my jokes. Besides, I've always believed God to have a marvelous sense of humor. Why not bring it along to Sunday Mass?

"But it was your eyes that finally got me out of the pew and in here on my knees. You've got kind eyes, Father, the kind of eyes that smile. You don't seem like all the other priests. That's what made me take the chance and come here today. I thought you would understand. At least, I hope you will."

I blow out a long sigh, stretch out my legs. Okay, obviously we're not talking about me.

"I'm probably doing this all wrong." She hesitates, her voice wistful. "I know the church has rules about the way they like things done, including the way you should make a confession. But I'll admit it, Father. I've never been good at following the rules."

A rebel when it comes to the rules? That makes two of us. I've had enough skirmishes with the diocese about insisting I enforce archaic church rules to last me a lifetime.

Pick your battles with the bishop carefully, I tell myself.

One confrontation at a time, my friend Father Ray tells me.

One day at a time, my program tells me.

"You're doing fine," I assure her, "although some people find it easier talking face to face. Come around the screen, if you like. I have another chair over here."

But I'm not holding my breath. Despite my attempts to convince them otherwise in my two years here as pastor at St. Mary's of the Lakes, parishioners are bent on adhering to tradition.

I blink as she scoots around the panel and suddenly stands in front of me.

"I'm Gina," the young woman says, extending a hand. "Gina VanBrabant."

The firm handshake comes as a surprise, as does the break in anonymity. People who show up for confession don't shake hands, much less introduce themselves.

Nor do the priests.

"I'm Father Greg Kozminski."

"Yes, I know." She sinks into the chair facing me. "I've been coming to Sunday Mass here in James Bay since Joe and I moved to town."

I've noticed her in church for the past several weeks, a silent lone presence in one of the side pews. A tangle of black curls frames her face. A shy smile tugs at one corner of her mouth. I catch the glint of a diamond wedding band on her finger. She's married? In those flip-flops and worn jeans, she looks barely old enough to be out of high school, let alone someone's wife.

But even in the dim glow of the little lamp on the table between us, her face is pale. Dark eyes warn there could be trouble ahead.

"Your sermons are great. People probably think I sleep through them because I always close my eyes. But I learned long ago that's the best way to listen." A high blush rises on her cheeks. "I like to pretend you're talking directly to me," she confesses.

I knock down a quick swell of pride. My ego would love to claim a seat on God's throne, but I'm merely a voice for the words she hears at Mass. He's the One who put them in my heart.

"Glad you decided to forego the kneeler." I settle back in the hard wooden chair, encourage her with a smile. "It gets lonely on this side of the screen. Most people don't bother with confession anymore."

"Do you blame them? Who wants to admit you screwed up, much less tell a priest? It's bad enough knowing you're guilty."

Guilt and grief. In my twenty-five-years-plus as a priest, I've heard countless admissions of fear and loneliness rampant in people's hearts. Marriages destroyed by adultery, promising careers ruined by drinking and drugs, families torn apart by abuse. A priest gathers the darkness that collects in people's souls and hopefully helps them walk toward the light of forgiveness.

Though lately, fewer people seem interested in seeking out my help. What's causing them to lose heart? Am I trying my best? Is it me? The church?

God, help me to help this young woman choose the right direction.

"What brings you here today, Gina?"

Her gaze drops, coming to rest on the purple silk stole draped around my neck. The stole proclaims me God's representative on earth, capable of absolving her sins.

Suddenly the wariness is back in her eyes.

She fingers the wedding band, worrying it back and forth over her knuckle. "Father, do you believe in love at first sight?"

The question is a definite first in my confessional. I swallow down a smile. "I'm not sure I have an answer for that."

"I fell in love with Joe the day I met him. Mama always said that love is the greatest gift of all. And I believe, with all my heart, that's what Joe is… a gift to me, straight from God."

Her mouth twists. "Although my father doesn't think so. He has definite ideas about life and church, and the way things should be. *'How dare you think about dating someone like him?'* he said. *'He's not one of us, and I'll be damned…"*

She pauses, blushing slightly. "Sorry, Father Greg, excuse my language, but I'm just repeating my father's words. *'…and I'll be damned if I'll let my daughter marry one of them.'"*

Gina's eyes narrow. "You see, Joe's not an American, and he didn't grow up in this country. I don't think he realizes how intolerant some people can be. People like my father. '*He's not one of us....*' " Her face tightens. "I was done listening before he even said that. But then Mama cried and begged me to go see Father Michael, so I made the appointment. There's no way I could ever tell Mama *no*."

"Who's Father Michael?" I ask, though I've got a pretty good idea we're finally talking about the errant priest.

"He's the pastor back home in our parish between Ypsilanti and Ann Arbor." Gina's face scrunches in a scowl. "Joe and I kept the appointment, but I should have known it would end up being a waste of time. Father Michael was as bad as my father. Worse, even; you'd think at least a priest would have some clue about kindness and compassion. Father Michael was horrible when we went to see him. I think he actually enjoyed refusing to marry us."

"Did he give you a reason?" *He's not one of us...* Her father might be a jerk, but this Father Michael is a Catholic priest, trained to be open-minded. Catholic means universal, welcoming to all. No matter what a person's nationality or faith.

"He mentioned something about a six-month rule. Even after I explained that Joe and I had known each other for six months, Father Michael told us it didn't matter, he still wouldn't marry us. He said even if we were a normal couple, there'd be no getting around the rules." Gina rolls her eyes. "He especially seemed to love that part, bringing up the rules."

"I assume he was referring to the premarital counseling sessions," I say gently. "The six-month waiting period is customary."

Mandatory is more like it. When it comes to canonical laws, the Catholic church holds an exclusive copyright.

"Sorry, Father, I guess I didn't make myself clear. Father Michael said that even if Joe and I waited six months, he still wouldn't marry us."

I frown. That doesn't make sense unless there's a religious impediment she's not mentioning.

"He told us we had no business getting married. He said it didn't matter that Joe had already finished his university studies and had a good job or that I was in college, too. Father Michael told me I was too young to understand what I was getting myself into, and that the cultural differences would prove too great. He said that if I did go through with marrying Joe, I'd eventually end up sorry." Her eyes narrow. "Then he threw us out of his office."

I blink. "He did what?"

Gina nods. "Father Michael said if Joe and I were hell-bent on getting married, that's exactly where we would end up... in Hell."

I've stumbled across my share of coldhearted guys wearing the collar throughout the years, but this Father Michael sounds like a holier-than-thou jackass, the kind of priest that gives the rest of us a bad name. And as for cultural differences? No one deserves to be treated the way Gina's described, no matter who they are or where they're from. We've got to be dealing with another faith for her father to be so harsh, her mother so upset, and the priest so adamant in his refusal to marry them.

A radical orthodox faith.

"Joe and I were married two months ago in a civil ceremony in front of a judge. Definitely not the wedding I always dreamed of, but definitely the right man," she says. "I love Joe with all my heart. And I know God was there with us in the courtroom that day, no matter what anyone thinks—including my father or Father Michael. I believe God lives in people's hearts, not in some old church or what some stuffy priest says.

Gina's hand flies to her mouth. "Holy crap! No offense, Father. I didn't mean you."

"No offense taken." I chuckle softly. She's a delight. "Believe it or not, I've bumped into a few of those priests myself."

More than a few.

"Joe is the most positive loving man I've ever met. How anyone could hate him for what he is is beyond me. What makes people think they have the right to judge?"

Religious intolerance. How many wars have been fought throughout history because of that very thing? There's a big Muslim population in downstate Michigan, especially near the university towns. If things were bad before the terrorist attacks in 2001, the fragile truce that now exists between Christianity and Islam barely borders on civility. It's hard to believe the world—even in modern-day America—can be like that, especially tucked away like I am in this small Northern Michigan town. But every visit home I make to see Mom downstate serves as an instant reminder that people haven't let go of their fear or anxiety. You feel it everywhere: restaurants, shopping malls, even in the grocery store. People keep their distance. The distrust and apprehension is there in their eyes, and the quick turn of their heads as they encounter men with swarthy faces and women in head scarves, some shrouded with face veils.

Not one of us.

What the hell does it matter who or what a person is? Muslim, Jewish, Protestant, Catholic. We're not defined by a country or a religion.

One man at a time. One heart at a time.

"Life is short enough as it is," Gina says. "There's no time or room for hatred."

"The world would certainly be a wonderful place if everyone thought that way," I agree. "Unfortunately, hatred exists—so much of it because of religion."

She eyes me carefully. "What do you think, Father?"

Do I tell her the truth? That she's sweet, spirited, and a bit of a rambler? If I was smart, I'd tell her to phone the rectory for an appointment, then send her on her way with a penance to say some prayers for her father, Father Michael, and other priests like him. Gina hasn't done anything wrong except skirt a mere technicality mandated by the church.

Although I'm sure if Bishop Holden heard me label marrying outside the church to be *a mere technicality* he would vehemently disagree.

But this isn't the time or place for a theological discussion about the shortcomings of the Catholic church. That's a topic normally reserved for debate with my good friend Father Ray over a leisurely dinner, not something to discuss with a vivacious young woman in my confessional late on a Saturday afternoon.

Not with Mass starting soon.

"The church teaches—"

"I don't care about the church." Black curls swing as she shakes her head. "I trust you, Father Greg. That's why I'm here. I want to know what you think."

How do I admit the truth? I'm a priest, but I'm still just one man. The Catholic church isn't interested in my opinion, nor what Gina thinks, either.

As a priest, as a Catholic, it's a hard reality for me to accept. Hearing any of it isn't going to help her.

But God help us all if the church and its priests dominate to the point that has people afraid to question authorities or search their own hearts.

"The Catholic church is not a democracy." I weigh each word carefully before I speak. "The rules exist for a reason."

She sits forward in her chair, a little of the snap disappearing from her eyes. "Are you telling me you agree with Father Michael? That Joe and I were wrong? That despite what Father Michael said and did, we shouldn't have broken the rules?"

While I don't know the details of what went on in that office with that particular priest, one thing I do know: the church and its rules are damn good at breaking people's hearts.

"Perhaps it would be easier if I put it this way," I say gently. "Ultimately, God is the only judge."

"But—"

I hold up one hand and she sputters into silence.

"And I believe," I continue, "be it right or wrong, that each of us is called to live our lives in a way so that when we finally stand before Him, we are able to honestly say *I did my best and was guided by love*."

"But that's it exactly!" Her eyes shine with a fierce intensity. "It's all about love, isn't it? I knew you would understand."

Her face loses that battered look, like she's found what she came looking for. But at what expense? My gut twists. Maybe it was a mistake, admitting how I feel. My personal beliefs don't belong in the confessional. But how can I let her walk away without hope?

"I don't care one bit about my father, but I haven't found the courage to tell Mama yet. Bad enough she thinks Joe and I are living together. It will break her heart when she finds out we got married outside of the church."

Gina draws in a deep breath, taking up all the air in the small space between us. "That's the other reason I'm here. I want to have our marriage blessed. In church. Maybe this weekend? After Sunday Mass?"

The look on her face is so determined and the trust she's put in me so complete that I long to say yes.

Even though I know it's impossible.

"I'm afraid it's not that easy. These things take time," I say carefully. "The church law is very specific. Marriage is a sacrament not to be entered into lightly."

"But Joe and I are already married."

"Yes, I know, but—"

"Shouldn't that make things simpler?"

It's easy to understand her frustration. Hell, I get frustrated, too, even after all my years as a priest. I still butt heads on a regular basis with the church hierarchy over rules and laws that no longer make sense. I keep waiting for things to change, but how long is it going to take? The Catholic Church is a marvelous institution for upholding tradition merely for tradition's sake.

But at whose expense? At how much heartbreak?

"What if I told you I'm going to have a baby?" Her chin tilts upward. "Would that make a difference?"

Babies trump all. Is she telling the truth or playing the sympathy card to get what she wants? God knows it would not be the first time I've been drawn in by some parishioner who showed up with a sad story.

"I am pregnant, Father," she says, her eyes softening. "I would never lie about something like that. Though I'll admit finding out about the baby was a surprise. But Joe is so pleased, and so am I. It's like God told us that, in spite of everything that's happened, we made the right decision and that things will be okay. That's why I want to have our marriage blessed in church, and I want our baby baptized. More than anything, Father Greg, I want to make things right with God."

She blinks once, twice, and her eyes lock on mine. What's her story? Is she telling the truth or hiding something from me? I search her face, but all I see is honesty, hope, and a plea for help.

Call me a fool, but I want to help. Ray would call me more than a fool. He thinks I'm a pushover, too easy on people, and in all honesty, he's probably right. I can be naïve and too trusting at times. Over the years, I've oftentimes ended up sorry for the things I've done, and the people I've tried to help.

But doesn't everyone deserve the benefit of the doubt? And there's something about Gina that makes me want to believe she's telling the truth. My gut tells me I can believe her.

And I would do anything to wipe away that dark smudge of pain in her eyes.

"What about your husband? Is he agreeable to all of this?"

"We haven't exactly talked about it," she hedges.

I eye her for a long moment. "Did you tell him you were coming here today?"

She shifts in her chair. "Not exactly."

I sit back, consider the options. It doesn't require a degree in theology to see how much she loves her husband. Gina dredged up the courage to seek me out, despite the damage caused by Father Michael. She's turned to me for guidance and expects me to supply some answers. But I don't want to make matters worse, say the wrong thing, and cause her to bolt.

Priests carry so much on their souls, things whispered under the seal of the confessional. Sometimes I feel like I'm drowning under the weight of the sadness surrendered. People expect me to listen, to give wise counsel. But how do I know I've said the right thing? The church has given me the authority to sit in judgment, to counsel them on what to do. But what if I'm wrong? Who am I to judge?

"Please, Father, can you help us? I promise we'll do whatever you say."

What business do I have instructing someone like this young woman how to live her life? Perhaps if priests were allowed to marry, if I'd been permitted to have a family of my own, things would be different. I've honored my vocation for nearly thirty years, and my love for God has deepened, but so has my frustration with the church. The divisiveness tears at my heart. Perhaps that is the worst of all—the necessity of remaining separate, of withholding myself from the rest of the flock.

Jesus spoke of finding the lost sheep. But what of the shepherd? Who goes searching for him when the shepherd feels lost?

Gina isn't here to hear my truth.

That sometimes I feel like a fraud.

That sometimes I feel like ripping this Roman collar right off my neck.

"Tell Joe I want to meet him." I suddenly decide. "Bring him to Mass. The three of us can chat after that."

"Thank you, Father." The sudden glow on her face reminds me of a radiant Madonna. "I knew coming to see you was the right thing to do. Joe and I belong together; you'll see, once you meet him. He's the right man for me. My father was furious when he found out we were dating, and he threw me out of the house. Mama begged him not to, but he wouldn't listen." Her eyes disappear in tiny black slits. "He never listens."

She blinks fast, and I worry there'll be tears soon. When women cry in the confessional, it's usually because the hurt is too huge to hold inside.

I hand her a box of tissues as the church bell tolls the quarter hour. It's my cue to head up front to the sacristy and begin preparing for five o'clock Mass. I hear muffled sounds as the church fills up. People shuffle in the back door, coughing, chatting with the ushers as they grab bulletins.

But I am not going to abandon Gina. It won't be the first time Mass is five minutes late. Besides, they can't start without me.

"I hate the way he makes me feel—resentful and mean." Her fists ball in hard little knots. "I hate him. I think I've always hated him."

"Hate is a powerful word," I say gently.

"Are you saying it's wrong to feel the way I do?"

"No, of course not. A person has every right to their feelings. All of us are human. Even your father," I add.

"Hate the sin, but love the sinner?"

"Something like that."

"But how is that fair?" Her eyes blaze. "Why should I be the one who has to forgive? My father refuses to accept Joe. He's the one at fault, not me."

"But you're the one who came to confession," I point out. "And like it or not, lots of things in the world aren't

383

fair." I cringe as words I myself hated hearing as a child spout from my own mouth. "And it doesn't sound like your father is interested in changing," I add.

"That's an understatement," she mumbles.

"Then the change will need to start with you. Pity the man he is, Gina. Pity the way he lives his life. But most of all, remember to pray for him."

"Prayers won't do him any good," she predicts. "I could spend all day on my knees and it wouldn't make a difference. He'll never change."

"Never is a long time. People have a way of coming around." I've seen hard-core Catholics crack following the birth of their first grandchild, despite the stigma of an interfaith marriage.

"You don't know my father. He'll never forgive me for marrying Joe. And once he finds out about the baby, he'll figure out some way to keep Mama and Donny out of my life. Besides Joe, Mama and my little brother are the only family I've got."

She balls up a tissue and rolls it around in her hand. "Tell me the truth, Father. Will God forgive me for marrying outside the church? For the way I feel about Father Michael, and for hating my father? I hate the way he treats Donny and how he ruined Mama's life. But I refuse to let him destroy mine, or Joe's life, either. Maybe it's for the best that we're far away from him. Joe's never met my father. He would never understand if I told him even half of what my father said."

Gina shudders. "That I'd been raised to know better, that people are meant to be with their own kind." She struggles to swallow, like the words are a thick clump in the back of her throat. "He said… that Joe and I being together is a sin against God."

And Gina dared to break the rules.

Poor kid. She's had a rough time of it, brought up in a traditional Catholic family headed up by a bully who used rage and religion to keep his family in line.

"I'll help in any way I can," I promise, "starting with marriage preparations. We'll take it from there, then work on the baptism. Meanwhile, you go home and talk with Joe. Tell him you came to see me today. Bring him along to Mass. Let him see what's involved with the church. And if he's interested in taking instructions, I'll be happy to help with that, too."

Gina blinks. "Instructions?"

"If Joe would like to join the Catholic faith," I explain.

"But…" Two bright spots flame on her cheeks. "I'm sorry, Father, I thought you knew."

Knew what? Something's not right.

"Joe is just as much a Catholic as you or me," Gina says. "The reason my father hates him is because Joe is black."

I trudge across the parking lot after Mass, headed for the rectory, my thoughts still on Gina. With no black families living in town, and—save for Gina and Joe—no interracial couples, either, the two of them should prove an interesting addition to our summer-resort community. Our country has come a long way, especially now we've witnessed an African American president in the Oval Office. But I'm not foolish enough to think the barriers and bigotry have disappeared. Gina and Joe will need plenty of support.

Especially since her father has disowned her.

Especially with a baby on the way.

Especially after that bumper sticker I saw on a car in downtown James Bay the other night.

Never apologize for being white.

The rectory back door slams behind me, a noisy reminder I promised Mom this morning that I would speak with the janitor about having it fixed. If I don't talk to Vince soon, she'll be sure and remind me.

I glance down the long, narrow kitchen, poke my head in the empty dining room. The massive table wears a snowy white tablecloth and is neatly set for two.

Obviously my plans to take her out for dinner tonight after Mass have changed.

I wander into the front entry. "Mom? Where are you?"

"Upstairs." A voice drifts from above. "I'll be right down."

I hang over the railing, watching as she grips the banister and slowly makes her descent. Despite the quilted pink housecoat, she looks regal as a queen. That glorious cloud of white hair crowning her head still surprises me. Sometime during the past year, she let her hair go. When did that happen? How could I have not noticed? How much happens to those we love while we're too busy worrying about other things?

"Gregory, how many times do I have to tell you not to slump?" she says as she reaches the bottom step. "You'll ruin your posture."

"I think it's a little late to be worrying about that now," I say, straightening to my full height of six foot three.

She gives an affectionate rap on my shoulder. "What did I teach you? *Never say never.* It's never too late for anything."

I plant a soft kiss on her cheek. "I'm fifty-four years old, Mom. Maybe it's time you quit telling me what to do."

"I might be an old lady, but I'm still your mother," she chides. "Remember all those years you spent hunched over the piano, and I would tell you to sit up straight? I don't want to see my effort wasted. You would understand these things, Gregory, if you had children of your own."

I hold back a sigh and a twinge of longing for something I've never had, that will never be. A Catholic priest is a spiritual father to everyone, but a biological father to no one. What do I know about married life or babies either, for that matter? My knowledge of infants comes mainly from the baptismal font, where the vast majority usually dissolve in a fit of red faces and piercing screams while I'm baptizing them. Plus, I'm an only child. There will never be any nieces or nephews for me to cuddle.

"Ever wish you and Pop had had more children?"

She halts in the doorway. "Good Lord, Gregory, where do you come up with these things?"

"Just wondering." I trail her into the kitchen.

"What would I have done with two or three more children? You were bad enough." She opens the cupboard and pulls out a skillet. "Once you learned to walk, you never sat still. I was constantly chasing after you. And after you learned to talk? All those questions. *Why, Mama*? You never stopped. It was always *why, why, why*?"

A faraway look flits over her face. "You asked so many questions, sometimes I was afraid I would run out of answers."

With anyone else the words would be hurtful, but the playful smile and gentle look in her eyes tells me I am loved.

That I have always been loved and cherished as a gift from God.

I lean against the counter, watching as she opens the refrigerator and whips out a bowl of eggs ready for scrambling. "I thought we were going out to dinner."

"I thought so, too. But Mass started late, remember? And now it's already past seven o'clock; I changed my mind."

She whisks the eggs in a deft movement, adds a few drops of milk. Butter sizzles in a slow dance inside the skillet as she adjusts the burner. "What happened tonight, Gregory? You never used to be late with Mass."

Do I admit the truth? I was waylaid by two females; one confession by a wild-eyed beauty named Gina before Mass, and one long chat in the sacristy afterward with a frosted blonde named Lila.

Maybe it's best if I keep my mouth shut.

"I got a little sidetracked."

"And I got a little hungry," she says matter-of-factly, popping slices of bread in the toaster. "Besides, there's nothing wrong with eating in. You should save your money instead of spending it on me. And it's Saturday night. Knowing this town, the restaurants are already crowded. The last thing I want is to sit around waiting for undercooked and overpriced food."

"I was going to take you to Chuck's Tavern and Grill. You seemed to enjoy it the last time you came for a visit."

Mom wrinkles her nose. "That place is fine if you're in the mood for a hamburger or fried fish. Which I am not." She halts, skillet in hand, and peers up at me. "And what's wrong with scrambled eggs? You liked them enough when you were growing up. Or has that changed, too?"

"Never," I assure her as she spoons golden mounds of eggs evenly between our plates, adds toast and fresh tomatoes slices. "You make the best scrambled eggs in the world."

She thumbs my cheek with a quick smile. "That's what I like to hear."

I carry our plates into the dining room and we take our seats at the long table with me at the head and Mom on my right. We bow our heads and I offer a simple prayer. The zesty smell of lemon polish mingles with a sweet whiff of strawberry jam as I slather my toast. "I thought you told me you were going to spend this afternoon resting, not cleaning."

She blinks with innocent eyes. "All I did was dust."

I glance around the room. The chandelier sparkles, the sideboard gleams. I know my mother all too well, but she doesn't know herself. At seventy-eight years old, she has yet to learn her limits.

"I've been thinking maybe I should stay a little longer," she muses. "It might be a good idea. This place needs a woman's touch. And you need someone to take care of you, Gregory."

God help us both. I love my mother, but I need my own space. Space without her constantly in it.

"There's no need for you to worry about me. I'm perfectly capable of fending for myself. I know how to cook. You taught me, remember? Besides, I have a housekeeper."

She sniffs. "I've yet to see evidence of that. What's her name?"

"Martha. She comes in once a week, on Mondays."

"Well, whoever this Martha person is, she could use a lesson in proper household management," she says with a shrewd look. "I'm surprised you haven't already had a fire in the kitchen, the grease on the stove was that thick. I must have spent an hour scrubbing it down."

"Come on, Mom, don't go blaming Martha. Remember, this is a big house. She does the best she can."

Built over a century ago, the rectory originally would have housed two or three priests, plus a few associates. Nowadays, I'm left to ramble alone in this drafty old building.

"I'm lucky to have her," I add. "It wasn't easy getting Martha to come in and clean for what the church can afford to pay her."

"One would assume she'd be grateful for the job. Think of how many people in today's economy are looking for work." Mom nibbles at her toast. "And speaking of grateful, I hope the people in this parish appreciate having you as their priest. You're working too hard, Gregory, and I'm worried about you. Just think of everything you did today. First, that fancy wedding, then confessions, and Mass tonight. Plus, the two you'll say tomorrow. By the way, you did a nice job with your homily this evening. Very effective."

"Thanks, Mom. I try my best."

And try even harder when she's here. Mom plants herself firmly in the front pew every time she visits, just like she did at Mass tonight. And while her presence can be comforting, it's also a distraction.

Sometimes I wonder if it might be easier to connect with my parishioners if Mom sat further back.

Maybe in the last pew?

Not that I would suggest she move. I might be the priest, but she is my mother.

"How was the wedding this afternoon?"

"The usual." I spread jam on a second slice of toast. "The bride's father gave her away. The mother cried. The groom looked nervous."

"I notice they kept some of the flowers on the altar. Those roses must have cost a fortune."

I shrug. "Knowing that family, they can afford it. It was quite the lavish affair."

She eyes me over her cup of tea. "What about the reception?"

"They're having it at the Yacht Club."

Her eyebrows lift. "And you're sitting here in the rectory eating scrambled eggs? You'd think people, especially those with money, would have better manners. Don't they know the priest should always be invited to these sorts of things?"

I swallow down the truth along with a bite of toast. Not only did I receive an invitation, the bride's mother was gracious enough to include my mother, too. But I begged off, pleading a prior engagement. I'm sure Mom would have been thrilled to accompany me to the Yacht Club, but today's wedding was one I was glad to be done with. The lavish church ceremony and reception were two years in the making. The bride's jewel-encrusted dress easily cost thousands.

But despite the premarital counseling and the numerous sessions the three of us spent together, the bride's constant nagging and the groom's blithe disregard soured me months ago on this particular couple. Totally wrapped up in themselves, not in each other.

I give them one year, maybe two, at most. And that is being generous.

Perhaps Gina and Joe did themselves a favor. Not that I'm an advocate for young people running off and getting married outside the church. But somehow I have got to figure out how to get engaged couples to concentrate on what matters most: the love between a man and woman, rather than the pomp and circumstance they think is due the bride and groom.

Especially with the divorce rate in this country hovering near fifty percent.

Mom settles back in her chair. "By the way, what is the name of that little blonde who was up there on the altar with you during Mass?"

I scrape up the rest of my eggs, trying to remember which kids were on the schedule to serve tonight. We've got a full roster, girls and boys alike. Finally I recall the two lanky young brothers, one of whom yawned all the way through Mass. "There weren't any girl altar servers tonight."

"No, I'm talking about that woman who helped during communion."

This time there's no need to think. "That was Lila Carter. She's one of my sacristans."

Thank God for Lila. She was in the sacristy while I was in the confessional with Gina. Lila made sure the wine was poured, the hosts were out, the altar servers weren't goofing off. With Lila around, things always go smoothly.

"That's right, I remember now," she muses. "Lila Carter. She came up after Mass and introduced herself."

The mild smile on my mother's face sends shivers up my neck. I've seen that look before. Suddenly, every instinct I have goes on high alert.

"She certainly knows her way around the altar, doesn't she?" Mom nibbles at her toast. "And it's obvious she wants everyone else to know she knows it, too."

I eye her carefully. "Lila is a very nice woman. I'm sure you'll see that for yourself once you get to know her."

"Really? How interesting you should say that, Gregory, especially since I have no intention of getting to know her. Why should I? Pushy, that's what she is. I know her type. Women like this Lila person are always up to something." She peers at me over her tea cup. "And just so we're clear on the subject, I have no interest in having dinner with her, either."

"What are you talking about?"

"She invited us for dinner tomorrow night. Something about a regular Sunday-night thing between friends." She sniffs. "Can you imagine?"

Actually, I can. I'm a frequent visitor to Lila's home nearly every Sunday night. She's a wonderful cook, gracious hostess, and one of the most generous people I know. Her Sunday evening get-togethers are a highly sought-after invitation in our little town. A priest learns early to be cautious around women, but with Lila there's no need. Our friendship is an easy one, based on similar ages, mutual respect, and devotion to God.

Plus our seats across the table from each other every Thursday night at our weekly AA meeting.

"Don't worry, Gregory. I realize this woman is one of your parishioners. I made sure to be very polite. I thanked her, and said that we were very busy. And I told her that since I would be in James Bay for only a few more days, we had other plans."

Even in her late seventies, Mom, a retired schoolteacher, still relishes being in control. She might not have control of her classroom anymore, but she's still got me.

"Lila does a lot for the church. I find her to be a great help."

"Just be careful you don't allow her to become too much of a help. Granted, she's not as young as some, but she's still an attractive woman, Gregory, and you are a priest. Never forget that. I've seen women like this Lila Carter before. They're always after something. Watch yourself, son. You don't want to end up sorry. Don't give her an opportunity to take advantage."

"Duly noted." Somehow I choke down the last of my toast. The thought of Lila having designs on me is almost too much to swallow. Lila carries a sweet serenity about her, not to mention she is the soul of discretion.

"And hopefully, Gregory, you will not make me out to be a liar. When I told her we had other plans, I meant it. I've already been here two days, and I've barely seen you. First you had that funeral yesterday morning…"

I blow out a sigh. "It's not my fault if someone dies—"

She tsk-tsks me into silence. "And then you spent all Friday afternoon working on your homily, plus that wedding this afternoon and Mass tonight. I know you're busy, Gregory, and your parish only has one priest." She pauses. "But you only have one mother."

Mom's an excellent navigator on the Catholic highway of guilt.

"Let me get through tomorrow's Masses and then we'll spend the rest of the day doing whatever you like," I promise. "Would you like to take a drive? The autumn colors are starting to turn."

"What about Raymond? I was hoping to see him while I'm here."

Father Ray Davis, one of my oldest friends since we roomed together during seminary days, has always been a special favorite of Mom's. With his parish only twenty-five miles away, it's an easy afternoon drive.

"I'll call Ray tonight," I say. "If he's busy, maybe the three of us can do something together Monday."

"Isn't that the day your housekeeper comes?" Mom rises from her chair and stacks our plates. "If you're afraid to have a little chat with her, Gregory, I'll be more than happy to help. I've seen evidence of mice in this rectory, and that is completely unacceptable. I raised you better than that. Don't forget, I'm coming for Christmas. I have no intention of putting up with rodents, even if you are my son." She clucks her tongue. "Just think what your parishioners would say, hearing your mother was here for the holidays and had to stay in a hotel."

I hold back a smile. Guaranteed they wouldn't care. Plus, Mom would enjoy room service, and I'd have the luxury of peace and quiet.

"I'll speak with Martha on Monday morning," I say, "as soon as she gets here." I take the dishes from her hands and place a gentle peck on her cheek.

"Promise?"

"Yes, Mom."

"Good." She nods. "And Gregory? One more thing…"

"What's that?"

"That janitor of yours. Does he work on Mondays, too?"

"Vince?" I eye her carefully. "Yes, he does. Why?"

Smiling sweetly, she turns her head and nods.

My heart sinks as I follow her gaze and spy the faulty kitchen door.

Looks like Monday morning, I'll be having a little chat first with Martha, then Vince.

Unless, God help all three of us, Mom gets to them first.

CHAPTER TWO

"So, Mrs. K., let me get this straight. You fired the rectory housekeeper?" Father Ray settles back in his chair with a sly wink for me.

"Well, of course I didn't fire her," Mom says, blinking innocently. A little too innocently, if you ask me. "Martha quit on her own accord. I merely suggested that she might want to be a little more thorough when she cleaned. Is it my fault she took offense when I mentioned seeing evidence of mice droppings in the kitchen cupboards?"

Her nose wrinkles slightly. "Besides, I would never have taken it upon myself to tell her to leave. That's not my place. And certainly not my job."

I break out in a loud fit of coughing. It's pretty obvious whose job it is she's referring to. Once again, I've come up lacking in the my-son-the-priest-does-a-fine-job-managing-his-staff-BUT department.

"I merely pointed out a few things to her," Mom continues. "How was I supposed to know that Martha would quit? But as Gregory's mother, it's my job to do what I can to make his life easier. And personally, I think he's better off without her. Meanwhile, that rectory he's living in is an utter disgrace." She brushes a few bread crumbs into a neat little pile. "The paint is peeling off the walls, and the carpeting needs to be replaced. You've been there, Raymond. What do you think?"

"Truth, Mrs. K.? The place is a dump." Ray drains his Manhattan and signals the waitress for another drink. "Greg deserves better, but we're dealing with the church, remember? It takes money to make things happen."

"It always comes down to money, doesn't it?" Mom blows a delicate sigh that I know is aimed to raise my spirits. Too bad it can't raise the balance in the parish checkbook. "You'd think people would want to do better by their priests, especially seeing how you boys are responsible for them. They should take care of you. If they don't, what's to guarantee you'll be around to take care of them?"

"You can't blame the parishioners, Mom," I remind her. "The economy's not doing great."

"That's got nothing to do with it," Ray says. "People get wrapped up in their own little world. They see what they want to see, and hear what they want to hear. Give them a little push, Greg, and tell them what you need. Most people are glad to help once they know the situation."

"You're saying that Gregory simply needs to give his parishioners a little nudge?" Mom muses.

"Whoa, come on now—" I sputter.

"You know, Mrs. K., you might have something there." Ray eyes me over the table as the waitress serves his drink and provides us with dessert menus. "Greg's not much for entertaining, and I doubt anyone's been inside the rectory lately. Maybe if people had a chance to tour the place, they'd see how bad it is and do something about it."

Mom's eyes brighten. "Raymond, that is a wonderful idea."

I squirm in my chair. The look on her face scares the hell out of me. It's one of those why-didn't-I-think-of-this-sooner? expressions I learned to dread growing up. Like when I was nine and she bought me the cowboy outfit for Halloween when what I really wanted was an astronaut suit. Or when she volunteered to chaperone the St. Francis Eighth Grade Winter Dance when I'd already made up my mind I wasn't going.

Me, dance with a girl? No way.

Especially with my mother watching from the sidelines.

"I've just had the most marvelous idea." She beams at both of us. "I'll host an open house at the rectory. Doesn't that sound perfect? We'll serve coffee, fresh fruit, and pastries. And with the rectory right next door to church, everyone will come. Especially if we have it after Sunday Mass."

If I don't stop her, she'll be off on another of her tangents. "Mom, you know I love you, and I appreciate you wanting to help, but I don't think—"

"But that's the beauty of it, Gregory," she says, stopping me with one of those withering schoolteacher glances that come from years of dealing with recalcitrant students. "You don't have to think. In fact, you don't have to do anything except show up. I will take care of everything."

Mom in charge? The thought scares the hell out of me. I turn to Ray for help, but he merely winks.

Some hell of a friend he's turned out to be. My mother would never be running with this whole invite-the-parish-to-breakfast idea if he hadn't encouraged her by opening his big mouth.

"Mom, please, I'm telling you it won't work. You don't understand—"

"What I don't understand is why you think this will be such a problem," she primly announces.

She'd understand plenty if the situations were reversed. Mom loves her privacy, but mine vanished the day I was ordained. With a priest on call twenty-four seven and a faulty lock on the kitchen door, I'm continually clueless as to who's going to drop by next. I come in after morning Mass, there's a casserole waiting on the kitchen counter. I go out for groceries and an irate parishioner gives me holy hell at the checkout counter because we called another plumber rather than him when a church toilet needed repair. I sit down to watch the evening news only to hear the doorbell ring and find a parent sobbing at the front door, begging me to help get his daughter into rehab again.

I have no privacy, no life of my own. What I do have, according to Mom, are mice scampering through my kitchen cabinets.

"I don't understand why you're being like this. Then again, you always were a stubborn little boy. Why can't you just say *thank you* and let it be?"

I look to Ray for help but he merely shrugs, and sips his drink.

I'm on my own.

"Mom, I don't mean to seem ungrateful. But it's not right."

"What's not right?" she demands. "I don't understand."

I blow out a deep breath. If there was an easier, softer way, I'd take it. "You just can't walk in and take over like this."

"And why not?" Her face and voice are stony. She is not used to being challenged.

And I'm not used to challenging her. It's the stigma of an only child.

"For one thing, we're talking about the rectory, not the church," I say gently. "How do you think it would look if my mother is the one asking for money to fix up the place where her son lives?"

She sits back, hand to her throat, and pauses. "Why, I never thought of that," she says after a moment. "You're absolutely right, Gregory. Appearance is everything. Especially when it comes to asking for money." Her face softens and she pats my hand. "I'm sorry, sweetheart."

"No apology necessary. I know you only want what's best for me." I swallow down the shame over having foiled her scheme.

Then her eyebrows knit together and my heart kicks into overdrive.

"I don't know why I didn't think of this in the first place," she abruptly announces. "It's the perfect solution. Your parish has an active Rosary Altar Society. All I have to do is contact the right women. They'll be more than happy to host the event."

It's worse than I thought. Sixty ladies in the RAS, most of them retired, with every good intention of helping me out. And Mom directing from the sidelines.

It's all I can do not to bury my head in my hands.

"When do they hold their meetings?" she asks.

Ray grins, eyeballs me over his drink. We both know if I don't tell her, she'll discover it for herself easily enough. The information is listed on the cover of our Sunday bulletin.

"The first Monday of every month."

"I had planned on going home after this weekend, but this changes everything," she decides. "There's nothing on my schedule that can't be moved. My pinochle club doesn't start up again until mid-October, and the hospital guild should be able to manage without me for the next few weeks." She nods, her mind made up. "I'll plan on staying until I make sure everything is organized."

Thanksgiving is still more than a month away, but I feel like a trussed-up turkey ready to be popped in the oven. Guaranteed once the RAS ladies get wind of her idea, they'll be all over the rectory and they'll eat me alive.

My mother will be the one wielding the carving knife.

She rises with a regal smile. "Would you boys excuse me? I need to powder my nose. And if that waitress comes back, please order me an orange sherbet."

I grab Ray's arm as soon as her back is turned. "What the hell do you think you're doing, encouraging her like that? You know I couldn't care less about new carpet or furniture."

"Whoa, easy there, Greg." He raises a hand in protest. "She's only trying to help."

"Trying to ruin my life, you mean." I rake my fingers through my hair, wait as the waitress clears the remains of our dinners, takes our dessert orders. "What am I going to do? God knows I love her, but she's driving me crazy. I can't get any work done with her around. I was counting on her being gone by the end of the week, but after tonight..." I shake my head. "Obviously that's not going to happen."

"At least not until you get the carpet replaced or hire a new housekeeper." Ray prods me with a grin. "Did she really fire Martha?"

"Don't remind me," I mutter.

"Your mom's got moxie, I'll give her that. Still, Greg, I'd count my blessings if I were you. She's got your best interests at heart. We should all be so lucky."

"I know," I mumble as the guilt sets in. Ray's parents have been dead for years, and his relationship with his two younger brothers isn't what you'd term the best. They've been estranged for years—from Ray, as well as the church.

"Okay, I get it. And you're probably right about Mom, too. But this crazy idea of hers about hosting a fundraiser to fix up the rectory is a waste of time. Why spend the money on carpet and paint when we've got tree roots clogging the sewer lines? Most of the windows need to be replaced. And as for the electrical wiring..." I roll my eyes. "I said a Hail Mary every time I turned on the bedroom air conditioner last summer."

"Praying it would work?"

"Praying I wouldn't fry in my sleep." I throw him a gloomy smile. "The garage door opener has been broke for months. I have to get out of the car and open the door if I want to park inside. And I haven't used the fireplace since I moved in. It's in such bad shape, I don't dare. If we had the money, I'd get it fixed or block it off. Every winter we lose heat straight up the chimney."

It's not my imagination, either. I've kept a close eye on the utility bills, despite Cynthia Whitman's best efforts to guard her turf. Our parish secretary has bleached-blond hair, beady brown eyes, and a holier-than-thou attitude that told me from the get-go she believes I'm clueless about everything except how to find my way around the altar.

No doubt Cynthia would be surprised by how much I do know. She's a nosy gossip, not to mention a snoop, and reports on a regular basis to her old boss, Father "Mac" MacAfferty, about the happenings at his former parish.

Plus, grouses to him about the shortcomings of her current boss.

Me.

"Renovating the rectory could end up costing us six figures," I say. "The church doesn't have that kind of money. That crazy MacAfferty put the place in debt with his remodeling project a few years ago."

God's house deserves the best, and I suppose I should be grateful. The renovations are stunning, befitting a landmark such as Our Lady's, a Gothic beauty over one hundred years old. With a soaring ceiling, painted murals, gleaming wooden pews, and glorious stained-glass windows, Our Lady's is a showcase for Catholics, pre-and-post Vatican II. But Father Mac didn't do us any favors by sinking our parish over a million in debt.

And with the lousy economy, business leaving town, jobs disappearing, and houses falling into foreclosure, I'm the one responsible for coming up with the funds to make the mortgage payments. With a monthly price tag of ten thousand dollars, it's a struggle.

"Even if Mom does somehow manage to raise a few thousand dollars, why should I spend it patching some holes? What that rectory needs is a bulldozer razing it straight into the ground."

Then a wild thought suddenly bulldozes its way straight to the front of my brain. "What if we tear down the rectory and turn it into a parking lot?"

Ray stares at me like I've announced I've decided to run for Pope.

I lean forward, charged with an energy I haven't felt in months.

"Think about it. It makes total sense. The diocese keeps talking about consolidating parishes. We don't have enough priests and soon they won't have a choice. Our Lady's is one of the largest churches in the diocese. I can't see them closing us down." I feel the grin spreading across my face. "And with more parishioners, naturally we'll need more room for parking. With the rectory gone, we connect the space to the existing parking lot. Voila, all our problems solved."

"And where exactly do you intend to live?" he calmly asks.

"Who cares? I don't need much—just a small apartment where I can store my books, eat, and sleep."

Ray chuckles. "Good luck convincing the bishop to buy into that one."

"You think Holden won't go for the idea?"

"It's not the bishop I'm worried about," he says. "That's the original rectory, correct?"

"Yes, but—"

"Forget it, Greg." He eyes me over his empty glass. "You're living in a shrine."

"What's that supposed to mean?"

"Your parishioners' grandfathers and great-grandfathers built that house. Any of them get wind you're thinking about tearing the place down, you can kiss your Sunday collections good-bye. Not to mention, they'll go straight to the bishop. And guaranteed, Holden will back them one hundred percent. He's not going to expose himself to controversy, not when he's only two years away from retirement."

Much as I hate to admit it, Ray's analysis is probably dead-on. Bishop Holden runs a tight diocese and doesn't put up with anything that causes storm clouds in a parish. His priests are under orders to deliver sunshine and blue skies, no matter what the cost to their parishes or them personally.

For me, that means more mice taking up residence in the rectory.

Unless I plan to increase the budget, seal the cracks, and call in an exterminator.

"Maybe you could talk to Holden," I suggest. "You're good at schmoozing."

"Sorry, Greg, but I can't help you. I've been out of his good graces since I did that live television interview about Lenten practices without first clearing it with his office. Christ, for all the grief Holden gave me, you'd think I'd been on the national news instead of some local station nobody watches.

"Ah, well, no great loss." Ray lifts a shoulder, rattles the ice cubes in his glass. "The less Holden and the diocese see of me, and me of them, the better off we'll all be." He grins. "Maybe you should send your mom over to argue your case. Women like her—devoted, diehard Catholics—are hard to resist."

"I'm sure she'd do it, but I don't need the grief," I mutter. "Holden would either canonize her or throw her out."

Ray leans across the table. "What's got you in such a sour mood tonight? And don't give me that crap about your mom staying for a few extra days. You're blessed to have her, and we both know it."

I ponder my friend across the table. Thank God—thank God! for Ray Davis. We've been best friends since hooking up as roommates our freshmen year in high school seminary, and our weekly Monday-night get-togethers have been a bright spot in my life for years. Lately, one of the few bright spots. I would trust him with my life.

But even Ray would probably find it difficult to grasp something I barely understand myself.

The vague restlessness. The sense that something isn't quite right. The longing for something I can't name. I've experienced feelings like this before, but normally the melancholy dissolves like an early morning mist in the wake of brilliant sunshine. Except this time. I can't even blame it on the weather, for we've experienced a glorious Indian summer for the past several weeks. There's no hint yet of a biting wind that precipitates the plummet from the glory of autumn into the dead of winter.

But there's already a winter chill settling in my heart.

I try to shake off the gloom and doom and focus on my friend, but it's hard to gather my thoughts. They scatter like the dry autumn leaves racing around the foundation of the rectory. Which reminds me, Vince the janitor and I need to have a little talk. If he doesn't get at those leaves before the snow falls, they'll end up in moldy piles rotting against the basement windows. Come spring, we'll have a mess.

"Greg, my friend, I think you need a vacation. How about we take a trip to Las Vegas? Prices are pretty reasonable right now; we could snag a couple of hotel rooms, do some gambling, play a few rounds of golf."

"I don't golf," I remind him. "And Vegas is a little rich for my blood."

"You'd be surprised how cheap it is."

"You'd be surprised how broke I am."

I don't carry the sin of envy on my soul, but I don't have the options Ray was born with. He comes from family money and can tap into unlimited resources whenever the spirit moves him. Ray is a trust-fund baby, but I'm on my own. There'll be no *mother house* like the nuns have, welcoming me home upon retirement. And God help the priest who hasn't seen fit to fund his 401K or sock away enough to buy himself a little condo. He'll end up at the mercy of some young upstart with a righteous-ring-around-the-Roman-collar attitude. Mandatory retirement and no place to retire means Senior Priest status, qualifying you for nothing more than a spare bedroom in a drafty rectory and the not-so-welcome privilege of being assigned the early Mass on Sunday mornings.

"Greg, you can't let this stuff get to you. Screw the rectory. For that matter, screw the bishop, too. Holden's a blowhard. What do they tell you in that twelve-step program of yours? *Easy does it.* Good advice. Let's take some time off, the two of us, and plan that getaway. It doesn't have to be Las Vegas. We'll go someplace warm. Wherever you like. My treat," he adds.

I catch sight of Mom slowly weaving her way back between the tables. Ray catches my look, grabs my arm. "We'll even invite your mom," he offers.

As usual, Ray is being his usual generous self. Somehow I manage a smile for my old friend.

"Thanks, but I'm not sure bringing Mom along qualifies as a vacation. Besides, I can't get away right now. Not with the holidays coming."

"Your mom's a gem, and we both know it," he reminds me. "Though you're probably right about the timing."

With the leaves already off the trees, Advent isn't far off. Normally I enjoy the four weeks the church spends in joyous preparation anticipating the Lord's birth. But this year even the mere thought of putting up a Christmas tree sounds like major work.

Then again, maybe if I string enough lights, the circuits will overload and the rectory might catch fire. All my problems would be solved in one big blaze.

Merry Christmas, me.

"We'll take that vacation, Greg, sooner or later. Meanwhile, try to relax. Let your mom help you out. And if you're looking for an angel to kick in some funds, why not hit up that girl in your parish who won the lottery? What was her name?"

"Lucy Carter," I mumble as Mom reaches the table.

"What are you boys whispering about?" she says as Ray and I both stand.

I keep quiet. One mention about Ray's vacation idea and Mom would have the three of us booked on a Caribbean cruise before tonight.

"Just a little gossip between friends." He gives me a quick wink as he holds out her chair.

"Anyone I know?" she inquires brightly.

"Lucy Carter," he says.

"Bishop Holden," I counter simultaneously, wishing Ray would learn to keep his mouth shut.

She eyes him as he pushes in her chair. "Is this Lucy Carter any relation to Lila Carter?"

"You've met the mysterious Lila?" His eyebrows lift. "Wow, Mrs. K., I'm impressed."

It's all I can do not to give him a good swift kick under the table.

"Oh, I've met her," she says, her lips pursing in a thin line. "Not that I had much choice, seeing how she came up and introduced herself after Mass last weekend." She frowns. "And what exactly do you mean, *mysterious*?"

I shoot Ray a say-one-more-word-and-you're-a-dead-man glare.

"*Mysterious* in that I've never met her," he say smoothly. "I was beginning to think she didn't exist."

"Oh, she's real enough," Mom says with a slight sniff. "And attractive, too... not that you boys would be interested, of course. But I know her type. Very forward, very pushy. She's the type of woman who thinks highly of herself and thinks everyone else should, too."

I sputter over my water glass. Pushy? Lila is anything but. Attractive, yes; anyone with eyes could see that. God created man, then in His wisdom gave us women to add beauty to our lives. Lila Carter is beautiful, but she's also a good friend, a trusted volunteer, and the soul of discretion. She's the type of woman anyone—including a priest, including me—would feel comfortable with. I would trust her with anything. Lila is beautiful, compassionate...

Maybe it's better not to trust her.

"She might be pushy, but she also has plenty of money," Ray advises. "Her daughter Lucy won seventy million dollars in the lottery. They both belong to Greg's parish."

"I remember you mentioning something about that." Mom turns to me. "Perhaps I should contact this Lucy and see if she might be interested in donating..."

"No," I state flat-out. "You are not to ask Lucy for money. She's been more than generous as it is. She just bought new Advent vestments for our parish."

Ray throws me a sharp stare. "The ones you were drooling over in that little shop in Rome? Those vestments cost five thousand dollars."

The pilgrimage we shared last spring seemed far removed from the reality of everyday life until last week when the unexpected shipment arrived. Unzipping the vestments from the thick, protective bag was like unearthing shrouded memories of the narrow, bustling streets of Rome crowding in the shelter of the Vatican walls. The soaring ceilings of the Basilica Major, the smell of incense, the church bells tolling.

I swallowed down a lump in my throat as I slipped the rich, embroidered vestments over my shoulders.

I am the Alpha and Omega... He who believes in me will never die.

But do I believe anymore?

Have I lost faith in God? In church?

Or faith in myself?

"I'll give you credit, Greg," Ray says. "You know how to make things happen. Bravo, for asking Lucy to pick up the tab."

"But I never asked," I protest. "They simply showed up on the FedEx truck one day. Somehow she knew what I wanted. It was like a miracle." I think a long minute. "I guess it *was* a miracle."

"Miracles don't just happen," Ray scoffs. "At least, not in my parish."

"Lila might have mentioned something," I admit. I remember flipping through the church catalogue with Lila one day, pointing out the vestments shortly after my return from Rome. Did I lament the cost? Somehow Lila must have known, but it's hard to remember. We chat about so many things. Lila has frosted blond hair, peaceful blue eyes, and a fragrant serenity that drifts around her like a heavenly cloud.

"Well, if Lucy Carter bought those vestments, there is no reason that you can't ask her to buy new carpet for the rectory," Mom states firmly. "Meanwhile, what is all this talk about the bishop? The grief the two of you have given that man over the years, you're lucky he hasn't fired you both."

"I'm sure the thought has occurred to him," Ray says.

"And replace us with what? There aren't enough priests to go around. Besides," I add, "we don't work for Holden."

"And who exactly do you think we work for?" Ray asks with a smirk.

"I thought we were working for God."

He slaps his hand on the table and barks with laughter. "Good one, Greg. I'd love to be around when you inform Holden you've got a new boss."

The waitress is back with Mom's sherbet, more coffee for me, pie and another drink for Ray. Mom eyes my coffee cup as she spoons her sherbet. "All that caffeine isn't good for you. You won't sleep tonight."

You should have ordered dessert instead," Ray says.

"I don't need the extra calories." I pat my stomach. "I'm trying to lose a few pounds."

"You still jogging?" He grabs his fork and attacks the thick slab of apple pie in front of him.

"Not as much as I would like. The older I get, the easier it is to slough off, especially once the cold weather sets in. Besides, I seem to have misplaced my running shoes."

I cup my hands around my mug, watching as Ray makes quick work devouring the pie guaranteed to add another notch to his already ample girth. With all the boozing and eating he does, he's a heart attack waiting to happen.

I sip my coffee, keep my mouth shut. It's Ray's business how he chooses to live his life.

"Don't worry, Gregory, I'll find your shoes," Mom says. "What about you, Raymond? Are you into this jogging craze, too?"

He chuckles. "Are you kidding, Mrs. K.? Do I look like a health nut?"

"Well, I just wondered," she says. "Gregory always says it helps him relax."

Ray fingers his glass. "Let's just say I relax with a little help from my friends."

Jim Beam and Jack Daniels—exactly the kind of friends I don't need. I did my time slumming with the best of them. When I moved on to washing down my lunch every day with straight vodka in a coffee cup, I figured it was time to find some new friends.

Mom finishes her sherbet in silence, but I can guess the conversation going on in her head. *My son, the priest; my son, the alcoholic.* She's always been ashamed of me. Mom does not like me broadcasting the fact that I'm an alcoholic. But it is what it is, and I am who I am. I am in recovery and a better person for it.

And hopefully a better priest.

Our bill paid, we're in the lobby walking toward the door when a woman's voice, friendly and familiar, floats over my shoulder.

"Father Greg?"

I halt, turn, and see Gina VanBrabant beaming up at me.

"I almost didn't recognize you." Her words spin through the air in a dizzy rat-a-tat. "You know how you see someone you know, only you can't remember how or where you know them because they're not dressed?"

Her face immediately reddens. "I mean, you're in regular clothes. You're not wearing your Roman collar."

I can't help grinning. "Even priests take a break from the uniform now and then. Mondays are my day off."

"It's funny to see you dressed in regular clothes, just like me." Gina glances down at the skirt skimming just above her knees and grimaces. "Then again, I guess not."

"Good thing. I'd look pretty stupid in a skirt. I've got horrible-looking knees."

Gina giggles. "Father Greg, you're too funny."

She is as pretty and vivacious as I remember from in the confessional the other day. Long dark curls encircle her head like a crown. Her skin shines in a honey-colored light that puts me in mind of a golden Madonna.

"I'm so glad we bumped into you tonight. Now I can introduce you to Joe."

She pulls forward a tall, slender man with handsome features, dark hair cropped close to his head, and rich, brown skin that puts me in mind of cocoa mixed with bittersweet chocolate. "He actually accused me of making you up, seeing how I've talked about you so much."

"My wife likes to tease, but I assure you Gina has said only good things." Joe extends his hand. "It is my pleasure to meet you, Father."

"Likewise." His accent puts a decidedly European twist to the King's English.

I turn to Mom and Ray and make the round of introductions. For once, they're both reserved, unlike Joe and Gina, whose happiness is contagious. To be young and in love; what a blessing. Marriage is a vocation, a gift from God between two people who choose to love, honor, and respect each other all the days of their lives.

More than twenty-five years ago, I made a choice, too, dedicating myself to the service of God through vocation to the priesthood. I chose the church, and I thought it would be enough. For years, it has been.

But is it anymore?

"You two look like you're out celebrating something special," I say.

Joe and Gina trade simultaneous smiles more brilliant than the luminous beams from the overhead chandeliers.

"Congratulations," I offer. "What's the occasion?"

Gina smiles shyly, and the swift intimate look that passes between them nearly brings me to my knees.

Love between two people needs no occasion.

"I've been telling Joe about everything you and I discussed," she says. "We're very anxious to get started with our marriage preparations."

Mom pats my arm. "Raymond and I will wait outside."

I nod absently, watching them go. "Phone the rectory and talk to Cynthia. She keeps my appointment book. Tell her I said to make it sometime this week."

Gina's face falls. "I was hoping we could do it sooner, with the baby and all."

Her eyes are so trusting, as if she believes I can work miracles. But we're dealing with the church. The Vatican hasn't changed much in two thousand years, and no matter what I do, there'll be no miraculous intervention for Gina and Joe.

Yet something about this young couple stirs something inside me. A whisper of hope, a faint remembrance of something that touched me long ago.

"All right, let's shoot for tomorrow," I suddenly decide. "Normally I try and keep Tuesdays free. I've got hospital calls in the morning, then Mass at the nursing home. But I'll make time for you in the afternoon. How does three o'clock sound?"

Joe glances at Gina. "I would have no problem leaving work early."

"I'll pencil it in the calendar as soon as I get back to the rectory," I promise.

"We appreciate you making time for us, Father," he says.

Gina beams. "I knew coming to see you was the right thing to do. You made all the difference."

I push aside a warm rush of pleasure. "I haven't done anything."

"That's for us to decide, don't you think?" Gina leans over and catches me in a brief hug. "Thank you, Father."

They head into the dining room and I stroll out the door. A trace of her perfume lingers on my jacket, and I sniff it, hug it closer. Is this how other men feel—proud, happy, content, with daughters of their own? Gina is old enough to be my daughter. What a blessing she is, this young, vivacious woman who is a delight to all.

But the faint fragrance fades as I step out on the sidewalk and squint against the setting sun. Who am I kidding? I'm not Gina's father, nowhere close.

"That was quite the cozy little picture," Ray says as I join him and Mom in the parking lot.

His comment annoys me for some odd reason. "Knock it off, Ray."

"Pretty girl. Someone from your parish?"

"New in town." I zip my jacket against the cool night air. "Newlyweds, both Catholic, married outside the church. They want to have their marriage blessed."

"Good luck with that one."

"And what is that exactly supposed to mean?" I ask as I open the passenger door for Mom.

He shrugs. "I wouldn't exactly call them the All-American couple."

I eye Ray carefully. "Right. Her husband is from Belgium."

"That's not what I meant."

I've known Ray since we were teenagers, but suddenly the man in front of me seems like a stranger. "When did you become a bigot?"

Mom wags a finger at both of us. "Now, boys, no fighting."

"Just an observation, Mrs. K.," Ray says with a faint smile for my mother and a meaningful look for me. "Look, Greg, I don't mean to cause trouble. But in case you haven't noticed, James Bay is a white-bread kind of town. In fact, I would venture to say that goes ditto for Northern Michigan."

"Raymond, it's been lovely seeing you again. Take care of yourself." Mom kisses him on the cheek and slides into the passenger seat.

I struggle not to slam the door. Ray's comments irritate the hell out of me. He's never been one to hold back his opinions, but normally his observations on church, clergy, and controversy coincide with my own.

But not tonight.

Why should it matter if Joe is black and Gina is white? It's no one's business—Ray's, mine, or even the church's—whom people choose to love or marry. Each of us is free to make our own choice. Isn't that what free will is all about?

Ray slides behind the wheel of his luxury sedan. "Let's get together for dinner next week," he calls through the open window as he backs up.

I turn the nose of the car around and follow him out of the parking lot. Mom sits beside me, hands folded in her lap.

"And what about you? You're awfully quiet." I finally grind out. My voice is harsh, and I know she's probably offended. But after my unexpected exchange with Ray, it's all I can do to keep my temper in check. "Anything you'd care to add?"

"About what?" She blinks in the shadow of twilight.

"Don't play games with me, Mom. You know what I'm talking about." I grip the wheel so tightly my fingers go numb.

She slips against her seatbelt, turning toward me. Her eyes are hooded in the growing darkness, but I know she's watching. Probably trying to figure out the best way to broach exactly how she feels without making me mad.

Or making me madder than I already am.

"They seem like a nice couple," she finally says, "especially the girl. Very sweet. But Raymond is right. An interracial couple in James Bay? It won't be easy for them. You know how people are. There aren't any black people in this town."

"What's that got to do with anything?" My anger erupts without understanding. "Don't tell me you've become a bigot, too?"

"You asked what I thought, and I am trying to tell you," she says in a stiff voice. "But I will not sit here and be insulted by my own son. If that is the way you intend to act, we might as well stop this conversation right now."

Fine. Let her stew. But if she thinks I'm apologizing, she's got another think coming.

We drive another few miles. The green glow of the dashboard and dim light from the overhead streetlamps casts an eerie silence between us.

"I don't think you realize what having a couple like that in your parish will mean," she finally says. "There are going to be problems, Gregory."

"Why should there be problems? Joe and Gina are just people, like everyone else."

"Yes, but they're different," she says. "And *different* means problems, no matter what. Everyone will be watching, no matter how sweet the girl is, no matter how intelligent or handsome her husband seems. You know how people are. They'll be watching the two of them, and they'll be watching you, too. You're the priest, Gregory. You'll set the tone. Mind what you say, no matter what you think."

"What I think shouldn't make one bit of difference."

"But it will. I'm not saying what they did was right or wrong. Although if it had been me, I never would have made the mistake she did and married outside the church. And while her husband seems like a nice enough man, I never would have married a man of… color."

I shoot her a fast look.

"But that's just me," she adds quickly. "I'm an old lady and the world is a different place now. What they choose to do is their own business. But no matter how much the world has changed, this isn't New York City or wherever he's from. James Bay is a small town. People here will need time to adjust."

Silence surrounds us as I round the corner and pull up in the rectory driveway. I cut the engine and sit behind the wheel, staring at the garage.

Mom watches me from the safety of her seatbelt. "Aren't you going to get out and open the door?"

"I don't know." I fold my hands across my lap. "Maybe I'll let the car sit out here all night. Maybe I'll let it sit outside all winter."

"You're still mad, aren't you?" she says. "You always were a stubborn little boy."

My jaw clenches. "I am not a boy anymore, Mom. I'm a grown man."

"I know that, sweetheart." Her voice softens. "Gregory, I did not mean to upset you. I am only saying, as your mother, that you should be careful. Don't get people riled up. Don't upset anyone. Please, son, be careful."

But maybe I'm tired of being careful. Maybe I'm tired of doing what I'm supposed to do, of telling people what they want to hear, of doing what they think I should do.

Maybe I'm tired of following the rules.

Maybe it's because I'm getting older.

Or maybe it's something else.

Maybe it's time I started breaking a few rules myself.

KATHLEEN IRENE PATERKA

www.ingramcontent.com/pod-product-compliance
Lightning Source LLC
Chambersburg PA
CBHW021423240626
47153CB00001B/3